The Perilous Deep

The Perilous Deep

A Supernatural History of the Atlantic

Karl Bell

REAKTION BOOKS

Published by
REAKTION BOOKS LTD
2–4 Sebastian Street
London EC1V 0HE, UK
www.reaktionbooks.co.uk

First published 2025

EU GPSR Authorised Representative
Logos Europe, 9 rue Nicolas Poussin, 17000, La Rochelle, France
email: contact@logoseurope.eu

Printed and bound in Great Britain by Bell & Bain, Glasgow

A catalogue record for this book is available from the British Library

ISBN 978 1 83639 090 9

Contents

NOTE TO READERS

All translations are mine unless otherwise indicated. I have lightly edited and updated the orthography, punctuation and capitalization of early modern English and explained obsolete words within brackets. Biblical quotations are from *The New Oxford Annotated Bible*, 5th edition. All dates are CE (AD) unless noted as BCE (BC).

Introduction: Casting Off

The Atlantic: vast, turbulent, deep and dark.

Like the fabled sirens' song, such qualities call to the human imagination, making the ocean both a powerful story-making and storytelling environment. Appearing deceptively timeless upon the surface, it is full of historic tales of supernatural powers, monstrous encounters, strange omens, unearthly experiences, accounts of tragedy and ghostly returns. Thanks to popular films and other fictions, even twenty-first-century landlubbers, people largely disconnected and remote from the ocean as a reality, are familiar with some of its more famous denizens: the doomed captain of the *Flying Dutchman*, the monstrous Kraken, the elusive sea serpent, mysterious and alluring mermaids.

Our familiar histories of seafaring tend to be dominated by heroic naval battles, brave explorers pushing themselves to the limits as they seek unknown horizons, and bold pirates to whom our historical fantasies have probably granted a little too much swagger. We are drawn to the nostalgic romanticism of the age of sail, its stolid trading ships forming the links in economic chains that would come to bind the world into a globalized market in the eighteenth and nineteenth centuries, and later to the grand luxury of ocean liners that tamed the ocean into a playground. This is a history that has long sat well with us, a history of human ambition, daring, enterprise, progress, prosperity and conquest, one in which we gradually came to claim a mastery of the seas.

Often told through accounts of larger-than-life figures, the ocean was a place to explore, seek treasures, gain fame, or extend the power and reach of one's country. Engaging as it may be, this history speaks to only a particular representation of seafaring, one tidied up in retrospect, bolstered by fiction and often veneered with national mythmaking. Such a portrayal conceals histories of monotonous duty and hard labour, diverts attention from the Atlantic as the site of a tricontinental slave trade that lasted for over three hundred years, and leaves little space for considering such things as the place of fear or the fantastical within the maritime world.

This book embarks on a different type of maritime history, one that draws attention to a more muted engagement with the ocean, to stories and ideas that have largely been pushed to the fringes of official histories, rendered a curious footnote in our understanding of the maritime world, and rarely appear on maps or charts. A history of the supernatural Atlantic makes us reconsider our historical and human relationship to the ocean. While it does not necessarily seek to contradict those more familiar nautical, naval and imperial histories, it provides an important cultural dimension to seafaring that has previously been downplayed as 'superstition' or dismissed as former ignorance. It is a fluid tale that churns together supernatural beliefs and practices, imagination and storytelling, psychology and emotion, the pragmatism of life at sea lashed to the popular metaphysics of how the ocean was understood as a place of diabolical forces, divine retribution, inhuman marvels and unknown terrors.

Such a consideration seems timely, given our growing awareness of and unease about ecological concerns. While most environmental talk is about going green, it has been recognized that we also need to go blue, addressing the issues of warming oceans, melting polar ice caps and the future effects that these things are going to have on both human societies and marine ecosystems. An exploration of supernatural and fantastical ideas about seafaring, the ocean and its mysterious inhabitants helps us understand the ways in which past societies expressed, understood and responded to their own environmental concerns. Powerful and volatile, the ocean has been a site of threats and uncertainty down through the ages, and our dialogue with it stretches back to ancient seafaring civilizations. The vast expanse, unknown depths and frequent dangers of the ocean have inspired a rich medley of omens, ghosts, monsters and strange encounters for centuries.

It is perhaps only in the period that forms the central focus of this book, the mid-eighteenth to the mid-twentieth century, that technological and industrial developments have encouraged self-congratulatory 'modern' societies to feel increasingly detached from the natural world. For most of us today, the ocean exists far removed from our daily lives, a largely unconsidered source of food and the main means of transportation by which our feverish consumer cultures are sustained. We may splash around in the shallows at the beach on holiday. A few of us may venture beneath its waves to scuba dive or take a floating hotel across its surface on a luxury cruise, and some still make a living from extracting fish, gas or oil from what has become an industrialized space. Yet put any of us in a small vessel and place us out of sight of land, open to the elements and tossed by swelling waters that are no longer blue but black down to their sunless depths, and no doubt we too would begin to feel ourselves small, vulnerable and in need of some good fortune. Confronted by the oceanic vastness that stretches beyond sight and aware of the fathomless deep beneath our thin hull, our minds may also be inclined to dredge up old stories and the monsters that come with them; things we have never heard directly but that are nevertheless familiar to us from films that endlessly play to our fears and fascination with the ocean.

Much of what follows is based on accounts of maritime folklore, its tales, beliefs, practices and ideas. There are some tricky issues to navigate when drawing upon such material. Since it is often derived from oral accounts, one has to allow for the fact that this rich haul includes more than its fair share of exaggeration, supposition, misunderstanding and speculation, most of it subsequently put down in print by scholars or journalists who never witnessed any of it for themselves. We have to consider how that classic (and perhaps largely fictive) source of such lore, the salty old sea dog, taken with his opportunity for an audience, may have been happy to embellish his accounts so as to hold its attention a little longer. Many of the sources used in the following chapters suggest that such information did not spew from a grizzled old mariner acting as a convenient fount of folklore. More often it was gleaned piecemeal from the coastal communities in which mariners lived while ashore. Local clergymen were frequently important figures in the process of information gathering, serving as mediators between their communities and the enquiring folklorist.

This means that the original source or origins of the account are usually lost to the historical record. We merely inherit the retellings. This book does not seek to whittle away those elaborations to reveal some unchanging core 'truth' at the heart of accounts or stories. For the most part, such 'truths' were highly subjective, and different listeners would likely take different things from the same tale. Nor is it about mimicking the nineteenth-century folklorists' fascination with tracing the origins of tales and legends. While setting certain ideas and beliefs in a longer historical context, it seeks to work with and keep intact the concerns or wonders that such accounts promote, to consider, regardless of their factual accuracy, what purpose such ideas and stories served. In doing so we can appreciate the way they speak to larger 'truths' about our relationship with the ocean, with connections between land and sea, leaving and returning, life and death. On the one hand, these stories and ideas articulated threats and anxieties about the power, violence and sheer unpredictability of the ocean, a potentially perilous space full of omens and dangers. On the other, they provided a sense of protection, insight and knowledge, things that helped foster a feeling that seafarers might have some influence over the marine environment and, if carefully observed, might enable a safe return to land.

While seeking to use folklore as an undervalued aspect of maritime working life, we have to appreciate that it does not provide a direct and unproblematic insight into the collective imagination or an occupational worldview. The piecemeal nature of nineteenth-century folkloric collecting can distort, both leaving and obscuring gaps in folkloric knowledge. Such accounts can provide us with something of the range of beliefs and practices, but not all sailors went to sea with knowledge or awareness of them all. While there may be things that never made it into print or historical archives, there is also the distortion that comes from historians being able to amass a potentially wider range of information that was exchanged by mariners themselves. Also, we have to make distinctions between different states of folkloric material, whether it is 'living' (actively used and believed in), 'retained' (former practices that may still be observed but without genuine belief) or 'recorded' (captured by folklorists but possibly no longer 'live', with informants often distancing their own commitment to such ideas by locating their accounts several generations in the past).[1] In turn, folklorists consumed with capturing 'fragments' of older supernatural mentalities and stories before they disappeared beneath the onslaught of modern industrial society frequently failed to credit them with contemporary significance or application.[2]

We must also be wary of assuming that such accounts originated from an oral culture. There was not a simple, unidirectional move from oral tale to literary account in all cases. With growing popular literacy and increasingly cheaper printing costs in the nineteenth century, it was common for people to first encounter ideas associated with maritime folklore through street ballads, serialized penny fiction or newspapers. The notion of mermaids, sea serpents or phantom ships was just as likely to be encountered ashore and then taken to sea as it was the other way round. With a few exceptions, my aim is not to untangle the oral or literary origins of most accounts. While there is credible historical detective work to be found in such an undertaking, and while recognition of that entanglement of influences is important, it is the stories' cultural functions at sea and ashore that are my principal concern here.

For seafarers they were a way to articulate anxieties and concerns in a dangerous environment, and a means of placating such unease, as much through an appreciation of omens, observances and ritualized behaviours as through one's seamanship. They were a cheap and available form of entertainment to bind maritime communities together aboard ship and in ports, a common currency of cultural exchange that conveyed lessons and fostered a shared understanding of the maritime world. Given that mariners were repeatedly required to reconstitute themselves into new, often multinational crews, this body of nautical lore operated like a form of cultural glue. Similar tropes and beliefs were carried on all the oceanic tides of the world, although they usually took local colour and shape. Ashore, maritime folklore helped express the strangeness of seafaring and the marine environment to landlubbers, albeit with the likely possibility of some exaggeration and leg-pulling at the expense of their audience.

Land dwellers were not simply passive absorbers of mariners' supernatural worldview, for much of what sailors took to sea originated in the anxieties of the coastal communities from which many derived. More broadly, tales of sea monsters and mermaids became entangled in scholarly and scientific debates of the time and were used by cultural commentators and critics as a way of portraying those who laboured upon the waves. Writing of sailors' 'superstitions' in 1880, William Jones declared that their

> isolated occupations and peculiar mode of life render them more susceptible of fanciful impressions. Although the boldest men alive in action, yet they are frequently the very abject slaves of superstition . . . The surrender of [the sailor's] belief in the supernatural will probably be one of the last strongholds of superstition, for the obstinacy of his character will hold out long.[3]

Such a view did much to help create the idea of the sea and seafaring as something separate, mysterious and utterly alien to the experience of land dwellers.

With varying degrees of nostalgia, the default view of most later nineteenth- and twentieth-century critics was to dismiss maritime folklore as merely a lingering haze of ignorance and superstition.[4] As we will see, this formed part of a nineteenth-century move towards disenchanting the ocean, dispelling its myths and mysteries to portray it as a space that was subject to the brute power of steamships, the ingenuity of transatlantic telegraph communication and the critical scrutiny of natural science. Into the mid-twentieth century books of maritime folklore often adopted an evolutionary rhetoric, portraying sailors as superstitious dwellers in a marine wilderness, deprived of the supposedly civilizing, modern influences of Western urban society. This 'othering' of sailors was made easier by them being a largely invisible workforce. Vital links in the development of a modern, transoceanic economy, they conducted their work out of sight and far away. Such a view ignored the fact that those engaged in transatlantic voyages were more likely to gain a cosmopolitan experience of that modernizing world than provincial landlubbers who may never have ventured beyond their hometown.

Geographically, this book focuses on the Atlantic Ocean and some of its tributary seas, ranging from the frigid waters of the North Sea to the stormy South Atlantic, from the Cape of Good Hope to Cape Horn. While it mainly draws upon northern European examples, a transatlantic scope allows us to engage with the maritime folklore of Europe, Africa and the Americas. It makes no claim to being either an encyclopaedic survey or a continent-by-continent gazetteer. The Atlantic is vast and the coastlines of western Europe, west Africa and the eastern seaboard of the Americas run to many thousands of miles. Instead, it uses pertinent examples to illustrate and reflect on the ideas, beliefs and tales that sluiced back and forth across the Atlantic world.

Historically, the book mainly focuses on the mid-eighteenth to the mid-twentieth centuries. On the relatively few occasions where historians have seriously engaged with maritime folklore, they have tended to concentrate on eighteenth-century Anglo-American mariners or nineteenth-century French fishermen.[5] Adopting a broader chronology enables an exploration of maritime supernatural ideas over a period that saw a changing relationship between technology and the maritime environment. Those who dismissed maritime folklore promoted a simplistic narrative that the shift from sail to steam to diesel marked an end to sailors' previous sensitivity to weather and the changeable seas, and to the body of omens and supernatural observances and protections that accompanied it. Such ideas were increasingly presented as the useless cultural detritus of an age that was being romanticized and distanced, even though sailing ships continued to ply their trade into the early twentieth century. No longer working with the winds and tides, the steamship was a statement of blunt industrial power. While certainly not immune to the power and ferocity of the ocean, steamships could bullishly plot their course across its expanse in a way that sail ships could not. The later nineteenth-century's technological and imperial ambitions bred an attitude of mastery over the ocean. This hubris informed both the proclaimed unsinkability of RMS *Titanic* and the shock when the Atlantic swiftly proved such claims wrong. Knowing the harsh realities of the ocean, mariners did not necessarily buy into such assertions, and their supernatural beliefs continued to address underlying anxieties about the precariousness of life at sea.

This book draws upon a wide range of historical sources to access these tales, ideas and motifs. The nineteenth-century growth of popular newspapers and the development of folklore as a scholarly discipline both helped generate the evidential sources from which much of this study is built. Yet engagement with aspects of the maritime supernatural took many forms in this period. This ranged from street ballads to scientific reflections on marine biology, mariners' memoirs to court cases, advertisements for displays of live and 'real' mermaids to paintings and poems, and literary tales that range from the Gothic fiction of Edgar Allan Poe to the weird fiction of mariner-turned-writer William Hope Hodgson. All highlight that a supernatural maritime culture was generated and digested ashore as much as it was made by mariners cooped up on ships far from home. It also illustrates that while the issue of genuine belief was frequently downplayed in the nineteenth century, there was certainly no shortage of interest in the supernatural maritime world. Even as critics and commentators advanced their claims about living in a modern age, using supposedly declining belief in 'superstitions' to illustrate notions of Western advancement, it proved difficult to let the alluring enchantment of the maritime supernatural slip into the past.

This wealth of historical evidence highlights another issue that needs to be kept in mind. These sources reflect a predominantly white, male authorship or perspective, largely of western

European or North American origin. While transatlantic crews were often drawn from many countries and races, the evidence that we draw upon is second hand at best, frequently more. The voices of female and non-white mariners are rarer in the historical records drawn upon here. No doubt, if those more marginalized voices could be retrieved, they would both reiterate many elements of that collective supernatural worldview shared by seafarers and add their own important perspectives.

The following chapters are ordered in such a way as to take the reader on a seafaring voyage into the supernatural and monstrous Atlantic, confronting its magic and its many strange denizens and geographies before returning home to our much-haunted coasts. Starting with how the sea was viewed and understood as both a natural and supernatural place, we then consider how seafarers (and sea fearers) tried to magically protect themselves from it through a rich mix of charms, spells, omens and ritual observances. Once at sea, sailors entered a realm of supernatural beings, objects and entities, including merfolk, ghosts, phantom ships and sea monsters. They also encountered weird oceanographic spaces, underwater worlds, strange islands, mysterious places where the maritime world appeared to ignore the rules that governed the rest of nature. Having encountered the strangeness of the maritime imagination, we return to shore, exploring coastal folklores rich with supernatural tales and haunted by the spirits of the dead that washed up ashore. We end by voyaging out of the eighteenth and nineteenth centuries to consider how their maritime horrors, monsters and dangers have been updated as nautical Gothic and weird fiction tales, and, later, as cinematic wonders.

In undertaking this voyage, we will explore why these stories were told, how they evolved, were repeated and updated, and what fears and desires they helped to express. Despite wondrous accounts of monsters and merfolk, it will be seen that they were linked very much to how mariners operated in the mundane world, how the ocean made them feel, and a search for some sense of understanding and influence within it. As such, this is not just a history of seafaring. Our voyage encompasses histories of emotion, imagination, psychology and cultures, of technology and science, of a marine environment that extends beyond meteorological conditions or nautical phenomena, that goes beneath those surfaces to appreciate how the Atlantic was perceived, imagined and felt. In doing so, we can come to appreciate the profound psychological influence the marine environment exerts on the human mind. Beneath the change from sail to steam, beneath stories of magic and modernity, this is a history of how the Atlantic Ocean has long moved, awed and affected us, even as we have increasingly come to affect it.

1
Seafaring and Sea Fearing

In a December 1873 lecture entitled 'The Storm-Tossed Sons of the Ocean', Reverend T. Greenbury claimed that 2,000 ships and 1,000 lives were lost annually on British coasts. Transatlantic crossings were equally fraught with risk. Greenbury read out a list of nine ships involved in the corn trade that had been lost in just two months, all of them embarking from America. He noted that 'The very element to which the sailor trusted was the very cause of his greatest danger,' for life at sea involved scorching heat, freezing cold, torrential rain, sleet and frost, being beset by storms or becalmed in the doldrums. It was a working life based on navigating extreme physical dangers. Greenbury was keen to play up the drama and tragedy of seafaring, his lecture intended to raise funds for a sailors' orphans' home and a sailors' mission in Hull, England.[1] Yet the dangers of seafaring were very real. In a bad year, four or five of the hundred vessels that voyaged across the Atlantic to Newfoundland's Grand Banks as part of the late nineteenth-century French fishing fleet could be lost. It has been suggested that as many as one in three sailors died in their first decade as mariners.[2]

The physical extremes of the ocean and the very nature of the ocean itself fostered a sense that it was simultaneously a natural and supernatural environment, a place where distinctions between the two blurred and were lost. The ocean was never just a physical space of currents, tides and storms, but a domain of spirits, gods and higher powers that were responsive to the character and actions of the humans who ventured upon it. When living and working in such a primordial environment, waves and storms obtained supernatural motivation or meaning beyond the mundane. Maritime space was understood as a place where divine and diabolical forces intervened, or where the elements themselves were sentient and alive. The Atlantic's surging force, visually imposing vastness and unseen depths have long exerted a powerful influence on the human psyche, meaning the history of seafaring has always been one of both physical and psychological confrontation. As this book will demonstrate, vast bodies of water stimulated fear and wonder, and, in turn, have fostered imaginative responses and supernatural thinking. Such ideas suggest a seafaring mindset that was always more inclined to view the ocean as malign rather than benign.

Engagement with the ocean imposed a recognition of human limitations and insignificance. Unlike our assertive place in the landscape, most notable in the growing urban centres of eighteenth- and nineteenth-century Europe and North America, in the Atlantic humankind was never more than tiny, isolated motes amid the vast, non-human expanse of water. Published in 1757, Edmund Burke's *A Philosophical Enquiry into the Origins of Our Ideas of the Sublime and Beautiful* described these feelings of fear, awe and a challenged sense of self in terms of the sublime. The vastness of a mountain range or the power and majesty of the ocean fills the mind and stretches our ability to comprehend it. Burke argued that things that exceed our knowledge or cognition – ideas such as eternity or infinity, or confrontation with the imposing scale and dimensions of nature – are sources of the sublime. Exploring its psychological effects, Burke argued that this stimulated a sense of delightful terror if viewed from a certain (safe) distance. Closer, its dangers became 'simply terrible'. Declaring the ocean 'an object of no small terror', Burke's treatise marked a key eighteenth-century advancement in understanding the affective power of nature upon the mind.[3]

Far less philosophical in its approach, Frederick E. Bolton's rather eccentric, wide-ranging 1899 article on 'Hydro-Psychosis' provided a summary of an investigation he had conducted into how water made people feel. In terms of reactions to water in general, his respondents noted that they liked to be near water. It encouraged feelings of happiness or reverence and seemed to sympathize with people's moods and thoughts. Yet this rather pleasant response disappeared when it came to the sea. One respondent noted that they 'always feel as if the water were alive and sending out its arms for prey', another that it 'seems like a great monster which would not hesitate to wreak its vengeance upon anything within its reach'. Echoing Burke's sublime, the open sea made one person 'feel insignificant, stricken with awe, as though the supernatural were in the water'. It made some turn their thoughts to 'the God of the universe and of nature', while another suggested more vaguely that it was 'representative of great persons, their silent yet powerful actions, [compelling] me to submit to nature's plan'. We do not know who Bolton's respondents were, but it was noted that these feelings, prompted when simply observing bodies of water, were intensified when afloat upon their surface. There, the devout and the atheist were both inclined to turn to prayer for protection, for the ocean made them feel God's power made manifest.[4] It is little surprise, then, that in addressing the sense of individual insignificance and lack of control that arose when confronted by the ocean's size and power, eighteenth- and nineteenth-century mariners imbued the marine environment with a sense of hidden, supernatural forces that operated behind and through nature.

Beyond the visual and psychological impact of the ocean's surface, its depths also exerted a powerful draw on the mind and imagination. Since it was a space where the seen and known reached their limits and faltered, seafarers were inclined to populate the unknown, unseen deep with things that they most feared. As depicted in older maps, a recognition of limit and knowledge was usually marked by the presence of monsters, and as will be seen in Chapter Five, such ideas long continued to apply to the Atlantic's depths. Sunlight penetrates oceanic waters to depths of between 200 and 1,000 metres. When we consider that the average depth of the Atlantic is just under 4,000 metres, extending at its deepest, the Puerto Rico Trench, to a depth of 8,605 metres, much of the ocean exists in a vast and eerie darkness. Our fear of the dark (nyctophobia) and fear of open or deep water (thalassophobia) combine to express the primal unease humans can feel at sea. As air breathers heavily reliant on vision for protection, the deep is anathema to the sun-lit, land-based lives we have evolved to lead. It is often understood as an otherworldly realm, a barren place of loss, wreckage and decay. Even marine scientists, seeking to calibrate the levels of darkness within the deep, drew upon mythological underworlds for their darkest classification. Beyond the abyssal zone (3,000–6,000 metres) lies the hadal zone (6,000+ metres), taken from Hades, the Greek god of the underworld. Such a description echoes the ideas of eighteenth- and nineteenth-century mariners who, referring to the deep as Davy Jones's locker, viewed it as a dark aquatic underworld of the dead.

Earlier scientific understandings of the deep encouraged strange and macabre ways of envisioning what lies beneath the waves. It had been believed that different objects naturally sank to different depths, to a point where water density would prevent them sinking any further. Only gold was heavy enough to reach the ocean floor. The hierarchical ordering that accompanied such an idea would have created stratified layers within the deep, with a layer of human corpses hovering above wooden wrecks, and, lower still, a layer of cannonballs or anchors.[5] Such an idea supposedly persisted into the later nineteenth century, when HMS *Challenger* conducted its deep sea exploration (1872–6), both in the name of scientific enquiry and, more pragmatically, to better understand the ocean floor for the laying of the transatlantic cables that formed the nineteenth century's basis for our modern communications network.

Ancient Gods, Goddesses and God

Seas and oceans have long been perceived as the domain of gods and powerful spirits. The sheer physical presence and power of the marine environment stimulated a sense of supernatural excess. This made it an elemental testing ground in which seafarers had to contend with forces, natural and supernatural, that might punish their intrusion upon the waves by wrecking their vessels and taking their lives. As archipelago and island cultures, the sea played on the ancient Greek imagination. Noting that 'It is only a step from simile to metaphor, from metaphor to personification,' William Chase Greene argued that Greeks perceived natural elements like the sea as sentient beings, and later as personified deities that required placating.[6]

The shift from a diffused sense of animism to a specific deity that could be revered but also appealed to and possibly negotiated with was seen in the genealogical development of Greek sea god dynasties. An earlier god, Oceanus, was little more than an embodiment of the animated power and vastness of the sea. Mimicking human rulers, he had a palace, said to be 'far off to the west', placing it towards if not in the Atlantic from the Greek's Mediterranean perspective. The later gods and goddesses show a richer and more sophisticated imagining of the sea's nature. Rather than just representing the power of the sea, Poseidon's moods supposedly influenced it, linking mind and environment once again, and thereby offering a psychological explanation for the sea's turbulent and shifting nature. His wife, Amphitrite, daughter of the Oceanid Doris, linked Poseidon's Olympian family to Oceanus' older dynasty. As Greene notes, the Greeks took man as 'the measure of all things; when they animated the sea it was by anthropomorphism'. In reflecting humans, the Greek sea gods also reflected their cultural mores, familial relations and marriage customs. Addressing the various moods of the sea, the Greeks gave a name and presiding deity to each. The fish god, Nereus, was an old man who represented the sea's more benevolent nature. His daughters, the Nereids, represented other aspects: Galene personified calm weather, Thaumas the sea's majesty, and Phorcys its more frightening aspect.[7]

The Greeks tended to view venturing upon the sea as a personal negotiation with these aquatic divinities, for mariners' courage to cross it might provoke their wrath. This, according to William Jones's dose of late nineteenth-century condescension, resulted in mariners of the ancient world conducting 'their voyages in a vague mist of capricious doubts and fears, omens and prognostics . . . Every object that met their gaze was endowed with some miraculous agency for good or otherwise.'[8] Ancient mariners read the marine environment for signs, not just of the weather but simultaneously for clues as to what that weather suggested about how the gods viewed their presence at sea.

In terms of classical Greek literature, this maritime struggle against the will of the gods is best depicted by Homer's epic poem *The Odyssey,* estimated to have been composed between 750 and 650 BCE. Although contained within the marine microcosm of the Mediterranean, Odysseus's island-hopping trials and tribulations, his encounters with monsters, gods, demi-gods and magical beings on his long journey back to his family on Ithaca, provided a key Western blueprint for oral and later literary supernatural maritime adventures. One may not be able to go so far as to claim that it had a significant influence on the maritime folkloric imaginings that washed out into the Atlantic in the wake of European ships seeking the new world, but it certainly echoed and possibly provided a source for some of the more fantastical features of such tales.

Belief in marine gods provided a way for people to interpret and make sense of phenomena in the ocean's changeable and potentially hazardous environment. A space in which deities might intervene, for good or bad, could be negotiated through appeal to or shows of reverence towards the gods. Notions of sea deities expressed an appreciation of the non-human vitality of nature, forcing seafarers to confront something vastly larger and more powerful than themselves. Yet, perceived as the realm of gods, it was also a way of bringing the ocean back to a human frame of reference, where the supposed capriciousness, rage or benevolence of the sea could be understood in terms of human motives and emotions. As a place where human culture was stretched thin, akin to that of a maritime frontier, stories and beliefs could often supplement a lack of knowledge and certainty, with gods at least imposing some sense of order and meaning on the turbulent seas.

By the medieval and early modern period, Europeans viewed the North Sea and then the Atlantic through a more Christian interpretation of the world. Into the eighteenth and nineteenth centuries one still finds sailors referring to Neptune or Poseidon, but not in terms of actual belief. Rather, references to mariners as 'the sons of Neptune' was an evocative epithet that enabled sailors to be viewed and to view themselves as modern practitioners of a long and ancient seafaring brotherhood. However, the eighteenth and nineteenth-century Atlantic remained a space in which supernatural influences could intervene. From a Christian perspective, the ocean was a providential space where God could directly intervene to test or punish seafarers. Such ideas were part of the Protestant mental universe in the eighteenth century.[9] This was reinforced by the Bible, the key source of Christian authority for Protestants, and frequently the most common text used if one were to learn to read in this period.[10] Psalm 107 declares that 'They that go down to the sea in ships, that do business in great waters. These see the works of the Lord and his wonders of the Deep.' The psalm states that God commands the winds that stir the waves. When their ships are plummeting from mountainous peaks into deep troughs of dark water, sailors cry out to God, who, hearing their appeals, calms the storm, stills the waves and delivers them from terror into safety.[11]

Eighteenth-century preachers in coastal regions were apt at adapting parts of the Bible that best spoke to the occupations and concerns of their congregation or seafaring community.[12] Protestant sermons frequently presented natural disasters such as storms, earthquakes and shipwrecks as a divine response to sailors' sinful behaviour, so that the sea and weather became supernaturally weaponized as expressions of God's will and judgement. While this may not seem too far removed from ancient Greeks incurring the wrath of Poseidon, an interventionist Christian God at least gave religious-minded sailors some sense of influence over their fate. While they might be tested due to their past behaviours, it was in their power to repent, reform their ways and live more godly lives. Catholic sailors were inclined to fall back on piety acquired ashore, seeking protection from the ocean's dangers through appeals to the saints or the Virgin Mary. The patron saint of seafarers was St Nicholas, and eighteenth-century Catholic mariners from a range of European countries sought his miraculous aid, especially in causing storms to abate.[13]

Stories of shipwrecks caught the popular imagination of landlubbers. The suggestion of supernatural intervention, the tragedy of the dead and sometimes the gruesome details of those who survived the initial sinking made for an enticing tavern tale or a more literary concoction. Shipwreck accounts were widely and cheaply available as broadside ballads and chapbooks. Amy Mitchell-Cook has charted the shifts in the presentation of American shipwreck narratives between the seventeenth and nineteenth centuries. In the seventeenth century God was presented as both the cause of shipwrecks and the power that ensured the survival of those who made it back to shore. Eighteenth-century accounts often presented a more secularized account of wrecks and their victims, but the nineteenth century blended these approaches, combining godly interventions with an appreciation of human tenacity.[14] Printed accounts enabled endless speculation about divine intervention and free will, the power of nature (and possibly the supernatural powers behind it), and the skills and character of mariners when faced with dire circumstances. For the religiously inclined, shipwrecks were moral and spiritual lessons about the importance of faith, the power of God and the providential nature of the ocean. Religion and providential thinking were things that mariners acquired ashore as much as at sea, something that connected them to their land-based communities.[15] As we will see in various chapters, this is but one of many examples that challenge the mistaken notion that sailors were somehow a breed apart, members of an isolated, separate culture forged purely at sea.

Overt displays of piety could generate divisions aboard ship. Piousness fostered a sense of superiority, creating tensions in crews who, by the nature of their work, were heavily reliant on working in close collaboration with one another. This was demonstrated in the memoir of John Nicol (1755–1825), a literate Scottish sailor. Initially very pious as a young seaman, he gradually let his onboard Bible reading slip to fit in with the rest of the crew. Denominational differences could also divide crews. The late eighteenth- and nineteenth-century journals and autobiographies of Protestant mariners often reflected the anti-Catholic views of the period, with authors being critical of their 'superstitious' and credulous

French, Irish, Italian and Spanish crewmates. Nicol's autobiography gives an account of British Protestant crew members' dislike of Portuguese Catholic sailors who, when a fierce storm arose during at Atlantic voyage between Rio de Janeiro and Lisbon in 1792, abandoned their watch and posts. They sought out the onboard priest and knelt down at the quarterdeck while he sprinkled them with holy water. While the Catholic sailors seemed resigned to die, the four Protestant sailors were left to struggle with steering the ship and handling the sails as the storm raged around them.[16] From their perspective, the religious attitudes of the Portuguese crew members actively added to the dangers facing the ship. From the Catholics' perspective, it was a Portuguese vessel with a Catholic priest on board. When the storm hit, he had offered the Catholic sailors the last rites and helped prepare them for death. They had believed the storm had been sent, possibly by the Virgin Mary or the saints, because a Catholic vessel had taken on heretic Protestant crew members. Each saw the other as the problem.

The Devil and Davy Jones

While open to godly intervention, the ocean was also a diabolical realm too. In the folkloric imagination the Devil was as active at sea as he was on land, being particularly inclined to hurl storms at vessels carrying clergymen. Seeing malevolent purpose behind wind, waves and storms, sailors supernaturalized nature, granting its forces and phenomena personalities, so that a demon might create powerful gales or currents to drive a ship onto rocks or reefs. These demons were thought to be particularly active on holy days. According to French lore, one should avoid going to sea on All Hallows' Eve (Halloween), as the air would be full of them. In Ireland, it was dangerous to go fishing in Wexford Bay on St Martin's Eve, for on that particular day the demon who lived in the area was said to have sufficient power to grab and drown all fishermen who intruded into it. At the Cape of Good Hope a demonic figure called Adamaster was said to bring winds to destroy ships and would sometimes board vessels to take away the most evil members of the crew.[17] While conforming to folkloric accounts of the Devil as punisher of the wicked, this particular figure seemed to be a bastardized folkloric version of Adamastor, a mythological giant from the epic Portuguese poem *The Lusiads* (1572), written by Luis de Camões. Adamastor personified the Cape of Good Hope and the forces of nature faced by the Portuguese sailors who first tried to round it, thereby crossing from the Atlantic into the Indian Ocean. In this instance, a literary text seemed to provide inspiration for oral tales relating to the Cape.

The Devil was also imagined as a sailor. A French legend tells of how the Devil built a three-masted ship with wood from hell. Satan's crew consisted of those who had died as sinners. They engaged in acts of piracy until St Elmo sunk the vessel. The Devil

Unknown artist, 'Demons of the storm', illustration from James W. Buel, *Heroes of Unknown Seas and Savage Lands* (1891).

escaped by swimming away, but his hell ship was said to sometimes rise from beneath the waves at night, the vessel burning bright and reeking of sulphur. As we will see in the legend of the *Flying Dutchman* in Chapter Four, tales of sinful crews doomed to sail forever upon the seas denoted a kind of nautical purgatory, one in which dead sailors, especially cowards, thieves, murderers and sinners, were punished by serving an eternity before the mast. Yet, as the twentieth-century maritime folklorist Horace Beck noted, when mariners referred to ghost ships they meant one thing, when they referred to a devil ship they meant something else: not just an encounter with the dead but with the damned and the Devil himself. Beck's engaging *Folklore and the Sea* (1973) provided two accounts, from Newfoundland and the West Indies, where a devil ship was rammed and disappeared or driven off by making a lot of noise.[18]

Demonstrating the way maritime folklore often adapted and twisted ideas away from religious doctrine, the figure of Davy Jones also served as a nautical substitute for the Devil. In an 1889 article in *All the Year Round* it was suggested that 'Davy' may have derived from the West Indian word 'Duffy', meaning ghost, or the Sanskrit word 'Deva', from whose corruption we derive the word 'devil', while 'Jones' was a corruption of 'Jonah'. As such, 'Davy Jones' was an evil spirit who brought misfortune to ships and crew.[19] Mention of Davy Jones can be found in Tobias Smollett's *The Adventure of Peregrine Pickle* (1751). Here he is described as 'the fiend that presides over all the evil spirits of the deep, and is often seen in various shapes, perching among the rigging on the eve of hurricanes, ship-wrecks, and other disasters to which sea-faring life is exposed'.[20] The idea of a shapeshifting 'fiend' clearly positioned him as a maritime variant of the Devil for eighteenth-century readers.

Davy Jones was said to haunt the Atlantic as far back as the sixteenth century. Described as 'a giant breathing flames from his nostrils, having enormous eyes, and three rows of teeth', this imagery seems to owe something to a legacy of medieval demonology, suggesting an even earlier incarnation.[21] His strong association with the Devil meant that mariners' reference to 'Davy Jones's locker' may once have suggested a dark underwater hell from which there was no escape. If so, that idea seemed to have weakened over time. While the term 'Davy Jones's locker' was still common slang in nineteenth-century maritime culture, it seemed to be simply used as a colourful synonym for the deep.

This connection between Davy Jones and the Devil was demonstrated in what turned out to be a case of mistaken identity. Reverend Daniel Tyerman and George Bennett recorded the following account, told to them during their sea voyages on behalf of the London Missionary Society between 1821 and 1829. An officer once sent a boy up the mizzen mast to untangle a rope that had got caught at the top. He swiftly descended again, almost falling in his haste. Trembling, he announced that he had 'seen "Old Davy" aft the cross trees'. He described 'the Evil One' as having a huge face, pricked ears and 'eyes as bright as fire'. Two or three other sailors were sent up the mast, each returning to claim they too had been glared at by 'Old Davy'. When the mate climbed the mast, he discovered Davy Jones to be a large horned owl. The owl was brought down and 'Old Davy' was adopted as one of the crew. It was noted that if the owl had flown off, the impressionable young crew members would have forever believed it to have been a 'supernatural visitant' rather than just a bird.[22]

While his is a familiar name in maritime lore, as a character Davy Jones appears oddly absent from folkloric narratives in the Atlantic world. As the piece in *All the Year Round* noted, by the nineteenth century sailors made little mention of Davy Jones as an individual, but only mentioned him in reference to his 'locker'. It was the deep, not the demon, they remained concerned about. One of the few places where he was represented as a distinct character

John Tenniel, 'Davy Jones's locker', engraving from *Punch; or, The London Charivari*, CIII (10 December 1892).

at sea (rather than in literature about it) was in the traditional ceremony surrounding the crossing of the Equator. This served as a rite of passage or sea baptism for new sailors. Although Europeans officially crossed the Equator in the 1470s, it was not until the late sixteenth century that the Dutch developed a line-crossing ceremony, with British ships adopting a ceremony by the 1670s. It continued to be observed by nineteenth-century passenger sailing ships and has even continued in a milder form and as an entertaining distraction on modern leisure cruise ships.[23]

The ceremony involved a mock rebellion by new sailors (known as pollywogs). Neptune and his court then appeared on board to put them on trial. Davy Jones often took the role of the Devil or the judge and was therefore instrumental in dispensing humiliating punishments. Crew members dressed up for the roles, with Neptune often being the oldest sailor aboard, and Amphitrite, his wife, usually being a young sailor in drag. The rest of Neptune's court consisted of an odd, carnivalesque group including a scribe, barber, doctor, navigator, chaplain, jester and the Devil. New sailors had to endure ritual humiliations, being physically assaulted, made to wear their clothes backwards, blindfolded and coated in substances that represented excrement. The pollywogs were presented to Neptune by more experienced sailors and were forcibly dunked in water as their final initiation as fellow 'shellbacks'. Such an experience served as a memorable reminder of older oceanic deities and demons.

Sentient Seas and Sailors' 'Superstitions'

Alongside but often more muted than these predominantly Christian notions was a view that the ocean was also a place of elemental spirits. Such ideas are often little more than fragments gleaned from folkloric accounts and investigations. For example, J. A. Teit claimed that Shetland Islanders believed in a great sea spirit that would punish those who mocked or spoke disparagingly of it. The 'da mokkl sea-trow' or big sea troll was understood to be 'a kind of evil spirit that haunted the deep', one that could raise storms or bring misfortune upon fishermen. When at sea Shetland fishermen considered themselves surrounded by potentially hostile sea spirits and were aware of themselves as intruders upon that space.[24] Echoing this, the folklorist Christina Hole noted how the changeable nature of the sea meant that mariners, fishermen and coastal communities had long 'tended to regard it . . . as a living, thinking entity, rather than as a mere natural expanse of salt water', a thing capable of thought and feelings.[25] Seas and oceans possessed the dual nature of an unstable god or a human tyrant, capable of giving, providing food and a livelihood, yet equally capable of cruelly taking away, punishing and killing.

On the west coast of Ireland tales were told of an avenging wave. Shea, a fisherman, once killed a mermaid, even though she had begged him for her life. When he next put to sea the wave came at him, topped with lightning. Suddenly struck by a guilty conscience for what he had done to the mermaid, he turned his vessel and tried to reach the shore, but he and his crew were drowned. Unsatisfied with these deaths, it was said that the avenging wave similarly threatened Shea's direct descendants whenever they put to sea.[26] Clearly the Atlantic waters had a long memory and held grudges.

Linked to that was the belief that the sea deserved its due. In Shetland and other islands in the northeast of Scotland this found rather callous expression in the belief that one should not save a drowning man. It was thought that to cheat the sea of one death would require another in recompense. Tales were told of how the rescuer of a drowning man had himself drowned within a year. While not an unlikely prospect for Scottish fishermen, this helped imbue the sea with sentience, one that remembered and sought to redress perceived insults.

The winds were also granted a sense of animism and had a particularly contrary nature. Mention of fair winds while at sea was thought to be unlucky, as the wind might change simply to show that it could. As we will see in Chapter Two, sailors understood the wind to be capricious and easily provoked. This animistic belief extended to sailing vessels, too. Robert Southey noted how sailors 'ascribe consciousness and sympathy to their ship', claiming 'She behaves well,' giving the ship personality and vitality.[27] The ship's bell was thought to represent the vessel's soul. If it rang of its own accord, it was taken as an omen of disaster, and there was a belief that it always rang, like a dying cry, as a wrecked ship sank beneath the waves.[28]

This understanding of waves and winds highlights an odd contradiction in the mariner's mindset. Viewing the sea as a sentient environment that needed to be respected and placated both intensified an awareness of it as a vast and powerful non-human entity while also anthropomorphizing it by projecting human-like qualities and motivations onto it. While grappling with their insignificance amid the vastness of the Atlantic, mariners also continued to believe that the ocean was responsive to the past sins or smallest actions of the minuscule, individual human beings that moved across its great surface. Such notions suggested that nature was not simply oblivious to mariners and that their misfortunes were not pure happenchance. Rather they promoted the more unsettling idea that the ocean was paying attention and might be consciously out to get them.

These views did not simply disappear in the nineteenth century or with the gradual passing of the age of sail. As part of the lecture with which this chapter opened, Reverend T. Greenbury declared that sailors did not tend to be atheists, but that they were not strictly Christian either. He went on:

> the mighty ocean . . . that vast, that deep, that illimitable ocean, was ever speaking to [the mariner] of the great Creator. The sailor had so constantly before him the evidences of Divine power that, wicked though he might be, he could not become an atheist, but often went to the other extreme and became exceedingly superstitious, believing in signs and omens, ghosts and goblins, flying Dutchmen, and so forth.[29]

This body of belief and an instinct to interpret the unusual through a supernatural lens was never far below the surface. This is seen in an account of the mysterious ringing of a bell aboard a British frigate in the Atlantic. Appearing in the *Bristol Mercury* in June 1855, the incident was vaguely situated as having taken place 'some years ago', aboard a frigate 'manned by four hundred of Old England's hardest seamen'. Becalmed in the middle of the Atlantic, hundreds of miles from land and without any other ship in sight, the crew heard a ringing of bells. Attempts to locate the source of the ringing came to nothing, for it was eventually worked out that it was not the frigate's bell they could hear. Talk turned to 'an invisible power', with the quarter master solemnly declaring, 'unless it was a freak of old Neptune, Davy Jones, or the Flying Dutchman, he did not know who [rang the bell]'. The ringing periodically continued, even though the bell was in sight and nobody was nearby. Neither the officers nor the rank-and-file seamen could explain the source of the mysterious ringing.

Eventually the ship's purser challenged the supernatural speculations by claiming the clouds must be funnelling the sound of another ship's bell from far away. The sailors dismissed this more mundane interpretation as stupid and suggested that the purser would be best to stick to his job 'and serve out better baccy and slops'. The journalist noted that the sailors 'preferred to believe in the impossible rather than in the probable', and that night the strange ringing encouraged 'more yarn about supernatural events than had been heard for months before'. One crew member declared that he had once seen the *Flying Dutchman*, another, a mermaid. After another day, another ship eventually came into sight. They confirmed they had rung their bell as part of the ceremony of crossing the Equator two days earlier, thereby proving the purser's theory correct. Despite that, the piece concluded that 'there were score of sailors in the frigate – bold, hardy, strong-willed men – who resolutely refused to believe, and to the day of their death were doubtless prepared to maintain that the ship's bell was rung by supernatural agency.'[30]

One must be cautious with taking such an account at face value. It lacks specific details, including a precise date or the name of the ship. No crew members were identified, other than through generic references to 'one old forecastle' or their rank. The journalist clearly places words in the sailors' mouths without providing any indication of the story's source. This depiction is linked to a popular portrayal of 'Jack Tar', the archetypal British naval seaman of the late eighteenth and early nineteenth century. Often presented as daring and fearless in battle, he was frequently portrayed as a naive innocent ashore. Recent scholarship suggests that seamen were far savvier than they have been credited for when in port. However, the journalist's emphasis on the crew's broad desire to reject the purser's more scientific claim in favour of their own supernatural interpretations and prejudices played into that rather childlike image.[31] This created a contradictory image, for the ultra-masculine naval seaman, stereotyped as a drunken, brawling, whoring ruffian, was also understood to be highly sensitive to omens and quick to fill the maritime environment with supernatural forces and influences.

Telling Tales: The Function of Maritime Folklore on Ships

The sailor's worldview has been said to combine 'the natural, the supernatural, the magical, and the material'.[32] This tended to give maritime lore a very pragmatic dimension. Rather than viewing it, as contemporary critics did, as mere 'superstition' or ignorance, it is better understood as both an important psychological aid and cultural means of confronting the many dangers of seafaring, a way of operating as part of a shipbound community and as a member of a broader, international maritime culture. How did this supernatural culture operate and what functions did it serve for mariners?

Given the potential for religious denomination or national or ethnic identity to foster divisions in crews, folkloric ideas provided a shared culture that sat above such concerns. They provided an alternative way of talking about the concerns created by life at sea, a body of lore that was commonly referenced without necessarily requiring belief. Rather than a rigidly structured, coherent system of dogmatic beliefs, it was a rich but looser collage that referenced animism, magical thinking, religion and folklore. Its supernatural and marvellous elements informed an occupational worldview that helped bind mariners together, variously serving as a means of warning, explanation or instruction. It was broad and adaptive, formed and inherited as an unquestioned mishmash of ideas from the past and many places. Such a mindset could accommodate the idea of godly intervention, the influence of the Devil and vaguer aquatic spirits that stood outside or pre-dated Christianity without contradiction. It can be understood as a vernacular form of religiosity, one in which there was no holy book and no clergy, simply the supernatural yarns and anecdotes traded between itinerant mariners and the metaphysical ideas that such tales reinforced. The Atlantic was an important conduit in the transportation and transmission of these stories and beliefs. The Grand Banks drew cod fishermen from England, Ireland and France, and tales told in Newfoundland have been linked back to similar accounts told by Catholics in Ireland and communities in the West Country in England.[33]

Historians have recognized the important role played by maritime folklore on board ships. Brian Rouleau has convincingly argued that it served to dampened potential tensions and provided a means of expressing a sense of community and its concerns.[34] Chris Magra has highlighted its value as a shared means of understanding and dealing with the unpredictable and potentially dangerous nature of life at sea.[35] While we may now view much of it as maritime whimsy, there were pragmatic applications and concerns underlying why people exchanged their titbits of nautical lore. Long hours of labour and watch routines meant storytelling did not necessarily occur daily. As seen with the above story of the mysterious ringing bell aboard the frigate, a round of such tale swapping could be triggered by unusual or inexplicable events, when mariners felt compelled to move beyond their mundane knowledge and interpretations and grasp for more supernatural ones.

Without stories to distract them, bored, restless and long-confined sailors might have directed their attentions to more destructive behaviours. In the long crossings back and forth between France and Newfoundland's Grand Banks there were necessarily periods where there was little work to do, and crews needed to find ways to entertain themselves. While there, extremely bad weather might prevent fishing but intensify the unease that came with being cooped up aboard ship. Stories became a welcome distraction. They also served to reinforce a sense of the seafaring community's own identity, with fishermen's stories often depicting landlubbers as despised and cowardly characters.

Stories were a cheap currency that could be easily exchanged, with new crew members learning both tales and the art of telling them from more experienced mariners. In this way, mariners expanded their storytelling repertoire as they served on different ships. This was particularly significant for cabin boys, who were often subject to brutality at the hands of older sailors. They were an easy target for their weary or frustrated crewmates. If cabin boys were permitted into the exchange of stories, being able to entertain their crewmates may have deflected their violence.

Some officers were also inclined to make an example of the youngest crew members rather than directly tackle older, tougher sailors. In the eighteenth- and early nineteenth-century French fishing fleet that worked the Newfoundland Grand Banks, there was a superstitious belief that hitting cabin boys could variously raise or calm the winds as needed.[36] Letellier, a young mariner from Normandy, used the telling of stories to divert his shipmates from bullying him. Writing of his first two voyages to the Grand Banks in 1876 and 1877, he explained that it was tales told by ex-sailors working on his family's farm that initially encouraged him to go to sea.[37] Once aboard, he could use those entertaining stories to make himself useful to the crew and thereby gain acceptance as one of them. The problem for cabin boys was that they were typically inexperienced seafarers, their store of nautical tales often small unless obtained, as in the case of Letellier, before coming aboard. Even then, it could take time for them to be accepted into a crew of hardened mariners, let alone given an opportunity to tell them a tale.

George Cruikshank, 'Saturday night at sea', illustration from Thomas Dibdin, *Songs, Naval and National, of the Late Charles Dibdin* (1841).

Tales could also be a means of conveying practical information about seafaring occupations. On the Dingle peninsula in the west of Ireland, stories became a way of teaching young fishermen the nature of the work, the weather and the sea, how to understand the behaviour of fish and how to handle a boat.[38] Supernatural stories were memorable ways of reinforcing lessons about danger and safety at sea. As we will see in Chapter Four, ghost stories were particularly useful in this regard, along with helping seafarers maintain a sense of connection to loved ones back on land. Ghost stories of lost or drowned sailors allowed them to talk about such experiences via the supernatural rather than directly. The pronounced masculine culture of the sailor meant they were expected to be brave but in a stoic way, facing danger and then laughing it off after they had survived.[39] In this context, folkloric accounts became an oblique way of expressing common anxieties shared by seafarers, one that allowed them to be discussed without risk to their masculine identity.

This reticence about talking directly about fears and dangers was itself part of the mariners' culture of solidarity.[40] Its existence was suggested by an account in Irish poet William Butler Yeats's *The Celtic Twilight* (1893). Recording the folkloric yarns of his informant, Paddy Flynn, Yeats told of a Captain Moran whose 'sea captain's prayer' was to maintain his composure in the face of certain death. Moran demonstrated a tough, stoic streak that he similarly demanded of his crew:

> Why, sur, we war in mid Atlantic, and I was standin' on the bridge, when the third mate comes up to me lookin' mortial bad. Says he, 'Captain, all's up with us.' Says I, 'Didn't you know when you joined that a certain percentage go down every year?' 'Yes, sur,' says he; and says I, 'Aren't you paid to go down?' 'Yes, sur,' says he; and says I, 'Then go down like a man, and be damned to you!'[41]

The idea of telling tales to talk about things indirectly also took on a political dimension aboard ship. The chain of command between officers and seamen was rigid, unquestioning obedience was expected, and any suggestion of protest was likely to be harshly punished. Direct criticism of officers could be deemed insubordination, but to do it collectively through the guise of stories enabled seamen to express their desires, grudges and expectations of both officers and fellow crewmates. The historian David Hopkin notes how French mariners told fairy tales that ostensibly talked of things unreal and far away. Their stories contained fanciful maritime features such as 'magic islands, fairy crews, [and] demon ships' but no mention of the real challenges they faced. Yet behind the veil of metaphor, these tales were ways of talking about injustices, power and survival, issues pertinent to the experience of mariners aboard ship.[42] They might give insight into the type of leadership they valued and the type they despised. As will be seen in Chapter Four, ghost stories could become a way of vicariously imagining the punishment of a bullying crew member or officer, often receiving their comeuppance at the hands of some vengeful spirit.

Officers were known to listen in on the crew's storytelling, and Hopkin argues that telling tales became a form of indirect communication and negotiation between them. The power of supernatural stories was that they could suggest ideas that could easily be withdrawn as a *mere* tale or fantastical nonsense. It was hard for such ideas to be pinned down as mutinous, as they could be dismissed by crewmen as just an entertaining yarn. As interesting as Hopkin's notion of 'disguised negotiation' is, it depends on a level of knowingness that is extremely difficult to gauge.[43] Tales were often not written down, let alone people's interpretations of them, so it is hard to know whether crewmen and officers all got the point of the stories or took the same meaning from their underlying messages. This interpretation also raises another concern. Understanding such tales as purely coded complaints and anxieties about mundane reality risks diminishing the power of the supernatural within those stories and thereby depleting the sense of maritime enchantment that they fostered. Storytelling was an important way of imagining different possibilities, retaining the ocean's sense of wonder and mystery in a period when an emphasis on rationalism, economic globalization and scientific exploration sought to dismiss such ideas as hokum.

Some of these functions of supernatural maritime folklore can be seen in other aspects of onboard culture, such as the singing of shanties. The use of these work songs peaked between 1820 and 1860. Performed by crews to coordinate their labour when operating sailing ships, they naturally excluded officers. This gave the common seamen an opportunity to express their identity, hopes, discontents and values. Shanties often spoke to a nostalgic sense that the past had been better than the present. They gave voice to dissatisfaction at being far from home and having to endure hardship and strict discipline aboard ship. Like storytelling, they enabled mariners to express concerns about dangers and death, but also provided escapism in songs about beautiful women, travel to exotic lands and debauchery ashore. Some even referenced features of maritime folklore such as the *Flying Dutchman*. As in the exchange of folk and fairy tales, it was difficult for officers to crack down on this, for the shanties helped facilitate the very labour that sailors were grumbling about. Neither shanties nor maritime folklore were purely the creation of people at sea. Both tended to be exchanged in ports, and while some shanties may have owed a debt to broadside ballads, the tropes of nautical ghost stories may have been informed by similar stories heard in taverns ashore.[44]

In an occupation where sailors frequently changed vessels, captains and crewmates, the sharing of tales of strange experiences and sightings at sea helped them repeatedly reformulate themselves into a new workforce for the duration of a voyage. Such practices informed a worldview and a marine community that understood the ocean as both a natural and supernatural space. Maritime folklore moved with the mariners and was circulated by them; they were its network, generators and transmitters. This meant that its common features, ideas and tropes became internationalized and transoceanic in the developing global economy of the late eighteenth and nineteenth centuries.

While the exchange of stories may have helped foster a sense of a seafaring community, mariners often held differing views on the folkloric ideas being shared. Beyond autobiographies and memoirs by the likes of John Nicol, Charles Tyng, George Little and Richard Henry Dana Jr, all of which would have been written with an awareness of a likely audience, evidence of these personal opinions is scarce. One might reasonably assume that some might believe, others might choose to suspend disbelief and entertain such ideas, while yet others might simply tolerate them as part of shipboard gossip. Belief was not necessarily required for the soft power and influence that could be exerted through maritime folklore. In his memoir of early nineteenth-century seafaring, the American sea captain Charles Tyng told how as a younger mariner he had served on a ship unloading cargo in Havana. The crew had created a story of it being haunted by 'an evil spirit'. The vessel was leaky, and the story helped justify deserting a dangerous ship, its unpleasant captain and their contractual obligations. Many of the crew, drawn from several nations, deserted in their first week in port.[45]

Like belief, the issues of truth and accuracy were not that important to the functions of storytelling. Sailors' tales and accounts operated perfectly well and were even enhanced when deliberate exaggeration, barefaced lies and leg-pulling were all churned into the mix. The pragmatic attitude demonstrated by Tyng's crewmates was echoed by a piece in the *Western Mail* in October 1870. Referring to an incident in which sailors had refused to sail on a ship from Cardiff that had subsequently sunk, it was noted that while mariners might generally be considered a 'superstitious class', they often proved to be 'neither superstitious nor foolish, but shrewd men of the world, whose wits are sharpened by experience'.[46]

The eighteenth-century Enlightenment promoted the advancement of rationalism as a way of dispelling and moving beyond the supposed ignorance, irrationalism and superstition of the past. In the later nineteenth century, European and North American theories of cultural evolution tended to associate animistic and magical thinking with non-Western peoples. These trends informed a 'modern' divide between 'primitive', 'superstitious' beliefs and increasingly secular Western attitudes, between the heart and distant fringes of their empires. However, as seen in this chapter, Western sailors disrupted this divide as they travelled around those empires. Although they were keen observers of the marine environment and its meteorological phenomena, their emphasis on observation could lead to decidedly unscientific ideas about omens and the operation of the supernatural. Inspired by the primal nature of the ocean and its threats, they sailed upon waters that were simultaneously natural and supernatural. In such an environment, a rational, disenchanted 'modern' view of the world often struggled to find purchase.

Writing in 1937, Robert Hadfield claimed that the development of steam and motor-driven vessels, luxury cruise liners and global communications had caused modern readers to lose sight of the awe and terror the oceans had once evoked in seafarers.[47] Such a statement was simply an update of earlier nineteenth-century assertions that technological rationality would ultimately eradicate belief in the supernatural. Those developments may have gone some way to distancing twentieth-century seafarers from some of the dangers faced by their ancestors, but they could never wholly disconnect them from the psychological influence of an oceanic environment determined by the power and vagaries of elemental forces. As we will see in the next chapter, despite the modern era's ongoing technological developments in ship design, propulsion, navigation and communication, the challenges of seafaring (and sea fearing) long continued to be navigated through a rich body of lore, one full of magic, rites, observances and omens.

2

Maritime Magic and Omens

There was once a Scottish trader who bought the wind. Old John McTaggart purchased it from a local woman who was said to have power over such things, and therefore had more than a whiff of witchcraft about her. For his money, the merchant received two pieces of string, each containing three knots. Setting out from Kintyre in his little smack, he undid the first knot on one piece of string. His sails suddenly filled with a good breeze, causing his vessel to pick up speed. Yet the merchant was a man in a hurry – time was money – and so once in midchannel he untied the second knot. The steady breeze became a gale, pushing the smack ever faster through the churning waves. Approaching the coast of Ireland, the impatient merchant untied the final knot. The gale transformed into a fierce hurricane. The raging winds roared ahead of his ship, smashing some of the homes on shore. Aware of the power he had unleashed, and having learnt his lesson, he took care to untie only the first two knots on his journey home to Scotland.

As folkloric accounts go, this is little more than the bare bones of a story that could be transposed anywhere. It is vague in its dating, its biographical details and even its Irish location. Yet these stripped-down essentials, easily adapted to any locality, were an important part of the way migratory tales travelled. Similar accounts are found as far apart as Finland and the east coast of Massachusetts.[1] Despite its skeletal state, it points to important aspects of this chapter. It shows us mariners' desire to control the elements and bend nature to human will. It speaks of ordinary people resorting to magic, and of a knowledge of how and from whom such magic could be purchased. With echoes of Johann Wolfgang von Goethe's 1797 poem 'The Sorcerer's Apprentice', it also indicates how employing magical power did not guarantee a desired outcome: nature could be altered by magic, but that was not the same as control. This tale is also a good example of why we need to be cautious about the conclusions we draw from folkloric accounts. Compared to undoing Old McTaggart's knots, it is considerably harder to unpick the extent to which sailors genuinely believed in the efficacy of 'buying the wind' or whether it was more of a symbolic practice, merely a totemic hope for a fair breeze.

Neither religious faith nor trust in a sturdy ship and competent crewmates was necessarily enough for seafarers risking their lives in the Atlantic. Into the nineteenth century and beyond, mariners of all types went to sea with an armoury of magical charms, customary rituals, practices and observances, all of which sought to temper their concerns about and gain some influence over capricious seas and hostile oceans. While distinctions were sometimes made between the 'superstitions' of coastal fishermen and those of 'deep blue' mariners engaged in transatlantic voyages, the bulk of maritime folklore spoke less to specific seafaring occupations and more to the shared danger of the sea or ocean as a working environment. As seen in the last chapter, that environment was subject to supernatural forces, but it was also one in which careful observance of omens and the policing of one's own actions and words might allow for a degree of human influence, too. The Scottish poet and novelist Sir Walter Scott captured the supernatural richness of the nautical mind in his 1813 poem *Rokeby*. In canto 2, he declares that during the middle night watch:

> seamen love to hear and tell
> Of portent, prodigy, and spell:
> What gales are sold on Lapland's shore,
> How whistle rash bids tempests roar,
> Of witch, of mermaid, and of sprite,
> Of Erick's cap and Elmo's light;
> Or of that Phantom Ship, whose form
> Shoots like a meteor through the storm.[2]

Although Scott was referring to the seventeenth century, we will see that much of this could still be regarded as 'living' folklore at the time the poem was penned.

As Fletcher S. Bassett's compendious study, *Legends and Superstitions of the Sea and of Sailors in All Lands and at All Times* (1885), indicated, variants of these beliefs and practices were commonly shared by the maritime labour force of many seafaring nations around the world and down through the centuries. Nineteenth-century journalists and commentators on folklore and 'popular credulity' frequently portrayed sailors as among the most superstitious of occupations, 'superstitious' being used as a derogatory term. As late as 1923, the *New York Times* could declare that 'as superstitious as a sailor' was a proverbial phrase known to every nation that bordered one of the seven seas, although its article suggested that diesel engines, iron hulls and modern radio had done much to erode the older body of 'superstitions' that had accompanied the age of sail.[3]

While this was a common point of commentary, there is little to suggest that sailors were necessarily more superstitious than those in other potentially hazardous occupations, although the collective body of maritime lore appears richer and more extensive than that relating to soldiers or miners. Nor were maritime magical practices solely the furtive product of sailors' isolation at sea. Going all the way back to the initial stages of shipbuilding, this rich body of occupational folklore had land-based origins too. It was rooted in the anxieties of the coastal communities from which sailors and fishermen were often recruited and in which they lived while ashore. As such, our examination of maritime magic will begin on land, with consideration of how mariners prepared themselves for the dangers they would face once afloat.

Maritime Magic: Prevention, Protection and Bending Luck

Maritime magic and magical thinking offer us a way into understanding something of the psychological experience of seafaring, both for sailors and their land-based families. It certainly spoke to fears, but also to a sense of optimism that humans could obtain some influence over the unpredictable ocean. The greatest fear in venturing to sea was obviously drowning. In one way or another, most magical protection, ritualized practices or reading of signs and omens was directed towards avoiding the storms and misfortune that might result in the sinking of a vessel. Crew members who went into the Atlantic waters faced hypothermia and drowning. Those who were fortunate enough to make it into boats, if available, might endure horrific physical and mental ordeals from which not all survived. Nineteenth-century shipwreck narratives and an increasingly sensationalist press told of the limits to which survivors could be pushed. In the case of the sinking of the *Mignonette* some 1,600 miles northwest of the Cape of Good Hope in July 1884, this included starving sailors killing the cabin boy and resorting to cannibalism in order to survive.

To avert these frightening scenarios, sailors often carried charms to protect themselves. As was the way with folk magic, this usually involved taking natural or everyday objects and giving them supernatural meaning and potency. Fish bones, shells, coral or dead seahorses might all serve this purpose. These may have been found objects that were kept for protection, but they could also be purchased from cunning folk. Cunning folk were enterprising Jacks or Jills of all magical trades, and those who lived near or among coastal communities and seafarers were unlikely to miss a trick when it came to plying their magical skills for a fee. In 1873 a local cunning man, 'Dr' John Thomas, warned a sailor from Penryn, a fishing port in Cornwall, that a mysterious woman whose name began with an 'A' was working magic against him, with the intention of drowning him. Betting on the daily risk faced by the sailor and letting him fill in the blanks regarding whom the woman might be seemed a useful way of drumming up some anti-witchcraft trade. Coastal cunning folk might also manufacture protective charms for seafarers. One such example held in the Museum of Witchcraft in Boscastle, the 'hammer of Thor', was made by a Cornish wise woman, the reference to the Norse god clearly intended to offer protection from storms.[4]

A particularly popular form of maritime charm was a caul. Through the principle of sympathetic magic, of like for like, it was reasoned that the membrane that protected the baby in the womb would protect a sailor in the ocean. This connected to a broader folkloric belief that a child born with their caul intact would be blessed with a life of good fortune. These were often sewn into a sailor's clothing so that he would never be without it when at sea. Newspapers continued to publish notices of cauls for sale throughout the nineteenth century. One was advertised in *The Times* (8 May 1848) for six guineas, coming with the appealing claim that it had protected a sailor throughout his forty-year career at sea, and that he had finally died safe at home and in his own bed. Yet the value of noting this seems to jar with a contradictory belief that the caul's protection would remain effective as long as the child from whom it had been taken remained healthy. Illness or decline in health would result in the caul changing, becoming crispy or flexible as the person's health shifted. This would negate the value of passing a caul on from father to son.[5] Another was sold for five guineas in Plymouth's *Western Daily News* (9 February 1867), and three were advertised in the *Liverpool Mercury* in 1873 for prices that varied from 30 shillings to four guineas. No small sum, given a mariner's wages.

As indicated through these prices, cauls declined in value over the course of the middle decades of the century. An article published in the journal *Folklore* during the First World War noted that the sale of cauls had declined in the later nineteenth century. However, prices and sales suddenly revived as submarine warfare became part of that conflict.[6] When circumstances shifted and the likelihood of drowning increased, supposedly fading 'superstitions' could make an abrupt return. This continued into the Second World War. The folklorist Christina Hole told of how 'In 1944, an Oxfordshire woman known to me, whose son was born with a caul, was offered £10 for it by the midwife, who wanted it for a sailor friend. She refused to sell it, however, preferring to keep the immunity for her own child.'[7] Hole claimed the power of the caul extended beyond the individual sailor who possessed it, for the ship he served on would never sink while he was aboard.

While cauls and charms were the best-known protections from drowning, there seem to have been many other local examples. When the model barque was periodically taken down from the top of St Thomas's Cathedral, Portsmouth, for cleaning, local mothers would place their children in it, believing it would protect them from drowning.[8] Portsmouth was Britain's principal naval town, and many of its young boys might eventually serve in the Royal Navy.

This was but one of a range of seemingly bizarre rituals and superstitions that stretched back to the building and launch of a vessel. During construction of ships in Germany, Belgium, the Netherlands and Scandinavian countries, it was a traditional custom to put into a ship a small piece of stolen wood, nothing larger than a plug or plank. This would supposedly 'give the ships the nature of a thief: quick-running, especially at night'. Stolen nails or other pieces of iron or steel would also serve to negate or protect the vessel from witchcraft. Henning Henningsen suggests this was simply the extension of a land-based custom of burying coins, iron, bones or stolen timber into a new building, to protect it or to bring good luck.[9] Conversely, a death or accident during the building of a ship was thought to taint it with bad luck, although it is not clear how sailors would have been aware of this.

The idea of blessing a new ship at its launch dated back to antiquity. The notion of christening a ship updated and made respectable an ancient practice of giving libation. As William Jones noted, 'On the completion of a ship, it was decked with garlands and flowers, and the mariners adorned with crowns. It was launched into the sea, with loud acclamations, and other expressions of joy, and being purified by a priest . . . it was consecrated to the god whose image it carried.'[10] Despite their renowned reluctance to have a woman on board, sailors supposedly preferred a ship to be christened by a woman.[11]

The naming of ships was equally fraught with risk as there were superstitions surrounding lucky and unlucky ship names. It was believed that the name of sailing ships should not be changed, although it was acceptable to change the name of a steamship. Given the technological shift from sail to steam in the nineteenth and early twentieth centuries, this suggests an accompanying shift in attitude and perception. Sail ships had character and individual personality, whereas steamships were perceived as more functional, utilitarian vessels. In the Royal Navy, ships named after snakes were considered unlucky. In 1890 HMS *Serpent* was wrecked on the Spanish coast on her first commission and was followed by the loss of HMS *Viper* and HMS *Cobra*. In 1928 a new submarine had its name changed from *Python* to *Pandora* (not a great improvement, unless we associate Pandora with hope rather than the disaster she unleashed).[12] Given the misfortunes suffered by ships of all names, one can only speculate that such a belief may have been fostered by vessels named after snakes being more memorable than others.

Once afloat, sailors would add their own good-luck tokens to the vessel. The tradition of placing coins beneath the mast of a ship dated back to at least the Romans. For commercial vessels this seemed to be an encouragement of wealth and fortune, with the idea that the coin symbolized the making of more. Fishing boats leaving harbour in Kings Lynn, Norfolk, England, would pin a coin to the mast to bring a good catch. A similar practice could be found in naval ships intended for battle. The officers of the USS *New Orleans*, built in 1934, 'placed 10 pennies beneath the foremast, and 2 dimes, 3 nickles and 28 pennies at the heel of the mainmast'. The destroyer *Shelton* was given a new mast in San Francisco in 1951. Since it had not been possible to locate a silver coin dated to that year, one from 1950 was placed underneath.[13] Similar practices have been recorded in England, Denmark, Norway, Sweden, Finland and Germany. In Germany the tradition seems to be that coins should be as old as possible, and preferably foreign. In many European countries there was an emphasis on silver coins or other silver objects, thought to have a protective influence against the evil eye, witchcraft and lightning.[14] Similarly, many sailors fixed a horseshoe to the stern post for good luck: this was said to be a popular practice among English sailors, especially after Lord Nelson had one nailed to the mast of HMS *Victory*.[15] A horseshoe fixed to the mast with its ends upwards would ensure the safety of the vessel. Countering the image of the superstitious common sailor, it is worth noting the involvement of officers in these practices.

Navigating Bad Luck and the Taint of Misfortune

As seen in the shifting shipwreck narratives of the seventeenth to nineteenth centuries, deities and spirits did not have total control over a sailor's fate. While God, the Devil or some oceanic spirit that may have pre-dated Christianity could intervene, sailors still believed that attention to luck and omens could grant them a degree of influence and a chance to avoid misfortune. Magical protection could and did fail. Hard experience taught that the ocean would have its implacable way and take its fair share of ships and crews. However, it at least encouraged a hope that the odds could be nudged in the sailor's favour. To do so they had to contend with the nature of bad luck. Misfortune tended to have an insidious quality that would taint and linger, rather than being simply confronted or avoided.

Writing about Scottish fishing communities in 1881, Walter Gregor recorded that a boat that had been wrecked and cast ashore after its crew had drowned would be left to rot. The local community would not even use it for firewood, emphasizing that such ideas were not confined to those who took to the sea, but were similarly found in the coastal communities to which they belonged. It was noted that they were willing to sell the boat on to fishermen from another village, thereby removing the tainted vessel from their locality.[16] This pragmatic callousness was seen in the aversion to saving a drowning man in Shetland, other islands of northeast Scotland and Cornwall. It was variously believed that the man saved would eventually do harm to his rescuer, or that the sea was owed its due. Cheating it of one life would result in it taking another.[17] In many cases, it was thought that the rescuer himself would be the object of the sea's anger and it would be he himself who was destined to drown.[18] In such a case, the taint of misfortune would shift from the drowning individual to a would-be rescuer. This was a fear seen in several late nineteenth-century cases in Orkney. In one a boatman refused to row out to a drowning man and removed the oars from his boat so that others could not. In another incident, three men watched their neighbour drown, not from to a lack of courage or compassion, but because of 'a far deeper-seated terror of the sea's vengeance'.[19] On a more practical level, it was also a way of rationalizing not leaping into icy cold waters to save a fellow crewman or villager. It was a matter of self-preservation.

The taint of death extended to mariners' reluctance to have dead bodies on board ship. Again, the principle of supernatural sympathies seemed to apply: like attracts like, so death would attract death. If a body was brought home rather than being buried at sea, then it had to lie across the vessel, never end on. It also had to leave the ship before the crew when the vessel reached port. In a piece in the *New York Times* in 1897, James J. Ferris, an old American sailor, claimed, 'They don't make any better sailors the world over than the Scandinavians, but they are loaded to the guards with superstition.' He recounted how when sailing up from the Gulf of Mexico his three-master encountered a squall and a young man fell from the yard and died. The three Americans in the crew were all for returning his body to Maine. When they stowed the sailor's corpse on the forward deck, the 'ghost-fearing Scandinavians' refused to do lookout duty, and the presence of the body seemed to encourage unrest among them, to the point where Ferris claimed, 'It took all the arsenal we had aboard . . . to keep them down until we reached New York.'[20]

In 1898 the *Chicago Daily Tribune* claimed that when dead bodies were transported as cargo they were often listed on invoices as either 'statuary' or 'natural history specimen' so as not to stir the superstitious unease of crew members.[21] A similar unease could be found among Scottish islanders. A boat that had carried a coffin was deemed unlucky. The Reverend MacDonald noted that when a woman died on the Outer Hebridean island of Eriskay, her coffin was put in a small boat completely unsuitable for the job of taking it to the mainland, rather than in her family's fishing boat.[22] For all the bonds of love, the family did not want the corpse to taint the vessel upon which their livelihood depended.

As with the physical dangers of the sea itself, mariners could be beset by ill luck from all directions. Certain days of the week were deemed unluckier than others, and launching a ship or starting a voyage on a Friday was particularly unlucky. Infused with apocryphal religious ideas about it being the day of Christ's crucifixion and other folkloric ideas surrounding bad luck on Fridays, this was very much a land-based notion that informed maritime activities. In December 1892 the *Chicago Daily Tribune* recited a popular but most likely invented account that has been cited in both Britain and the United States. Sounding like an exaggerated joke that may have been misconstrued as fact, it reported that 'a skeptical Massachusetts captain . . . back in the early years of the republic' decided to test the superstition to breaking point. He contracted the construction of a new ship on a Friday, and the keel was laid on a Friday. The ship, obviously named *The Friday*, was launched and loaded on a Friday. The ship even employed a cook called Friday. A symbol of defiance and freighted with ill luck, the ship finally sailed on its first voyage on a Friday, heading for a port in the West Indies. It was never heard of again.[23]

Such an observance suggests that sailors continued to pay lip service to a calendar of holy days and days of religious significance that had waned on land through the seventeenth and eighteenth centuries.[24] The first of April, supposedly the date of Cain's birth and Abel's death, 31 December, said to be the day of Judas's birth, and Candlemas, 2 February, were all considered ill-omened by mariners. The association with biblical villainy seemed to taint the days. Yet, demonstrating the practical function of such beliefs, this seemed to enable sailors to apply a degree of collective pressure, possibly even a refusal to work. An account in the *Leeds Mercury* in February 1858 claimed that the recent launch of *The Leviathan* in Deptford, postponed from a Saturday to a Sunday due to high winds, 'could have been easily launched on Friday, but for the blind superstition of sailors with respect to that day'. It was suggested that captains would often look for an excuse not to put to sea on a Friday, thereby avoiding the ill fortune that was believed to accompany such a day.[25]

Maritime folklore also required sailors to navigate through a host of people who could encourage or attract bad luck. Physical appearance was important, and there was often a literalness to some interpretations. Someone who was cross-eyed or had a squint was suspected of possessing the Evil Eye. Yet those who had been crippled from birth were thought to be under God's protection and therefore good luck to have on board.[26]

It is often stated that mariners did not like to have women aboard ship, and yet no convincing explanation has really been presented for this. The presence of women may have potentially disrupted a predominantly homosocial environment, and the practical explanation for this prejudice was that women would distract mariners from their work and thus invite accidents or injury. Yet scholarship has suggested that women were not as absent from the maritime world as previous histories would suggest.[27] There are vaguer notions of feminine sympathies between women and the ocean. Perpetuating a bunch of contemporary gender stereotypes, the character of the ocean supposedly mirrored the presumed instability of women (and vice versa), both understood as changeable, tempestuous, alluring yet dangerous. Yet with the contradiction that can arise in any large, eclectic body of lore, the birth of a baby on board ship was deemed good luck. While the nature of women may have been viewed suspiciously for its affinities with the sea, the role of woman as mother and life giver was both traditionally acceptable and a counter to the concerns about death considered above.

Clergymen were also considered unlucky. While sailors were generally renowned for being a blaspheming, irreligious bunch, this was not necessarily anti-clerical so much as pragmatic. As God's agents, priests would provoke storms and tempests sent by the Devil to destroy them, causing sailors to be caught in the theological crossfire. As seen in Chapter One, the Devil was understood to be an interventionist entity who took a personal interest in the ship's passenger log and the maritime travel arrangements of the clergy. It has also been suggested that the presence of a Christian priest might provoke the older gods of the sea, although this tends to be broader speculation rather than anything verified by sailors themselves.[28] In the minds of those within a masculine occupation such as seafaring, clergymen were often associated with the feminine sphere of life, possibly leaving them open to the same prejudices that mariners directed at women. Certainly they had no place among the crew. More obviously, priests were associated with funerals, thus bringing on board that feared taint of death. It was noted that while the sailor was often understood as heroic in battle and in the face of physical dangers, he 'shrinks with indescribable apprehension on shore at the sight of a coffin'.[29]

Whatever the mixture of prejudices and anxieties, mariners were strongly opposed to priests and clergymen at sea. Scottish fishermen were said to actively avoid using the words 'priest', 'minister' or 'church' while working. Transoceanic mariners were also wary of having clergymen as passengers. The folklorist Christina Hole stated, 'A friend of mine sailed to Canada in 1920, in a ship which developed a heavy rolling motion. This discomfort was unanimously blamed by the crew upon the presence of some Trappist monks on board.'[30] In a newspaper article from 1923 it was noted, rather tongue in cheek, that two clergymen were lucky that it was the twentieth century, and that sailors' superstitions were not as strong as they once were. The son of the

Methodist bishop from Ohio and a clergyman from Dartmouth were travelling to Europe on the *West Campgaw*. When they began singing hymns, the sailors warned them they were 'just tempting the devils of the deep'. Unfortunately, the clergymen continued to sing, and crewmen supposedly attributed to this the following two days of gales, and then fog for another day or so while in 'a region infested with icebergs'.[31]

Unlucky individuals who brought or attracted ill fortune were called Jonahs. While the Jonah of the biblical story was not unlucky as such, the most memorable feature of his account was strongly linked to the dangers of seafaring. Jonahs were sometimes found among the mariners' ranks themselves. In an unusual (if historically imprecise) nineteenth-century case, a sailor on an American vessel, the *President*, believed himself to be the cause of a fierce storm a few days out from Charleston. Blaming this on his own sinful life and clearly nursing a very guilty conscience, he threw himself overboard. The storm abated. When the ship was beset by storms on its return journey to New York, the crew sought out the dead sailor's belongings and threw his chest overboard. Again, the storm subsided. When a squall blew up as the ship was approaching New York, the crew searched the ship once more. They found one of the dead man's shoes and cast it overboard. In this case, the ability to attract misfortune extended beyond the man himself to his possessions.[32]

As the *New York Times* noted in 1884, such superstitions were not confined to crewmen. 'Even old sea Captains, who have risen from foremast hands, are not entirely free from these prejudices, although they deride them in theory.' In one case an old sea captain identified the wayward son of a clergyman as the Jonah that was creating ill luck on his ship. The young man had a reputation as a womanizer and had been encouraged to take to a life at sea for a time. The voyage was a long one and beset by misfortunes. Near the end of the voyage the ship was becalmed for nearly two weeks. At one point, when the captain was on deck, it looked as if a breeze might stir, but it failed to materialize. Looking around, he saw the clergyman's son scrubbing the decks nearby. The captain angrily declared, 'I never will have a fair wind as long as I keep such a fellow like you on board. I believe you are the Jonah of this ship.'[33] In both these cases, the Jonah was associated with a sinful past that would incur the punishment of God or the forces that controlled the maritime elements.

Jonahs illustrate how beliefs that helped bind crews together through a common supernatural culture based on observance, omens and actions could also reveal the darker side of shipboard communities. They exposed a tough, anxiety-inducing working environment that could lead to crews turning inward, singling out one of their number as an explanation and scapegoat for misfortune. This was a potentially dangerous situation for the identified crew member, especially if a ship was mid-ocean and officers were not strong enough to maintain discipline. However, a Jonah did not necessarily have to be human. The *Weekly Irish Times* reprinted a summary of a news story in the *Eastport Standard* in 1886. The steamship *New Brunswick* had recently suffered several difficult voyages. It had been confronted with storms and headwinds in journeys between St John and Boston, and was delayed in reaching Eastport. Both officers and crewmen concluded there must be a Jonah on board. The culprit was identified as a stray hen that had escaped from a coop that had been transported as freight some time earlier. The escapee had been placed in a box by a deckhand and kept on the main deck. A marine superstition held that if a hen is carried under a tub with its head down, the vessel will encounter headwinds. Given that the hen was kept in a closed box, the sailors assumed this amounted to the same thing. The deckhand was forced to put the hen ashore, and thereafter the steamship met with better weather.[34]

As this incident shows, the notion of Jonahs accompanied and adapted to the transition from sail to steam. This allowed such ideas to continue into the twentieth century. Hadfield cites the case of the unnamed wife of an American naval lieutenant who survived the sinking of the *Titanic* in 1912, was on board the *Lusitania* when it was torpedoed by a German U-boat in 1915 and was on RMS *Celtic* when it collided with the *Anaconda* of the American Diamond Line in 1927.[35] The vagueness of biographical detail makes this story rather suspect. If true, the woman could be labelled a Jonah, although her remarkable ability to survive this string of nautical disasters could equally be read as testament to her good fortune rather than bad.

While Jonahs could be magnets for misfortune, maritime folklore suggests all mariners policed their own actions so as to avoid inadvertently provoking the elements. It was considered bad luck to whistle on a ship if the wind was blowing. Following the magical principle of like for like or imitative magic, it was feared whistling could cause a storm to blow up. Granting the wind sentience, it was suggested it would take the whistling as a challenge, or, if sent by the devil, would be considered a mockery that might provoke a fierce response. When the wind was 'asleep', it was suggested sailors could summon a breeze by softly whistling, but some believed it helped if it was accompanied by encouraging words such as 'Come along, old chap, come along, old boy.' As such, whistling had to be carefully calibrated to the sailors' needs and the weather conditions. A gentle whistle would encourage a stiff breeze, but anything more exuberant would summon a gale. Alternatively, if sailors deliberately wanted to create a breeze, both Scottish and German sailors were said to scratch the mast with their nails. Such accounts suggested sailors had some responsibility for changes in the winds, and therefore some influence over them.[36]

If whistling failed, mariners could resort to a more direct way of 'buying the wind'. In one, described as 'one of many poetic fancies', mariners who found their vessel becalmed would throw a few pennies into the water. If the wind picked up within twelve hours, it was taken as a sign of their having purchased it.[37] Failing that, it was believed that cutting one's hair could influence the wind. In 1921 a group of hardy Scandinavian sailors arrived in New York harbour with close-cropped hair. The captain said the ship had been beset by a tempest for two days, failing to make any progress towards their destination. The crew recalled this 'old superstition' and had their hair cut. The storm abated before this impromptu round of barbering ended.[38] French maritime folklore suggested that some sailors could control the wind through a ring worn on their little finger. Yet this power came with a catch: they must never be more than three months at sea at a time, and no longer than three days ashore. If not, they would pay for it with their lives.[39] Such a restriction echoed the restless lives of mariners. We will return to this idea of the seafarer in constant motion when we consider the *Flying Dutchman* and its ghostly kin.

There are obviously questions about how much any of this was genuinely believed. As previously suggested, belief (and disbelief) was not necessarily fixed, and scepticism could turn to at least entertaining such ideas if they looked to threaten a ship or extend a voyage. In one incident, recounted in 1884, but supposedly having taken place 'a few years' earlier, an American vessel was returning to port from a voyage around Cape Horn. 'Patsy', an old sailor who expressed a desire to extend the voyage to eke out more wages, was seen to go to the forecastle one evening during the dog watch and began to whistle. He also gestured at the points of the compass, as if to summon a wind. One of the ship's boys observed this and informed his crewmates that the old sailor was 'engaged in a diabolical attempt to charm up a head wind'. The crew reacted angrily, and some even spoke of throwing what the journalist termed 'the objectionable wizard' overboard. It was noted that Patsy's crewmates had previously declared that 'whistling or any other action on the part of mortals could have no effect whatever upon the wind', and yet they seemed to hurriedly change their mind when it looked as if his efforts could delay their return to port.[40]

For fishermen, this policing of one's actions extended to the specific words used while at sea. William Jones claims that into the eighteenth century Norwegian and Scottish fishermen avoided naming the objects used in fishing 'for fear of exciting the attention or covetousness of evil spirits'.[41] Such a constraint makes one wonder how they could have actually conducted their work without the occasional verbal slip. Nineteenth-century Cornish fishermen would not talk directly of rabbits, whereas Scottish fishermen avoided the use of certain words: 'minister', 'kirk', 'swine', 'salmon', 'trout', 'pig' and certain family names were not to be mentioned. When using a church as a landmark, they would not refer to it as a 'kirk' but as a 'bell-hoose', and would call a minister 'the man wi' the black quyte'.[42] While the avoidance of church and priest references may link to mariners' dislike of clergymen mentioned above, the reason to dread naming certain animals is not clear. Again, this is due to the nature of the material we are drawing upon. The associations would not have been random but, inheriting only fragments and shadows of beliefs and ideas, we have a record of the taboo words, not the thinking behind them. This taboo most likely stems back to concerns about bad weather, for finding a dead hare on board ship was taken as a sign of a coming storm. In Forfarshire it was said that if a hare crossed the path of some fishermen on the way to their boat, they would choose not to sail that day.[43]

Fishermen seem to have been particularly sensitive to any encounter or person who might jinx their efforts. A chance meeting with red-haired or cross-eyed women, hares or pigs could all cause them to abort their efforts for the day, certain that the prospects of a good catch had been ruined or the likelihood of some misfortune was too high. Within the supposedly superstitious ranks of all seafarers, fishermen were presented as the most intensely superstitious of all of Neptune's sons. While they might not necessarily venture into the depths of the mid-ocean, their vessels were smaller and more vulnerable than transoceanic ships. They also had to negotiate the unruly elements, Atlantic storms, treacherous coastal waters and constant uncertainty of the catch upon which they and their community's livelihood depended. For example, the family-based mackerel fishing on the Dingle peninsula on the west coast of Ireland mainly consisted of small three- or four-man crews in open boats, working long, ten- to twelve-hour shifts. They often conducted drift net fishing at night, sometimes 6 or 7 miles from shore, in a craft that might only have had oars to get them home.

Within Scottish fishing communities, there was a custom of racing to the fishing fields on New Year's Day, for the winner was said to be assured of a good catch that year. Another custom was to draw blood on New Year's Day to ensure a good catch. This could result in fishermen out on the shoreline with guns. In a critique of the domestic violence that could exist in isolated fishing communities, William Jones suggested that this drawing of blood could extend to a fisherman beating his wife to ensure a good catch in the year ahead.[44] Coastal communities were likewise bound by certain restrictions when the fishing fleet was out. People had to avoid pointing at the boats at sea with a finger, a gesture that may have symbolized a directed curse, but rather had to use the whole hand. Nor should the boats at sea be counted, for it would bring ill fortune to their number.[45] Such ideas suggest that for all their precautions fishermen were not purely in control of their own luck, but could be influenced by the remote actions of those ashore. They were also a reminder that the fortunes of fishermen and their land-based families were bound to one another as parts of a fishing community.

Witchcraft and Prejudice at Sea

Much of what has been examined so far has focused on prevention, protection and defence against misfortune. However, maritime magic also included elements of threat and attack. As seen in the account that opened this chapter, some witches claimed to be able to sell the wind, a vital commodity for sailors who sought swift travel and insurance against finding themselves becalmed miles from land. Selling the wind may sound like a joke at the expense of the mariner, but, as seen in the array of beliefs and practices just outlined, it speaks to a yearning for influence over the unpredictable marine environment. Yet a person who could bind the wind in knots could equally use it to generate storms and cause havoc and harm. Just as inland dairy farmers had believed witchcraft could stop cows from producing milk or butter being churned, so coastal communities believed a witch could prevent fishermen catching fish or summon gales to destroy their vessels. A bewitched boat that was unable to catch fish would swiftly bring poverty to a family, while storm-damaged vessels might cause an entire community to suffer. Such was the threat presented by what Lizanne Henderson has termed the 'elemental witch', a particular type of malevolent magical practitioner versed in the manipulation of wind, weather and sea.[46]

There were historical precedents to encourage a belief in the remote reach of witchcraft at sea. In 1591 Agnes Sampson confessed to placing a spell on King James VI's ship as he returned to Scotland from Denmark. Sampson had supposedly caused the winds to delay the king's ship while the others in his company moved on unhindered. Such paranoid thinking seemed to inform James's claim in his book *Daemonologie* (1597) that witches could 'rayse stormes and tempests in the aire, either upon Sea or land'. According to James, one could tell a witch's tempest from a natural one because it rose suddenly and violently but tended to be brief. Sampson went on to claim that she and her coven had met the Devil at sea; he was said to resemble a large haystack that rolled upon the waves. The witches then boarded a ship and, invisible to the crew, drank its supply of wines. When they grew bored, Satan sank the ship, sparing the witches but drowning the crew. One should keep in mind that such an account, with its references to more continental European ideas about diabolical pacts and covens, was obtained through torture.[47]

If belief in a witch's power to raise storms had diminished by the nineteenth century, the idea that they could take away fish remained. Witchcraft beliefs were generally becoming more private and personal by the second half of the nineteenth century, but fishing communities could still reveal glimpses of wider collective belief. In 1845 a fisherman assaulted a woman in Portmahomack, Easter Ross, Scotland, cutting her above the brow. Prompted by the belief that causing a witch to bleed would break her spell, he blamed her for his failure to catch herring and the loss of his nets. Illustrative of wider consent for such ideas, his crew had refused to sail with him until the witch's curse was broken. When a fishing boat had been 'overlooked' by a witch, a ritual to remove the malevolent influence could require the participation of a good number of people. A noose large enough to pass the boat through would be made on the halyard, a rope used for hoisting a sail. The noose would then be put over the prow of the boat, pushed under its keel, and the boat would sail through the rope, removing the evil that had been cast upon it.[48]

Writing in 1899, psychical researcher Ada Goodrich-Freer related a case of witchcraft in the Outer Hebrides. A man referred to only as 'C.' was going to church one Sunday morning in Kiloanan (*sic*: Kildonan, South Uist) when he encountered two women, a mother and daughter. They were 'actively engaged in framing witchcraft by means of pieces of thread of various colours'. He smashed their strange apparatus and reprimanded

Illustration of a Tempestarii or storm witch, someone who uses magic to affect the weather, 19th century.

them for their evil plans and for undertaking such actions on a Sunday. The women asked him not to reveal what he had witnessed, promising to provide him with magical protection if he maintained their secret. After mass, the man told others of what he had seen and done. Later, as he was about to sail to the mainland, 'a black crow settled on the mast of his boat and a storm rose in which he perished'. Using the tale to indicate that seeking out such information was not without its risks to the folklorist or psychical researcher, Goodrich-Freer concluded, 'The story is not only true, but of recent occurrence.'[49]

In an account from the west of England in 1865, Robert Hunt suggested that the magical practitioner could even be a fellow crewmember. He stated that he had 'lately received the story from Mr T. Q. Couch of Bodmin', Cornwall, and that it relayed 'a very common superstition'. The crew had suspected that one of their shipmates was a wizard. Following a quarrel and threats of revenge, the sailors were gathered towards the front of the ship. The suspected wizard was not with them, but a toad fell into their midst. One of the sailors threw the toad into the fire in their shelter. The creature struggled in the flames and then flung itself away from the fire. Another sailor then grabbed the toad and threw it into the sea. Shortly afterwards, the suspected sailor appeared. He was soaking wet, and claimed that in a drunken state he had first fallen into a fire at a beer shop and then fallen overboard from the boat. Whether the toad was to be understood as a familiar connected to the wizard or the wizard himself transformed into animal form, the connection between their recent ordeals by fire and water was taken as proof of his wizarding ways.[50] This association between misfortune and animals at sea informed nautical superstitions. A witch's ability to raise storms could transfer to their onboard familiars. Swedish sailors were said to refuse to have a black cat on board, for 'it carries storm in its tail'. Scottish sailors believed that having a white dog and a black cat on board a ship at the same time was bound to result in a voyage of squally weather, although such a belief was not necessarily linked directly to witchcraft.[51]

In Europe, the one group of sailors that were most commonly associated with witchcraft were Finns. As *The Standard* reported, 'There is an absurd dread and superstition lingering among sailors respecting Russian Fins, and it is believed by foolishly incredulous mariners that they can draw blood out of a ship's mainmast.' Such concerns seemed to extend across the Atlantic to American crews. In *Two Years Before the Mast*, Richard Henry Dana gives an account of a Black cook who was afraid of a Finn's magical abilities, and a captain who confined a Finn to the forepeak until he conjured a favourable wind.[52]

This was not necessarily an idle superstition. In a grim case that was widely reported across the British press in April 1867, Charles Anderson, a Swedish sailor, was brought before the Old Bailey court in London for the murder of his shipmate James Marchien. Both had been serving on the *Raby Castle*, a British vessel that was near Cape Legullas on the south coast of Africa at the time. Anderson, an able seaman and carpenter's assistant, was prone to odd behaviour such as laughing and talking to himself and tended to be a loner, but was said to know right from wrong. Marchien was described as 'a mulatto' from St Lucia, but Anderson seemed to have become fixated on the idea that he was a Russian Finn. On the night of 24 November 1866, having completed his watch on deck, Anderson went to Marchien's bunk and attacked him from behind with an axe, his blows almost severing the man's head. He was swiftly apprehended and placed in irons. The press made much of the sailors' superstition that it was unlucky to have a Russian Finn on board. According to the *Pall Mall Gazette*, the presence of such individuals was 'likely to lead to the destruction of that vessel'. This prejudice against Russian Finns was raised by Anderson's defence, but it did not merit further mention in the court record. According to press reports, Anderson claimed that if he had not killed Marchien 'the ship would have gone on the rocks, and they would have all been lost'. Anderson's state of mind had been central to much of the testimony provided by other crew members, but any attempt to formulate a case of diminished responsibility on the grounds of insanity were ultimately rejected. Anderson was initially sentenced to death, but his punishment was commuted to transportation to Western Australia later that year.[53]

The Finns' negative associations with witchcraft seems to be informed by ethnic prejudices. Neither Scandinavian nor

Slavic, Finns possessed an uncertain, outsider identity within Europe at this time. Part of the Russian empire but not seen as wholly European, they could be distanced through an association with magic, especially as Western Europe was placing emphasis on a self-image of enlightened rationalism. One has to consider whether this maritime prejudice was used to conceal a more blatant racial antagonism, something that again hints at the possibility of muted tensions aboard ship.

Transatlantic crews often consisted of a rich mix of nationalities and peoples drawn from many continents and countries. Terms like the 'sons of Neptune' can encourage a false sense of unity, for transatlantic sailors were an endless churn of individuals who reconstituted themselves into crews. Each mariner was a product of a regional, national and possibly imperial culture, and in such circumstance one's identity as French, English or American could become more important, not less. Divisions could surface, especially when crews were under duress. An old American sailor, James J. Ferris, was free and easy with his stereotypes and claims about mariners from other parts of the world in a piece in the *New York Times* in 1897. He noted that while superstitions had ebbed with the age of steam, there were still enough of them among merchant mariners 'to make the Captain's life a merry-go-round'. Suggesting that officers were having to navigate this web of beliefs, omens and observances into the late nineteenth century, he was particularly critical of Italian, Spanish and Portuguese sailors. He told of how when a liner, *Leona*, reached New York the previous year the Italian sailors refused to touch the thirteen dead bodies that had been stored in the forecastle following a terrible fire in steerage. He claimed that Italian mariners believed that touching a corpse would cause its ghost to haunt them. While noting that they were keen to resort to appealing to the Virgin Mary during storms, he also suggested that Italian sailors could rise up and smash all the images of the

Virgin Mary on board if she did not provide timely aid or intervention. Whatever the faults of the Italians, Ferris stated that 'when it comes to an all-around moss-grown stock of superstitions, the Spanish sailor gets the medal.'[54] While supernatural ideas informed a shared maritime culture that might sit above certain differences such as religion, Ferris's comments suggest that they also actively fed into prejudices about the degree to which mariners of certain countries were prone to 'superstitious' beliefs.

An Ocean of Omens

Once at sea, the sailor was sensitive to all manner of nautical and meteorological omens, seeking to glean some forewarning of danger and misfortune. In a 1900 article about sailors from Bangor, Maine, a series of short accounts gave repeated examples of incidents when a sailor who read the signs or heeded a message either got off or never stepped on a vessel that sank shortly afterwards. Such signs might include noting rats leaving a ship, a dream of death or, in one case, a ghostly visitation from a sailor's mother, who had been dead eight years. Giving no indication of where these accounts had come from, the newspaper seemed to be reinforcing such ideas rather than chastising sailors for holding to them.[55] Press accounts noted that the belief that rats leaving the ship portended misfortune not only lasted longer than most other maritime folklore but was considered a common fact rather than a superstition. There was a pragmatic rather than supernatural explanation to this, with rats moving away from leaking parts of the ship, especially from the bilges, where they might conceal themselves. It spoke to the poor condition of the vessel, its unseen weaknesses adding to the risks at sea. In this way, omens of ill fortune could be fulfilled.

Some of the few non-aquatic animals to be observed by mariners on their transatlantic voyages were birds and this gave rise to a rich body of ornithological superstitions and divination. On the coasts of North America fishermen looked for the appearance of the osprey in summer, as British fishermen looked for the gannet, both taken as signs of the commencement of the fishing season on their respective coasts, Similarly, the sighting of terns portended a prosperous fishing season. By contrast, stormy petrels were said to portend dreadful danger for 'the mariners of all nations'. Like the flocking of seagulls in harbour, they were taken as a warning of coming storms.

In the early evening of 12 September 1857 Captain Johnson of the Norwegian barque *Ellen* was standing on the quarter deck when a strange bird about 1½ feet (45 cm) in length and with a wingspan of 3 feet (90 cm) flew around and then at him. When he tried to grab the bird, it bit him and other crew members who attempted to restrain it. They eventually succeeded and the captain had the bird decapitated and its body thrown overboard. However, he took the appearance and attack as an omen. Based on this, he changed course, from just north of northeast to east, and it was this unplanned and unintended course adjustment that led to him discovering a sinking steamer, the *Central America*. He conveyed its 49 crew and passengers to New York, where he made his declaration about this odd incident. The captain said the bird was 'unlike any bird I ever saw, nor do I know its name', but it had dark grey feathers and an 8-inch (20 cm) beak that contained teeth 'like a small handsaw'.[56]

Certain birds were not to be killed, for it was feared that to do so would result in misfortune. Petrels, also known as Mother Carey's chickens (said to be a corruption of *Mata Cara*, or Virgin Mary), were one such bird, said to contain the transmogrified souls of dead mariners.[57] Similar ideas applied to gulls and albatrosses. A single gull flying in a straight course at sea was said to be the reincarnated soul of a drowned sailor following the corpse it had once inhabited as the body drifted along the seabed. Coastal folk took a gull flying against the window of a house as a warning that a family member was in danger at sea.[58] The albatross was said to fly further from land than any other bird and thus sailors tended to grant this remote connection to land superstitious significance. The landing of an albatross on deck was taken as an unfortunate omen and, as shown in Samuel Taylor Coleridge's haunting poem *The Rime of the Ancient Mariner* (1798), to kill such a bird was thought to bring adversity and punishment. If birds contained the souls of former seafarers, then to kill one would harm a fellow mariner. Worse yet, those souls were said to be those of wicked sailors condemned to continuous motion. This both explained why not all mariners' souls were transferred to sea birds and enhanced the curse brought down on one's head by ending the damnation of an evil doer.[59] It also spoke to the future fate of current sailors, emphasizing, as many nautical ghosts did, that even after death mariners were destined to dwell in the maritime environment in which they had lived and toiled. Like many aspects of maritime magical thinking, we can view this belief in birds containing transmogrified souls as an attempt to impose our anthropocentric thinking on nature by seeing something of ourselves within it. While it was never voiced in reports, the bird that so persistently sought to draw the Norwegian captain's attention seemed to embody something of the soul of a mariner seeking to aid those who faced drowning.

The superstition surrounding albatrosses was updated in several press report in *the Chicago Tribune* in 1890. An English barque, the *Selkirkshire*, anchored in Brooklyn, New York, recounted how in travelling from Australia to England two crewmen had caught and killed a huge albatross. When they set it out on deck, it was said to have a wingspan of 20 feet (6 metres). The long bones had been removed from the wings to dry. The sight appeared to have a disturbing influence on a crewman named Alec. In a fit of madness attributed to the tropical sun, he placed his arms in

Gustave Doré, 'It ate the food it ne'er had eat', engraving from Samuel Taylor Coleridge, *The Rime of the Ancient Mariner* (1876).

the holes left by the removal of the bones, leapt onto the railing and threw himself into the sea, supposedly declaring, 'Who says Alec can't fly?' A lifebelt was thrown to the man, and the second mate fixed one to himself and heroically jumped into the rough sea after his deluded crewmate. An initial attempt to launch a lifeboat failed when it was smashed against the side of the ship. A boat was eventually launched from the yard arm. Working their way through a fog, the rowers eventually found the second mate half dead from exhaustion. Twenty feet from him was Alec, saved from drowning by the albatross's large wings keeping him afloat on the turbulent waves. The two men were pulled into the boat, but Alec jumped overboard a second time. When they retrieved him again, a crewman knocked him unconscious with an axe. With the lifeboat half full of water and the ship out of sight in the fog, the mariners rowed for five hours before finally sighting the ship, muttering darkly about Alec and the trouble he had caused. The captain ordered the albatross wings to be thrown overboard. When Alec regained consciousness, he immediately tried to stab the fourth mate, forcing the crew to place him in solitary confinement. He was committed to an asylum when the *Selkirkshire* reached England. While often keen to claim that maritime superstitions were fading out, the journalist could not help but suggest that Alec's sudden mad turn was linked to the death of the albatross, and that the incident had borne out the old superstition about harming the bird. It concluded that the crew would 'never fool with another albatross'.[60]

Within the sea itself, the appearance or actions of animals could also bode good or bad fortune. If cuttlefish swam near the surface, it was said to be a sign of coming storms. Porpoises were considered lucky and not to be harmed. It was suggested they kept sharks away from the ship, although how was never explained. While a potential threat to mariners, sharks were also understood as omens of death, and were said to know when a person was close to dying and to follow ships that contained such individuals. Such actions were more likely due to sharks' superior sense of smell than anything supernatural, this being their primary sense.[61]

Similarly, while sometimes granted a frisson of supernatural meaning, predictive observations at sea often arose out of many years of maritime experience. To the new sailor or the landlubber, the experienced mariner's knowledge of nature, attuned to meteorological signs and oceanic phenomena through a lifetime at sea, could appear to verge on supernatural insight or predictive power. Even so, that did not ensure a consensus when it came to interpretation. This is best demonstrated through differing views on St Elmo's fire, an electrical phenomenon that sometimes played around the masts and upper rigging of ships. Some European sailors took it as a positive sign of the protective or benevolent presence of various saints, but French sailors believed the lights were the souls of drowned mariners trying to get back on board ships they had once served upon. American sailors were said to believe that if St Elmo's fire illuminated the head of a sailor working in the masts, then his hour of death was near. If the lights remained high in the mast, it was a good sign; if they descended, this presaged storms, their severity gauged by how low the lights reached.[62] Interpretations may have varied, but the unusual phenomena encouraged mariners of many nations to invest them with predictive meaning.

Intended to give mariners a sense of influence over the dangerous environment in which they lived and worked, these beliefs and practices spoke to a powerful anthropocentric instinct: a desire to believe in human influence over nature, to be able to read its signs and to avert its dangers. Confronted by one of the greatest forces of nature, mariners gambled on omens and a hidden, supernatural web of influences to bring them safely back to shore. It is notable that actions meant to actively encourage good luck seem fewer than those to avert misfortune. This suggests a mentality that was permanently tilted towards pessimism, for while careful observance of signs might forewarn of calamity, the prospect loomed heavily in the mind of mariners. The mass of omens, observances and magical protections considered in this chapter suggests a perpetual struggle against a hostile environment. Even breaking a mirror on board ship was considered unluckier than doing so ashore, suggesting that the marine environment naturally enhanced the misfortune such an accident would bring.[63]

While often kept muted beneath a focus on nautical skill, technology and seamanship, there was a more anxiety-ridden experience that encouraged mariners to heed observances and practices to avert potentially fatal misfortune. Magical thinking has long been understood as a response to hazardous environments, be it down mines, on battlefields or on the ocean. Mariners' actions and beliefs can be understood as a search for human agency in changeable and potentially deadly conditions. As this chapter has suggested, this amounted to managing the randomness of misfortune, avoiding the worst of fates and placating the unpredictable nature of the ocean. Regardless of the transition from sail to steam, the fundamental awareness remained that the ocean was an environment that human ingenuity and technology could cross, but that it was not and never could be our 'natural' environment. Oddly, this sense of exclusion seemed to foster a compensatory instinct, a strong anthropocentric understanding of our relationship with the sea. As we saw in Chapter One, as a moral or purgatorial space, the ocean was believed to be responsive to individuals' past actions or sinful characters. This was extended through magical thinking to an understanding that good or bad things happened at sea because of what mariners or their loved ones in coastal communities did or did not do. While the dangers of storms, sinking and wrecking were natural, their cause or occurrence was given supernatural meaning, connected to something as seemingly trivial as pointing at a boat out at sea. Far from a sense of detachment from nature, this showed the human psyche deeply connected to a marine environment that was understood as highly sensitive to human actions and minutely responsive to the smallest gesture or wrong word. While granting mariners a sense of influence and significance within the volatile maritime world, it also bound them with numerous restrictions and made them responsible for any infractions.

As suggested above, magical belief was fluid and unfixed within the maritime community. While most often associated with the able seaman or common sailor, we have seen that officers sometimes shared these ideas, while not all within the humbler ranks necessarily did so. Nor is it likely that the rich body of lore that scholars can glean from a multitude of sources would have been known by crews, let alone consciously observed in its entirety. To navigate its many signs and restrictions would have required the presence of mind and self-discipline of monks, something hard to maintain in such an active and lively occupation as seafaring. But these things lay submerged and were easily retrieved as explanatory reasons for misfortune, after the event as much as before. Even in offering some explanation of why ill fortune fell on some and not others, they helped make sense of the capricious nature of maritime dangers. This collection of charms, omens and observances helped get crews out to sea and offered some sense of protection and influence once there. Yet that was only the start of their journey into the supernatural Atlantic. Ahead of them lay an oceanic realm of supernatural beings, ghosts, phantom ships and monsters.

3
Supernatural Beings and Fishy Tales

On 29 July 1857 readers of the *Dumfries and Galloway Standard* would have encountered the following declaration by two fishermen from the Argyllshire coast in Scotland, in a piece simply titled 'A Mermaid':

> We, the undersigned, do declare that on Thursday last, the 4th June 1857, when on our way to the fishing station, Lochindaal, in a boat, and when about 4 miles s.w. from the village of Port Charlotte, being then about six p.m., we distinctly saw an object about six yards from us, in the shape of a woman, with full breast, dark complexion, comely face, and fine hair hanging in ringlets over the neck and shoulders. It was above the surface of the water to about the middle, gazing at us and shaking its head. The weather being fine, we had a full view of it, and that for three or four minutes. – John Williamson, John Cameron. – Islay, June 9, 1857.[1]

That was it. No editorial comment, no reflection. Just a statement of having seen a mermaid. Such a public declaration in the mid-nineteenth century may appear odd, especially when a real-world sighting conformed so closely to a very idealized image of such creatures. Yet this highlights how the status of mermaids as real or fictional was still uncertain in the nineteenth century, and how, true to their hybrid form, mermaids can be understood as products of land-based as much as maritime cultures.

What lies behind the mermaid's popularity and cultural familiarity? Ask anyone to name a creature of maritime folklore and the most likely answer will be 'mermaid'. When one searches through the nineteenth-century press, references to mermaids far exceeded any others element of maritime folklore, running to thousands rather than hundreds of entries. They are the most common maritime folkloric figure depicted in art and literature of this period. They are also the subject of more scholarly reflections and interpretations than any other maritime figure, with a notable increase in such interest in the twenty-first century.[2]

Perhaps more than any other chapter, this one engages with transcultural interactions and adaptations. It is in ocean-dwelling creatures like the mermaid and the marine goddesses from which they evolved that we see the cultural influences of Europe, Africa and the Americas bleeding into the Atlantic, mixing and cross-fertilizing. The mermaid was a highly adaptable symbol of both fusion and division, the meeting of the civilized and bestial, above and below, the familiar and different, possessing a strange hybridity that both attracted and unsettled. The mermaid personified the association between the feminine and the marine environment, being understood as simultaneously alluring and dangerous to a predominantly male gaze, be it mariners at sea or artists ashore.

The term 'mermaid' is only the most well known of the names given to the many aquatic beings who dwelt in the Atlantic Ocean. Like mermaids elsewhere, the merrows or moruachs of Irish lore came from the sea to gain the affections of men. They were said to sometimes marry men from coastal families but could also drag them down to their death beneath the waves. Illustrative of their pre-Christian origins, it was said that the sound of church bells could scare them off, while a man who wore a crucifix would be protected if merrows sought to drown him. Scotland had the Ceasg, a mermaid that could grant wishes to those who captured her and guide fishermen to the best fishing grounds, but who also had a reputation for swallowing men alive. In the waters off Brittany, the Morgan or Morverch (sea-women or sea-daughters) were said to live in opulent palaces beneath the sea. One also finds a diversity of names for the mermaid in the Caribbean, with mahmys in Jamaica and the Lasirenn in Haiti.

Bishop Erich Pontoppidan referred to both the Hav-mandem (merman) and Hav-Fruen (mermaid) in his *Natural History of Norway* (1755), and Iceland had the marmennill, another male water dweller.[3] Although less frequently seen, mermen were certainly not unknown in maritime folkloric accounts. Unlike the mermaid, which was often found on the coast, mermen rarely came ashore. It was suggested that while mermaids were beautiful, mermen tended to be ugly and lacked their companions' seductive charms. In Shetland folklore the merman was said to have a darker complexion, with hair and a long beard of black, brown, red or grey. By comparison, mermaids were fairer in complexion, more Scandinavian perhaps, with lighter skin, long yellow hair and finer features.[4]

Alongside these humanoid figures, the North Atlantic was also home to supernatural, shape-shifting aquatic horses such as the Icelandic Nickur, the Shetland Kelpie and, more commonly found in salt than fresh water, the Tangi. The Tangi was said to be a small, dark grey horse usually found on the seashore, although it could appear as a good-looking young man. He was believed to try to seduce young women, just as mermaids were said to seduce men. The Tangi made its home in caves along the shoreline, or in the water beneath high cliffs. Fishermen claimed to have seen the Tangi at night, aglow with a blue light, moving up and down the cliffs. When it moved fast, flames would dart from beneath its hooves. It was said that the Tangi could find anything thrown into or lost in the sea, no matter the depth. Demonstrating its supernatural powers, it could cast a spell on people and animals by repeatedly circling them, causing insanity that would result in its unfortunate victim throwing themselves from the cliffs, drowning themselves to escape their torment. Yet the Tangi was also susceptible to certain weaknesses, including fire, knives (or iron), or hearing the name of God or its own name spoken. Smaller half-horse, half-fish creatures were said to have been caught by fishermen in deep waters around north and east Shetland and off the coast of Norway, supposedly as late as the 1870s and '80s. Their small size led to the idea that they may have been the Tangi's offspring. Blending the lore of mermaids and the Tangi, the Norwegian water horse known as 'Nok' was said to play music in the water, with the effect that all who heard it would be turned mad.[5]

Supernatural sea-dwellers took other forms too. Again, Shetlanders spoke of sea trolls or sea trows, their maritime folklore clearly having a strong Scandinavian influence that connected the fantastical imaginary of Iceland, Norway, the Faroe Islands and Scotland. The term 'sea troll' seems to have been loosely applied to a range of underwater entities. It could allude to sea fairies, but equally when a whale ripped through the fishing nets it might be said to be a sea troll, or possibly an agent of the Devil that had taken whale form. Another type of sea trow took the form of a wailing woman whose forlorn cries could be heard by fishermen whether they were close to shore or far out to sea. Much like the Banshee, her crying portended suffering, loss or sorrow for those who heard it.[6] Water sprites, like fairies, were uncertain companions at sea, for while they were said to bring good luck to fishermen, they were also sometimes said to lead seafarers to their deaths. If caught in the nets, the water sprite would rip them open and free the catch, for water sprites were said to rule over the fish.[7] As suggested here, mariners' and coastal dwellers' understanding of most sea beings was defined by ambiguity, an awareness that they, much like the seas and oceans themselves, could variously be benevolent or malevolent, could give or take, reward or harm.

Mythic Origins and the Evolution of Merfolk

Belief in mermaids and mermen was widespread and longstanding. Writing of sea superstitions in 1920, Doris Blake claimed, 'The antiquity of the belief in mermaids and mermen is beyond finding out. It can be traced from age to age through every nation.'[8] Much of this can be traced back to ancient mythologies. Mythology involves symbolic and conceptual thinking, where the non-human, be it monstrous or divine, often acts as the personification of an idea or, in the case of seas, a vast space. In attempting to comprehend and explain the might and temperamental nature of the seas in terms of gods or goddesses (or at least a realm ruled by them), ancient cultures created hybrid images of human and fish. Atargatis, a fertility goddess of ancient Syria, offers one of the earliest divine models for the mermaid. In the first century BCE she was described by the ancient Greek scholar Diodorus Siculus as having a woman's face but the body of a fish.

As we saw in Chapter One, the Greeks also had their own marine deities, although one has to move beyond Poseidon and Amphitrite to their offspring, Triton, to draw a step closer to the anthropomorphic fish being. He transformed from an underwater man to having more piscine features, along with a sea-coloured beard and hair. His name, initially used in the singular but later in the plural, was still used as a naturalist's alternative term for amphibious humanoids into the eighteenth century. In addition, there were the seawater nymphs known as the Oceanids, and the Nereids, female sea dwellers who accompanied Poseidon and who were often depicted by artists as beautiful, often semi-nude young women. Their association with the sea led to poetic elaborations, and they acquired fish-like lower bodies and sometimes green hair.[9]

Over time, these Mediterranean minor deities merged with Sirens. This was a rather odd combination, when we consider that the original Sirens were monstrous harpy-like bird-women, were not necessarily connected to the sea, and lacked the bewitching singing voice that they were later granted by poets such as Homer. The discord between folkloric, literary and pictorial depictions of the Sirens has been a source of scholarly debate, with some pointing out that while Homer gifted the Sirens with the power of mesmeric song, he did not physically describe them as either birds, human or fish, or any combination of those things.[10] Addressing the Sirens' folkloric origins, Leigh Hunt proposed that their myth arose from an allegorical representation of a particular dangerous coastal location where the sound of the wind among cliffs and rocks sounded like song, a combination of sweet music and a treacherous terrain.[11] Eventually, elements of fish-tailed goddesses, the Nereids and Sirens blended into the ideal of the beautiful young mermaid who could be both alluring and deadly. The idea of the beguiling Siren was adopted by later sculptors, painters and poets, who turned them from squawking bird-women into fish-tailed temptresses with flowing hair and a seductive song. With a complex genealogy that blends myth, folklore, art and literature from many countries, it has been noted that it is almost 'impossible to trace any clear line of descent' in the cultural evolution of the mermaid.[12]

Medieval European learned elites reverentially granted the works of ancient writers great authority. Pliny the Elder, an imperial Roman administrator and the author of the *Natural History*, had recorded accounts of Tritons, Nereids and a merman or 'sea man' in his work of AD 77, and he remained a key authority on naturalist knowledge through to the early modern period.[13]

His work was first published in 1469, shortly after the development of the printing press, and a popular translation by Philemon Holland was published in 1600. Pliny's scholarly respectability helped underpin the fact that

> The Middle Ages were too fondly in love with fable to neglect a legend that appealed so vividly to the imagination. They seized upon it eagerly; they put aside every fact that was likely to clear up the mystery, and every Western nation created for itself a water-spirit. In France, it was the Siren; in Scotland, the White Lady; in England, the Mermaid; in Germany, the Nix or Ondine; in the Netherlands, the Merminne or Neck.[14]

This was informed by the idea that ocean life mirrored that of the land, so that one encountered the nautical equivalence of terrestrial life forms in merpeople, seahorses ('Equus Neptuni'), sea cows, sea dogs and so on.[15] This notion may help explain why so many water dwellers reflected either humans or horses, one of the most important animals in medieval societies. Coastal-dwelling Celtic communities, like the peninsula and archipelago-dwelling Greeks, also had stories about the marine versions of land-based animals. Such ideas persisted into the sixteenth century, with Ambroise Paré's *On Monsters and Marvels* (1573) containing a section on sea 'monsters' that were analogous to land creatures. Rather than mere reflections of the surface world, Paré's fledgling scientific work presented them as rare marvels, signs of 'the incomprehensible power of Nature and God' and the rich variety of forms they allow to thrive.[16]

This religious link is seen in the fact that some marine creatures were described as having a curiously ecclesiastical bent. In 1546 a 'sea monk' nearly 8 feet (2.4 m) long was captured in waters between Sweden and Denmark. It was said to have a long,

Plate from Gaspar Schott, *Physica curiosa, sive mirabilia naturae* (1667) depicting: I. a triton; II. a sea monster in the likeness of a monk; III. a sea man in the dress of a bishop; and IV. a sea satyr.

hooded garment, like a monk. The creature was sketched and Christian III of Denmark had the images sent to the Holy Roman Emperor. The 'sea bishop' was also said to exist. Humanoid in form, its name derived from its head, which was shaped like a mitre. When it was brought before some Catholic monks, it made a gesture that was interpreted as a plea for freedom. Upon its release, it was said to have made the sign of the cross before disappearing beneath the waves.[17]

These ideas were contemporaneous with the stories of transatlantic mariners in the Age of Discovery. Boria Sax claims this was a period when our modern image of the mermaid emerged, the result of increasing maritime trade conducted by cosmopolitan crews that exchanged their countries' stories about mysterious sea-dwelling people.[18] Christopher Columbus's crew claimed to have spotted a mermaid, as did Captain John Smith when leading his expedition to America in 1614. Smith supposedly saw a woman in the water with large, expressive eyes and long, green hair. Drawn to her beauty, he pursued her in a boat until she dived beneath the water, briefly exposing her fish tail as she made her escape.[19]

By the seventeenth century, there had been a considerable transition, with mermaids shrinking from goddesses, demi-gods and monsters to playful and enticing water maidens. The idea was widely circulated and promoted in maritime culture, not just through stories but as ships' figureheads, tattoos, on scrimshaw, and on inn and tavern signs. As folklore rather than myth, the mermaid took on a humbler function. She was linked to mariners' imaginative engagement with a marine environment that could be both alluring and lethal, where supernatural interactions supposedly occurred in everyday lives, and where accounts of having seen a mermaid stood as a marker of an old salt's great experience.

Sea Dwellers and Supernatural Powers

Mermaids possessed innate powers that can be understood as supernatural, some of which derived from their aquatic otherworldliness, but sailors also projected certain powers onto merfolk. While it was the mermaid's beauty that often first caught the eye, it was their singing that held the attention. Their enchanting and hypnotic song had the power to override reason and cause those under its influence to follow them underwater, there to be drowned and possibly devoured. Their singing was said to lure men and seals, although there is little mention of it having the same effect on women. Perched alluringly by a rock pool or in the surf, mermaids' song can be understood as a hunting technique. Some of their other inhuman powers derived from their lives underwater. Mermaids were said to be able to speak many languages, as mariners from all nations passed over their undersea domain. This talent was aided by preternatural hearing that allowed them to listen to conversations ashore.

Beyond these innate abilities, mermaids, like fairies, had the ability to grant wishes and magical powers to humans. In the nineteenth-century Cornish 'Droll of the Mermaid', the mermaid bestows on the man who finds her trapped and cut off from the water anti-witchcraft abilities and power over familiar spirits to provide him with 'all I desire to know for the benefit of others'. In effect, this story uses the mermaid to explains how the Lutey family, of whom the man was an ancestor, gained a local reputation for being magical practitioners. Those supernatural abilities would continue in his family forever, although there was a cost. The man disappeared with the mermaid nine years later. Whether he drowned or lived beneath the waves with the mermaid is left unclear, for she had earlier alluded to an ability to transform him into an underwater dweller by cutting gills into his neck. However, every nine years after, one of his family members drowned. The sea gave, but it took in return.[20]

Sailors also projected supernatural precognition onto mermaids and took their actions as omens of good or bad fortune. If a mermaid was sighted but looked or moved away from a ship, all would be well. If the mermaid looked at it directly, or moved towards it, it boded ill for the future, with storms or some misfortune likely to beset the vessel.[21] If caught by the nets or hooks of fishermen, mermaids were known to ask for release, offering to bestow on them good luck or to tell the future of the crew by way of a reward. If they were not freed, or if harm was done to them, then bad luck was likely to befall the fishermen. This was the fate that befell a North Shetlander who accidentally caught a mermaid on his hook. When he brought her alongside his boat, she begged not to be harmed. The fisherman, for no explicable reason, ignored her entreaties and stabbed her in the breast before releasing her back to the water. Shortly after the mermaid had sunk beneath the waves, a fierce storm brewed and the fishing boat barely made it back to shore. The fisherman, said to be thereafter haunted by his callous action, later drowned. While such a fate was always a risk, the story connected the fisherman's actions towards the mermaid with his eventual death at sea, much as witchcraft stories connected subsequent misfortune to an encounter with a witch.

The supernatural abilities of mermaids were upstaged by another type of sea dweller known as Finn-men. Rather than having the fixed human–fish hybridity of the mermaid, Finn-men could shift between human and seal form. In the latter form, they could move at fantastic speeds through the water. Some tales indicate that this was a physical transformation, while others tell that Finn-men, like certain merfolk beliefs, adopted a skin or covering that enabled them to travel and breathe underwater. Victorian scholars debated whether this sealskin transformation may have derived from stories about Finn-folk who arrived from Norway or even further afield in animal-skin kayaks.[22]

This led to tales of Finn-men being mistakenly attacked and wounded when appearing as large seals. Like mermaids, this was deemed unlucky for the assailants. In one account, a group of Shetlanders were hunting seals with guns. Every time they took aim at one particular seal, their weapons misfired. Eventually the hunters took this as a sign that the seal was a disguised or transformed Finn-man who was using magic to prevent the guns from firing properly. Realizing the potential risk they were taking, they stopped shooting. In another case a Shetlander discovered a large seal sleeping among rocks on a beach in eastern Shetland. He stabbed the animal with his knife, but the seal got away, slipping into the sea with the knife still in its body. When the Shetlander later called on an elderly friend in Norway, the old man asked if he had lost a knife on a certain beach on a certain day. He then returned the weapon to the Shetlander, adding, 'It would not have been so bad if you had not twisted the knife when you put it in.'[23] Such tales can be understood as a variant of folkloric tales in which the true identity of a witch is revealed by somebody wounding a hare and then discovering a woman who had recently received wounds in an equivalent place on her body.

Said to reside in coastal areas of western Norway into the late eighteenth century, if not later, it was also said that Finn-men lived underwater in a place called Finfolkaheem, and, during the summers, on a floating island called Hildaland. Scottish tales suggest that Finn-men were known to abduct unsuspecting girls from the shore, if they turned their backs to the sea. However, they were generally seen as positive rather than malevolent magical practitioners, although such abilities tended to make people wary of them. Finn-men were powerful wizards, capable of making themselves invisible at will. They could understand the language of birds and animals, and some could transform into ravens or porpoises. They could also control the weather, either bringing storms or calming the winds. Although Finn-men were often viewed with suspicion or fear, Shetlanders were known to pay them for a rich range of magical services. They could also provide magic charms to bring good luck or to protect from misfortune or illness, break spells placed on bewitched cattle and counter the malevolent magic of fairies. They could also locate objects lost underwater and knew where stolen goods were to be found on land or sea. In short, they duplicated and exceeded many of the services that human 'cunning folk' claimed to be able to provide. Their ability to foretell the future and misfortunes was particularly detailed: they knew the fate of sea vessels and when people would sicken or die, where best to catch fish and how many would be caught. Given this, Shetlanders travelling to Norway were known to consult with Finn-men about the future or have their fortunes told. While often small in stature, of a swarthy complexion and with skin blemishes that gave them a notable appearance, some chose to not draw attention to themselves or their powers, quietly living with and marrying into Shetland communities.

Associated with the North Sea and the Baltic, especially in the waters between Scotland and Norway, Finn-men were not the same as the Finlanders, who were commonly associated with witchcraft at sea, although there was obviously scope for confusion in the use of the names and their shared connection with magical powers. Writing in 1918, J. A. Teit recorded that some years earlier, when a Shetlander met with a Dr Westermark, a Finlander, aboard a steamer, he advised that when the visitor landed in the Shetland Islands, he should not say he was a Finn. It was suggested that the steamship passenger might want to say he was a Swede or Scandinavian instead, as this would not prompt the suspicion that was directed towards Finn-men.[24]

Dissecting Mermaids: Allure and Anxiety

Much like their joined human–fish form, merfolk were a hybrid of enchantment and unease, the desired and feared, known and unknown, surface and depth. The superficial appeal of mermaids always came with concerns about what might lie beneath, the purpose that evident allure served. Mermaids were imagined as sexually appealing. The idea of beautiful, long-haired young women preoccupied with accoutrements of mirrors and combs emphasized their femininity, but their frequent nakedness, and, variously, their vulnerability, nonchalance or active efforts at seduction struck a less conventional chord. Their physical appeal was offset by the fact that their lower fish body denied the very lusts that may have fed into such stories. Mermaids could promise the wonders and riches of unknown hidden realms, the call of the wild and an escape from the burdens and responsibilities of the surface world, but this would leave humans vulnerable to drowning, and possibly to being eaten. Even if the idea of a marriage was feasible, the surface dweller would be an outsider, likely to be reduced to a novelty, pet or ornament. The very source of fascination, the draw of the other world, was also the dividing line that, stories suggest, could not be permanently crossed.

Any notion that mermaids were just the fantasies of sexually frustrated sailors cooped up for too long together at sea is too simplistic. Isolation within an all-male working environment may well have bred a desire to see women at sea, but what then was the sense in making such fantasies fish from the waist down? If such creatures appealed, it was perhaps because, while resembling humans, they were fully adapted to the ocean environment. The experienced mariner may not feel like an intruder at sea, might even come to consider it his home, but as a creature of the land, it was not and never would be his natural environment. The hybrid merfolk were fantasies of unfettered freedom, able to dwell in an environment that, as much of the lore in this book suggests, inspired anxiety and fear in those who originated ashore. Stuck on their ships for many weeks, the temptation to follow mermaids beneath the waves was seafarers' equivalent of our fantasies of flight, both being imagined escapes from our bounded limitations. Perhaps somewhat darker, one could also understand the lure of the mermaid as a fantasy of a beautiful death, of a willing escape through drowning from weeks of confinement aboard ship. The mermaid's strange hybridity served as an ideal of marine adaptation. Blending the mind and reason of the human(oid) with a body fashioned for life underwater, the mermaid had uninhibited access to the ocean in a way humans could only dream of.

In Irish lore, some merrows were said to be human children who, victims of shipwreck or sinking, had been saved from drowning by merfolk. Taken beneath the waves to Tír fo Thuinn, they forgot their human origins. These tales clearly served to temper grief at young, innocent lives lost at sea. It was said that if these adapted merchildren should step foot on land again, they would remember their former lives and be forever exiled from life beneath the seas. While merfolk could commonly traverse sea and land, often appearing at the coastal boundary of each, such stories suggest a sense of division rather than liminality. Human children-turned-merrows could only ever be inhabitants of one world or the other, not both.

This fantasy of adaptation to escape death appears on a larger, more tragic scale in the context of the transatlantic slave trade. The Atlantic colluded in hiding the unknown number of bodies of slaves, both dead and alive, that were cast overboard. One idea, a comfort against the grief and loss of such actions, was that those who were treated in such a callous fashion transformed into merfolk. In this way the ocean became an aquatic afterworld, a place of altered life and resurrection in a form that would permit them to live and live free in the Atlantic's vast expanse.[25]

African slaves also brought their belief in water spirits with them, adapting river goddesses to the ocean and to the various lands in the Caribbean and Americas where they were taken. The Simbi, nature spirits from West Africa, were both a connection to a distant home and a symbol of hope and aid under the conditions of slavery. The South Carolina Lowcountry was one such place where Simbi were relocated, becoming spirits of rivers and streams in the American South. While an image of a white, Western mermaid has come to dominate European and North American accounts, these other mermaid-like figures can be understood as expressions of cultural resistance and adaptation. Having lost their freedom, and suffered slavers' attempts to discard their culture and identity in their long wake back across the ocean, to enslaved peoples stories and beliefs were luggage that could not be taken away in the cramped and filthy confines of the ships. Powerless to bring freedom or an end to suffering, the Simbi at least provided a familiar and comforting figure in a new land.[26]

Another water spirit figure to cross the Atlantic from West and South Africa, from the Ivory Coast, Nigeria and Senegal, was Mami Wata. In Africa she had been a river goddess, but her role grew and adapted to fit the needs of slaves. 'Mami Wata' may be derived from pidgin English of 'Mother Water', meaning the African spirit was known by a foreign (English) name, although this European etymological origin has been contested by some African scholarship. Mami Wata combined the duality of the ocean, capable of being both a provider and a threat. She sometimes abducted swimmers or people in boats and took them to an underwater spirit realm. If allowed to return, they did so with renewed spiritual knowledge and often a dramatic improvement in both their wealth and beauty. Mami Wata was associated with lust and sex, but also with healing and fertility that linked her to the fecundity of the ocean. This duality extended to gender, for while she was usually depicted as female, she could also take male form. Mami Wata was more than a mermaid, but, like European tales of mermaids, she is often depicted with long hair and holds a mirror, a link between present and future that echoes the fortune-telling abilities of merfolk. This suggests a degree of creolization, of African and European ideas of aquatic beings mixing in Caribbean culture.[27]

The dominance of a male, predominantly heterosexual gaze may have been a feature in determining the imbalance between mermaid and mermen sightings, although that does not explain why mariners were more inclined to see the opposite sex than their own. Ultimately, the emphasis on the feminine water dweller, particularly the mermaid, seemed determined by her acting as an anthropomorphic representation of the ocean itself. The ocean was often understood as possessing a changeable feminine nature, nurturing and providing, yet also tempestuous and dangerous; it was the womb from which all life had originally derived, and the tomb to which seafarers could be confined. The ocean's greater fecundity of life compared with that found ashore furthered its identification as an essentially feminine space. Again, the mermaid was an important representation of this. Mermaids were not conventionally fertile, for merchildren were even rarer than mermen, but their human–fish appearance spoke to the ocean's ability to produce rich and varied forms of life that were not found on land. The high seas were often depicted as a place where male mariners went to escape problematic relationships or nurse a broken heart. Surrounded by male company, crews formed a small masculine enclave in a ship that was often designated a 'she', in an environment commonly associated with female characteristics. As we have seen in previous chapters, mariners tended to be rather pragmatic in their approaches to the maritime supernatural, less inclined to abstract, symbolic thinking. Yet it is important to distinguish between the alluring idea of the mermaid and its familiarity within transatlantic culture, and those notably fewer accounts that purport to be actual mermaid sightings.

The intriguing otherness of the mermaid's hybrid form was also a source of anxiety in an eighteenth- and nineteenth-century world that sought to advance a neat and orderly categorization of the natural world as a scientific means of understanding. The mermaid represented a figure existing at human–piscine boundaries that should never even meet. The division between those forms, and their segue into one another in the mermaid, disturbed the efforts of Enlightenment science to impose order on the world, unsettling notions of species and drawing attention to the animal nature beneath our flattering sense of human civilization.

Despite the physical allure of the mermaid, their biology meant they were figures of sexual frustration rather than wish-fulfilling fantasies for sailors. Seductive but chaste, the mermaid as teasing temptress played into an element of misogyny that would have been inclined to fester in a predominantly homosocial environment such as that found on board ship. Shared stories of mermaids would reflect the prejudices as much as the hopes of the group, likely amplified by the sense of confinement on a vessel. Mermaid stories spoke to a distrust of feminine wiles, deception about their true natures, motives and appearance. The idea of a creature that appears human but with a concealed animal lower half of their body is seen in the monstrous Lamia of Greek mythology and the medieval romance of Melusine. They also spoke to an unease when confronted by an assertive female sexuality that was not tempered by European society's cultural constraints. Through such depictions, the mermaid as a temptress preying on men's weaknesses could be framed as feminine monstrosity rather than masculine failings.

The qualities that allured and unsettled were two sides of the same coin. To follow the mermaid was to take a swim on the wild side, with both the freedoms and dangers that came with it. Like the sea, the mermaid was dangerously enthralling, powerful and untamed. The message that came from tales of the Sirens, from the torment of Homer's Odysseus tied to the mast onwards, was not that beautiful women were making themselves available to mariners. Odysseus' heroism lay in his power to resist such appeals, or to suffer their enchantments and continue on his way. The lesson was to hold to one's sense of duty, purpose and responsibility, to value reason over instinct, to consider the welfare of fellow crew members, and not to be lulled by supernatural song or sexual attraction.

Seafarers lived and worked between two domains, the ocean serving as the contact point between a masculine-dominated surface world and a feminine-dominated underwater world. While mermaids and men may have been intrigued by the existence of each other's realms, venturing into them rarely proved rewarding. Tales told of terrestrial husbands who became little more than pets or trophies underwater, while mermaids who came ashore tended to become worn-down wives who harboured a sad longing for a return to the ocean. This is seen in the tale of the sea woman of Haarlem, although she does not marry. The initially intriguing strangeness of the sea woman who was found stuck in a broken dyke between the Dutch towns of Campen and Edam gradually ebbed once she had been 'acquired' by some viewers from Haarlem who had come to see her. She was dressed as other women, learned to eat meat and was taught how to spin. A previous urge to escape back to sea gradually dwindled into acceptance of her fate. Living in Haarlem for fifteen years, she even acquired a reverence for the cross and was buried in a local churchyard.[28] The sense of enchantment rarely lasted, either for the one that ventured into the other world or those who accommodated them. Like the Sirens' song, the promise lay in the enticement, not the consequences.

Eighteenth- and Nineteenth-Century Accounts and Sightings

Much of the above represented a romanticized, often artistic or literary, depiction of the mermaid. This contrasted dramatically with ongoing 'real' sightings and accounts derived from oral culture. The 'real' mermaid frequently failed to live up to the beautiful ideal of myth. These parallel representations went back some way. In *Speculum Regali*, a twelfth-century Icelandic text, a mer-creature from Greenland known as the Margyzr was described as a female 'monster' with 'a very horrible face, with broad brow and piercing eyes, a wide mouth and double chin'. She had 'breasts and bosom like a woman, long hands and soft hair', although her hands were webbed. From the waist down, her body resembled 'a fish with scales, tail and fin'. Tending to appear before heavy storms, when the Margyzr played with fish in her hands or threw them towards the ship, it was taken as a sign that the vessel would lose several crew members. If it threw the fish away or turned away from the vessel, then it was a good omen, and everyone would make it through the coming tempest.[29]

It has been suggested that 'real' mermaid sightings declined after the fifteenth and sixteenth centuries, a result of sailing ships increasingly moving away from hugging the coasts where possible, with nineteenth-century steamships accelerating the shift in trade routes.[30] Such a theory is obviously based on the assumption that mermaids were essentially coastal rather than deep-water creatures. Added to this, from the seventeenth and eighteenth centuries a growing scepticism might have discouraged people from voicing their accounts of mermaid experiences, although here the historian is confronted with the challenge of proving an absence as proof of change. Despite these developments, accounts continued into the nineteenth century, and often from people who, by social status or maritime experience, might be deemed credible witnesses.

In his *Natural History of Norway* Pontoppidan states that the most recent sighting of a merman he had heard of was in 1723, a mile from the coast, near Landskrona, Sweden. It had been found floating like a dead body on the water. When it dived and reappeared, several witnesses saw a figure that resembled 'an old man, strong limb'd, with broad shoulders', though they could not see his arms. His head was quite small, and he had 'a meagre and pinched face, with a black beard'. His skin was described as 'coarse, and very full of hair'.[31] Despite being aware of and seeking to cut through the distortions and exaggerations of storytelling, Pontoppidan did not interrogate the truth of this particular account. Occurring only thirty years before he published his book, this relatively recent eighteenth-century account seemed to carry more weight for him, not having had time to morph into something more fantastical.

In 1810 two merchildren were found among rocks on the Isle of Man in the Irish Sea. This was a rarity, even among merfolk sightings. Three 'respectable tradesmen' from Douglas, searching for sea birds, were drawn to the cries of one, the other having died, its body lacerated from wounds received in the violent gale that had presumably driven them ashore the previous night. The surviving child was taken to Douglas. It was described as just under 2 feet (60 cm) long from the top of its head to its tail. Its skin was a pale brown, its tail scales violet, its hair green and gelatinous to the touch, like seaweed. It was kept in a tub of seawater, where it was happy to swim about, eat shellfish and take small amounts of milk and water.[32] Despite the mention of respectable tradesmen, the account was reported by somebody who was not present at the discovery and conveyed, in a letter that was printed by several regional newspapers, as second-hand information. The persistent problem with 'real' sightings is that we only have the witnesses' word for it, or, in this case, someone else's. The lack of verification meant merfolk continued to float between belief and scepticism, reality and fantasy.

In 1823 six fishermen from Yell in the Shetland Islands caught a mermaid 3 feet (90 cm) long, with the upper body of a humanoid, and a face described as like that of a monkey. The creature had stiff bristles on its head, but its lower body was smooth and grey. One might easily assume them to be describing a seal, but the fishermen claimed they would have certainly known the difference. It took them three hours to untangle the creature from their lines and remove the hook that had entered its body, so their observations were not hurriedly made. As a Mr Edmonston noted, in passing on information of the account, the usual dismissal about the 'excited imagination' of fishermen, or the misreading of something glimpsed in the water, could not be levelled at them in such a case. He added,

> Not one of the six men dreamed of a doubt of it being a mermaid, and it could not be suggested that they were influenced by their fears, for the mermaid is not an object of terror to fishermen; it is rather a welcome guest, and danger is apprehended from it experiencing bad treatment.

This may explain why they laboured to free it and subsequently release it back into the water. Given the fishermen could easily be subjected to ridicule and a questioning of their occupational knowledge, there seem little point in deliberately fabricating such a tale.[33]

The lives and actions of merfolk were elaborated upon in Shetland lore. Described as quite small but well proportioned, their fondness for music, singing, dancing and storytelling made them strongly akin to land dwellers' notions of fairies. They were believed to be like surface dwellers in their homes beneath the waves, but when they wanted to travel through the water their lower bodies transformed into that of a fish, or they adopted a 'fish-like covering' that protected them from the extremes of the deep water. This covering was removed from the head and shoulders when on the surface, suggesting that it was required for them to breathe underwater, and was completely removed when ashore. There was debate about whether merfolk could survive long ashore or on the surface of the sea, for their bodies were conditioned to the atmospheric pressures of deep water. Those that spent any great time ashore were said to grow sad, pining for the sea. Blurring with elements of selkie legends, this could become a form of terrible grief if the coverings that permitted their return to life beneath the waves were taken from them. It was said that when fishermen were near the merfolk's homes they would play tricks on them, removing bait or fish from their hooks and fixing their lines to rocks or seaweed. In such ways, mermaids could be blamed for mistakes and accidents with the fishing lines or even the failure to secure a good catch.[34] Shetlander ideas about merfolk were echoed in Irish beliefs that the merrows wore special items to enable them to travel through water. Around the coasts of Kerry and Cork, they were said to wear a red cap called a cohuleen druith. In Ireland's more northern waters one finds the echo of Finn-men and selkie legends, with merrows wearing sealskin coats or cloaks.

While this suggested a belief in merfolk persisted in Victorian Britain, folklorists tended to frame such claims through several common ploys. First, they were often presented as *lingering* beliefs that lacked genuine conviction and contemporary relevance. Second, such ideas were distanced spatially, associated with the Celtic fringe of Ireland or the remoter parts of Scotland, or else temporally, as in Robert Hunt's recording of mermaid tales from 'old Cornwall'. These accounts seemed to exist independently of the mermaid in mythology or literature. While those who had received a classical education at nineteenth-century British universities may have been familiar with the works of Hesiod, Homer and Ovid, most common sailors and fishing communities were not. Rather, the folkloric mermaid was understood as a rarely seen but possible reality of their working environment, part of the lived experience of fellow mariners, rather than some mythological or poetic invention. While mythology, poetry and folklore all used the term 'mermaid', they did so in different contexts and did not necessarily refer to the same thing.

Mermaids and Science in the Eighteenth and Nineteenth Centuries

Despite a popular fascination with natural wonders, marvels and monstrous aberrations in early modern European culture, belief in mermaids and other fabulous creatures was changing by the turn of the eighteenth century.[35] Rather than simply dismissing such ideas as past ignorance, there was an increasing desire to subject the likes of mermaids to rationalized understandings, and to engage with the natural realities that had become obscured by the accrual of supernatural tales. Eighteenth-century Europe turned its attention to what Vaughn Scribner has termed 'the science of wonder'. This saw naturalists begin to treat once fabulous creatures as valid topics for scientific examination. In particular, the seemingly amphibious mermaid held the possibility of important insights into the origins of human land dwellers. Such ideas courted controversy, for some eighteenth-century naturalists were willing to suggest that Adam, the first man, had been preceded by a mermaid or triton.

This scientific consideration meant rejecting what was seen as supernatural absurdities and artistic elaborations such as enchanting songs and knowledge of the future. It presumed that much of what had been described was simply mistaken observation, inflated by mariners' love of telling tall tales. Mermaids' hands may have still appeared in eighteenth-century cabinets of curiosities, those odd meeting places of natural science and sensational wonders, but exactly what they were the 'hands' of was increasingly open for discussion. As part of that debate, eighteenth-century naturalists began to move away from a previous dependence on the revered texts of classical authorities such as Pliny. Instead, they adopted more rigorous scientific approaches involving the sharing of knowledge and information through a network of written correspondence and learned societies, the development of detailed drawings and descriptions, the preservation of specimens, re-examining historical accounts and, with the eighteenth century seeing a second age of European exploration, travel across the oceans.

Noted naturalists in North America and Europe, including Cotton Mather, Carl Linnaeus, Erich Pontoppidan and François Valentijn each sought to probe at the realities beneath the myths and legends of mermaids. In 1716 Mathers wrote of a mermaid seen in 1610, when a Captain Richard Whitbourne had been exploring Newfoundland. Somewhat later, Linnaeus urged the Swedish Academy of Science to capture a mermaid sighted in the Baltic Sea near Nykoping, Sweden, in 1749. He and his student Abraham Österdam later published *Siren lacertina*, a collection of historical mermaid sightings, in 1766. Eighteenth-century British, European and American newspapers reported mermaid and triton sightings, demonstrating a willingness to publicly discuss such creatures in journalistic and scientific debate. In a piece about contemporary mermaids in the Aegean Sea in the *Gentleman's Magazine* in May 1775, it was proposed that mermaids could be divided into different races. Echoing eighteenth-century Europeans' crude notions of racial hierarchies, it was proposed that a specimen found in 1774, described as handsome, fine-featured and with blue eyes, was akin to the Caucasian race. This contrasted sharply with a taxidermized specimen displayed at a fair in Saint-Germain, Paris, in 1758. The 2-foot-tall (60 cm) creature had been stood erect, as if balanced on its tail, and its ugly facial features were contorted into a grimace. Its darker skin led a journalist to claim that it could be compared to the 'Negroid' race.[36]

These initiatives developed further in the nineteenth century. Around the mid-century, as the developing science of palaeontology promoted the idea of extinct former species and Charles Darwin advanced a theory of evolution based on environmental adaptation, mermaids offered interesting thought experiments regarding both. The mermaid, in its human–piscine form, suggested a former point of evolution, a possible missing link between marine and terrestrial worlds and therefore an ancestor from which humans had emerged. Such an idea had been proposed by Benoît de Maillet in his *Telliamed* (1748). H. Brink-Roby has suggested that Darwin's evolutionary theory granted new credibility to the likes of mermaids, although Darwin's critics used the mythological nature of such hybrid creatures to undermine his theory.[37]

If merfolk were a living species, then, the logic ran, the growth of transatlantic trade and shipping would have led to an increase in sightings in the eighteenth and nineteenth centuries. Instead, most naturalists had to turn to scattered historical accounts for description of such creatures. Merfolk's long history in the cultures of many seafaring countries around the world encouraged the possibility that they had once been a real species that had gone extinct, living on only, perhaps surrounded with a haze of supernatural elaborations, in myths and legends. Some felt it was time for biological sciences to either provide the scientific basis for such tales or to dismiss them as mere fabulations.[38] This was not easily achieved, in part because nineteenth-century naturalists could not agree on what mermaids were or, if presumed extinct, had been.

It did not help that, in an age that prized empirical evidence and the proof of one's own eyes, taxidermied mermaids became popular attractions. A male specimen was displayed in London in 1795. Bald, horned and ugly, it was very much an animal rather than an alluring humanoid. Most nineteenth-century examples were similarly far removed from the expectations of legend and literature. In 1836 the *Saturday Magazine* described one being exhibited in a glass case in one of the leading streets in London's fashionable West End. It was described as having 'the head and shoulders of a monkey, which was attached to the dried skin of a fish of the salmon kind with the head cut off, and the whole was stuffed and highly varnished, the better to deceive the eye'.[39] A Dutch vessel had supposedly taken it from a native Malacca boat whose crew were said to use it as an idol or representative of their gods. Some of these fake mermaids were said to originate in India and Japan. In one case, an enterprising Indian fisherman had made a mermaid from the bodies of an ape and a fish and exhibited it with the promise that, if touched, it could cure diseases. Whether it was the unusual sight or the magical claim, his attraction drew large audience until a European man bought it for a large sum and brought it to Europe.[40] As curios brought back to Europe from overseas, they may have had the allure of the exotic, but these ugly, wizened concoctions certainly lacked any supernatural aura.

Perhaps the most well known of these fakes was the 'Feejee mermaid'. Arriving in London in 1822, it became a popular sensation that summer, promoted in newspapers and periodicals, and even being drawn by the noted Georgian illustrator George Cruikshank. It also divided scientific opinion, with Dr Rees Price open to the idea that it might be evidence of a missing evolutionary link, and Sir Everard Home assuming it to be a hoax. The scepticism of naturalists and journalists did nothing to dent its popularity among those who were willing to pay their half-crowns and shillings to gaze upon the grotesque. However, after Home exposed it as a fake in December 1822, its exhibition at the respectable Turf Coffeehouse in St James Street closed down the following month. That did not mark the end of the Feejee mermaid, for it then toured the provinces until 1825. When it was displayed in a tent at Bartholomew Fair in London, the picture outside was of a beautiful mermaid with the obligatory comb and mirror. Punters were obviously in for a shock when, lulled by the promise of beauty, they came face to face with a shrivelled, shrunken amalgam of ape and fish. Always having an eye for money-making attractions, the American entertainment entrepreneur P. T. Barnum eventually purchased it for his museum.[41]

The exposure of one fake did not prove that mermaids had never existed. As such, the debate between naturalists continued into the later nineteenth century. Championing a dismissive, rationalist line, Henry Lee took the view that every mythical creature of the seas had its origin in the misunderstood sighting of a natural animal. Supposed 'mermaids' had simply been seals, walruses, manatees or dugongs, all of which could resemble human faces and human movements from a distance. Sea lions, porpoises and dolphins were later added to this list of marine animals that had helped sustain accounts of mermaids.[42] The bristly muzzle of the walrus or dugong could resemble a bearded man, while manatee females had 'breasts' or mammae for feeding their young, a feature that may have led Spanish and Portuguese mariners to refer to the manatee as the 'woman fish'. Mocking the idea of the mermaid's enchanting beauty, Lee noted how imaginative a sailor must be if, 'having been deprived for many months of the pleasure of females' society, [he] could be allured by the charms of a bristly-muzzled dugong, or mistake the snorting of a wallowing manatee for the love-song of a beauteous sea-maiden'. In such cases, an awareness of mermaid legends may have helped fill in the gaps when a humanoid face was glimpsed in the water, thereby encouraging further accounts of merfolk.[43] There was no room for accepting the scientific existence of an amphibious humanoid in Lee's reductive view. For him, merfolk were nothing more than repeated cases of mistaken identity: nature enriched by a sprinkling of fables and lies. This became the dominant view, for unlike the uncertain, cryptozoological status of the sea serpent in the nineteenth century, the impossibility of living merfolk seemed to be based on the point that they were both too close to humans and too inexplicably different to be considered real.

Making Mermaids

The mermaid was an invention of land-based culture as much as a maritime one. Indeed, sailors' accounts of mermaids are disproportionately few compared with their cultural expressions ashore, where they appear with greater frequency than any other element of maritime folklore. Despite the scientific musings about mermaids, most nineteenth- and early twentieth-century land dwellers accepted the idea of the mermaid without needing to believe in its reality, and certainly without ever having to encounter sailors' tales of such. If anything, not existing only seemed to enhance mermaids' appeal. As taxidermied specimens demonstrate, there was a desire to bring the mermaid ashore in the nineteenth century as part of a manufactured enchantment. This took many forms, in art, performance, literature and advertising.

Writing in 1875, Armand Landrin noted how the mermaid had become favoured by 'romancists and poets'. There is some truth to this, with Victorian luminaries such as Alfred, Lord Tennyson, and Matthew Arnold penning works on mermaids and mermen.[44] They were also portrayed by artists of the Pre-Raphaelite movement in Victorian Britain. There was a residual fear of the mermaid in some of this art. This did not just capture mariners' concerns from the stories and legends of the past, but spoke to more contemporary concerns about female sexuality and gender relations. The Pre-Raphaelite artist Edward Burne-Jones created markedly different depictions of mermaids. In a series of watercolours made between 1880 and 1890, he presented groups of mermaids, possibly mothers and children, passively standing in the waves. While presenting the idea of the mermaid as nurturing, and as part of a sisterhood, there seemed little need for mermen. It had been suggested that as a hermaphroditic being, mermaids might be able to produce offspring without the need of a male, a process known as parthenogenesis. While some Victorians may have been inclined to view this as an ideal representation of motherhood, a marine version of the Virgin Mary, others may have questioned where this left (mer)men and the patriarchy. If mermen tended to remain physically remote in many folkloric accounts, their limited presence in Victorian art suggests they were also remote in the minds of artists and the broader cultural concerns their work reflected.

In *The Depths of the Sea*, painted in 1887, Burne-Jones presented a darker vision. A femme fatale of a mermaid stares out at the viewer as she clings to her male victim beneath the water. As she holds him close to her, his arms seemingly bound, there is a disturbing sense that she is possessing the surface dweller without having any affection for him. The depiction of a male watery sacrifice, indicated by his lack of struggle and the fact that he may already be dead, is a relative rarity given the subgenre of Victorian painting that portrayed tragic female deaths by drowning. These famously included literary characters such as Ophelia, painted by Burne-Jones's Pre-Raphaelite predecessor John Everett Millais, or romanticized depictions of fallen women who sought escape from broken hearts or prostitution by throwing themselves into the Thames at night. Yet poetry and painting helped distance the mermaid into a conscious fiction, a poetic fancy rather than a maritime reality. This is evident in Burne-Jones's painting. There is tragic beauty in the doomed man's drowning. Such a romanticized notion was far removed from the grim horrors that sailors sought to avoid with magic, rituals and omens. Yet, resonating with sailors who may have taken to sea to get away from some failed relationship, it has been suggested that Burne-Jones's cold and deadly mermaid was informed by a misogyny that derived from his own personal relationships with women.[45]

Other Victorian artists seemed less troubled by mermaids. Evelyn de Morgan's *The Sea Maidens* (1886) presented them as a wholesome sisterhood, naked to the scaly waist but, to the modern eye, appearing as an oddly sedated mermaid girl band. In a 1900 painting by John William Waterhouse, a mermaid is absorbed in that typical behaviour of combing her long hair, seemingly startled by the viewer's gaze rather than plotting anything sinister. These safer, more passive, less monstrous images stood in marked contrast to both the sinister mythological currents swirling in Burne-Jones's painting and the hideous 'real' creatures that were to be found in contemporary fairs or exhibitions.

The mermaid found a role in a popular culture hungry for new sensations. There was something of the freak show in Harry Phillips' exhibiting of a 'living mythological mermaid', first at the Brighton Aquarium, and then at the Albert Palace and the Royal Aquarium, London, in 1886. For the price of sixpence, viewers saw a beautiful mermaid in a water tank, surrounded by living fish. A piece in *The Era* declared that, rather than believe it to be an illusion, they would prefer to 'believe the other way'.[46] Other promotional material praised the quality of an illusion that 'conjures up reminiscences of the sirens'. This modest spectacle was upstaged by 'Neptune's Daughter', a musical extravaganza at the New York Hippodrome Theatre in November 1906 featuring a real pool. Dancers were dressed as mermaids who encourage a

ROYAL AQUARIUM.

IN THE GALLERY NEXT THE CENTRE STAGE.

HARRY PHILLIPS'

LIVING

MYTHOLOGICAL

MERMAID.

Four Months in the Pavilion, West Pier, Brighton.

Exhibited Five Months at
ALBERT PALACE,
Six Months at
PAVILION, Jetty Extension, Margate,
Fourteen Months at
ROYAL AQUARIUM.
Four Months on GRAND PIER, BRIGHTON.

Exhibited Five Months at
ALBERT PALACE,
Six Months at
PAVILION, Jetty Extension, Margate,
Fourteen Months at
ROYAL AQUARIUM.
Four Months on GRAND PIER, BRIGHTON.

Submerged in a Glass Tank with Live Fish.

A FEW PRESS NOTICES.

" . . . The wonderful 'Mermaid,' which is sure to be the talk of London."—*Bell's Life*, October 4th, 1886.

" We may especially recommend to the notice of those who patronize the Palace the real live Mermaid, exhibited by Mr. Harry Phillips. There is no mistake this time, and we absolutely decline to credit the exhibitor, who is himself a Tyrolean and character vocalist and ventriloquist, when he tells us that it is all an illusion. We prefer to believe the other way. There, in a glass tank, with sticklebacks and gudgeon for her companions, sits the lovely creature, very beautiful as to her head, with its lovely flowing hair, and very fishy as to her tail. She looks quite bewitching, and she smiles so graciously, that the spectator at once conjures up reminiscences of the sirens, and lingers long and admiringly upon the scene. All should see the real live Mermaid."—*Era*, April 24, 1886.

" The Aquarium has recently obtained a new attraction in the person of a good looking living Mermaid. The entirely novel illusion displays a lady in a recumbent attitude and apparently at ease in all the surroundings of an ordinary Aquarium. Fish are seen swimming, and all sides of the tank are open to the inspection of visitors. The illusion, which is cleverly contrived, is the invention of Mr. Harry Phillips, and is well worth going to see."—*Brighton Gazette*, February 17th, 1886.

On View all day, in the Gallery next the Stage.

Admission 6d. No Waiting.

BURT & SONS, 58, PORCHESTER ROAD, BAYSWATER, W.

Advertisement for Harry Phillips's 'living mythological mermaid' at London's Royal Aquarium, 30 October 1886.

lovelorn sailor to join them in Neptune's kingdom below. Set in Brittany, with an orchestra providing the sound of a storm, and with shifting sets featuring a coastal village and painted waves, it was an elaborate production. Watching a rehearsal of the show, the journalist was informed that the dancers, practising in their bathing suits, 'would look more like real mermaids at the performance' but would not have fishes' tails, 'because a chorus girl, not being by nature fishy, would probably find such a contrivance an impediment to aquatic feats'. The show concluded with the sailor being persuaded to follow the mermaids beneath the waves and into the pool, there to marry Neptune's daughter. The final scene featured a ballet of 250 female dancers representing the various inhabitants of the sea, their costumes having fins on the arms, scaly tights and finned pleats in their skirts.[47]

Literature co-opted the mermaid as it did the fairy in the nineteenth century, their fantastical otherness often being harnessed to a yoke of moral instruction for young readers. Hans Christian Andersen's 'The Little Mermaid', one of his best known 'fairy tales' (first published in 1836 and translated into English in 1846), can be read as a rather dark vehicle for promoting the period's feminine virtues of devotion, self-sacrifice, conformity and silence. For the love of a prince, the mermaid (unnamed until Disney called her Ariel) is willing to sacrifice her tongue and beautiful singing voice in exchange for legs that will cause her pain but enable her to go ashore. When the prince fails to recognize her and marries someone else, the mermaid cannot bring herself to kill him, as urged by the sea witch who had created the potion that transformed her. She jumps off the ship that is carrying the prince and his new bride and, no longer a mermaid, dissolves in the foam. Aware that this strikes a downbeat note, Andersen ends by allowing the mermaid to escape death: she instead becomes an aerial spirit who has been put on the path to obtaining a soul for the sacrifices she has made.[48]

Although promoting a very different message, this instructive purpose can also be seen in a *Boy's Standard* story, 'Jack Jones' Adventures among the Mermaids', from 1891. Sailing from Liverpool to South America, the younger members of the crew get Jack Jones, an aggressive and ill-humoured sailor, drunk and play a prank on him. With a mermaid inventively fashioned from canvas stuffed with oakum, some rope and paint, they convince him that a sea nymph has brought a message, and he hears a feminine voice singing 'The Fairy Tempter'. Jones imagines he sees a dozen nymphs jeering at him, while Neptune glares at him in the background. Davy Jones and Mother Carey warn him never to bad-mouth them again, for they are sailors' 'blessed sea protectors'. Left naked, drunk and confused on the cabin floor, Jones, we are told, will change his unfriendly ways in future.[49]

The mermaid followed a similar trajectory to the taming of Victorian fairies, at least ashore. As indicated at several points in this chapter, the two had longer cultural affinities, with mermaids presenting similar dangers to fairies in attempting to lure people from the human to the non-human world, an experience that frequently involved transformation and some form of loss. Fairies and mermaids were also linked by at least one theory of their origin. It was proposed that fairies were the undecided angels in Lucifer's rebellion in Heaven. Neither good enough to stay in heaven nor evil enough to be condemned to hell, they had instead fallen to earth. Those that were banished to the remote and hidden parts of the land became fairies, while those that fell into the ocean depths became merfolk. Neither were believed to have souls, the achievement of which underpins Andersen's Little Mermaid's desire to secure the love of the human prince. Both had the more sinister, capricious elements of their former natures removed in later nineteenth-century reimaginings. Fairies generally became smaller and more appealing as they shifted from folkloric reality to children's literary fiction, while mermaids became beautiful and innocent.[50]

This is seen in late Victorian advertising. Stripping away any remaining notion of mermaids as deceptive, flesh-eating creatures, advertisers appropriated the old idea of their supernatural powers to lull and lure to their own secular needs. The mermaid's eye-catching visual appeal and frequent semi-nakedness was used to sell goods ranging from mineral water to hair products to tobacco. They also helped to sell places, as the tourist industry developed in this period, with bays, coves, caves, rocks and pools in locations such as Cornwall and Devon in England, and northeast Scotland being associated with mermaids. A similar drive developed later in the West Indies, with only one of fourteen mermaid-named locations dating back before 1900, and only a further three before the Second World War. There was clearly a degree of deliberate invention going on, most likely in the name of tourism. Of course, older associations were not necessarily free of similar accusations. As Simon Young has noted, while such placenames cannot be taken as evidence of former belief, they at least show a willingness to encourage discussion about mermaids.[51]

As seen in this chapter, the Atlantic was populated by an array of aquatic humanoids, with cultural genealogies that wove together ancient myths and classical texts, tall tales, mistaken observations, deliberate hoaxes, rumours and folklore. For mariners, they served as symbols of the unknown, the possibility that there were things, rarely and briefly sighted from ships, that existed beyond the limits of their knowledge. They were to eighteenth- and nineteenth-century seafarers what extraterrestrials became to twentieth-century aircraft pilots. Such encounters were ways for mariners to mark their difference from both greenhorn sailors and landlubbers alike. They enabled them to speak to a range of maritime experience that could include the rare and marvellous, to having directly seen things (supposedly) that land dwellers only encountered in manufactured form, as literary fictions, artistic portrayals or faked entertainment.

The mermaid created ashore, and especially in the nineteenth century, was knowingly engaged with as a fiction, yet one that had undergone its own evolution. By the end of the century, it had largely swallowed its mythological maritime forebears – nymphs, tritons and water sprites – and had knapped all the hard edges and horrors off its own folklore. More titillating than seductive, more cheery than flirtatious, often more fixated on her own beauty (hence the comb and mirror) than other people, a once-powerful symbol of the ocean's allure and anxiety had been watered down into a spectacle, an amphibian storybook fairy, a glamour model bent to the service of modern advertising. For land dwellers at least, this seemed to speak to a sense that the oceans had been tamed and no longer held anything to fear. As the following chapters suggest, mariners maintained a very different view.

4

The Haunted High Seas

Captain Vanderdecken was a stubborn man. When a fierce storm blew up at the Cape of Good Hope, most other mariners would have relented, sought safe harbour and waited for it to pass. Not so this seventeenth-century Dutch sailor. He took it personally, pitting himself against the forces of nature and God, assuming the latter had placed the storm in his path. The gale grew worse, his crew shrank back in terror, but Vanderdecken would not be turned from his course. Instead, he boldly vowed he would make his way around the Cape if it took him until Doomsday. Sea and storm churned in a maelstrom, and with the ship threatening to break apart, a glowing figure, said to be the Holy Spirit itself, descended from the clouds and stood before the crew. As if that were not a sign that Vanderdecken was pushing things a little too far, the captain threatened to shoot the divine visitant if it did not leave his vessel. Good to his word, when it did not reply, he fired a shot. His pistol sounded, but it was the Dutchman who cried out, finding the bullet had wounded his own hand. Having grown used to controlling his crew with physical violence, he then tried to strike the glowing figure, but his arm instantly withered.

The Holy Spirit had had enough. In punishment for his defiance Vanderdecken was condemned to sail for eternity, never sleeping but always on watch, unable to eat or drink but always hungry and thirsty. His ship would never be allowed to reach port, and he would never know calm seas or fair winds again.

In a twist of Vanderdecken's defiant words, he would sail until Doomsday.[1] From this almost biblical encounter between man and God, the legend of the ship, the *Flying Dutchman*, grew. Like barnacles on a hull, it accrued details and backstory over time, becoming an omen of misfortune to all who caught sight of it: a seventeenth-century ghost ship haunting the nineteenth- and twentieth-century Atlantic.

Just as old buildings encourage tales of haunting, so the long history of seafaring in the Atlantic Ocean gave rise to accounts of phantom ships. Such tales are found in the coastal and nautical folklore of Ireland, Britain and France, down to the dangerous waters of the Cape of Good Hope in South Africa. On the other side of the Atlantic they are found around Cape Horn in Chile and up through the West Indies, the Gulf of St Lawrence and the eastern seaboard of the United States and Canada. As is the case ashore, the willingness to believe in ghosts, or to be open to stories of their existence, continued for longer than a (public) belief in magic. Claims about magic were largely based on unprovable connections between cause and effect. A curse could be followed by misfortune, but it was an act of association and belief that connected the two. Ghosts at least required some evidence, however vague or speculative, be it a manifestation, moving objects or sounds. As late as 1942 Mass Observation surveys conducted in wartime England indicated that 40 per cent of men and more than 50 per cent of women believed in or at least were willing to entertain supernatural ideas, with ghosts, omens and premonitions being the most cited examples.[2]

Much of nautical ghost lore was not based on first-hand observation (or at least cannot be verified as such), but on accounts likely heard from others. As with most other supernatural nautical ideas, it was ordinary sailors rather than officers who tended to say they had seen ghosts aboard ship or sighted phantom ships. This should not be taken as evidence that the common sailor was naturally or necessarily more superstitious than their officers. Officers might have been more inclined to withhold or not openly express their opinions, whereas crewmen might exchange accounts of ghostly happenings as part of the onboard currency of storytelling. Crewmen were also more likely to be in parts of the vessel that officers did not frequently visit and were primarily responsible for conducting the four-hourly watches that had to be conducted around the clock. As such, common sailors were more likely to experience unusual sights or sounds to which officers were not privy. Wilbur Bassett, bringing some of his own prejudices to bear, drew a distinction between the supernatural inclinations of sailors from different nations rather than different ranks. He claimed, 'American and English sailors had more education and less superstition, more fear of ridicule and less ready fancy than their Gallic mates.' They were less likely 'to give out the fancy of another as the truth', so that on the occasions when they did talk of having seen a ghost ship 'we may be sure the story is worthy of inspection.'[3]

As seen when considering the broader functions of storytelling in Chapter One, these accounts were not necessarily true, but nor were they just invented entertainments for the purpose of simply whiling away the time on board ship. This chapter begins by investigating the *Flying Dutchman*, not simply because it is the Atlantic's most developed phantom ship legend, but because it provides a means of exploring the interaction between nautical and land-based influences, and between oral and literary cultures. It will then examine how ghost stories were a means of talking about the dangers and strangeness of life at sea, a way to convey practical and moral lessons aboard ship, to manage the grief around lost loved ones at sea and ashore, and ultimately to preserve highly fabulated memories of life and death in an environment where history struggled to leave a visible mark on ever-shifting waves.

Constructing the *Flying Dutchman*

As we have seen, the ocean was understood as a place subject to divine and diabolical intervention. Heaven and hell pressed close upon the Atlantic waters. In this popular theological framing, a crew damned to sail the seas forever were in an aquatic form of purgatory. Their punishment took on Danteesque dimensions, plagued by foul weather, working an eternity before the mast, always hungry and thirsty, perpetually moving, forever denied the safety and rest of reaching port, land and home. The crew of the *Flying Dutchman* were even denied interaction with other sailors, for that engagement would bring misfortune to passers-by, and attempts to communicate with loved ones via letters would drive the unwitting messengers mad. This curse deprived them of hope and divine forgiveness, making the ocean hellish. Such tales suggest that the worst fate that could await mariners was a gruelling afterlife of servitude that was essentially the same as when they were alive, unable to escape the tyranny of a harsh captain, the confinement of their ship or the ocean itself. Ships, so often symbols of freedom, became in these tales a form of incarceration, endlessly voyaging but never arriving at a destination, a collective wooden coffin that trapped the crew together beyond death.

As a story, the *Flying Dutchman* was constructed from various elements, including land-based legends, nautical accounts and literary influences. Vanderdecken was but one of several legendary maritime figures who were cursed to wander the seas. Earlier examples included the legend of Reginald Falkenberg. The tale relates to the castle of Limburg in the Netherlands where two brothers, Waleran and Reginald, had both sought the affections of Alexia, the daughter of the Count of Cleves. Waleran won, but jealous Reginald murdered his brother and Alexia in their bed on their wedding night. Marked by his brother's bloody hand,

Falkenberg fled to a forest, accompanied by two lights. Travelling on, he eventually reached the coast and found a boat waiting for him. A mysterious boatman rowed him out to a sailing ship, but once Falkenberg was aboard the boatman disappeared. The ship then sailed itself, with Falkenberg spending six hundred years sailing around the North Sea without a steersman. The accompanying lights became two spirits that played dice for the soul of this sea-bound wanderer.[4] Just as Falkenberg was physically marked by the sin of his brother's murder, the bullet wound in Vanderdecken's hand was a cumbersome reminder that his state of damnation was also self-inflicted.

Another influence was the tale of the Dutch mariner Bernard Fokke, a skilled but brutish seventeenth-century sea captain. He was thought to be in league with the Devil, such was his ability to complete voyages at speed. He made the trip from Batavia, Java, to Holland in ninety days and appeared immune to the dangers and misfortunes that beset other mariners. When he eventually failed to return from a trip to the East Indies, it was presumed that the Devil had claimed his soul, forcing him to wander the seas around the Cape of Good Hope. There was an imperial dimension to the tale of Fokke, for the Cape of Good Hope was a gateway to the Netherlands's eastern empire in the seventeenth century. His story evoked the former maritime dominance of the Dutch East India Company, established in 1602, a rival to the English (1600) and French (1664) East India Companies. Echoing the older story of the Wandering Jew, an individual who could not die but suffered an eternity of wandering for his insult to Christ, the European focus of Falkenberg and Fokke's legends laid the blueprint for the *Flying Dutchman*'s cursed captain. R. L. Hadfield claimed that while literary tales such as Frederick Marryat's *The Phantom Ship* made Vanderdecken's name the most famous, 'the actual legend on which Captain Marryat based his story are not so widespread as those of Falkenberg and Fokke.'[5]

The *Flying Dutchman* legend may have originated as oral tales exchanged between sailors, but it eventually caught the attention of and was substantially fleshed out by literary-minded landlubbers too. Tracking its literary genealogy back to the late eighteenth century, it appeared in George Barrington's *A Voyage to Botany Bay* (1795), was mentioned in Thomas Moore's 'Written On Passing Dead-Man's Island in the Gulf of St Lawrence, Late in rhe Evening, September, 1804', and found mention in Sir Walter Scott's notes for his poem *Rokeby* (1813). Scott, a hugely popular writer of his day, promoted the idea that to see the *Flying Dutchman* was a harbinger of ill fortune. Vanderdecken's name was central to a May 1821 *Blackwood's Edinburgh Magazine* story entitled 'Vanderdecken's Message Home; or, The Tenacity of Natural Affection'. Published anonymously, it gave an account of seeing the ghost ship off Cape Town, South Africa.[6] Vanderdecken was also the captain's name in an anonymous 'penny blood' publication titled *The Flying Dutchman; or, The Demon Ship* (1830). The subsequent success of Marryat's novel *The Phantom Ship* (1839) and Richard Wagner's opera *The Flying Dutchman* (1843) cemented Vanderdecken at the centre of melodramatic stories that were not simply about damnation but also redemption.

Wagner's opera granted Vanderdecken a periodic opportunity for salvation. Permitted to come ashore once every seven years, he must find the love of a faithful wife to lift his curse. The opera's drama revolves around this possibility when he seeks the hand of Senta, a Norwegian sailor's daughter. When Senta's former lover urges her to take him back, Vanderdecken, believing his curse will never be lifted, reveals who he is and tells her of his curse. He leaves, and in a desperate attempt to prove her love and save him Senta throws herself into the sea. As the *Flying Dutchman* sinks beneath the waves, Vanderdecken and Senta ascend to heaven, her sacrifice having released him from his curse.

Thereafter, nineteenth-century accounts refer to the *Flying Dutchman* and sometimes Vanderdecken (with a blurring between whether the 'Flying Dutchman' refers to the ship, its captain, or both), but it is only journalistic reports that occasionally mention Falkenberg or Fokke. This suggests that the transition of story elements became a two-way process. Literary depictions, inspired by oral tales, seemed to have subsequently fed back into and coloured some of the later folkloric accounts. In this way, maritime folklore was neither purely the invention nor solely for the consumption of seafarers. This makes it extremely difficult to untangle how far subsequent sightings were informed by oral or literary influences.

Beyond oral and literary tales there was a third element in the mix. For those who may not have been inclined to attend Wagner's opera or to read Marryat's novel, the popular theatre provided a way of accessing the story of the *Flying Dutchman*. The 1830s and '40s were marked by both an increasing interest in the nautical novel and plays set at sea. The Bowery Theater in New York even built a pool on stage in 1840, so as to be able to delight audiences with stories of smugglers, pirates, witches, shipwrecks, storms and naval battles. Pre-dating both Marryat and Wagner's works, Edward Fitzball's *The Flying Dutchman* was a very popular melodrama that ran in theatres in London, Boston and New York from 1827 to the 1850s.[7] It is unclear if Wagner knew of Fitzball's more populist production, but it introduced Vanderdecken as being enslaved to Rockalda, an evil spirit of the deep. Vanderdecken is permitted to return to earth once a century to find a bride, although he must not speak and, as a spirit, he appears surrounded by blue flame. For dramatic purposes, it was best to give Vanderdecken an opportunity to be redeemed, rather than suffering the endless torment he was said to endure in maritime legend. In this play he has to contend with other suitors for the hand of the heroine, Lestelle Vanhelm. Eventually taking her back to Rockalda's undersea cavern, he fights with a young naval officer who also loves Lestelle. Vanderdecken cries out, and, breaking the rule that he must not speak, vanishes to return to his evil master.[8] The story appears to have been popular, for a new pantomime, *Harlequin Billy Taylor; or, The Flying Dutchman and the King of Ratitongo* (Rarotonga in the Cook Islands), was licensed for London theatres in December 1851.

Despite the rich backstories provided by fiction and theatre, most maritime accounts display little concern for who Vanderdecken was or how he got there. With a pragmatism frequently seen in mariners' approaches to the supernatural, the main concern was what a sighting meant for those who saw it. Here the *Flying Dutchman*'s appearance lashed together past, present and future: a vessel from the past is seen in the present and taken as an omen of future misfortune. In foreshadowing a storm or ill fortune, mariners were haunted by the ever-present dangers in their future as much as by a vessel from the past. That the *Flying Dutchman* brought misfortune in its wake also suggested that such an unfortunate fate was predestined and inescapable.

Terrestrial ghosts tend to disturb merely through their unsettling presence, but they are usually weak and faded entities, lacking volition and fixed to a particular location. By comparison, some nautical ghosts possess dynamism and purpose, the *Flying Dutchman* being a particularly distinctive example. It actively sailed, roaming far and wide, according to accounts. Fitting with a pessimistic attitude that underlies many of the beliefs and practices explored in previous chapters, it also fed into mariners' sense that the marine environment and its supernatural inhabitants were out to get them. The *Flying Dutchman* had a predatory nature, as if it were hunting the living and spreading its misfortune among them. It was said to be part of Vanderdecken's curse to terrorize sailors by bringing squalls and wrecking ships, making the *Flying Dutchman* not merely a harbinger of ill fortune but its cause too.

Ghosts often fail to recognize the living or exist out of joint with the present, but Vanderdecken actively sought interaction with nineteenth-century seafarers.

To do this the *Flying Dutchman* had a chameleon-like ability to change shape, supposedly six times a day. Accounts variously describe it as looking like 'a heavy Dutch vessel . . . a light corsair', corvette, brig, schooner or frigate.[9] This meant mariners could claim many different ships were the *Flying Dutchman*, its identity not revealed by its design so much as its eerie qualities of sailing against the wind, or being beaten by a gale that did not affect those who observe it. This potential for almost any phantom ship sighting to be associated with the legend may help explain why the *Flying Dutchman* seemed to roam so widely, being sighted from the Cape of Good Hope to Cape Horn, in both the North and South Atlantic. The purpose of this shapeshifting deception was to hail passing vessels and request them to take letters from the *Flying Dutchman*'s damned captain and crew. This was a common maritime practice, especially when ships were engaged in transoceanic pursuits such as whaling. In *Moby-Dick*, Captain Ahab's ship, the *Pequod*, has a 'gam' with another ship, the *Town-Ho*.[10] These social meetings between passing ships provided a brief opportunity for an exchange of news, information and letters that could be taken in the direction of home.

Accepting letters from Vanderdecken was said to bring madness to those who touched or read them. Some accounts suggest they would also bring destruction to the deceived ship, causing the vessel to dance in the air and then turn over, pitching the crew into the sea.[11] Vanderdecken's intentions can be read in several ways. The more forgiving one is that he and his crew sought to pass on letters to their long-dead loved ones, to finally achieve contact with land. Such was the nature of their curse that these efforts were forbidden, causing others to pay a heavy price by becoming embroiled in this corrupted correspondence.

Indeed, if Vanderdecken even stepped foot aboard another vessel its wine would sour and all its food rations turn to beans. The more critical version is that Vanderdecken malevolently and wilfully sought to do harm and pass on a little of the misfortune he had long endured. In this way, his deadly letters represented a physical manifestation of his ill will towards the living and the innocent. Either way, communication with the damned was to be avoided at all costs.[12]

This Gothic curse seems to have been a later elaboration that grew from literary fictions of Vanderdecken, for in most oral accounts the *Flying Dutchman* was usually sighted remotely, and then rarely. Literary sources tended to indulge in the horror of closer encounters. In *The Phantom Ship, A Nautical Ballad*, a ship sights the *Flying Dutchman* as it comes around the Cape (presumably the Cape of Good Hope, although it is not stated). Rather than trying to avoid it, the crew seeks to board the legendary vessel. Taking a rowing boat, they draw close enough to see 'the grisly sailors pacin' to and fro'. Their captain has a conversation with Vanderdecken, but what was said between them is not told. Returning to their own vessel, a gale picks up, reiterating the idea that the *Flying Dutchman* heralded a storm.[13] Clearly literary, musical and theatrical works pandered to a desire on the part of audiences to see the damned, whereas mariners out in the Atlantic were more inclined to pass the *Flying Dutchman* at a distance and as swiftly as possible.

Vanderdecken tends to steal the limelight. There is little mention of his crew, other than their general character and torments. When the Holy Spirit damned Vanderdecken, he removed the original crew from the ship, with the unexplained exception of a cabin boy, who was physically transformed so that he sprouted horns from his forehead, grew fangs, and his skin became like that of a sea creature. Thereafter, Vanderdecken gathered his damned crew from the rogues, cowards, sinners and shirkers of the maritime world. They were condemned to drink nothing but gall and chew heated iron as food.

Crews of sinners were common in tales of ships of the damned. On a large ghost ship seen off the coast of Brittany, those sinners were tormented by demonic dogs that prevented their escape. It too was forced to sail eternally, never finding port or dropping anchor.[14] One can see the value in officers, masters and mates allowing such stories to be perpetuated. While sounding a little too medieval to be real for most nineteenth-century mariners, they offered a colourful warning to those who did not work hard or follow orders, or who might be inclined to mutiny and murder. Like Vanderdecken's hubris, their laziness, disobedience and immorality might condemn them to a nautical afterlife of eternal toil, where hell was reimagined as a ship forever cast upon a punishing ocean.

Maritime Anxieties: Speaking through Ghosts

Like many maritime supernatural ideas, ghost stories were strongly linked to the concerns of working in a dangerous and unforgiving environment where death could be but a wrong footstep away, a fall from icy rigging, a slip overboard or some other mishap. Regardless of a mariner's skill and experience, the shipwreck remained a persistent risk. For naval mariners, there were the additional dangers involved in combat at sea. The possibility of grievous and fatal injury and the prospect of drowning silently haunted mariners. To sail the ocean was to pass over an unseen graveyard of rotted corpses and wrecked ships, from the innumerable maritime conflicts, tragedies and accidents that had sent vessels, crews and passengers to the depths. With an estimated 3 million wrecks in the world's oceans, the Atlantic is believed to contain more than any other. Notable areas include an estimated 5,000 ships off the North Carolina coast, and thousands more in the famed triangle between Bermuda, Florida and Puerto Rico.[15]

Where death dwells, so too one finds ghost stories. This applies as much to ships and shorelines as it does to hospitals, morgues or graveyards. Nautical ghost lore suggests that the ocean was a place where the boundaries between life and death were thin, and where interactions between the two flowed back and forth. As seen in previous chapters, the afterlife might take different forms for dead seafarers. Their souls might transmogrify into the bodies of gulls or albatrosses, or they might appear as the lights of St Elmo's fire. Of those that returned, coming back as a ghost was but one possibility. Yet all these tales alluded to the idea that the mariner's soul or spirit would remain closely bound to the marine environment in which they had lived and worked. Aboard ship and ashore, a culture of telling ghost stories both expressed and helped temper concerns about danger, death and the distance between loved ones at sea and on land.

It is not a coincidence that stories of ghost ships tend to cluster around areas known for dangerous waters, histories of shipwrecks or piracy, or locations where wreckers were active: Cape Horn, the Cape of Good Hope, the Georges Bank, the mouth of the St Lawrence, around the Hebrides, along the Cornish coast. Ghosts are created by powerful tragedies and dramas, or at least their retrospective back story requires something of that nature. On land or at sea, not everyone returns as a ghost. Those that do often have a connection with murder, suicide or other types of violent and untimely death, such as industrial accidents. The suddenness of their demise seemed to leave their ghosts connected to the world from which they had been so swiftly dispatched. The same dramatic explanation can be applied to ghost ships themselves, with the vessels in question being the site of great violence, accidental collisions and shipwreck. Those that safely made it home to slowly rot in harbours or estuaries rarely became ghosts. It was the drama of the open sea that made them.

The nature of death at sea also encouraged the idea of restless spirits. Whether lost to the waters or buried at sea, corpses were unfixed in the marine environment. Bodies may have been weighted to sink them into the depths, but it was not the same as the sense of fixity and rest that came with burials on land. The lack of a 'proper' burial for those who drowned at sea left their bodies adrift and their spirits wandering.[16] Ghost ships were similarly created when a vessel's crew escaped, and the ship sank 'alone'. Granting it a sense of sentience, the restless ship would then return, looking for a crew.[17] Such ideas spoke to the symbiosis between mariners and their vessels, each requiring the other to fulfil their purpose.

Haunting requires a sense of a past, yet the passing of time is not obviously visible on the ocean's constantly shifting surface. This can encourage an illusion of timelessness, of an environment free of involvement in historical change. This is a persuasive but deceptive idea. As our current environmental concerns show, our oceans are deeply bound to the consequences of historical change. While the ocean surface may act as a site of continual erasure in terms of human passage, a concealed history exists beneath the waves. The physical remnants of histories of warfare, misfortune, exploitation, industrialization and pollution are all interred in the graveyard of the deep. Although hidden, they dwell in a dynamic environment, churned by currents, unsettled by tectonic disturbances, crushed by the weight of water, physically transformed by submersion in and incorporation into a subaquatic ecosystem.[18]

Ghost ships can be understood as a way of reflecting the passage of history upon the seas. The ghostly Elizabethan galleon, eighteenth-century slave ship and Victorian steam packet each evoked different ages of seafaring. Even the physical degradation of a ghost ship indicated the effects of time in a marine environment, made visible by the ragged state of the vessel's hull, deck or sails. This was the nautical equivalent of identifying the approximate age of land-based ghosts through reference to the clothes they wore. Yet the limitation of our historical imagination seems to determine which ghosts are and are not seen. On land, medieval monastic ruins may inspire the sighting of a ghostly monk, but people rarely see ancient ghosts. Beyond films or museum exhibitions, we do not know how to clothe them to recognize them as such. The same applies to the sighting of ghost ships, and mariners' knowledge of what older vessels might have looked like. The oldest ghost ships in Atlantic accounts tend to be described as old barques, vessels that dated back to the fifteenth and sixteenth century. Despite earlier Atlantic exploration by the Norsemen, there seem to be few reported sightings of spectral longships.

Phantom ships and maritime ghosts were not simply the product of nostalgia for a romanticized age of sail. While the nineteenth-century development of steamships may have encouraged a sense of detachment from the tides or winds, ghosts still got into these most modern of machines. The steamship *Great Eastern*, launched in 1858, was instrumental in laying the cables that formed the foundations of the nineteenth-century's transatlantic modern communication network. The ship had a reputation for being unlucky, having supposedly failed to launch properly from its slipway. It suffered an explosion, struck a reef and caused accidents with other ships, and over time at least thirty of its crew were killed. Seeking to explain why it had such poor luck, a story evolved that a riveter had fallen into the bottom of the ship and died during the vessel's construction, his corpse being concealed when the stokehold's floorplates were sealed in place. Other accounts said he had been accidentally sealed alive in the ship's double hull. Crewmen told of hearing the distant tapping of a hammer. While a passenger on board the *Great Eastern* in 1868, the French novelist Jules Verne was told yet more origin stories of the ghost, about a passenger who had got lost and died in the hold or an engineer who had been accidentally boiled to death.

Despite the crew's talk of a ghost, none was ever seen. The cause of the 'hammering' turned out to be a piece of metal that struck the side of the ship as it moved through the waves, but this did not dispel stories of the phantom riveter. When the ship was eventually broken up at Birkenhead in 1888 it was said that a skeleton was found in the bilge, a riveter's hammer beside it. While providing a macabre reason for an unlucky ship, the ghost of a dead workman does not stand up to scrutiny. It is unlikely that the riveter could have been killed or gone missing without somebody noticing, certainly not to a point where construction blithely continued and concealed the accident. More recent research that indicates no such remains were found when the ship was broken up, only that it was speculated that they would be.[19] Yet, regardless of their truth, these stories spoke to the idea that in the eyes of callous shipbuilders or shipowners, workers were anonymous and expendable. Deep at sea, far from home, mariners aboard the *Great Eastern* may have seen something of themselves in that dead man's unheeded hammering, their voices ignored in favour of developing transatlantic communication, their seemingly valid safety concerns ignored for the sake of commerce.

Mariners did not identify a phantom ship purely by its deteriorated form or antiquated design. Ghost ships frequently betrayed themselves through eerie qualities that jarred with seafarers' expectations. Some might appear in strangely localized weather, within fog banks on a clear day, or with their sails straining as if amid a fierce storm while the conditions around the observer's vessel remained calm. The *Flying Dutchman* was often said to be seen with its sails billowing or set for stormy weather in

J. W. Evans, 'The phantom burning ship', engraving from *Century Magazine* (July 1894).

otherwise calm seas.[20] Other ghost ships might sail against the wind, have a phosphorescent glow, pass in silence or vanish when approached. What was described as a French version of the *Flying Dutchman* was reported near St John's, Newfoundland, where an old French caravel was said to sail against the wind and tide. The ghost of *The Dash*, an American privateer in the 1812 war, was said to sail into the town of Harpswell backwards. The ship had originally been lost in a race to prove its superior speed. Becoming a harbinger of death, it would appear when a relative of one of the original Harpswell crew was about to die.[21] If ships sailing backwards evoked a discomforting sense of weirdness, the *Flying Dutchman* trumped them all. It was said to emerge from under the waves, its upper masts piercing the surface, followed by its deck and hull. This was a haunting reminder of all the dead mariners in the depths; such an unusual re-emergence marked both its supernatural character and the fact that it was part of the ocean in a way other ships were not. In these ways phantom ships evoked a similar eeriness to that which came when land-based ghosts passed through walls, defying expectations and the known rules of how one's physical environment works.

Perhaps the most spectacular were flaming ships, vessels that emerged from the sea or appeared on fire. Such vessels, mostly found in North American accounts according to Horace Beck, usually played out the scene of their original demise, reacting the 'death' of the ship. One such vessel was the *Young Teazer* in Mahone Bay, Chester, Nova Scotia. It had served as an American privateer in the war of 1812. Captain Johnson had previously been captured by the British. He was paroled on his honour not to bear arms against Britain again or he would be hanged. Ignoring this, he joined the crew of the *Young Teazer* and was involved in its attack on the town of Chester, Nova Scotia. The ship was eventually pinned in Mahone Bay by a British warship. While the *Young Teazer*'s captain tried to come up with a plan to escape, Johnson, knowing he faced the rope if taken by the British, went below and blew the ship up, killing all but six of the crew. Thereafter the vessel was often seen to appear, the glow of her fiery demise seen through fog or in bad weather, presaging a gale.[22] Such ghost ships were moving haunted houses, repeatedly re-enacting but never able to atone for a dreadful act.

These legendary tales were prompted by a colourful coastal history of privateering, wrecks and possibly smuggling, with wartime rivalries between Britain and the United States creating villains and characters seemingly deserving of eternal punishment. Such tales were notably coastal in nature and likely the product of landlubbers as much as mariners, evoking dramatic aspects of a rich economic and military history on the eastern coast of the United States. The tales also highlight a notable difference between European and North American phantom ships. The *Flying Dutchman* was exceptional in terms of the backstory that it accrued. Typically, phantom ships sighted by Europeans were unknown and anonymous. In North American folklore ghost ships often had to be named vessels, especially, as seen above, ones linked to major national events such as the 1812 war. Others were associated with renowned historical figures, with pirates being particularly popular, including Captain Kidd's *Quedah Merchant*, seen in Long Island Sound, and Jean Lafitte's *Fame* in Galveston Bay.[23] Such ghost ships spoke to a seeming need for North American phantoms to have some meaningful historical connection and significance. This can arguably be understood as an eastern-facing, nautical variant of the legend-making instinct that accompanied the creation of the 'Wild West'.

Why Tell Ghost Stories?

The longevity of certain ghost stories was not purely random. Like all cultural products, tangible or intangible, ghost stories served a purpose. Many of these functions were broadly similar on land and sea, but others took on additional meaning in the marine environment or within the rigidly disciplined, hierarchical structures of life aboard ship. Ghost stories had long had a moral purpose, linked to the exposure of crimes or injustices. Traditionally, it was only once those wrongs had been put right that ghosts could be released from the torment of repeated return. Yet they could also serve practical lessons and provide comfort for those at sea. Ghost ships might warn sailors of storms. Stories involving ghostly mariners who died by being washed overboard, falls from the rigging or in shipwrecks served as a way of talking obliquely about the ever-present dangers involved in maritime labour. While tainted with sadness, there was also some comfort in the trope of the ghosts of mariners appearing before loved ones ashore at the moment of their death, or those loved ones appearing aboard ship when they died, despite their being separated across the vast distances of the Atlantic. Such stories encouraged a sense of strong emotional bonds between those on land and at sea.

As we saw earlier, ghost stories could provide a way of talking about authority and the abuse of power on board ship. They enabled those with very limited power within a rigid hierarchy to voice concerns about bullying officers or crew members in entertaining and memorable ways. This is seen in an account in Walter Scott's *Letters on Demonology and Witchcraft* (1830). Bill Jones, an elderly sailor on a slave ship out of Liverpool, was subject to bullying by the ship's rather temperamental captain. While at sea, an argument about Jones being a lazy worker escalated into the captain shooting and killing him. As he died, Jones vowed he would never leave the captain. Soon afterwards, crew members began to see Jones's ghost on board. Eventually the captain confided that the dead man's ghost was always at his side. This conformed to the notion, familiar from Shakespeare and other Jacobean tragedians, that ghosts were manifestations of guilty conscience. Tormented by the ghost, the captain eventually threw himself overboard. Yet even as he was about to sink beneath the waves, the captain declared that Bill Jones's ghost was still with him and would presumably accompany him down to Davy Jones's locker. In another account, also from the early nineteenth century, a drunken captain killed his cabin boy and, as a result, was forced to sail forever. To enhance his punishment, the corpse of the murdered boy followed in the ship's wake, its glowing body a constant reminder of the captain's crime. Addressing the harsh regimes and bullying that crewmen might have to endure aboard ships, such tales also offered the vicarious pleasure of supernatural retribution upon cruel shipmates or tyrannical officers.[24]

While we tend to associate ghosts with fear, some ghost stories could offer reassurance or comfort. Unlike the *Flying Dutchman*, not all phantom ships portended ill fortune. Some accounts promoted the idea that ghostly mariners sought to help and guide the living, thereby sustaining a sense of brotherhood beyond death. In one case, two small vessels left Broadsea for Aberdeen at the same time. During the voyage, they were separated in a gale. When one reached the difficult harbour entrance at Aberdeen, her crew were pleased to see their former travelling companions ahead of them in the dark. It was only after they had safely followed the boat into the harbour and secured their vessel that they realized their companion was no longer ahead of them. It was later found that the second boat had gone missing in the gale.[25]

In Heyst, Belgium, fishermen told of a ship, the *Concordia*, whose appearance at sea warned of a coming storm. The ghostly captain was said to know the weather, and the sight of his ship would urge fishermen to make for shore in good time or not venture out in the first place. Such tales spoke to fishermen's awareness of their vulnerability compared with transatlantic sailors, for their vessels were smaller and not as swift as sailing ships. They needed to read the signs sooner and make for the safety of the shore before a storm hit.[26] While the *Flying Dutchman*'s appearance was taken as a portent of predestined doom, these stories suggested that ghost ships might intervene to avert disaster, helping mariners avoid misfortune, if they heeded the warning. Such a tale chimed with the belief that the spirit world had access to knowledge of the future that the living lacked. This idea arose in spiritualist séances in the nineteenth and early twentieth centuries, with séances during the First World War sometimes including an element of prediction and foretelling rather than simply seeking to connect with loved ones after their death.[27]

A common narrative trope in folkloric tales, songs and ballads was the ghost that traverses the oceans, connecting land and sea, the living and the dead. Sailors were said to have seen visions of loved ones at the moment they died ashore. In return, the ghosts of dead mariners sometimes made their way back home. Such tales reinforced a sense of strong emotional bonds between loved ones, whatever the distance between them. Ghosts were a common feature of sailors' songs and this sense of connection often featured. In 'Willie O' the ghost of a drowned sailor returns to his lover, Mary, who is asleep at home. His watery grave has drained the colour from him, but Mary does not seem frightened by this. He talks about their courtship, providing comfort and consolation, until a cock crows at dawn and he disappears. Such comfort clearly had to look beyond the disconcerting horror of being confronted by the revenant of a loved one who shows up at the door in the dripping wet clothes in which they had drowned. The willingness to even imagine such an encounter and draw comfort from it spoke to the power of emotional longing, pain and loss. This connection between the living and dead is also seen in the ballad 'Far, Far at Sea', although the ghost is less comforting than in 'Willie O'. A woman dreams that her lover has been lost at sea. A voice whispers the news in her ear, and when she wakes the phantom presence still haunts her thoughts, causing her to cry out in terror, just as her lover had as he sank beneath the waves.[28]

A well-known broadside ballad, 'The Yarmouth Tragedy; or, The Constant Lovers', from around the 1730s, went further than informing about a death at sea, seeking instead a reunion within it. Nancy and Jemmy, two young lovers from the coastal town of Yarmouth, Norfolk, are prevented from marrying by Nancy's parents. Her merchant father sends Jemmy overseas to Barbados, promising he can have his daughter's hand when he returns. Nancy's father pays the boatswain to kill Jemmy on the return voyages and he does, pushing Jemmy overboard so that he drowns. Jemmy's ghost appears before Nancy, asking her to join him in his 'watery tomb'. Nancy drowns herself in the sea and three days later they are seen in one another's arms, floating by the ship Jemmy had been returning on. The sight prompts the boatswain to confess to the murder and he is hanged from the ship's yard arm.[29] Such a story illustrates a popular, sentimental strain in some ghost stories and songs, promoting the idea that love can transcend death.

As in life, the relationship between the living and dead, between those at sea and ashore, was complex. While ghosts could provide a comforting farewell, there could also be a darker, more vengeful dimension to the end of a relationship. The ballad 'The Dreadful Ghost' tells of a sailor who leaves a woman pregnant, abandoning her by escaping to work at sea. The woman commits suicide and returns as a vengeful spirit hellbent on punishing her ex-lover's wrong. She tracks down the sailor's ship at sea, appearing before it in a small boat. The captain tries to protect the sailor, telling the spirit the man she is looking for has died. Indicative of the spirit world knowing more than the living, the ghost knows the truth and threatens the captain not to get in her way or she will summon a storm that will leave him and his crew 'slumbering in the deep'. The captain's attempted defence of his crewman may illustrate the tightknit homosocial environment on board ship, but the ghost's threat of supernatural power overturns those loyalties when all are at risk. The ghost forces the sailor to step into her boat, which then sinks into the ocean in flames. Making sure the listeners of the ballad get the message, as the ghost sinks from view, she warns the watching crew, 'Sailors all who are left behind, never prove false to young womankind.'[30] The song 'Cruel Ship's Carpenter or Pretty Polly', similarly features a sailor's dramatic punishment at the hands of a wronged ghost, ending with Polly's ghost physically tearing apart the man who killed her and her baby.[31]

Despite the overlap in themes and concerns, and the possibility that songs sometimes fixed in lyrics a version or versions of a folkloric ghost tale, there are differences between telling

THE SAILOR AND THE GHOST;

A whimsical Ballad.—As sung by Mr. Moody, Mr. Suett, and Mr. R. Palmer.

'TIS of a sailor this song I write,
Who on the seas took great delight,
The female sex for to beguile,
At length two were by him with child.

He promis'd to be true with both,
And bound them safe all in an oath,
To marry one, if he had life,
And one of them he made his wife.

The other, being left alone,
Said, oh! you false deluding one,
By me you've done a wicked thing,
Which public shame will to you bring.

Then to a silent wood she went,
Her public shame for to prevent,
And soon she finished up the strife,
And cut the tender thread of life.

She hang'd herself upon a tree—
Two men, a hunting, did her see—
Her flesh by birds was beastly tore,
Which griev'd the young mens' heart full sore.

Straight way they went and cut her down,
But in her breast a note was found;
The note was written out at large—
Bury me not, I do you charge:

But on the ground here let me lie,
When every one that passeth by
May, by me, a warning take,
And see the folly when 'tis too late.

So, as he is false, I will be just,
And here, on earth, he shall have no rest.
So, as she said, she plagu'd him so,
Till, at last, to sea he was forc'd to go.

As he was on his main-mast high,
A little boat he did espy;
And to prevent the wicked thing,
It made him tremble every limb.

Down on the deck this young man goes,
And to his captain his mind disclos'd;
There is a spirit coming hence,
I pray you stand in my defence.

Upon the deck the captain goes,
And there he spy'd a fatal ghost;
Ghost.—"Captain (said she), you must and can
"With speed help me to such a man."

Capt.—"In St. Helen's this young man dy'd,
"And in St. Helen's his body lies.
Ghost.—"Captain (said she), do not say so,
"He is dwelling down in your ship below:

"And if you stand up in his defence,
"A mighty storm I will send hence,
"Will cause your men and you to weep,
"And leave you sleeping in the deep."

Down from the deck this captain goes,
And brought this young man to his foes.
She fix'd her eyes on him so grim,
It made him tremble ev'ry limb.

It was well known I was a maid,
When first by you I was betray'd;
I am a spirit, come for thou,
You baulk'd me once, but I'll have you now.

Then, to preserve both ship and men,
Into a boat they forced him;
The boat sunk down in a flame of fire,
Which made the sailors all admire.

MORAL.

All you that do to love belong,
Now you have heard this mournful song,
Be true to one, lest ill betide,
And don't delude poor woman kind.

Published 25th March, 1805,
BY LAURIE AND WHITTLE,
NO. 53, FLEET STREET, LONDON.

Unknown artist, *The Sailor and the Ghost: A Whimsical Ballad*, 1805, engraving.

tales and singing songs or ballads. The latter were often products of landlubbers rather than sailors themselves, and could be presented to a very different audience, in a different context and for a different purpose. While historians have access to song lyrics, we have little or no knowledge of how a ghost song was introduced to an audience: whether it was performed on board ship, in a tavern or at home, whether any knowing asides were made during the performance, or any commentary, by performer or audience, given afterwards. Much like the accounts gleaned from folklore collections, this makes it difficult to gauge the attitudes, let alone the beliefs, of performers or audiences.[32] Aboard ship or when well liquored up in a port's tavern, the telling of a ghost story could have a confessional element to it, being used to admit to and validate one's belief in the supernatural through recounting a specific experience. Such an act required an element of trust in the audience, with the assumption that the teller would not be roundly mocked, but that his tale might lead to contributions from others, encouraging a dialogue about such matters. By contrast, songs, shared, borrowed and formalized, were far less personal. With an explicitly performative element to them, they did not require any degree of supernatural belief on the part of performers or audiences. As seen with the development of Vanderdecken's literary backstory, what these ballads show is that mariners' ghost stories may have been informed by influences from land, not simply oral tales traded at sea. In referring to migratory legends, folklorists have appreciated the interaction between oral and literary cultures but have tended to underestimate the complicated and messy interactions between terrestrial and maritime cultures. While the component themes, patterns and symbols of migratory legends have been systematized and classified, that schema does not address the fact that such stories rarely migrated in neat, linear journeys across oceans.

Beyond speaking to individual relationships, ghosts, as entities of the past in the present, also addressed concerns about collective memory and loss. Writing in the *Evening Standard* in 1910, one journalist suggested that the story of the *Flying Dutchman* served as a memorial to the sense of loss that accompanied all sunken ships. It spoke to the longing for the return of mariners who would never step ashore again. He declared the tale was 'not an idle superstition' but

> tells of the aching hearts of the long absent; of the wild desire to win home across the wide world to home and loved ones . . . of the passionate thoughts and of the supreme confidence and of the unfailing hope of those ashore, who waited and watched for the missing ship. And as between the waiting Dutch and the Flying Dutchman, so may it always be between us and our missing ships.[33]

Tales of ghost ships became dramatic and memorable ways of memorializing nautical tragedies. For coastal communities that had suffered directly, the ephemeral existence and form of ghost ships and their ghosts reflected the simultaneous presence, absence and continuing existence of the dead in the minds of grieving relatives coming to terms with loss.

This process of memorializing maritime tragedies, from a historical event through to a ghost song, can be seen in the case of the *Charles Haskell*. During a fierce storm in March 1866 this fishing vessel collided with another, the *Andrew Jackson*, at Georges Banks, Newfoundland, causing the latter to sink with all on board. This soon took on a supernatural dimension, with the *Boston Investigator* reporting in April 1870 that ghosts from the sunken vessel had boarded the *Haskell* on her last three voyages to the Banks. On the last occasion, the ghosts had urged the *Haskell*'s captain to sail to Salem, the home of the *Jackson*, and when he refused, they all jumped overboard and disappeared near Eastern Point, Cape Ann. Rapidly gaining a reputation for being haunted, crews refused to serve on the *Haskell* and it was reported that she was left languishing in Gloucester harbour. This suggests how ghost stories could have real world impact, the *Haskell*'s haunted reputation having damaging economic consequences for the operation of the vessel. From this turn towards a nautical ghost story, the accident also inspired a poem in 1874, which subsequently formed the basis for a song, 'The Ghostly Crew'. The developing legend was that when the *Haskell* passed over the site of the accident, the drowned sailors from the *Johnston* (changed from the *Jackson*) would climb on board and take their positions, as if crewing the vessel that caused their deaths. They would take the ship into harbour and then, at dawn, climb back overboard. While the ghosts themselves did not appear to be vengeful, merely getting on with their work, their ghastly appearance was a reminder of the horrible fate that the *Haskell* had inflicted on them.[34] 'Nautilus', the contributor to the *Boston Investigator*, noted that the ghosts jumping overboard was something of a novelty in ghost stories and suggested that they were 'amphibious or marine spirits', their watery deaths enabling them to exist both in and out of the water.

Although rarer, ghost stories could also memorialize histories and incidents that those in Europe and North America might have preferred not to think about. Julia Mix Barrington has proposed that literary tales of ghost ships serve as a metaphor for the shame and revulsion of transatlantic slavery.[35] The slave trade certainly haunts the Atlantic as a lingering, long muted history of violence, exploitation and guilt that Western nations have struggled to confront. While such stories may abound in the coastal folklore of West Africa, the West Indies, South America and coastal areas of the southern states of the USA, this is not replicated in Anglo-American maritime folklore. One reason for this may be that the mariners' tales were likely to reflect their societies' popular attitudes and prejudices of the time. Those attitudes were inclined to view slaves on the notorious 'middle passage' across the Atlantic as property or cargo, and few accounts in maritime folklore bother to mention a ship's cargo. Western sailors' tales were nearly always about themselves in some way, about their concerns above and below deck, but rarely about who or what was in the hold.

Despite this contemporary blindness or indifference, one can still find occasional glimmers of awareness and remembrance. One account, lacking any specific date, told of how plague broke out on a slave ship crossing the Atlantic. The captain callously had two hundred slaves, both the dead and the infected, thrown overboard. That night, the dead slaves returned as ghosts, climbed aboard the vessel and frightened the crew into abandoning both the ship and their captain. The ghosts then tied the captain to the mast, the ship became a phantom, and it was said to haunt the site of the captain's murderous crime for years. Those who encountered it claimed to have seen the 'horrible, gibbering ghosts' of the vengeful slaves and the white captain still bound to the mast among their spectral throng.[36]

Some ghost ships alluded to older collective memories associated with the Atlantic's maritime history. Another European inspiration for the damned seafarer was Dahul, a pirate said to operate off the Algerian coast. He commandeered a Spanish brig and terrorized the seas between Gibraltar and the Azores, capturing, looting and burning vessels. His story reiterated many common Christian prejudices and rumours about North African Muslims, including the crucifixion of a Catholic priest, the killing and eating of a Spanish child and the idea that Dahul was directly in league with the Devil himself. An appeal from the tortured priest eventually brought God's judgement upon Dahul. Like Vanderdecken, he was condemned to sail the seas forever, tossed by the tides and winds, never to reach port, his crew, drawn from drowned mariners, exhausted by endless toil.[37] Informed by religious and xenophobic prejudices, the tale of Dahul created a supernatural bogeyman from the sense of threat presented to Europeans by North African raiders from the 'Barbary Coast' from the sixteenth century onwards.

Across the Atlantic, on the southeastern coast of South America, the Spanish spoke of a ghost ship associated with an evil Dutch captain and crewed by men that looked like corpses. The crew made no sound as they worked, and their vessel emitted a strange glow. The legend told of Don Sandovalle, a young Spanish nobleman who left Peru with Lorenza, his new bride, and a fortune. Their vessel never reached Spain. A Dutch ship captained by a man named Everts was known to roam between the La Plata River and the Cape of Good Hope, and it was believed he had attacked the Spanish ship, killed Sandovalle and tortured Lorenza by tying her to the mast of his ship and denying her water. She cursed the Dutchman and his crew to eternally sail the seas and it was his black-hulled ghost ship that continued to be seen off the southeastern coast of South America. Such a story served to retain Spanish memories of the Eighty Years War (1568–1648) with the Dutch, their colonial rivalries in the Americas, especially after the creation of the Dutch West India Company in 1621, and Dutch attacks against Spanish treasure ships.[38]

Rationalizing Ghost Ships and Disenchanting Ghosts

Like mermaids and sea monsters, nautical ghosts and phantom ships were subjected to a growing emphasis on disenchantment in the nineteenth century. Promotors of this mindset sought to dispel the allure of the supernatural through mundane, rationalized explanations, or at least to replace the awe of otherworldly phenomena with the marvels of nature and science. From the eighteenth century and through the nineteenth, critical commentators increasingly associated 'superstition' with ignorance, intellectual backwardness and erroneous thinking. When applied to phantom ships, mariners' supernatural interpretations were often explained as misjudgements or misperceptions encouraged by the nature of the marine environment. This was further hampered by the folkloric tales that sailors exchanged and carried with them, for such stories could colour their perceptions, leading them to interpret phenomena and draw conclusions that circumvented natural explanations in favour of supernatural ones. Mariners were familiar with the story of the *Flying Dutchman* and reached for it or something of its ilk as an explanation when encountering unusual sights or experiences.[39] For some at least, believing was seeing, rather than the other way round.

The urge to dispel ghosts as supernatural phenomena was evident in the early nineteenth-century development of apparition theory. In Britain works such as John Ferriar's *An Essay Towards a Theory of Apparitions* (1813) and Samuel Hibbert's *Sketches of the Philosophy of Apparitions; or, An Attempt to Trace Such Illusions to their Physical Causes* (1825) presented ghosts as internal 'mistakes' rather than external entities. They were the result of perceptual glitches, optical or neurological deceptions, or biological disorders. Charles Dickens incorporated such 'modern' thinking into *A Christmas Carol* (1843), when Scrooge speculates that the appearance of Marley's ghost may be due to his senses being disordered by poor digestion: 'You may be an undigested bit of beef, a blot of mustard, a crumb of cheese, a fragment of an underdone potato. There's more of gravy than grave about you.'[40] These publications and theories sought to pathologize ghosts, explaining them away as the result of cognitive impairment, mental stress or physical ailment. From this perspective, rationalized interpretations focused on the physical strains of maritime labour, explaining away mariner's accounts of ghosts as resulting from fatigue or exertion, even eye strain from being on watches for four hours at a time.

Marine meteorological conditions and the very nature of the ocean itself conspired to reduce, hamper or distort mariners' vision. The ocean's undulating surface worked itself into peaks and troughs that unsettle our land-based sense of a fixed horizon. The constant spray as vessels worked their way through the waves, the opacity of the deep and even the way sun- and moonlight reflected off the ocean's surface all encouraged the eye to be deceived. Speaking critically of sailors' credulity and supernatural beliefs, Stephen Fovargue's *New Catalogue of Vulgar Errors* (1767) noted how mariners were 'terrified at the thought of an apparition' and that 'Jack Tar' could be 'more frightened at the glimmering of the moon upon the tackling of a ship, than he would be if a Frenchman were to place a blunderbuss at his head'.[41]

Added to that were mists, sea fogs, sleet and the darkness of night in a vast space virtually untouched by the meagre illumination provided by ships. The ocean did much to obscure the clarity of vision, and where there were gaps or uncertainty, the mind was liable to fill them, often with resort to pre-existing ideas that might include supernatural encounters. Writing about meteorological phenomena and the *Flying Dutchman* in 1823, a contributor to the *Cambridge Journal* noted, 'the most intelligent naval officers, with whom I have conversed, seem to regard it as some waterspout, or else a cloud reflected in the mist, or some other atmospherical phantom, which the superstitious imaginations of the sailors have converted into a ship, and attached thereto the above fable.'[42] In January 1911 it was reported that a whaling steamer, the *Orkney Belle*, had been 5 miles from Reykjavik, Iceland, one evening. The captain and second mate were on the bridge when the sea mist suddenly thinned and they saw a sailing vessel coming at them, head on. The second mate threw the steamer hard to port and they narrowly missed a collision. While there was little to suggest this was anything more than a ship heading out from Reykjavik, Anderson, the *Orkney Belle*'s old carpenter, was quick to proclaim that they had had a near brush with the *Flying Dutchman*.[43]

If actual ships could take on a spectral quality at twilight, so too could natural features such as rocks. In a twentieth-century case a schooner left Grenada at dusk, heading for Carriacou, one of the Grenadine islands. Suddenly, under the light of the moon, the crew saw another ship, also a schooner, with no lights heading for them on a collision course. They tacked hard to miss the ship, but just as they settled upon their new course the mysterious vessel loomed again, once more heading for a collision. The schooner readjusted, but whether they turned to port or starboard, the dangerous vessel seemed to be rushing at them. This continued until morning, when the schooner found itself alone once more. It was suggested that rather than a ghost ship dangerously jousting with the schooner, the crew had seen two rocks known as the Leeward Rocks, which could resemble a schooner when seen in moonlight. Other accounts suggested that misperception could be aided by rocks covered in guano, their whiteness adding to the sense of sighting a spectral ship, especially at night. In such cases, the boundaries between the natural and supernatural blurred.[44]

Beyond these mundane features of the marine world, there were unusual but natural atmospheric phenomena that encouraged the idea of spirits and the sighting of spectral ships. We have already seen how mariners interpreted St Elmo's fire as the spirits of former sailors. The optical phenomena known as fata morgana, when a mirage of a ship out of sight may appear to float above the horizon, also contributed to accounts of phantom ships. In the Baltic in 1854, nineteen English vessels, still 30 miles away, were seen floating in the air. Other related phenomena included 'looming', when images of ships might be projected and greatly magnified against clouds or mist.[45] The realities of the ocean as a dynamic meteorological system granted scope for rationally explaining away ghosts. Yet as an environment that differed markedly from our land-based frames of reference, in terms of its movement, fluidity, density, mass and atmospheric interaction with water, air, light and heat or cold, it also stimulated supernatural interpretations too.

The use of the term 'ghost ship' broadened over time, and in so doing lost some of its overtly supernatural associations. The label was applied to derelict or deserted vessels discovered when the winds or tides caused them to drift into the increasingly busy shipping lanes of the nineteenth-century Atlantic. The 'ghostly' association arose simply from the eeriness of a vessel found dilapidated and abandoned. In this period, the most famous example of an empty vessel was the brigantine *Mary Celeste*. Having set off from New York City on 7 November 1872, it was found by a British ship abandoned 400 nautical miles from the Azores on 5 December. There was no sign of the ten passengers or crew. There was some water in the hold, but the ship was still seaworthy. A boat was missing, and the presence of personal possessions on the ship suggested those on board had left in a hurry. While the hasty abandoning of the ship remained a mystery, there was nothing to suggest this was anything more than another nautical tragedy in the mid-Atlantic. Regional newspapers in Britain did not pick up the story before mid-February 1873, with the *Exeter and Plymouth Gazette*'s article title of 'mysterious occurrence at sea' being typical of the way the discovery was reported as curious but in no way supernatural.[46] Interest was later stoked by 'J. Habakuk Jephson's Statement', an 1884 short story by Arthur Conan Doyle that purported to be an account of a survivor of a ghost ship called the *Marie Celeste*. The *Mary Celeste*'s extended fame seems to owe more to the reframing of the supernatural as the paranormal in the twentieth century. A cultural fascination with the unexplained, best seen in the twentieth's century's development of the idea of the Bermuda Triangle, led to the disappearance of the *Mary Celeste*'s crew being retrospectively claimed as an earlier example of maritime strangeness, albeit outside that notorious zone.

As with other expressions of maritime supernatural belief, the urge by some to rationalize and explain away ghosts and ghost ships did not mean that mariners necessarily abandoned such ideas. Accounts continued to appear, evolving with the times. Indicating the way that ghosts tend to be generated in dangerous and dramatic circumstances, the First World War stimulated new tales. The introduction of a ghostly form of warfare in the shape of submarines, the uncertainty of their presence haunting any transatlantic voyage, meant they too were incorporated into a twentieth-century updating of maritime ghost stories. Like the *Great Eastern*, the German U-boat *UB-65* appeared jinxed from its creation. Two workers were killed by a falling steel girder, and three more when they became trapped in a compartment with poisonous fumes. When the torpedoes were being loaded, one exploded, killing a further five men, among them the second officer. His ghost was subsequently seen on board by various crewmen, including the submarine captain. The captain was killed in a British air raid shortly after. Such was the talk of haunting that a pastor held an exorcism on the submarine, though it did little to improve morale. One gunner went insane, and one of the gun crew was washed overboard. Even accounting for the stresses and misfortunes of war, the submarine seemed to suffer unusual amounts of accidents and deaths. It eventually exploded on 10 July 1918, some reports saying near Fastnet Rock, the most southernly point of Ireland, others that it was nearer to the Cornish coast. Whether this was due to combat or a critical malfunction is not known.[47]

Disasters also continued to inspire ghost ship stories into the twentieth century. One of Britain's worst peacetime maritime tragedies occurred in the early hours of 1 January 1919. The *Iolaire*, a steam-powered yacht crowded with soldiers returning home to the Isle of Lewis from the First World War, struck rocks off Holm Point near the entrance to Stornoway harbour. Two hundred and five of the official 283 passengers aboard lost their lives, causing virtually every family on the Isle of Lewis to lose a male relative or friend. Such a grievous loss may have prevented locals from even wanting to introduce the whimsy that can accompany ghost stories. However, Captain James Buchan, one of American folklorist Horace Beck's informants, provides a remarkably similar account of a troop transport ship returning to Stornoway after the First World War. He said the weather was

Photograph of a 'ghost ship' in the North Atlantic, as described by the U.S. Coast Guard, 20th century.

calm, whereas the *Iolaire* had been struggling in foul weather in the dark, but the vessel similarly hit rocks in the harbour and sank with a dreadful loss of lives. Thereafter a white steamer was frequently seen to be heading towards the harbour before a storm.[48] Buchan lived at St Coombs on the Moray Firth, on the opposite side of Scotland to the Hebridean Isle of Lewis. If Buchan's white steamer was a ghostly version of the *Iolaire*, it seems that some ghost stories may originate in places removed from the location where a disaster occurs, a location where the loss ran too deep to move on to notions of hauntings. In this case Buchan seemed to be alluding to a real disaster to suggest it as a causal explanation for the white steamer's subsequent appearance.

In November 1927 the *New York Times* reported that the North Sea had its own *Flying Dutchman*, said to bring misfortune or even death to those who saw it. This phantom vessel was first reported by a British war convoy that left a Norwegian port in November 1917. The convoy consisted of twelve ships when it left Norway. Lieutenant Commander Fox of the *Mary Rose* later counted thirteen ships, the additional vessel suddenly appearing at the back of the convoy. It was described as 'a somewhat rusty craft whose name had been so obliterated by long service at sea that it could not be made out'. The mysterious ship had been with the convoy when it was first attacked but disappeared by the time the Germans had been driven off. The only vessel lost in the attack was Fox's ship, the *Mary Rose*. The mysterious vessel, described as 'a growing legend', had been sighted several times since 1917, each time bringing misfortune to those who saw it. Like the *Flying Dutchman*, it too possessed shapeshifting abilities, being variously described as 'a small warship . . . a rusty freighter, a battered schooner or a small sea-worn liner'.[49]

Ghost ships can be understood to represent sailors' tiny wooden worlds and the weak phantasmal presence of human technology and culture amid the immensity of the ocean. In the nineteenth-century maritime world, ghosts might also serve as metaphors for the mariners themselves, labouring away, links in the chains of imperial and global trade, and yet invisible to the landlubbers who were so dependent upon their toil. Alongside being a way to talk about shipboard conditions and the many dangers of seafaring, and a means of processing and remembering the tragedies, deaths and losses it could entail, ghost stories spoke to a deeper appreciation of oceanic haunting. The ocean killed and concealed, and its yawning depths were a measureless, hidden tomb. Blending the thalassic and the thanatic, ghost ships were markers in the endlessly shifting waters, memorates where there could be no memorials. The Atlantic's seemingly illimitable power to swallow – the dead, the wrecked, the very history of the surface itself – stimulated ideas of haunting but also hunger. While ghosts expressed certain unsettling elements of seafaring, so too did the notion that beneath those few feet of wooden or iron-clad hull there might dwell huge and powerful monsters with appetites as insatiable as the ocean itself.

5

Monsters of the Deep

On 20 September 1848 the *Daphne*, an American brig out of Boston, sighted a sea serpent near the Congolese coast. One of the ship's mates later described it as 'a huge serpent or snake, with a dragon's head' and a body about 100 feet (30 m) long. *The Daphne* brought one of her deck guns to bear and shot at the creature, then 40 yards from the ship. The shot struck its mark, for the serpent raised its head and wildly thrashed the water before plunging beneath the waves. *The Daphne* gave chase, the serpent moving at an estimated fifteen knots an hour, based on the several times it rose to the surface again. Eventually, with night descending, the ship's master, Mark Trelawney, had to abandon the pursuit and continued his onward voyage to Lisbon.

Although not as widely reported, this encounter came in the wake of the HMS *Daedalus* incident that had taken place the month before and about a thousand miles from where the *Daphne* tangled with the sea serpent. *Daedalus* was a Royal Navy ship, and when word got out that some of its crew had seen a sea serpent, it generated interest in the press. Initially, the *Daphne*'s account seemed to independently verify much of the detail mentioned in the *Daedalus* encounter, for the story had broken while the *Daphne* was still heading towards Europe. The *Daphne*'s description of the serpent's appearance closely matched and the distance between the two sightings led to speculation that it was even the same creature. However, some suggested that the rather more exciting *Daphne* incident, with shots fired and the pursuit of sea monsters, was a hoax, constructed in response to the appearance of the *Daedalus* story in *The Times* on 14 October.[1] Regardless of its veracity, it was illustrative of the way the *Daedalus* encounter initiated a trend in sea serpent sightings that would run into the twentieth century. These were accompanied by running debates about facts, fictions and misinterpretation, the competing appeal of rationalized understanding and unknown wonders, and the authority of seafaring experience versus learned scholarship ashore.

This chapter examines why mariners have long populated the deep with monsters, and how those monsters inherited from earlier times were made and unmade in the modern age. Mariners' claims about the existence of sea monsters were subjected to rational scrutiny in the later eighteenth and nineteenth centuries. Yet however much sceptics sought to explain past monsters away, the vast expanse and depths of the ocean meant the possibility and allure of their existence could never be completely dispelled. In this contradictory nineteenth-century urge to both discredit and enchant, two ancient sea monsters met with very different fates.

Sea monsters appear in so many different mythologies of the world that they might be considered a universal archetype of the human imagination, speaking to our fear and fascination with the power and mystery of the ocean, a place of monstrous energy and fecundity. Gigantic creatures such as the Kraken and the sea serpent spoke to an awareness of human frailty, smallness and vulnerability at sea, to a sense of intrusion upon a vast, non-human environment, and to the deep's powerful draw upon the imagination. Stephen Asma has observed how the imagination is used 'to establish and guide our own agency in chaotic and uncontrollable situations', and nowhere was this more pronounced than at sea.[2] Sea monsters express our most primitive thalassophobic fear: the alien creature that emerges from the darkness beneath, swift, huge, but rarely seen in its entirety, a monster of ferocious appetites. Such fears, repeatedly expressed in maritime lore, were encapsulated in the iconic poster for the 1975 blockbuster *Jaws*, where the shark is expanded to monstrous size, its huge mouth full of blade-like teeth. It epitomizes the image of oceanic predators buried deep in the minds of a land-based species that has grown accustomed to viewing most of the animal world from the top of the food chain.

Sea monsters express our limitations at sea, an awareness that while humankind may sail across the surface of the ocean, its claims to mastery of the waves amounts to little more than foam carried on powerful tides. The surface fosters a sense of knowledge and navigability, of tides, reefs, weather and currents. Yet that diminishes with a descent into the deep, replaced with a feeling of being exposed, vulnerable to whatever is better adapted to the darkness below. The deep may be a natural space, but it is understood, culturally and psychologically, through an emotional filter of unease, of obscurity and hidden secrets, a place of physical extremes largely beyond our capacity to explore it prior to the twentieth-century development of submersibles and deep-sea robotics. A place where imagination has always groped beyond the reach of knowledge.

The opportunity to speculatively populate the deep with unseen monsters was enhanced in the nineteenth century. The century was rocked by a series of scientific discoveries that fundamentally challenged previous understandings of space and time. Advances in astronomy opened deep space, showing the universe to be bigger than previously imagined. Geological and palaeontological discoveries revealed the vastness of 'deep time', transforming the world from the Bible's supposed 6,000 years of age to something many millions of years old. It also introduced the notion of extinct gigantic sea creatures, the marine equivalent of the dinosaurs. The deep sea also got deeper in the nineteenth century. Previously, sounding lines had been 200 fathoms (1,200 ft, 366 m) long, so anything that length had been considered deep. This understanding of depth was overturned by HMS *Challenger*'s mapping of the world's oceans between 1872 and 1876. A marine extension of the West's terrestrial exploration and imperialist drives in the second half of the nineteenth century, its study revealed the Atlantic to be miles deeper than previously imagined. It also contained the Mid-Atlantic Ridge, a predominantly underwater mountain range that was the longest in the world. Accompanying this was debate about whether life could exist at such depths. In 1843 the naturalist Edward Forbes advanced his 'Abyssus theory' that there was only limited diversity of life in the deep, and that it diminished the deeper one went. By his calculation, nothing could exist below 550 metres, such was the inhospitable environment and crushing weight of water. Such claims were subsequently overturned when Michael Sars, a Norwegian biologist, discovered a diverse range of sea creatures below that depth near the Lofoten archipelago, Norway, in 1850. Although rarely glimpsed, there was life at the bottom of the ocean. Unseen and unknown, who could say with certainty that the monsters of ancient legend did not still dwell there too?

Inheriting Monsters

The urge to dispel fabulous sea monsters in the nineteenth century ran counter to an earlier trend to enchant the seas with stories of monsters. These had been inherited from ancient civilizations around the Mediterranean and the seafaring cultures of the North Sea. Among the many fantastical monsters in Homer's *Odyssey* was the fearful Charybdis, a powerful whirlpool that sucked down the sea and any ships within its vicinity. Weaving monster stories around natural phenomena such as rock formations, whirlpools or reefs may have spoken to seafarers' animistic ideas about the marine environment, but those stories also helped mark out a geography of natural hazards in a memorable and thrilling way. The Bible was also another source of sea monsters. The story of Jonah recounts how he tried to escape God's command to go to Nineveh by jumping on a ship in Joppa and sailing overseas. When God sent a storm, the crew turned on Jonah as the cause and threw him overboard. Faced with drowning, God sent a 'giant fish' that swallowed him whole, a natural creature (later assumed to be a whale) being bent to supernatural purpose. After three days in the creature's belly, Jonah prayed, repented, agreed to the task assigned to him by God and was promptly vomited up onto dry land. Other biblical sea monsters such as the Leviathan resonated with Norse mythology's gigantic sea-dwelling serpent, Jörmungandr. These 'Great Fish' stories may have originated in Indian and Persian folklore and spread west to influence tales in Greek, Arabic, medieval Latin, Danish and English literature. Two tropes were often repeated in these tales: the giant fish mistaken for an island, and the ship's crew who are swallowed alive and must escape from the belly of the beast. Cornelia Catlin Coulter claimed the latter was probably already old when the Book of Jonah was written.[3] Such a tale forms a memorable part of Lucian's *True History*, a satirical parody of Homer's *Odyssey* and possibly seafarers' tall tales, written in the second century AD. A fantasized account of a sea voyage beyond the Pillars of Hercules and therefore out into the Atlantic, it includes an encounter with a creature 170 miles in length. It swallows the explorers and their ship whole. Within its belly they find an island formed from the mud it has swallowed, complete with a forest and human and animal inhabitants. They set fire to the forest and after twelve days the creature is sufficiently weakened by the pain for them to be able to prop open its jaws and drag their vessel out between the gaps in its teeth.

'St Brendan landing on a sea monster mistaken for an island', engraving from Caspar Plautius, *Nova typis transacta navigatio*... (1621).

Such stories remained popular into the medieval and early modern period in Europe. Medieval bestiaries presented the whale as a wily and treacherous creature that would allow sailors to anchor their ships to its back, thinking they had found land, and to light a fire so as to cook food, and then suddenly sink beneath the water, dragging crew and ships down with it. This mistaken island motif appeared in *The Voyage of St Brendan*, printed in an English version in the fourteenth century. An Irish monk and his followers voyage out into the Atlantic and mistake a huge sea creature for an island. They also face the possibility of being swallowed by a huge fish but, calling upon Jesus Christ, they are saved when a bigger fish rips their potential attacker in three before swimming away again.[4] The idea of the great fish mistaken for an island continued into the sixteenth century in wonder tales that illustrated the marvels of God's creation and His power over even the mightiest creatures of the ocean.

The early modern period's fascination with marvels and monsters accompanied the development of maps of the Atlantic.

This is best illustrated in the Carta Marina, Olaus Magnus's famous map of the northwest Atlantic (1539). Its depiction of the Norwegian coast, Iceland and the Faroe Islands writhes with a profusion of monsters, the physiognomic inaccuracy of some blurring distinctions between the real and imagined. Magnus's images of sea creatures attacking ships or one another served to reinforce the idea that the North Atlantic was a hostile environment full of struggle, danger and death.[5] As with consideration of the deep, attempting to map oceanographical spaces resulted in the imagination filling in the blanks that arose from uncertainty, rumour and speculation. The presence of sea monsters on maps has typically been taken as signifying a limit to one's knowledge, but this should not necessarily be taken at face value. As with coastal legends fermented by and perpetuated for the benefit of eighteenth- and nineteenth-century smugglers, sea monsters could serve as a way of warding off others from areas of value. What better way to discourage competitors from fishing fields than to have a fierce-looking sea serpent marking that location on a map? It is notable that as mariners' sense of control increased with navigational knowledge and more detailed maps, so by the late sixteenth century monsters gradually began to disappear from sea charts.

By the later nineteenth century, the fish mistaken for an island had largely become a literary allusion, one Victorian readers would have encountered in Sinbad the Sailor's first voyage, in the sixth volume of Sir Richard Burton's *The Book of the Thousand Nights and One Night* (1885). An odd case published in the press in 1891 also provided a modern update to the 'swallowed by a giant fish' trope. In February, James Bartley, a sailor on a whaling ship off the Falkland Islands, was said to have been swallowed by a whale that he and his crewmates were hunting. Believing Bartley had been lost when the whale struck his boat, his crewmates were surprised to find him alive in the stomach of the dead whale two days later. The whale's gastric acids had bleached Bartley's skin and left his flesh oddly wrinkled. Accounts suggest that the experience left him a raving lunatic for two weeks, but he eventually recovered from the horror of being swallowed alive.[6] The truth of this account has been questioned, with critics pointing out that only the sperm whale has a wide enough throat to swallow a man whole. Regardless of its accuracy, the sensational account still spoke to the primeval fear of being swallowed alive that had long been part of the tradition of sea monsters' tales down through the ages.

The nineteenth century embodied competing impulses of reason and romanticism, one encouraging the categorizing of all marine fauna to known classifications, the other perpetuating a desire to revel in the possibility of sea monsters. These set the mighty Kraken and sea serpent moving along opposite trajectories, the first diminished through rationalism and science, the second seeing a remarkable mid-nineteenth-century revival that proved impervious to the efforts to dispel it.

The Shrinking Kraken

The nineteenth century marked the demise of the Kraken as a legendary entity. It was not so much that it was no longer believed in as that an alternative, naturalized understanding of what it had always been took hold and demystified the stories that had accrued around such an evocative creature. Found in both Mediterranean and Norse mythology, it had once represented the embodiment of the incomprehensible size, power and strangeness of the ocean itself, and remained a representative of the monstrous aspect of the ocean long after European beliefs in ancient sea gods had been gradually washed away by Christianity.

Initially, the Kraken had been supernatural, in that it was thought to be a singular, possibly immortal being, much like one of the ancient titans. The Kraken was described differently in Graeco-Roman and Scandinavian cultures. Armand Landrin attributed this to the influence of different geographical and climatic environments on the nature of their peoples:

> Gloomy, terrific, and cold, the Scandinavian fable borrows its grandeur of character from the elements of awe and fear; gay, rich and graceful, the Greek fable attains the same end by making us dream. The North teaches us dread, the South, love.[7]

Both made much of the Kraken's huge size. Scandinavian nations told of a sea creature that was the size of an island, a mysterious monster that was never seen in its entirety but was a topic of dread and wonder for seafarers and coastal communities. Unlike the gods, its motives were not to be understood or humanized. It has remained the representation of the ocean's monstrous non-humanity.

Given the Kraken's colossal size, there is something rather sad about the fact that scholarly work on this fabulous beast tends to rest on a remarkably narrow range of historical references drawn largely from early modern churchmen. Much as in the 'Great Fish' stories, Olaus Magnus, Catholic Archbishop of Uppsala, Sweden, and creator of the Carta Marina, told of how fishermen had lit a fire on the Kraken's back, thinking it an island. The creature suddenly sank beneath the waves, the vessels were overwhelmed by waters and the fishermen drowned. Similarly, in the seventeenth century Bartholinus told how the Bishop of Midaros found the Kraken ashore. He mistook it for a large rock and, setting up an altar on it, performed a mass. The Kraken respectfully waited for the bishop to conclude the mass and step ashore before it slid back into the sea.[8] Once again, the aquatic monster mistaken for a land mass motif was at play, used in Bartholinus's apocryphal account to suggest that even the mighty Kraken respected the sanctity of Christian ceremony.

It was not a coincidence that the Kraken (and sea serpent) turns up in works by clergymen. There was a religious dimension to their talk of monsters. In an early modern culture fascinated by marvels and wonders, the natural and supernatural were both employed as demonstrations of God's glorious works. Everything in the world, even the gigantic Kraken, was part of a divine scheme, for such monsters served as what Stephen Asma terms 'living billboards for God's sublime creativity and awe-inspiring authority'.[9] The mid-eighteenth century saw the publication and then translation of two important works on natural history that featured sea monsters, both by Scandinavian clergymen. The second volume of Erich Pontoppidan's *Natural History of Norway* (1751, translated into English 1755) is most frequently cited in the case of the Kraken. The Danish-born bishop of Bergen and a member of the Royal Academy of Science at Copenhagen, Pontoppidan drew upon Scandinavian lore about the Kraken, but did not simply take it at face value. Instead, he cautiously took account of possible error, exaggeration and misperception, noting, 'If I was an admirer of uncertain reports and fabulous stories, I might here add much more concerning this and other Norwegian sea-monsters.'[10]

Indicative of an unease about deep water, Pontoppidan gave an account of how on hot summer days, Norwegian fishermen would sail out several miles to sea, expecting it to be 80 to 100 fathoms deep (480–600 ft, 140–80 m), but found it to be only 20 to 30 fathoms deep (120–80 ft, 37–55 m) and full of fish. This was taken as a sign that the Kraken was beneath them. If the water became shallower, the Kraken was rising, and the fishermen would swiftly abandon their work, take up their oars and retreat to a point where the water grew deeper again. The Kraken would never fully emerge and so, as Pontoppidan noted, had never been completely beheld by the human eye. Yet even that which was glimpsed spoke to an experience of awe and dread. Its upper back was said to be a 'mile and a half in circumference', and resembled small islands surrounded by seaweed, with larger risings like sand banks. As it rose, so

> several bright points or horns appear, which grow thicker and thicker the higher they rise above the water, and sometimes these stand up as high and as large as the masts of middle-sized vessels. It seems these are the creature's arms, and it is said if they were to lay hold of the largest man-of-war, they would pull it down to the bottom.[11]

When it sank back below the surface, the danger was just as great, for it created a swell and then a whirlpool as it descended, likely to pull all ships in the immediate area down after it.

Fellow Scandinavian clergyman and missionary Hans Egede was also instrumental in capturing and committing to print accounts of giant sea monsters. While the Kraken was usually associated with northern European waters, Egede's *Description of Greenland* (first published in English in 1745) gave an account of a similarly huge and frightening creature known to the coastal communities of Greenland as Hafgufa, meaning 'sea mist'. The shape, length and size of its body was such that it 'appeared more like a land than a fish, or sea animal'. Like the Scandinavian Kraken, it was thought to be a singular beast, for if it had bred such creatures would have emptied the seas of fish. Also like the Kraken, the Hafgufa was said to release a scent into the water that attracted fish and even whales. It would then swallow them all down like a whirlpool, its huge meal sustaining it for a year. Egede suggested that the Kraken and the Hafgufa were one and the same, although he thought both stories 'silly and absurd'. The suggestion was that Norse settlers in Greenland had brought their tales of the Hafgufa with them from Norway and Iceland. He claimed that Norwegian fishermen described the Kraken as having a body 'several miles in length'; it was a creature with many heads and claws that seized men, boats and all marine animals in its reach. Despite its monstrous size and power, Egede claimed that the Kraken could be turned from its terrible feeding by simply calling it by its name. The monster would cease its attack and sink back beneath the waves again.[12]

While his accounts of the Kraken and Hafgufa were rooted in unreliable and fabulous tales of the past, Egede did provide a more recent account of a 'most dreadful sea-monster' seen in south Greenland in July 1734. Although described as considerably smaller than the gigantic Hafgufa, it was still frighteningly large:

> This monster was of so huge a size, that coming out of the water, its head reached as high as the masthead; its body was as bulky as the ship, and three or four times as long. It had a long, pointed snout, and spouted like a whale; great broad paws, and the body seemed covered with shell-work, its skin very rugged and uneven. The under part of its body was shaped like an enormous huge serpent, and when it dived again under water, it plunged backwards into the sea, and so raised its tail aloft, which seemed a whole ship's length distant from the bulkiest part of the body.[13]

Often interpreted as a sea serpent sighting, the details of it being as bulky as the ship and possessing broad paws (fins?) and a body covered in rugged, uneven shellwork does not suggest something serpentine. It was likely a whale with barnacled skin, but this description of a hulking sea monster resonated with older accounts of the Kraken.

There were signs of the Kraken's decay in the eighteenth century, both in learned publications and among mariners. The Swedish botanist, zoologist and taxonomist Carl Linnaeus had initially given the Kraken some credence, including it in the first edition of his *Systema naturae* (1735) but removing it from later editions.[14] While most mariners were unlikely to be aware of the learned works of these eighteenth-century clergymen and naturalists, there does seem to have been a diminishing or at least a muting of belief in the Kraken by the turn of the nineteenth century. Like much maritime folklore, such belief was not necessarily dependent upon first-hand observation or encounter so much as the authoritative claims of more experienced shipmates. However, as references to it declined, so younger sailors were less likely to be initiated into its stories. The nineteenth century saw belief in a monstrously large creature continue under the Kraken's name but, importantly, it underwent a lasting transfer from the mythical to the natural.

In his memoirs of 1816, Thomas Holcroft addressed the topic of the Kraken, 'a subject which some naturalists have treated as absurd'. In a frank discussion about the Kraken with the captain and mate of the *Kennet*, both of whom had experience of navigating the Norwegian coast, the North Sea and the Atlantic, neither claimed to have seen it directly, but both 'immediately expressed their firm conviction of its existence'. This was based on it having been seen twice by other mariners in the past four years. Both sightings were based on speculation and extremely flimsy evidence. In the first case, a captain sailing through the Atlantic from Archangel observed rocks that were not on the charts. By the time a boat had been dispatched to examine this unexpected obstacle they had disappeared, the Kraken supposedly having submerged. Two-and-a-half years earlier, a Danish mariner had been sailing through the Firth of Forth on Scotland's eastern coast when he too encountered unexpected rocks in the water. Eventually summoning the courage to pass them, he told of what he had seen when he arrived in Dundee. Being disbelieved, he and his crew gave their testimony before a magistrate, a tactic later used by mariners on several occasions to bolster their claims about nineteenth-century sea serpents. Holcroft's informants then repeated, with unquestioning faith, familiar accounts of fishermen finding lots of fish on the back of the submerged Kraken, and their haste to avoid both its rise to the surface and the sucking whirlpool it created in its return to the depths. As Holcroft noted, 'These, you will recollect, are the old stories of Pontoppidan.'[15] One cannot discount the possibility that some accounts, possibly told as anecdotal experience, may have derived inspiration from historical scholarship.

Like many elements of maritime folklore, the Kraken came under a barrage of scholarly and scientific criticism in the nineteenth century. Dispellers of its former wonder and dread frequently put its existence and history down to mistaken observation, the play of fear and the unknown depths upon the imagination, and a tendency for mariners to exaggerate. Landrin noted that many ancient sea monsters had probably been based on natural creatures that were either carelessly observed due to fear or surprise, or magnified by the imagination and 'a natural love of the wonderful' into something monstrous and fantastical.[16] The naturalist Henry Lee whittled the Kraken down to 'a boorish exaggeration, a legend of ignorance, superstition and wonder', elaborated upon by poets.[17] A newspaper article from 1926 similarly observed that humans are prone to gross errors of observation when confronted with the unusual, and that even where they are accurate 'there operates subconsciously the motive of self-glorification in magnifying the details in narration, satisfying the appetite for the marvellous' among an audience.[18]

The attack on the Kraken in the nineteenth century did not rely purely on belittling it as a product of seafarers' ignorance and imagination. A second, more effective line of attack dispelled the legendary creature through admitting that mariners had indeed seen something natural but claiming that they had wrongly misinterpreted it. More and more sceptical of the existence of a creature of such abnormal size that it dwarfed all known marine fauna, nineteenth-century naturalists increasingly dismissed this legendary beast as a case of mistaken identity. At first this was based on typographical features such as sandbanks or rock formations, but in the nineteenth century it became focused on a particular creature, the existence of which possessed its own scientifically dubious, semi-mythical status until 1870. In 1857 Danish zoologist Johannes Japetus Steenstrup had theorized the existence of a giant squid, naming it *Architeuthis dux*. In the 1850s various parts of a large and as yet unidentified sea creature had washed ashore in Denmark, Jutland and Shetland, and had been found afloat in the Bahamas, but the existence of the giant squid was only confirmed when one attacked the French ship *Alecton*, a despatch steamer, as it was travelling from Madeira to Tenerife on 30 November 1861.

Lieutenant Bouyer and his officers and crew encountered the creature floating on the surface around noon that day. Bouyer identified it as a giant *poulpe* (octopus), 'whose existence seemed relegated into the regions of fable'. The crew shot at it, the bullets penetrating its soft flesh but appearing to do little harm. It then released the contents of its ink sac into the water, filling the air with a musky smell. Harpoons were thrown at it without effect and the creature dived under the ship, reappearing on the other side. Preventing his crew from attacking it directly in a small boat for fear of loss of life, Bouyer ordered a rope lasso to be slipped over its body. When the crew attempted to pull the creature on board its weight caused the rope to cut into its flesh, leaving a fin and part of its body on the deck while the rest slipped back into the water and disappeared. This evidence was viewed by the French consul in Tenerife ten days later, who subsequently notified the Paris Academy of Science. The creature's deep red body was said to be about 18 feet (5.5 m) long, not including its tentacles.[19] Sizeable, but no Kraken. If this partial evidence were not quite enough to confirm its existence, doubts were vanquished in October 1873 when a whole specimen was found on the coast of Newfoundland and brought ashore.

Rarely seen, and of remarkable size, the giant squid provided the basis upon which the Kraken legends could be reassessed and fitted into a known and natural order. Keen to suggest much of the Kraken legend had been based on mistaken observations, popular debunkers such as Henry Lee and John Gibson interpreted its thickening horns as tentacles, its musky scent and excretions that darkened the water to kill fish simply as the emptying of an ink sac. Confronted with a sea creature that was markedly different from the fish they typically caught, Gibson speculated that 'Ignorance and superstitious wonder, no doubt, led the Norsemen to exaggerate its size, and to clothe it with unearthly terrors.'[20]

Pontoppidan's account of the Kraken had foreshadowed this eventual reduction to a category of squid, having assumed it to be related to the octopus or starfish. Recounting a case of a Kraken found on the Norwegian coast in 1680, Pontoppidan told how the young creature had become stuck between the rocks and cliffs near the parish of Alstahaug. After trying desperately to use its long limbs to free itself, it eventually died there, its putrefying corpse filling the waterway and choking the air with the reek of decay. This incident not only challenged older ideas that the Kraken was immortal or unique, but radically reduced it in size. The reference to its long limbs suggests that the term 'Kraken' was, by the mid-eighteenth century, already being used as an alternative descriptor for a large octopus or cuttlefish.[21]

The Kraken's name was colloquially transferred to the giant squid after its discovery, and thereafter the legendary monster shrunk to a natural if remarkably sized sea creature. Referring to mariners' 'implicit confidence in the legend of the kraken or the horned giant', Landrin noted how several chapels in France contain votive tablets showing crews fighting it. One at the church of Notre-Dame de la Garde at Marseilles depicts combat with a squid on the South Carolina coast. Another at the chapel of St Thomas, at Saint-Malo, 'was placed there by the crew of a slave-trader attacked by a *polpe* when on the point of sailing from Angola'. He also noted that 'natives of the American coast speak of the terrible cephalopod; they are sorely afraid of it' though it was known to keep to the open sea.[22]

Sensational tales these may be, but they were no longer accounts of something that had once been considered preternatural and monstrous. Indeed, the Kraken's legend continued to diminish further, for it was not fixed specifically to the giant squid. Sensationalized encounters with giant octopus or 'devil fish' also became popular in the later nineteenth-century press and fiction and the name 'kraken' was sometimes linked to such tales of tentacular menace.[23] The containing of the Kraken within known (if expanded) categories of marine biology echoes the taming of nature narrative that was promoted on either side of the Atlantic by industrializing nations in Europe and the United States. Giant squid and 'devil fish' still evoked fascination and revulsion, but these 'Krakens' had been safely stripped of their mythical status, shrunken by a natural interpretation of where such legends may have originated. With a triumphant air of modern self-satisfaction, Henry Lee noted how,

> seen in the clearer atmosphere of our present knowledge, the great sea monster which loomed so indefinitely vast in the midst of ignorance and superstition, stands revealed in its true form and proportions – its magnitude reduced, its outline distinct, and its mystery gone.[24]

This disenchanting notion of monsters based on real sea creatures continued into the early twentieth century. In 1918 J. A. Teit described Shetlanders' belief in the Brigdi, a large fish seen in waters to the north and east of Scotland that sometimes attacked boats. Said to be one of the most dangerous creatures of the deep, local fishermen were known to make offerings of coins or pieces of iron to placate it. Yet Teit's informants, former Shetlanders who had emigrated to Canada, suggested that this fierce creature was probably just a basking shark, a large but harmless animal. Teit argued that Shetland folklore was basically Scandinavian in character, and this urge towards monster-making from real encounters could be understood as part of a rich tradition of fantastical storytelling within that old seafaring culture.[25]

In September 1920 a fisherman was attacked by a 'sea monster' while in his dory off Keppell Island near Hawk's Bay, Newfoundland. The creature reared up out of the water some 6 or 8 feet (1.8–2 m), revealing 'eyes like saucers' and four rows of teeth. It disappeared beneath the water, then attacked the small vessel from the other side. In one account it caught the fisherman's leg and started to drag him out of the boat until his trousers ripped. In another, he received a severe bite to the arm as the creature made repeated attempts to reach him where he lay in the bottom of the boat. Another fisherman in a motorboat came to help, and the sound of the engine seemed to frighten the creature away. Local stories had spoken of an 80-foot (24 m) sea serpent with a 'huge shovel-like head', but a journalist for the *Western Post* quickly supposed it to be a man-eating shark. Clearly reluctant to entertain fishermen's gossip, the journalist noted there were other reports that a monster had attacked a man and his son further north, killing the latter. He hoped 'that the true facts are not so serious'.[26] Such accounts clearly sought to strip away the distorting layers of exaggeration, storytelling and legend-making.

The Kraken had once embodied the fear and might of the oceanic sublime, and incredible tales of its colossal size had in turn spoken to feelings of human frailty and insignificance at sea. As it was reduced to a giant squid or octopus, knowledge tempered some of those fears, although encounters with such creatures remained newsworthy. Yet there was a sense that something had been lost in this process. In 1909 the *Sea Breeze* sounded a note of whimsical disappointment that whales, devil fish or even the sea serpent were 'nothing to the sea monsters of a former age when imagination and credulity were at their best'.[27] In their urge to debunk and dismiss sea monsters, nineteenth-century sceptics were prone to missing important insights into how seafarers' relationship with the ocean found expression through exaggeration and storytelling. Part of an age-old tradition, their sense of confrontation with the ocean's monstrosity, its non-human scale and dangers, was transformed from the natural into something more fantastical when monsters were evoked. Faced with a modern trend that sought to strip away mystery, ignorance and credulity, some sea monsters were ground down to the hard nub of facts. Such was the fate of the Kraken. The sea serpent, however, proved to be a far slipperier character.

The Ever-Growing Sea Serpent

In contrast to the decline of the Kraken, the sea serpent grew and grew in the nineteenth century, existing in a space of possibility between legend and marine (crypto)zoology. While never possessing the Kraken's original preternatural qualities, it could not be conclusively verified as a bona fide sea creature either. Like the Kraken, references to the sea serpent dated back to antiquity and could be found in both Mediterranean and Scandinavian cultures. The Old Testament spoke of Leviathan as a serpent or dragon of the sea, Aristotle's *History of Animals* mentioned sea serpents, although not necessarily giant ones, and the later scholarship of Olaus Magnus, Erich Pontoppidan and Hans Egede all made mention of huge sea serpents.[28]

Writing of the sea serpent in 1555, Olaus Magnus claimed that fishermen and merchant seamen on the Norwegian coast told tales of a creature 200 feet (60 m) in length and 20 feet (6 m) in diameter, which lived in the rocks and coastal caves near Bergen. This amphibious creature was said to slither ashore on summer nights, eating calves, pigs and lambs, but equally took to sea to feed on octopus and shellfish. Accounts suggested it had hair or a mane that hung from its neck, sharp black scales and 'flaming, shining eyes'. On those rare occasions when the creature rose its neck from the water and snatched crewmen from their vessels, Magnus viewed it as an omen, signifying some important change to the kingdom. For example, following the appearance of another serpent in 1522, said to be 50 cubits long, King Christiernus was banished from Norway and the country's bishops were persecuted.[29] In his *Natural History of Norway* Erich Pontoppidan obtained stories 'from credible and experienced fishermen and sailors', claiming hundreds had seen the sea serpent each year. Such was the sheer amount of testimony, the seafarers' certainty that it existed and the broad agreement about its description that Pontoppidan's initial suspicions about its existence were removed. He stated that the Norwegian coast was the only place in Europe visited by this 'terrible creature', and that it generally kept to the bottom of the sea, except in July and August, which was its spawning time. Pontoppidan accredited this arrangement to the wisdom of God, for it ensured the protection of mankind for most of the year.[30]

Despite Pontoppidan's claims about the sea serpent's territoriality, the idea of a giant sea serpent was also found in Native American artwork and culture of the northeast coast. This indicated that such ideas were not simply a European export but

Gustave Doré, 'Destruction of Leviathan', illustration from *La Sainte Bible selon la vulgate* (1866), vol. II.

reflected a more universal human unease about the inhabitants of large bodies of water. Such depictions appeared in petroglyphs or rock carving, such as those on the rocky outcrops at Machiasport, Machias Bay, in Maine, possibly the product of shamans of the Algonquin-speaking peoples of the region.[31] On their artefacts and items, the serpent often symbolized the power of evil, and tales of giant snakes and lake monsters were a familiar part of Native American (and Euro-American) legends.

During transatlantic voyages from the mid-eighteenth to the mid-nineteenth century, mariners and passengers on trade or transport routes were often drawn to sightings of strange and unusual fauna. For some, the range of marine life was taken as a sign of the variety of God's creation or the fecundity of the oceans, with rare sightings of flying fish, whales and sharks variously prompting wonder or fear. An entertaining diversion from the monotony of sea travel, such encounters also prompted reflection on the limits of one's knowledge and, most likely, speculation on what else may dwell beneath the waves or go unseen amid the ocean's vast expanse.[32] This scope for possibility and uncertainty meant that the sea serpent had both its believers and sceptics. In discussion with the same informants who had spoken to Thomas Holcroft of their belief in the Kraken in 1816, the mate, Mr Baird, told him of his sea serpent sighting midway on an Atlantic voyage to America. He described a fish narrow in the body but between 40 and 50 fathoms (240–300 ft, 70–90 m) in length. It had roused terror in the captain, who feared it would sink his ship. The captain and mate relayed other accounts of what they termed a 'sea-worm', claiming it could rise out of the water to the height of the main mast. Holcroft concluded that some mariners treated such tales as genuine truths, others as ridiculous falsehoods.[33]

Divided opinion meant the nineteenth century's sea serpent sightings, of which there was an increasing number from 1848 onwards, would revolve around the reliability of witnesses and who had authority when it came to interpreting such encounters. Any mention of sea serpents by sailors had to overcome the suspicion that they were either seeking to spin a tale for profit or attempting to hoodwink gullible landlubbers. In searching for authority in the matter, mariners' practical experience of the oceans was pitted against generally sceptical scientific scholarship, while other witnesses garnered authority simply from their social standing rather than their seamanship or specialist knowledge. This was demonstrated early on, in a series of sightings in Gloucester Harbour, near Cape Ann, Massachusetts, in August 1817. Under good weather conditions, fishermen purported to have seen a fast-moving serpent, the segments of its body rising and falling as it vertically undulated through the water. These claims led the Linneas Society of New England to send a committee from Boston to conduct a thorough investigation. Among their interviews with sea captains, ship masters and sailors, they also spoke to Colonel T. H. Perkins of Boston, who had seen the serpent through a telescope for a period of fifteen to twenty minutes. Perkins was described as 'a citizen of known integrity [who] could not be suspected of conniving at a fraud'. A serious-minded man, he was not the type to be duped either. While general descriptions tallied, there was disagreement over the serpent's length, with one witness described it as 50 feet (15 m) in length and deep brown in colour, another as 100 feet (30 m) long, with a head the size of a horse's but shaped like a rattlesnake. On several occasions the serpent was shot at from boats, and on the last, on 28 August, it finally disappeared amid speculation that it had been wounded.[34]

A widely reported encounter in October 1848 proved more significant in terms of encouraging and sustaining accounts of sea serpents. *The Times*, that benchmark of respectable Victorian journalism, printed an account of the sea serpent seen in the Atlantic by Captain Peter M'Quhae and the crewmen of HMS *Daedalus*, a

Royal Navy frigate. They had sighted a creature 'of extraordinary dimensions' some 350 miles off the west African coast. Around five in the afternoon, the weather dark and cloudy, the midshipman drew the officer of the watch's attention to something unusual approaching the ship. The officer and captain observed 'an enormous serpent', its long body beneath the water but with its 'head and shoulders' held 4 feet (1.2 m) above the waves. It moved fast, but passed so close under the *Daedalus*'s lee quarter that it was distinctively seen. M'Quhae noted that it seemed to be holding to a southwest course, moving with purpose at about 12 to 15 miles an hour. It remained in sight for twenty minutes, never submerging in that time, and thus providing ample opportunity for accurate observation. The sailors saw about 60 feet (18 m) of body near the surface, with an estimated 30 to 40 feet (9–12 m) more propelling it forwards beneath the water. The serpent was dark brown, with a yellowish white throat. It 'had no fins, but something like the mane of a horse, or rather a bunch of seaweed, washed about its back'.[35] With its head above the water, its jaws were said to contain large, jagged teeth, although this was not borne out in the sketch that the captain made for his report to the Admiralty, nor in the rather benign-looking creature that subsequently appeared in the *Illustrated London News* on 28 October 1848.

M'Quhae gave the names of officers and ranks of crewmen who had witnessed the creature pass by, and, along with his own eventual willingness to be associated with the sighting, it acquired a degree of credibility compared with the salty sea stories of drunken sailors. These were experienced and practical-minded Royal Navy mariners, men neither prone to being easily startled nor given to fanciful imaginings, and with little to gain from the publicity that their account received. The fact that the original press account was based on M'Quhae's report to the Admiralty further bolstered its credibility. It provoked a debate that ran in the 'Letters to the editor' columns of *The Times* for over a month.

Frederick James Smyth, 'The sea serpent when first seen from HMS *Daedalus*', illustration from *Illustrated London News* (28 October 1848).

Discussion initially addressed the accuracy of the data presented, with suspicion that the *Daphne* incident may have been a fabrication but that the *Daedalus* sighting could not be so easily dismissed. One naturalist suggested that M'Quhae had seen a large eel. Professor Richard Owen, one of Britain's pioneering palaeontologists, entered the debate in a letter to *The Times* on 14 November. With the recent display of a fake fossil skeleton of a prehistoric sea creature in London, and with the credibility of M'Quhae and his men going some way to compensate for a lack of physical evidence of a sea serpent, Owen was keen to assert an interpretation that would dispel the romanticism that surrounded the existence of such a creature.[36] He claimed that M'Quhae's crew had seen a sea elephant (or elephant seal). M'Quhae responded in *The Times* on 21 November 1848, countering that after his years of seafaring, he knew the difference between a sea serpent and a great seal. He noted that he and his fellow witnesses had not arrived at a kneejerk conclusion but formed their opinion after having seen the length of the creature and briefly debated it among themselves. He discounted the influence of imagination, optical illusion or even an awareness of Pontoppidan's work on the sea serpent, an account he claimed to have neither seen nor heard of prior to this discussion. The matter faded away without clear resolution, the debate left hanging on interpreting a negative: did a lack of sightings equate to the non-existence of the sea serpent?[37]

Sea Serpents in the Wake of HMS *Daedalus*

Following M'Quhae's account, sea serpent sightings increased on both sides of the Atlantic in the second half of the nineteenth century, driven in part by an increasingly sensation-hungry press that needed to fill print columns. These ranged from Table Bay in South Africa and the waters off the French and Irish coasts in the east, and from northeastern Brazil to Newfoundland in the west, with sightings occurring in inlets and rivers, on the coast and in mid-ocean.

In March 1850 an American newspaper, the *Christian Mercury*, reported on the sighting of a sea serpent in Port Royal Sound, Beaufort County, South Carolina. The Sound is a coastal inlet of the Atlantic and the estuary of the Broad River. First spotted by passengers aboard a steamer, the serpent later made its way up the Broad River, being sighted in one of its branches. It was described as between 120 and 160 feet (36–50 m) in length, its serpent-like head held 6 feet (1.8 m) above the water, its body appearing as a series of humps above the surface. The creature was followed for several miles along the riverbank, and when one of its pursuers shot at it with a rifle or shotgun it sank out of sight in the river. A plan was devised to capture the giant serpent, with two large flat-bottomed river boats being equipped with cannons. One was to pursue it from behind, the other to enter the river ahead of it, with a view to the two vessels trapping it between them and firing upon it. Rather ominously, the report noted, 'In this way he may be taken if, peradventure, he does not take them first.' This branch of the Broad River was quite narrow, no more than 330 feet (100 m) in width, and the newspaper predicted 'there is every probability of an animated conflict with this king of the waters within his own dominions.' Sadly, the outcome was not reported, although a later report claimed the adaptable sea serpent, seemingly able to traverse from salt to fresh water, had moved ashore at the mouth of Skull Creek.[38]

Later that year, in September 1850, and across the Atlantic on the Irish coast, another serpent appearance was distinguished by two developments. First, the witnesses belonged to 'the highly-respectable yacht-keeping class'. While working-class mariners might be dismissed as exaggerating old sea dogs, the class prejudices of the press tended to grant more weight to the testimony of the yachting set. Second, they claimed to have physical evidence, having retrieved a piece of scaly skin left when the creature brushed against some barrels. The article noted that it was the serpent's suspended status between legend and reality that fuelled the public's interest, urging them to rush to a conclusion one way or the other. Rather than persist with uncertainty, people, including learned professors, were willing to flesh out the limited data from scattered encounters with their assumptions and biases, enabling them to either rush to a conclusion 'that there is a sea-serpent frequenting the deep seas, and occasionally showing himself near Ireland or Norway; or else the opposite . . . that there is no sea-serpent'.[39]

The issue of witnesses' authority and reliability came up in later cases too. In December 1869 Captain Allen of the *Scottish Bride* gave an account of how he had encountered two serpents, an adult and possibly its offspring, at the edge of the Gulf Stream, some 200 miles from Delaware Bay on 23 November 1869. The paper did much to establish Allen as a credible witness, declaring him to be intelligent and experienced, having worked at sea since a boy, 'a thorough type of an American skipper, sharp, shrewd, bluff and honest', a man 'well known to the shipping merchants of New York'. Called to the deck by his second mate, Allen found the crew lining the starboard side of the vessel, observing the creatures. The sky had been overcast and threatened rain, but the sea was now calm and visibility was good. Four feet from the vessel, and several feet below the water, Allen observed a larger creature, 25 feet (7.5 m) in length, covered in 3-inch (8 cm) scales like a crocodile's, and with a tawny yellow underbelly. It had a large, flat head, and set in its sides were bright, shiny eyes that 'looked dangerous and wicked'.[40]

Allen wanted his crew to capture the creature but, the newspaper reported, they considered it 'something supernatural and were not disposed to meddle with it'. A boat was ordered to be lowered but, when the smaller companion alerted the larger, the two creatures abruptly dived down headfirst and disappeared into the depths. A storm broke that night and the crewmen refused to go up on deck without lanterns, fearing the serpent would attack them in the dark. Allen laughed off their fears, but even once the storm abated the next morning, the crew continued to dread the monster's reappearance until they sighted land the following day. Allen speculated that the creature had come up from Florida, where other shipmasters had spoken of similar creatures, drawn by the warm currents of the Gulf Stream. He reasoned that the creature was probably a deep-water animal and that the darkened skies had caused it to misjudge how close it was to the surface. Clearly invested in what he had seen, Allen used his nautical knowledge to explain the presence and location of the 'monster', rather than to explain it away.

Similar issues of the identified mariner's authority and character were evident in the case of George Drevar, captain of the

Pauline, an American barque. Around 11 a.m. on 8 July 1875, off the coast of Cape Sao Roque, Brazil, Drevar noted a commotion in the water. Observed from a distance, he saw what he later declared was a large sperm whale struggling with a huge serpent that had coiled its body several times around the cetacean and was crushing it like a boa constrictor. The two great beasts struggled for fifteen minutes, revolving in the water, disappearing beneath the waves for some minutes before resurfacing, still engaged in their struggle. Two other whales were observing the fight, thrashing their tails, causing the waters about all four creatures to froth wildly. Eventually the whale's tail uprighted in the water and then its body sank out of sight, presumably claimed by the victorious serpent. Drevar described the giant serpent as being darkish brown upon its back and white on its belly, having the colour and shape of a conger eel.[41]

Information about this remarkable encounter made it to the London press through a chain of informants. The crew of the *Pauline* had told some naval officers of their experience when they arrived in Zanzibar in October and those officers subsequently told E. L. Penny, a Navy chaplain. His drawing of an incident he

'Fight between a sea serpent and a sperm whale', engraving from *Illustrated London News* (20 November 1875), based on the drawing by Navy chaplain E. L. Penny of the *Pauline* encounter.

had not even witnessed was printed in the *Illustrated London News* on 20 November 1875. By his own admission, he had used some artistic licence, depicting the whale as further out of the water than it had been to clearly indicate how the serpent had attacked and killed it. In the second-hand account relayed to Penny, the serpent was said to have 'an immense head and mouth, the latter always open'. It was estimated to be about 150 feet (45 m) long, judging by the circumference of the whale it was coiled around, and about 8 or 9 feet (2.5 m) thick. Some of the *Pauline*'s crew saw the same or a similar creature on 13 July, 200 yards off the stern. Later the same day a few crewmen sighted it again, this time its body lifting 60 feet (18 m) out of the water and 'standing' perpendicular.

Drevar's credibility as a witness was important to such a fantastical account. He was variously described as 'a shrewd, hard headed scotchman' and 'a singularly able and observant man'.[42] To bolster their claims, Drevar and other crew members later swore an affidavit about the incident before a Liverpool magistrate when the Pauline arrived in that city.[43] This was a way of granting some legal recognition if not credibility to what could easily be dismissed as a tall tale. Like Captain Allen, Drevar also employed his knowledge of the ocean to both speculate and rationalize why the north coast of Brazil was particularly suitable for the sea serpent. A mid-torrid zone with warm waters suitable for breeding, the serpent's hunting grounds were protected by coral walls and numerous banks and reefs some distance from land. Drevar noted that it 'shows wit enough not to leave a secure home and go meandering about the ocean like other fish, to be captured and tortured for men's pleasure or profit'. San Roque was on the migration route for whales heading up into the North Atlantic, offering a good food supply for part of the year.[44] Aware that few people genuinely believed in the existence of such a creature, Drevar nevertheless began a correspondence with Albert

Gunther, curator of the Natural History Museum, and Henry Lee, author of *Sea Monsters Unmasked*. Lee suggested that what Drevar had witnessed was a giant squid, his preferred explanation for most sea serpent encounters. A later interpretation proposed that the *Pauline*'s crew may have witnessed mating whales, their overlapping fins being mistaken for coils in the thrashing water.[45]

Ultimately, Drevar and his crew did little to help their case, for their reflection took a surprising turn, leapfrogging maritime folklore to land on the biblical Leviathan. In a booklet privately published in 1889, the year before he died, Drevar repeated his claim that he had witnessed the Leviathan mentioned in the book of Job. Driven by strong religious convictions, he declared that God had been willing to reveal 'this greatest wonder of animated nature to me'.[46] This was later echoed by Drevar's second officer, J. H. Landells. Speculating that the serpent had swallowed the whale as a boa constrictor swallows a buffalo, he thought it not improbable that this was the Leviathan spoken of in the Bible.

This raises interesting questions about how witnesses arrived at their interpretation of a sea serpent. Open sea encounters like those of the *Daedalus*, *Scottish Bride* and *Pauline* were gauged against sailors' collective experience and knowledge, with the idea of a 'sea monster' being socially constructed and shaping an understanding of what was seen or remembered. Individual mariners were unlikely to leap to such conclusions or even voice claims about sea serpents if they felt their deduction would be met with ridicule from their shipmates. When it came to talking to others, collective testimony provided some defence against exposure. Captain M'Quhae had given the names or ranks of his fellow witnesses, and Captain Drevar and some of his crew had signed affidavits. Where this was not possible, other tactics had to be employed. On the afternoon of 5 August 1879 Captain F. J. Cox sighted a sea serpent 300 yards from his ship, then about 100 miles west of Brest, France. He described seeing something deep black and shaped like an eel raise itself 20 feet (6 m) above the sea. It was 5 feet (1.5 m) in diameter, but he could not gauge its length, much of its body being underwater. Seemingly unable to provide supporting witnesses, Cox drew upon the authority of his previous seafaring experience to carry his claim, declaring he had 'seen many kinds of fish and sea monsters, but never anything that could be called a sea serpent'.[47]

The range of views about the nature and existence of the sea serpent were expressed in a variety of tones. Some press accounts were presented as sincere and earnest, indicating the panic such encounters provoked. On 27 May 1899 the *Irish Times* gave a brief account of a sea serpent that had appeared in the midst of the fishing fleet at Kilbrannan, western Scotland, the day before. The fishermen resorted to boat hooks and oars to drive the creature off. The serpent, described by the fishermen as 50 feet (15 m) long, with 'an enormous back fin, a propellor-shaped tail, an ugly head, and hideous jaws', thrashed violently in the water and nearly capsized several fishing skiffs. The account was relayed by a correspondent from Campbeltown, Scotland, for publication in Ireland next day. Compared with the slow movement of accounts such as that of the *Daedalus* or the *Pauline*, both of which took months from the incident to their appearance in the press, by the end of the nineteenth century modern communication technologies enabled sea serpent reports to circulate faster and more widely than ever before.[48]

Other accounts adopted a more playful, ironic engagement with the idea of the modern sea serpent, knowingly suspending disbelief for the sake of an entertaining story. Even as the *Daedalus* sighting began to draw press attention in late October 1848, a letter to the editor of *Douglas Jerrold's Weekly Newspaper* suggested that the mechanically minded were taken with how such a creature could move at 15 miles an hour. The contributor presumed it must possess something like a screw-propeller (a recent nautical invention first used on the steamship *Archimedes* in 1839) in its tail.[49] In 1850 *The Leader* entertained the prospect that the sea serpent might be tamed in the future and taught to pull passenger-ships across the ocean. It was hoped that if such a day should come then the likes of Richard Owen, critic of the *Daedalus* sighting, would find himself 'sitting like a civil Neptune on the prow and waving his whip of seaweed over the prancing serpent'.[50]

By 1878 there was a good-humoured familiarity with the fact that sea serpent stories tended to appear in the late summer months. The *Daily Telegraph* commented, 'As usual about this time of year . . . our old friend the sea serpent has once more made his appearance.' This time it was off Ålesund on the Norwegian coast. Witnesses included Joachim Andersen, the Danish Consul. He was part of a boating party at Valdersund Fjord when the creature surfaced near the vessel. Estimated to be 20 metres in length and two-thirds of a metre in girth, its head was the size of a large dog. It had neither a mane nor scales. Not fitting the popular image of a sea serpent as an ill-tempered, meat-eating monster, the creature fled. The boating party pursued it for an hour before it disappeared. Word spread, and it was seen for the next two days, a fleet of boats joining the hunt. The piece ended with a tongue-in-cheek commentary on the impracticalities of capturing a sea serpent, suggesting a gun would be useless, a cannon on a small boat unmanageable, and nets and harpoons likely to be met with derision by the creature. It irreverently recommended using a torpedo, for on seeing it approach through the water the sea serpent would mistake it for a relative and welcome it with open mouth.[51]

Another example of the summer sea serpent story came in August 1885, when it was reported that such a creature had been caught alive and was being held in the Alexandria Basin, North Wall, Dublin. It was said to be 24 feet (7 m) long and 6 feet

(1.8 m) in circumference and ate a hundredweight of fish a day. It was supposedly captured by a Captain Steve Ascall near the Isle of St Kitt in the West Indies, with the loss of several lives. A special case was made, and it was towed across the Atlantic to Ireland. The captain was still deciding whether to exhibit the huge beast to the public as finding a suitable venue was both difficult and expensive. One suspects it was a cheap publicity stunt, for Mr James Millward, a known local entrepreneur, was said to be in discussion with the captain, with the hope of satisfying public curiosity and displaying 'this – for long considered mythical – monster'. Another newspaper, noting that it was satisfying to know the serpent was not a myth, felt its capture was disastrous for journalists, for such stories provided useful filler in the dull news season of late summer.[52]

The tourism potential in summer sea serpent sightings can be seen in an account from the seaside resort of Cushendall, Ballymena, Northern Ireland, in summer 1899. In the afternoon of 14 June inhabitants and visitors saw a huge sea creature bobbing about a mile out from shore in the resort's sheltered bay. The brownish creature was described as 50 feet (15 m) in circumference, with a large head like an elephant and fins 9 feet (2.7 m) long. It stayed in the billows for several hours and was seen by large numbers of people from the beach before it headed out to sea in the direction of Belfast. Some of the older fishermen said they had never seen such a large sea creature before, but its placid nature and movement seemed to match with recent sightings off the Scottish coast. One visitor, Andrew Ross, proposed a group of men should try to capture it using rifles and butchers' knives, a suggestion that was 'tabooed by "the salts".[53] Given the timing of the sighting at a seaside resort, one suspects that it may have been intended to draw visitors and drum up some summer trade. A piece in the *Sea Breeze* in 1926 suggested holidaymakers were not reliable witnesses when it came to sea serpent sightings, for their emphasis on leisure and fun meant they would not be in the right frame of mind to observe things in a cool and objective manner.[54]

Illustrated newspapers and magazines may have played a role in the differing fates of the Kraken and sea serpent. The later nineteenth century saw the development of cheaper newspaper publishing, improved distribution networks, the reprinting of stories between regional and national publications, and better-quality image reproduction that advanced a strong visual print culture. It is no coincidence that the *Illustrated London News*, established in 1842, opted to run numerous sea serpent stories (with illustrations) into the twentieth century.[55] Sea serpents could be imagined, described and depicted, conveniently drawing upon images of snakes, eels or even dragons. The range of sea serpent images in the later nineteenth century shows its enduring appeal to landlubbers. In advertising it became a shorthand for elusiveness or wonder, while in comic strips it was often the basis for a joke built around a case of mistaken identity. The Kraken was far harder to portray. It had never been glimpsed in its entirety, and its form had been neither easily recognizable nor broadly agreed upon prior to becoming fixed as that of a giant cephalopod in the nineteenth century. It defied representation, whereas any competent artist could grant the sea serpent a naturalistic image.

Despite witnesses and commentators using the shared term 'sea serpent', there was considerable variation in accounts during the nineteenth and twentieth centuries, suggesting that they were describing different types of creature. Many accounts described a serpentine animal that propelled itself forward with a rising and falling head motion, a creature that tended to have darker colouring above and paler colouring underneath. The length and girth of the body varied greatly, discrepancies easily arising from the fact that only part of the creature was usually seen, and that distance, elevation and weather conditions might all determine the accuracy of observation, as could the ability and experience of observers to judge unusual objects in the water. Yet while many observers alluded to eels, serpents or worms, a creature seen by a yachting party between Swampscott and Egg Rock, off the coast of Massachusetts, on 30 July 1875 was described as having a turtle-like head about 2½ feet (75 cm) in diameter. Its head protruding some 6–8 feet (1.8–2 m) above the surface, it was seen to have a fin on its back and some form of protrusion or flipper below its throat. The yachters had time to make their observations, for they tracked it for two hours, repeatedly shooting at it with a rifle, though with no evident effect, even when one shot found its mark. Two weeks earlier, a passenger aboard a ship travelling from Boston to Philadelphia had seen a similar creature being attacked by a swordfish. Like the yachting party, the passenger described a creature with a flat turtle-like head, a fin several feet down from the back of its head and smaller ones to the side, and shiny skin covered with large, coarse scales.[56]

This was markedly different from the creature observed off Sicily by the captain and officers of the royal yacht *Osborne* in June 1877. They described a creature 'of immense length, with a ridge of fins 15 feet long and 6 feet apart on the back. Its skin was smooth, not scaly, and it had a round head with jaws like an alligator's.'[57] This type of sea monster was mentioned in several accounts from the early 1930s, sea monsters receiving a renewed boost of interest from supposed sightings of the Loch Ness Monster in 1933, itself variously described as 'a huge, overgrown eel' and a 'strange fish . . . with a big head and back like an overturned boat'.[58] A December 1933 article in the *New York Times* recounted how Captain Werner Loewisch, a submarine commander during the First World War and still in active service in the German Navy, had seen a sea monster in the North Sea on 28 July 1918. His private diary recorded, '10 pm. Undeniably saw a sea serpent. I won't permit anybody to talk me out of it . . . It came in sight off the portside astern.' Loewisch elaborated, claiming that the creature was about a third of the length of his submarine (making it approximately 30 feet or 9 metres). Although the creature was seen at night in the North Sea, his account was remarkably detailed, noting that it had a flat, crocodile-like head, jagged points along its whole back, and four legs each with six webbed toes or fingers. Even accounting for retrospectively filling in details, such a creature did not fit the 'classic' image of a sea serpent. Second-guessing readers' likely responses, Loewisch stated that he had never suffered from hallucinations, and noted that the mate on duty also saw it. His account seemed to have been encouraged by another former U-boat commander, Baron von Forstner, claiming he had seen a 65-foot (20 m) 'submarine crocodile' in the Atlantic during the war.[59]

Rationalized explanations have been advanced for all of the more famous sightings of the nineteenth century, both at the time and since, although none so persuasively that they convinced people to stop interpreting strange sights at sea as giant monsters.[60] Besides a persistent desire to want to believe in such creatures, some of the rational interpretations could stretch plausibility. In one case John Gibson argued that the 'serpent' was a company of porpoises moving in single file, giving the appearance of the up and down convolutions of a gigantic sea snake. Others become so enamoured with a particular interpretation that it becomes their default explanation. This was seen with Henry Lee's willingness to explain sea serpents and Krakens as misunderstood encounters with giant squid, regardless of where they were sighted.

Those who entertained the idea of sea monsters in the nineteenth-century Atlantic, whether seriously or with ironic knowingness, tended to fall back on the nature of the ocean to justify their unwillingness to conform to the scientific rationalism of the age. The best expression of this comes from an unexpected quarter, namely John Gibson, a debunker and popularizer of rationalized interpretations of sea monster legends:

> With the sea occupying two-thirds of the surface of the globe and descending over large tracts to depths varying from two to five miles, it would be presumptuous for anyone to say that the ocean does not harbour in its recesses a great serpent-like monster still practically unknown to man.[61]

In a modern, industrial age, even on the well-established trade and migration routes of the Atlantic, the possibility of sea monsters served to challenge Western rhetoric about the mastery of nature in this period. While the Kraken may have been brought to heel by marine biologists, the slippery status of the sea serpent, always suspended somewhere between legend, misunderstanding and elusive reality, allowed it to continually hold out the promise of wonder in a world that sought to banish maritime mysteries of the past. 'Here be monsters' might have still defined the limits of one's knowledge in the nineteenth century, but the phrase no longer necessarily represented a marker of fear and unease. For those seeking to maintain a sense of enchantment about the ocean, the statement now carried a renewed thrill; a liberating sense that the vast ocean depths could always be imagined as possessing secrets and uncertainties that would forever elude the grasp of the modern world.

6
Weird and Enchanted Geographies

According to D. R. McAnally, the mysterious and enchanted island of Hy-Brasil appeared far out to sea to the inhabitants of Ballycotton, County Cork, Ireland, on the afternoon of 7 July 1878. Said to only appear once every seven years, it was described as rocky and rugged in places, but also heavily wooded with grassy meadows. The unusual arrival of this island in a known seascape led to hundreds of boats leaving Ballycotton to investigate, only to find that the island disappeared as they drew near. In the exchange of local gossip that followed, the island expanded, acquiring cities, cathedrals, towers, huge mountains and great plains. Countering this speculation and elaboration, Dennis Moriarty, an elderly fisherman from Ballyconneely Bay on the Connemara coast, claimed to know the history of the enchanted island, provided on good authority by fairies. The enchanted island was said to move around, seemingly as fond of seafaring as any sailor, for it had been seen along the length of the west coast of Ireland, from Cork to Donegal.[1]

Voyaging across the Atlantic in the nineteenth century, mariners sailed or steamed through the cultural flotsam of stories passed down through the ages. Remnants of myth, legend and folklore, the Atlantic was populated with paradisal and demonic islands, enchanted islands that appeared and disappeared, legendary lost lands, sunken civilizations and strange domains beneath the waves. Some were subject to supernatural forces, while others, such as the Sargasso Sea, were natural but mysterious and uncanny. That such tales existed in folklore with a degree of profusion is indicated by the inclusion in Stith Thompson's folklore motif index of marvellous places, motif F720, 'submarine and subterranean worlds', and F730, 'extraordinary islands'.[2]

Such tales were not simply the imaginative products of sailors seeking to express the strangeness of the marine environment to those ashore, though some accounts were rationalized as such. As the legends of Hy-Brasil indicate, many of them had originated in the maritime imaginary of landlubbers and in literature, not necessarily through the oral lore of seafarers. When these were projected onto and beneath the waves, these elusive spaces became a way of imagining the unknown beyond the horizon and within the ocean's depths. In the context of the Atlantic, this obviously includes the story of Atlantis and, from the mid-twentieth century, the sinister allure of the Bermuda Triangle, the latter familiar to us but not to the mariners of the late eighteenth to early twentieth century. Avoiding the swirling whirlpools of speculation that accompany both, this chapter focuses on Atlantis as an example of historical fascination and occult projection, and the Bermuda Triangle as a mid-twentieth-century reframing of the supernatural. Of all the places explored in this chapter, it was the Sargasso Sea that was perhaps the only one grounded in a modern maritime folklore, one that spoke to mariners' pragmatic concerns with risk and danger in a way that landlubbers' tales of the ocean did not.

Sea monsters may have expressed a fear of the Atlantic's vast, hidden depths, but its legendary geographies spoke to other sensibilities, to wonder, weirdness and longing. These lands were different from and often better than those known on either side of the Atlantic, places sufficiently remote that ideas of magical powers, supernatural entities, occult knowledge, lost treasures and a macabre oceanic graveyard could be safely entertained. Places that were hidden, could move or came and went, that were sites of strange forces and unexplained disappearances, provided a narrativized way of understanding the nature of the fluid, shifting oceanic environment. At the same time, these fantastical locations also marked a long history of the Atlantic as a space for the imaginary projection of hopes and fantasies, part of a long process by which we, as landlubbers, detached ourselves from the reality of the ocean.

Enchanted and Demonic Islands

Enchanted islands were often understood to be the abode of supernatural entities, be they demons or sorcerers. They might also function in strange ways, so time spent there was different from the outside world, or the island could appear and disappear, subject to magical forces.[3] Such stories were the product of literature as much as maritime lore, most obviously the islands ruled by Calypso and Circe in Homer's *Odyssey*, and the magician Prospero's island in Shakespeare's *The Tempest.* Many enchanted islands were imagined as verdant paradises, places full of livestock or fruit, reflecting the hopes, dreams and fantasies of earlier explorers who had voyaged out into the Atlantic facing an uncertain fate. Such ideas informed non-supernatural tales too, as seen in medieval accounts of the voyages of St Brendan, a famous seafaring monk of the sixth century. The paradise of St Brendan's Island has variously been associated with the Canary Islands, Madeira and the Azores, although it had disappeared from maps by the eighteenth century.[4] Such stories may have functioned as a psychological crutch, not only for sailors desperately hoping for a promising end to voyages full of risk and danger, but for the loved ones of those who never returned. The idea that they might yet be living in an island paradise provided a comforting fantasy. They may never return home, but maybe they had escaped being claimed by the cruel ocean.

Celtic tales of sea voyages, known as *imrama*, also told of paradisal islands in the Atlantic. The manuscript of Bran's voyages dates to the twelfth century, but the story had been developed considerably earlier.[5] Bran and his 27 companions encounter the sea god, Manannán mac Lir, and discover an island where there is no sickness, death, sadness or treachery. They pass this up to live on the Isle of Women but stay too long. Much like the land of Faerie, where time moves at a very different pace, when they return to Ireland after several years, the first man ashore instantly ages and crumples to ashes. The others tell their tale from the water and then head out to sea, never to set foot in Ireland again.[6] In another tale, set down in manuscript in the eleventh century but dating back to the eighth century, Maelduin voyages out into the Atlantic. He discovers an isle of demons who conduct a horse race, and another where there are giant ants the size of foals. He also visits an underwater land where people live in buildings.

From the sixteenth- to the mid-seventeenth century two islands north of Labrador, Newfoundland, were known as the Isola de Demoni or Isles of Demons. These names may have referred to Belle Isle and Quirpon Island off the northern Newfoundland coast, which were said to be haunted. A map depicted their inhabitants as horned devils with wings and tails and passers-by were subjected to the dreadful sound of their 'infernal orgies'. In a tale of the power of Christian faith, the tormented inhabitants were said to have turned to the Franciscan priest and explorer André Thevet to rout the demons, a feat achieved by his citing a passage from the Gospel of St John.

Thevet gave a further account of the Isle. In 1542 the French nobleman Jean-François Roberval had conducted an expedition to America. Among those on board was his niece, a young woman called Marguerite. While crossing the Atlantic she and a young gentleman, also part of the ship's contingent, became lovers. Discovering the affair, her disapproving uncle abandoned

Paris Bordone, *Neptune and Amphitrite*,
c. 1560, oil on canvas.

J.M.W. Turner, *The Wreck of a Transport Ship*, *c.* 1810, oil on canvas.

Jozef Israëls, *Fishermen Carrying a Drowned Man*, *c.* 1861, oil on canvas.

Painted sign outside the Museum of Witchcraft and Magic in Boscastle depicting fishermen buying a symbolic short piece of rope from a witch in hopes of a favourable wind.

William Holbrook Beard, *A Sailor's Delight*, 1891, oil on canvas.

George Cruikshank's etching of the Feejee Mermaid for the exhibition at the Turf Coffee-House, St James's Street, 1822.

Edward Burne-Jones, *The Depths of the Sea*, 1887, watercolour and gouache on paper, mounted on panel.

Evelyn Stuart Hardy, 'The Little Mermaid', illustration from *Stories from Hans Christian Andersen* (1890).

Charles Temple Dix, *The Flying Dutchman*,
1860s, oil on canvas.

Fata morgana in the coastal waters of Greenland, 2023.

Pieter Lastman, *Jonah and the Whale*,
1621, oil on wood.

Edgar Etherington, 'The Kraken, as seen by the eye of imagination', colourized etching from John Gibson, *Monsters of the Sea: Legendary and Authentic* (1887).

Stephen Reid, ‘There dwelt the red-haired ocean nymphs’,
illustration from T. W. Rolleston, *The High Deeds of Finn* (1910).

Poster for the film *Atlantis: The Lost Continent* (1961, dir. George Pal).

The legend of the Sargasso Sea, where all the wrecks of the ocean end up, illustration from *Allers Familj-Journal* (18 February 1925).

Poster for *The Bermuda Triangle* (1979, dir. Richard Friedenberg), documentary based on Charles Berlitz's book.

Bronze statue of Kópakonan, the 'selkie' or 'seal woman', by Hans Pauli Olsen, Mikladalur, Kalsoy, Faroe Islands.

St Guenolé, Abbot of Landévennec, saves King Gralon during the flooding of the town of Is, stained-glass window, Church of St Germain, Kerlaz, 1918.

Thorvald Niss, *The Drowned Man's Ghost Tries to Claim a New Victim for the Sea*, late 19th century, oil on canvas.

Davy Jones (Geoffrey Rush) in *Pirates of the Caribbean: Dead Man's Chest* (2006, dir. Gore Verbinski).

Poster for *Gorgo* (1961, dir. Eugène Lourié).

Marguerite, her lover and Bastienne, an old nurse who had enabled the lovers' affair, on the Isola de Demoni. Thevet told how their meagre dwelling was beset by hordes of demons. After they repented of their sin, although they were still living together, the Virgin Mary intervened, imposing an invisible barrier around their hut and driving off the demons. When the young woman became pregnant, the demons renewed their assault, keen to claim an innocent soul. The woman's lover grew sick and died, then her child, then the nurse, but she stood defiant, shooting at the demons. Although bullets could not harm them, she managed to shoot three bears that also threatened her. Eventually she placed her defence in the hands of heavenly forces who continued to protect her. She had to fend for herself for two years and five months before some fishermen saw smoke on the shore. Initially suspecting a trap set by the demons, they eventually summoned the courage to venture ashore, found Marguerite and returned her to France.[7]

The island of Hy-Brasil (or O'Brasil) was supposedly located west of Ireland, shrouded in fog, and, according to Aran islanders, only appeared once every seven years. It was most often seen from Inishmore, one of the Aran Islands, and off the Galway coast. It was described as 60 miles long, 30 miles wide and 'full of furies'. It was an issue of debate whether the island was hidden (and revealed) by God or 'crafty evil spirits' or was simply an atmospheric illusion caused by clouds and sea mists.[8] It has been claimed that it took its name from Bresal, an early Christian missionary thought to be buried there. It appeared on a Catalan map in the fourteenth century and thereafter on Spanish, Italian and French maps. Its reputation as an enchanted isle seems most pronounced in the seventeenth century. In 1636 a Captain Rich and several sailors saw an island with a harbour off the west coast of Ireland, but it vanished, a result of the island's sorcerer using magic to conceal it. In 1668 Morough (O')Ley was carried off to

O'Brasil by two strangers and kept there for two days. When he returned to the coast of County Galway, Ley claimed that he was given a medical text while on the island and used his newfound medical knowledge to make a living. The book is real and was likely inherited from his ancestors, who had practised medicine in Connaught, but scholars suspect that Ley used the link to the enchanted island to draw attention and attract trade. A variant of the story that says he was not to open the book for seven years after his return would have presumably caused a substantial delay in establishing his medical practice.

A Captain Nisbet was said to have landed on Hy-Brasil while travelling from France to Ireland in 1674. Initially lost in a cloud-bank, Nisbet's ship was driven upon it by a storm. Some crew went ashore, discovering a pleasant land of wood, green valleys, cattle, horses and sheep. There was a castle, but nobody responded to the sailors' attempts to gain entry. When they later lit a fire, there was a terrible noise that drove them back to their ship. The next day, they found an old man who said the island had previously been under magical enchantment by an enchanter or necromancer, but the spell had been broken by the fire's embers, making it visible and unable to disappear. The islanders gave Nisbet's crew gold and silver to take back to Killybegs in north-west Ireland. Despite the enchanter's spell being broken, the island was not seen again.

The status of Hy-Brasil grew more ambiguous in the eighteenth century. On a 1753 map by British cartographer Thomas Jefferys, it was labelled the 'Imaginary Isle of O Brazil', although 'Brasil Rock/Island' appeared on a Royal Navy chart as late as 1873. In her dissection of the Hy-Brasil legend, Barbara Freitag claims that its linking to Celtic mythology was largely a retrospective nineteenth-century development. While older tales spoke of enchanted islands such as Tír na nÓg, a place of perpetual youth, health and happiness, and the Isle of the Dead, both to the west of Ireland, they did not mention Hy-Brasil. Its history of mentions on maps seem to have prompted the need to give it a longer, more respectable genealogy. Freitag also interrogates the Captain Nesbit story, claiming it was derived from a satirical pamphlet that was taken as real, or at least became so in subsequent telling of the story.[9] Nineteenth-century stories helped revive interest in Hy-Brasil, with fishermen in Kilkee, County Clare, claiming to have seen it and that people had been lost trying to reach it. In his 1912 scholarly reflections on Hy-Brasil, Thomas Johnson Westropp ended the piece with the surprise revelation that he had himself seen it three times in his youth (implying it appeared more frequently than once every seven years), the last time in 1872. He described it as a dark island seen out west near sunset. It had two hills, one of them wooded, and in a low plain between them were towers and signs of smoke curling into the air, suggesting the island was inhabited. He claimed his mother, brother and several friends had seen it too.[10]

Alongside the appeal of stories of enchanted islands that appear and disappear there has been no shortage of rationalized explanations. Some relate to the nature of the oceanic environment that can obscure and distort perception. Cloud formations, fog banks and mirages formed from the conjunction of water and sunlight, or the 'floating castles' of the fata morgana, can all suggest land formations at sea, while undersea volcanic eruptions could temporarily bring landmasses to the surface before they sank from sight again. In earlier encounters, the surfaces and fissures of icebergs had been said to resemble ruined architectural structures, wrongfully giving rise to accounts of inhabited isles of glass.

Another explanation for moving and disappearing islands was the accuracy of relatively poor maps. Westropp suggested that interest in Atlantic islands barely existed before the twelfth century. In sketching out the cartography of a largely unknown expanse of ocean, legendary islands were often included alongside real ones, with one cartographer repeating or adding to the errors of a forbear. Prior to the accurate measuring of longitude from the 1760s, the location of islands on maps shifted, feeding ideas that they had appeared, disappeared or moved. Even when things had improved, islands could still appear and disappear without supernatural aid. The Auroras were three small islands in the South Atlantic first seen by the whaling ship *Aurora* in 1762. Sighted a number of times through to the end of the eighteenth century, they 'disappeared' after 1820. Their uncertain existence and disappearance was put down to mariners' misjudgements as to their location.[11]

One fabled location spoken of by British mariners in this period was a land to the west, a paradise of base desires. Fiddler's Green was the sailors' ideal of heaven, their counter to the dark, aquatic hell of Davy Jones's locker. It was said to be a place of boisterous leisure and no work, an endless round of grog, tobacco, food, music and willing female company. Sophia Kingshill and Jennifer Westwood suggest an earlier spelling of 'Fidler's Green' (with one 'd') may have referred to a sailor's word for a crab, suggesting an underwater location. This seems doubtful, given that tales of phantom ships often presented an afterlife at sea as a form of punishment. This doubt is bolstered by the fact that from the late eighteenth century, Fiddler's Green seemed to have been located not just on land but as far from the coast as possible.[12]

Where still known by the eighteenth and nineteenth centuries, most of these fabled islands were understood more as legends than real places. In the nineteenth century enchanted islands served as enclaves from modernity, places where supernatural powers and forces might be imagined as existing. These locations were disconnected and protected from the scepticism of the mundane world; they gained an additional allure as escapist fantasies from modernizing society, a way back to the seemingly unchanging lands of the past.

Worlds beneath the Waves

The Atlantic's mysterious geographies did not just appear on the surface of the ocean. Told as ways of imagining the unseen and unknown, maritime tales of underwater realms commonly mirrored land-based social structures, geographical features, animals and architecture, sometimes with the last substituting coral for stone as a token recognition of a radically different environment. They were also supernatural realms, for, much like enchanted islands, they were frequently the home of marine deities or magical practitioners.

Gods and goddesses of the seas and oceans had to dwell somewhere, and it made sense that the likes of Poseidon, Amphitrite or Triton would live in the element over which they ruled. For the Greeks, this tended to mean the projection of their social and political hierarchies into their envisioning of underwater domains, along with imagined palaces and servants; as above, so below. Similarly, Norse mythology had a maritime power couple, the sea god Aegir and his wife, the goddess Ran. They lived in Aegirheim, a grand, underwater hall with shimmering walls and banqueting tables stacked high with food from the ocean. In Sonatorrek (Loss of Sons), part of the thirteenth-century *Egil's Saga*, Ran, representative of the mysteries and dangers of the deep, casts her net over ships, drowning the sailors beneath the waves and taking their souls to Aegirheim.

The Celtic quest story of *The Tragedy of the Sons of Tuireann* told of an underwater island called Fianchaire or Fincara. This was reached by Brian, one of three heroic brothers, who fashioned a water dress and a crystal helmet and went exploring underwater. After a fortnight of searching, he came upon a glittering palace surrounded by sea flowers, the home of red-haired ocean nymphs. His retrieval of a spit made of gold enabled him to fulfil the requirements of his quest and return to his brothers waiting on the surface.[13]

Like these older European tales, the underwater underworld of Torngarsuk's 'lady daughter' in Greenland also originated in Inuit oral accounts, although it was relayed to a wider eighteenth-century European audience through its inclusion in Hans Egede's *Description of Greenland* (1745). Torngarsuk was, in Egede's Christian reading of Greenlanders' 'superstitions', a supernatural entity that was also associated with the malignant nature of water. Torngarsuk's daughter or 'grandame' was an underworld deity, a 'ghastly woman' who lived beneath the seas and ruled over all fish and sea-animals. Her dismal dwelling was guarded by seadogs, a term sometimes given to sharks, and only the angekkoks or Inuit shamans could speak with her, aided by guardian spirits called torngaks. She was said to enchant all sea creatures to her abode, thereby depriving the Greenlanders on the surface of food and their livelihood. It fell to the angekkoks and their spirits to venture into her realm and break the enchantment. This took a rather direct and brutal form, with the wizard having to grab the demonic goddess by the hair and beat her until she weakened enough that he and his accompanying spirit could snatch a charm that hung on her face. This was the source that held the fish near her undersea domain. Once it was removed by the angekkok, the sea creatures would escape its magical influence and scatter, swimming up into the waiting nets and harpoons of the hungry fishermen on the surface.

Situating great magical power and monstrosity beneath the waves, the story not only explained a temporary lack of fish, but offered the solution of human magical practitioners being capable of fighting the demon. It was a combat that went unseen, but victory would be measured by the return of the fish and the restoration of the fishing community's status quo.[14] The story can be understood as an undersea equivalent of the ancient Greek katabasis and anabasis, tales of a descent into the underworld and a return to the surface, usually with some form of prize or boon.

While ideas of underwater realms may have been informed by older, mythological tales of Mediterranean, Celtic or Norse cultures, mariners of the eighteenth and nineteenth centuries tended to demonstrate a more materialistic and prosaic imagining of subaquatic lands. Since they were aware of the valuable cargo that went down with sunken ships, underwater realms became a fantasy of lost and hidden wealth. Their tales often talked of gardens and groves, largely analogous with terrestrial flora rather than reflections of a marine environment. It was land-based experiences that informed the blueprint for underwater worlds, a projection of land beneath the waves rather than an attempt to genuinely imagine how the nautical environment would shape such a society.

Such tales could be elaborated upon if they served as an explanation for unusual phenomenon at sea. On the French coast, Breton lore told of a beautiful underwater garden owned by a water demon, a paradise where the souls of the pious who had drowned dwelt. The garden was bedecked in diamonds and gems that shone in the darkness of the deep, their reflection through the water making the sea appear to be on fire.[15] The garden's strange light was said to explain what is now understood as phosphorescent illumination in the water, caused by certain types of algae or decomposing vegetal or animal forms in the ocean.

The notion of underwater realms was a logical extension of maritime beliefs in the aquatic beings explored in earlier chapters. It was reasonable to assume that merfolk had to have somewhere to rest their heads. In the Cornish 'Droll of the Mermaid', a mermaid provides her rescuer with a description of her life beneath the waves with her family. It suggests a brutal, male-dominated society where her merman husband will eat her children if she does not return quickly with food, emphasizing the callous and predatory nature of oceanic life. The mermaid's habitation is a rather modest underwater cave, and suggests that mer-families exist in isolation rather than as part of a larger community. Yet emphasizing the notion of a harsh reciprocity where humans forcibly take things from the sea and the sea takes things back, the merfolk are provided for by the cargo of sunken ships that comes down to them on the seabed. Like the coastal wreckers who also profited from human misfortune, they are sustained by a scavenger economy. Such is human loss at sea that the merfolk's seabed realm is rich with gems, gold, silver and barrels of alcohol, which are all offered as a ploy to get the mermaid's human rescuer, a farmer, to join her beneath the waves. Resolving the issue of how surface dwellers could ever view this hidden world, the mermaid proposes making gill-like cuts under his chin, thus enabling him to breathe underwater.[16]

This transition into fantastical underwater realms, accessed at points in the mundane world and populated by non-humans governed by different rules, made these stories akin to terrestrial tales of Faerie. Visitors were changed by their experience, and in the story above, that would have required a physical transformation into something amphibious. Given the idea of and continuing belief in Faerie, even if attitudes were changing, the notion of hidden people living in strange societies and places underwater was not so odd. This parallel with Faerie is clearly seen in *The Fate of the Children of Turenn*. In their sea palace in Fincara, the sea nymphs are said to sing fairy music as they create embroidery with gold and jewels, the sound of their voices like chiming silver bells. As with the strange rules of Faerie, the sea nymphs do not speak when Brian enters their grand hall but watch him closely, and he in turn does not speak as he strides up to their great hearth and takes the golden spit. This act of boldness encourages the sea nymphs to let him have his prize, although they break the silence by telling him that, had they chosen to, the least of them could have killed Brian and his two brothers. Acknowledging their kindness, and having waited for them to speak first, he thanks them and bids them farewell.

This, then, was an additional form of storytelling stirred into the mix that formed supernatural understandings of the Atlantic's maritime places and spaces, a patchwork of models, ideas and influences drawn from mythology, legend, folklore and fairy tale. In Stith Thompson's index of marvellous beings, fairies (F200–399) are followed by 'spirits and demons' (F400), and then 'water spirits' (F420) such as nereids, undines, or water sprites, indicating a close taxonomical affiliation. The point is also illustrated by Hans Christian Andersen, a giant of nineteenth-century fairy-tale writing. Although not about a fairy per se, his 'Little Mermaid' story, another tale of transformation in order to move between land- and sea-based worlds, remains one of his best known 'fairy tales'.

Lost Lands: Atlantis

Despite being among the best known 'lost civilizations', Atlantis does not appear much in accounts of maritime folklore. It was, and remains, more of a scholarly fantasy, a historic mystery onto which a vast range of concerns – philosophical, political, social and occult – could be projected. Mariners seem to have been more concerned with pragmatic issues of danger at sea than academic speculation about lost cities beneath their keels. Mermaids, ghost ships and sea serpents were all sighted from the surface, and assessed for risk or as omens of misfortune, but unseen lands or submerged cities offered little in that regard. Talk of Atlantis may have added some colour and romance to sea voyages, but seafarers seem to have spoken of it in the same way as landlubbers, understanding it as a legend.

Atlantis's history is essentially a literary one, originating in two works, *Timaeus* and *Critias*, by the philosopher Plato. *Critias* was the more developed account, supposedly told to the Athenian Solon by an Egyptian priest. He described Atlantis as a confederation of rich, fertile and beautiful land, sheltered by mountains, growing wheat and fruits, networked with roads, canals and bridges, and populated with temples, palaces and harbours. The continent of Atlantis was said to lay in front of the Pillars of Hercules (the Straits of Gibraltar, at the mouth of the Mediterranean), and hence in the Atlantic. It was as large as Asia Minor and Libya combined. Governed by a race of people descended from Poseidon and his human bride, it had been an advanced and ideal society that lost its way. As the influence of demi-gods faded and was replaced by human nature, so they lapsed into decadence, and became an aggressive adversary that conquered parts of northern Africa as far as Egypt and the Mediterranean as far as Tyrrhenia. They finally met resistance from the Athenians, who drove them back, freeing those the Atlanteans had enslaved, and invaded Atlantis. Shortly afterwards, it was destroyed in a single day and night by earthquake and flood, a punishment of the gods.

It has been suggested that Plato's story was inspired by the volcanic eruption that destroyed the Aegean island of Thera around 1500 BCE. However, as with all theories surrounding Atlantis, the evidence barely extends beyond assertion. Used by Plato to praise his Athenian society and to teach a lesson about the inevitable decline of all civilizations, however wise and powerful they may appear for a time, it also seemed to inform an 'edge of the world' narrative. Ever since the fall of Atlantis around 9600 BCE, and down to Plato's time in the fourth century BCE, it was said to be impossible for ships to pass into the Atlantic due to the shoals of mud churned up by the sunken continent. Prior to that, as Plato claims in *Timaeus*, the Atlantic had been navigable.

Such a story justified why the ancient Greeks (and others) had not ventured extensively into the Atlantic by Plato's time.

Speculation about Atlantis continued through the medieval period and was revitalized by the European discovery of the Americas. Francis Bacon's *The New Atlantis* (1629) associated the lost continent with America. Contrary to the claims about Atlantis's aggression, Bacon's Atlanteans had little interest in the world beyond. Through 'Solomon's House', a museum and laboratory central to the life of New Atlantis, they examined nature to find a means of prolonging life, seeking social improvement through scientific enquiry. Such an ideal chimed with the scientific revolution that was developing at the time Bacon penned his work in the seventeenth century.

Nineteenth-century thinking about Atlantis was informed by Ignatius Donnelly's influential *Atlantis in the Antediluvian World* (1882). Donnelly, a populist Republican Congressman and fringe scholar, took Plato's allegorical story literally, viewing Atlantis as the wellspring from which many other ancient civilizations grew on both sides of the Atlantic. The continent's survivors had supposedly scattered to Central and South America, Africa and Europe, making Atlantis an origins monomyth for human civilizations on both side of the Atlantic. This deduction, he claimed, was based on shared cultural traits in art, science and religious beliefs, and evidenced by the common myth of a great flood in many world mythologies. He added that the mythological gods of the Greeks, Phoenicians, Hindus and Scandinavians were in fact misremembered stories of the Atlantean kings. Adding to his bold claims, Donnelly also suggested that Egypt was Atlantis's oldest colony and that its culture was a reproduction of that which had existed in Atlantis.[17]

Donnelly's ideas about Atlantis as a cradle of human civilization had been predated by Helena Blavatsky, the founder of Theosophy. In *Isis Unveiled* (1877) she described the inhabitants of

Atlantis as 'natural-born mediums', graced with abilities of remote seeing that were unhindered by distance or material obstacles, and of knowing all things at once. Echoing the moral decline suggested by Plato, Blavatsky claimed that Atlanteans, who did not have to struggle or sacrifice to gain wisdom or insight, 'unintentionally perverted their gifts to evil purposes'. Corrupted by the suggestions of an evil ruler called Thevetat, the Atlanteans became 'a nation of wicked *magicians*'. Similar to Donnelly, she suggested that the story of Atlantis was to be found hidden in biblical allegories about a race of giants born of fallen 'watcher' angels and women, and in the story of Noah and the flood. She also preceded his ideas of humanity's mono-origin, noting that ancient ruins in both Americas and in the West Indies were attributed to the submerged Atlantean civilization.[18]

Atlantis's lasting appeal down through the centuries lies in the way it serves as a lost highpoint of human wisdom, power and civilization from which we have fallen and never returned. Its lost knowledge may feed occult thinking but should not necessarily be understood as supernatural, rather just as incredibly advanced compared with our comparative state of regressive imperfection. That said, Blavatsky's occult connection remained a theme in literary fictions of the early twentieth century. Works such as Arthur Conan Doyle's *The Maracot Deep* (serialized 1928), Dennis Wheatley's *They Found Atlantis* (1936) and Dion Fortune's *The Sea Priestess* (1938) presented Atlantis as a source of occult and esoteric knowledge, a place of supernatural beings, the home of a race of astral projectors and the spiritual ancestors of reincarnated magical practitioners, respectively.

Late nineteenth- and early twentieth-century fiction added to our received image of Atlantis. André Laurie's *Atlantis* (1895), translated by Paschal Grousset as *The Crystal City under the Sea* (1896), gave us the subaquatic glass-domed city, an idea arguably informed by improvements in nineteenth-century industrial glass production processes and its use as an architectural material for the Crystal Palace that housed London's Great Exhibition in 1851. The use of domes to enable Atlanteans to breathe and to protect them from the pressures of the water also enabled writers to imagine Atlantis as a living city that had survived and prospered under the ocean. This stood in marked contrast to the eerily submerged Grecian relic visited by Captain Nemo and Professor Aronnax in Jules Verne's *Twenty Thousand Leagues Under the Sea* (1869).

Atlantis was also linked to surface politics. For example, David M. Parry's *The Scarlet Empire* (1906) used the undersea city as a way to express his strong anti-socialist views, a position informed by his role as president of the National Association of Manufacturers. Such an application added an early twentieth-century dimension to Plato's former thought experiment about utopian ideals, human hubris and the impermanence of any civilization, however great it may appear. By the early twentieth century there was also a sense that the whole surface of the world had been mapped. While Atlantis had not been found, theories over the past five hundred years had variously placed it in the West Indies, the Azores, the Canary Islands, on the mid-Atlantic ridge, in the Irish and Baltic Seas, at the North Pole and in Antarctica. As such, the Atlantic's traditional connection to the legendary continent became uncertain amid a mass of speculation. Nineteenth-century mariners' lack of discussion of Atlantis suggests that they were always more interested in what lay on the waves than beneath them. Atlantis, it seems, was for landlubbers.

Updating the Atlantic Weird

There were parts of the Atlantic that featured in mariners' understanding of the ocean's strangeness, dangerous locations where nature was believed to possess powers and influences beyond the normal, where different rules of time and space applied. On land, any unusual or distinctive geographical feature tended to accrue folkloric stories and so too do parts of the Atlantic Ocean. The Sargasso Sea, located north-northeast of Cuba, was known for its becalmed seas and the deadly, entangling seaweed from which it took its name. This combination threatened a grim death by stagnation, with a horrific decline through hunger, thirst and madness. A space natural but unusual, augmented by rumour and stories, the Sargasso Sea was part of modern mariners' living lore in a way that many legendary locations inherited from older, land-based tales were not. It served as the physical memory of the Atlantic, the place where things dead, wrecked, ruined and lost came to rest.

Somewhat like the sea serpent, the Sargasso Sea oscillated between sinister folklore and disappointing reality, although its creepy allure stretched into the 1930s. Writing up his findings from the HMS *Challenger* exploration, Sir Wyville Thomson described the Sargasso Sea as containing floating islands of weed between several feet and 3 yards across, although he claimed to have seen some of several acres' expanse, and speculated that the heart of the sea might contain larger masses. The weeds provided habitation for small fish, crabs and shell-less molluscs.[19] Yet nineteenth- and early twentieth-century accounts played up the Sargasso Sea's strangeness. In May 1897 *Chambers Journal* described it as an enormous mass of gulfweed where the flotsam and jetsam of the Gulf Stream accumulated, including the 'skeletons of ruined ships'. Not solid enough to walk on, yet too thick to enable the passage of a boat, the Sargasso Sea was described as 'a museum of unexplained enigmas', a rare fraction of the globe that was still largely unknown even though it was located in the centre of one of the busiest waterways in the world.[20] This element of the unknown encouraged the idea to stick. In 1905 the

London Journal referred to the Sargasso Sea as the Atlantic's graveyard, a place 'avoided with superstitious dread by all sailors of all nations'. The mass of ruined ships, said to be nine-tenths of the derelicts abandoned in the Atlantic, was known to sailors as 'the Death Fleet'. The ships were at all stages of decay, with some lying on their beam-ends, others bottom up, while others were as seaworthy as the day they launched. In another journal in 1906 it was described as 'the terror of the sailing ship', with one writer claiming, 'nothing of all he has to encounter on the wide Atlantic fills the experienced mariner with deeper dread than to be caught in this region . . . to avoid it he will steer hundreds of miles round to reach his destination.'[21] Better, it was said, to face hurricanes and storms than the dead calm of the Sargasso Sea. Robert Hadfield suggested that the superstitious had viewed the impeding seaweed as the work of demons, although how far back in the past such ideas may have existed was not made clear.[22]

These fantastical stories were put to the test in summer 1910 by the steamer *Michael Sars*, a Norwegian science ship, and found wanting. Rather than a vast, slowly swirling island of seaweed kept in place by its location at the point where the equatorial flow from the mid-west coast of Africa met the northward and eastern current of the Gulf Stream, they found only relatively small patches covering the surface. There was no graveyard of rotting, ruined ships enmired in its grip. The *Michael Sars*' crew included the eminent British hydrographer Sir John Murray. He reported that such tales may be favoured by fiction writers but were 'greatly exaggerated', for there was 'no warrant for the theory that any number of ships are held within the embrace of the weed that exists in this area'.[23]

Yet the idea was too appealing in its sinister, macabre imagery to let go. In a newspaper article from 1914, it was proposed that compressed blocks of Sargasso weeds could be used as a cheap substitute for coal, its abundance and rate of regrowth when cut making for a near-endless supply. The report described the Sargasso Sea as a mass of seaweed 3–4 feet (90–120 cm) thick and twice the size of Britain, with a thicker mass at its centre the size of Ireland. The idea of weed-covered derelict ships was also repeated, as was the claim that, existing several hundred miles south of the usual steamer routes between Britain and the United States, it was given a wide berth for fear of the weeds entangling their propeller screws.[24] These ideas led the Sargasso Sea to become a popular setting for weird nautical tales such as William Hope Hodgson's short story 'The Thing in the Weeds' (1916). Such fictions marked a shift in register from a supernatural Atlantic to one possessing an unsettling weirdness, if not in the massed vegetation itself, then in speculation about what lay hidden beneath.

A second expedition explored the Sargasso Sea in spring 1925. While waiting for the *Arcturus*, an American vessel, to reach its destination, newspapers repeated the familiar lore and legends, of a dreaded and mysterious 'almost land' that was a graveyard of ships and, according to tradition, the dwelling place of 'scarce-known monsters'. Despite the Sargasso Sea being relatively shallow, it was hoped the *Arcturus*'s use of dredging and trawling to explore beneath the weeds might result in the capture of a giant squid, an elusive creature usually found in deeper waters.[25] The *Dundee Courier* picked up on this ambition, sensationally claiming the giant squid was 'a man-killer' known to have capsized heavy vessels and strangled those on board. Straying beyond the natural into the vampiric, it claimed that the creature used its 'pump-like suckers' to suck out their blood. The suggestion that the seaweed might sit above the site of Atlantis was causally dropped in. It went on to explain how ships became stuck in the Sargasso Sea, finding themselves first becalmed, then surrounded by seaweed that glowed with an eerie greenish yellow phosphorescence at night, then, come morning, entangled. The whole sluggish mass slowly rotated, carrying with it the rotten corpses of animals, trees from Brazil and Honduras, boats from the West Indies and partially submerged wrecks. These vessels had been transformed into grotesque floating ruins, covered in barnacles, with weeds up to their scuppers, masts tilted at strange angles, the skeletal remnants of their crews still wearing the ragged clothing they died in. The newspaper ominously declared that hundreds, possibly thousands, had suffered such a fate. The article proposed a final horror, the existence of a huge whirlpool beneath the seaweed, a latter-day Charybdis that still occasionally drew in ships and held them in a strange 'living death'.[26]

This sensational hype was punctured again in July 1925 when the findings of the *Arcturus* were reported to the press. The project's lead, Professor William Beebe, told reporters in New York that the idea of a sea of seaweed in which ships had long become entangled was a myth, as was talk of 'terrible whirlpools' in the region. Like the *Michael Sars*, the *Arcturus* found only scattered islands of seaweed, though its crude methods of trawling had led to the discovery of many new specimens of marine life.[27] Yet even after this second round of scientific revelations, the press continued to push the sensational fictions. An article from 1930 still referred to it as a 'grim ocean graveyard', unchanged in the six hundred years since Columbus had encountered it on the way to the Caribbean, and repeated the claim that, when cut, the seaweed swiftly reformed behind a vessel and prevented its escape, granting it an impression of sentience, if not cunning. Doubts that even the largest ocean liner could make it through the seaweed meant that the Sargasso Sea marked an imagined space where the Atlantic might continue to humble the most modern and ambitious nautical technologies of the day.[28]

The image of a strange graveyard of slowly rotting ships bound in weeds faded when the Sargasso Sea was subsumed within the expanded field of Atlantic weirdness that became known as the Bermuda – or, more evocatively, the Devil's – Triangle. Located between the Florida coast, Bermuda, and Puerto Rico, and including the Sargasso Sea, the region had long been known for its dangerous waters and weather. The acquisition of a paranormal dimension to the region's missing ships and aircraft was largely a mid-twentieth-century development that retrospectively appropriated cases of 'disappearing' vessels as part of a supposedly localized phenomenon. While *Fate* magazine established the idea of this mysterious region in 1952, it was not given the name 'Bermuda Triangle' until 1962 by *Argosy* magazine. It was promoted to a wider public in Charles Berlitz's *The Bermuda Triangle* (1974), a bestseller that fed into alternative cosmologies, Forteana and conspiracy theories of the mid- to late twentieth century, variously linking its strange occurrences to UFOs, Atlantean laser weapons, time warps and interdimensional portals.

Coinciding with New Age interests bleeding through into mainstream Western culture, the shift in the frame of reference from the supernatural to the paranormal offered an updated and more palatable way to imagine otherworldly menace. Among its history of mysterious disappearances was the American Navy cargo ship *Cyclops*, which disappeared with all three hundred people on board in March 1918. In 1963 the *Marine Sulphur Queen*, a 7,000-ton tanker with a crew of 39, similarly disappeared, searchers finding only a single lifejacket and a man's shirt. Perhaps most famously, five U.S. Navy planes, Flight 19, took off from Fort Lauderdale on 5 December 1945 and disappeared after reporting compass failure and apparent disorientation regarding their location. Much like the mystery that accrued around the *Mary Celeste*, it has been suggested that this had nothing to do with paranormal influences and was a tragic case of pilot error.

The literature and theoretical speculation about the Bermuda Triangle is voluminous and spills beyond the chronological focus of this book. It is presented here as illustrative of the way in which a sense of the strange, sinister spaces of the Atlantic Ocean could be updated for modern audiences sceptical of older claims about the supernatural but still wanting to believe in powers, forces or locations that appeared to exist beyond the mundane world. This pseudoscientific trend or fashion marked a revived mid- to late twentieth-century attempt to navigate around a disenchanted worldview, using its processes of (speculative) rationalization to suggest not just space for but the central history-defining importance of Atlanteans or extra-terrestrials. This trend promoted an interest in paranormal forces and esoteric, hidden histories, with theorists often advancing elaborate, unifying and satisfyingly singular theoretical speculations built from a patchwork of empirical data and case studies selected from across a broad range of history. Regarding this fascination with the unexplained and anomalous, a sociological study of the period noted that 'Contemporary society is witnessing the rise of a vast current of opinion, or intellectual fashion, or social movement, which is providing people with "alternative cosmologies" to those offered by conventional religion and conventional science.'[29] Echoing mariners' earlier engagement with the ocean, these 'alternative cosmologies' offered reassuringly clear and total answers in a way both the complexities and the inadequacies of religion and science could not.

Enchanted islands and underwater worlds represented an imaginative colonization of the ocean, imposing human presence onto and under it. While seafarers were inclined to fill the deep with threat and danger in the shape of monsters, landlubbers filled it with fantasies of antediluvian power and technology, making the Atlantic the point of origin of modern human civilization across the planet. Yet Atlantis was also a reminder of the hubris and transience of once-powerful civilizations in an age shaped by imperialism. These fantasized geographies and strange spaces were also ways of imagining parts of the Atlantic that escaped modern maps, places where magical, supernatural or, in the twentieth century, paranormal forces may still be at play. There was an allure to thinking of the ocean as still containing gaps in knowledge: spaces and places where human understanding and influence reached its limits. These spaces and places were also oceanic geographies outside modern time. Islands that appeared only once every seven years operated according to temporal rules of their own, while the Sargasso Sea represented an atemporal space, unchanging other than in the number of ruined remnants of history that supposedly gathered in its imagined graveyard. Yet all seem connected through a longing for the past: fantasies of unseen societies and elusive, unconquered lands that held up a reflective mirror to both the intellectual and material gains made by and the imaginative and possibly spiritual losses sacrificed to nineteenth- and early twentieth-century modernity.

7

Coastal Folklore: Bringing It Back Home

Between 19 and 23 October 1888, the lighthouse keeper's house at Point Isabel, Brownsville, Texas, in the Gulf of Mexico, suffered a series of attacks by seemingly invisible forces. The residence, home to Mrs Schreiber, widow of the late keeper, suffered escalating assaults from shingle tiles, nails, oyster shells, clods of earth and eventually brickbats and pieces of scrap iron. Bricks were hurled through the windows. Drawn by the unusual activity, people had gathered, but they, like a local deputy sheriff who was sent to investigate, were unable to detect where the shower of objects came from. The 'superstitious mariners' of Point Isabel insisted it was the ghosts of sailors who had been drowned due to the lack of a beacon. During the Civil War, the Lighthouse Board had the lighthouse's illumination turned off during a dispute about land rights. This bred a legend that the lighthouse keeper, working with wreckers, had turned the light off, causing a schooner to wreck itself on the coast. The dead mariners had supposedly returned more than twenty years later to create a storm of poltergeist activity. That, or maybe certain locals were seeking to intimidate Mrs Schreiber.[1]

This strange incident from one of the most western points of the Atlantic world marks our return to shore, and to the distinctive nature and purpose of coastal folklore. As a liminal space between land and sea, the coast consisted of what we could term brackish folklore, the place where selkies, mermaids, sea serpents and ghosts ventured ashore and sometimes, by means of rivers, inland. As Mrs Schreiber's phantom assailants suggest, the shoreline was a place of supernatural return, a site of interaction between the living and the dead, and was therefore often marked by lingering melancholy and grief. Such hauntings extended to coastal legends about drowned villages swallowed by ever-encroaching waves, the phantom toll of their submerged bells a reminder of which was dominant in the tidal to and fro between land and sea. Yet it was also a location where more mundane but illegal activities such as smuggling or wrecking might be hidden by the creation of fakelore, consciously constructed folkloric tales that were intended to keep people away from certain parts of the coastline. Coming full circle, then, we return to coastal communities and ports as important sites of exchange, places where the import and export of supernatural narratives was conducted, a vital commerce that long sustained the notion of the maritime world as a place of marvels, magic and mystery.

Coastal Liminality and Landscape

Coasts are distinctive but in-between spaces, the meeting point not just of land and sea, but, in terms of ports, of the urban and marine, civilization and wilderness. The site of both leaving and returning, they were the places where ideas about supernatural seas could be acquired and where the imaginative flotsam and jetsam of maritime folklore frequently washed ashore again. As we have seen in previous chapters, that could variously mean mermaids sunning themselves on rock, sea serpents bobbing in bays or the drowned dead returning to console loved ones. The shoreline was a fluid, shifting boundary that marked both the border and a meeting point of the known and unknown, the regulated socio-economic order of land and the wilder, less predictable realm of the sea. Boundaries are frequently locations of unease and supernatural beliefs played a role in negotiating shorelines and coastal regions, locales where distinctions between land and sea, natural and supernatural met, melded and interacted.[2] As fringe cultures, coastal communities were subject to influences from both the hinterland behind them and the maritime world before them, the combination of which marked them as different to either.

Seas and oceans imposed themselves on the minds of coastal dwellers as much as seafarers. Their tidal presence and rhythm were intimately woven into the lives and deaths of coastal communities. The incoming tide tended to accrue positive associations, the ebbing tide negative ones. The tide was said to play a role in determining the gender of a baby, with boys tending to be born at high tide, girls at low, although this was contradicted by the belief that most births took place when the tide was nearly in. The child born on the ebbing tide was said to be more likely to have a life of bad luck. At high tide butter was said to require less churning and water boiled faster, suggesting life was easier during the incoming tide. It was said to be hard to die when the tide was coming in and that people tended to die on the ebbing tide. If an individual was ill, it was believed that if they held on until the tide turned, their chances of recovery improved. Reverend Walter Gregor, writing about beliefs in Rosehearty, Pitsligo, Aberdeenshire, in 1884, noted that it was believed that bathing in the sea when the tide was rising was good for you, but bathing when it was ebbing could be 'injurious to health', although how was not explained. Yet the reverse informed a practice in East Anglia where it was believed that a person suffering from whooping cough should be taken to the shore to meet the incoming tide. When the tide receded, it would take the illness with it.[3]

Similar beliefs applied to the beach and shoreline, too. In the Outer Hebrides it was not thought right to remove any fish found dead on the shore. This may have been informed by an idea that fishing should be a struggle, that one's catch should be won from the sea. A tale told of how three Eriskay men were landing a boat near the chapel house when they saw a dead salmon and some large trout on the shore. All rushed for the fish, but the one who took them regretted it, for shortly afterwards a near relative died. While there was no evident connection between these two things, it reiterated an idea that if things were taken inappropriately from the sea then it would take something back in return. According to Fletcher Bassett, English seamen were wary of picking up objects from wrecks on the shore 'for fear lest the drowned owner may claim his property and them with it'.[4] The message was that the easy gift cast ashore came with consequences.

Concerns about drowning were prevalent, forming a topic that pressed constantly upon the thoughts of costal and island communities. Scottish coastal villagers dreaded picking up drowned bodies or the vessels they drowned in if they washed up on the shore, for to do so might invite a similar fate. As with mariners, the fear was that death and misfortune was contagious. Ideas of drowning were even said to spill over into the interpretation of Hebridean islanders' dreams. To see water streaming down the inside walls of a house or, more obviously, to dream of being under an upturned boat presaged a drowning. To dream of a person dressed in grey foretold of sickness, misfortune or a voyage to sea, suggesting that the last was not much more desirable than the others.[5] This pervasive concern about misfortune and drowning fed into understandings of the various beings encountered on the shoreline – selkies, mermaids, even ghosts – all of which were said to have prophetic insight into the future. This projection of prognosticative powers on to those supernatural entities whom coastal dwellers might occasionally encounter reflects a deep yearning within their communities for foreknowledge or to know the fate of loved ones at sea. This was not solely a matter of affection. Death at sea had both a dramatic economic and emotional cost, with the loss of a fisherman and his vessel likely to plunge his widow and orphans into dire straits.

Coastal folklore expressed the concerns of local communities and also informed a local understanding of the land- and seascape in which they lived. Hebridean lore suggested that seafarers who lived on the Scottish islands took much of their understanding of supernatural forces from land. Islanders, regardless of whether they ventured upon the waves, were said to be fearful of any methods that could raise winds, for their islands were already subject to fierce gales and storms. Even if they desired to reach another island or the mainland, none would be so rash as to put a knife into the mast, a traditional method to summon a wind.

Hebridean islanders also shared seafarers' concern for seeking omens and signs in nature. This was seen with the construction of friths or horoscopes, often intended to find out what fate awaited absent mariners. In the late nineteenth century Catriona MacEachan, an elderly local woman, had been known for making such predictions. Rather than an astrological calculation as with other horoscopes, the caster would wake, say a prayer and a 'Hail Mary', close her eyes and walk to the doorstep of her cottage. She would then look out over the land or sea for signs of good and bad fortune. It was said that if the caster saw a woman it meant 'death or something equally bad'. There was some nuance added to this. A woman passing the doorstep was not so bad as one who was seen standing still, the latter being taken as a sign of certain death. Oddly, hair colour played a role in tempering the prediction, with women with dun-coloured hair being best, those with black hair 'fairly lucky' and those with red hair the worst. This negative association with women, possibly by female casters, suggests that mariners' dislike for women on ships was not purely the product of a homosocial culture forged by sailors but part of a broader folk cultural reading in which women were more inclined to be associated with misfortune. Men, by contrast, were viewed less harshly. If the caster saw a man or animal standing, it was a sign that a sick person would recover, but if the man was lying down the sick person's illness would continue.[6]

Like mariners unintentionally summoning a gale through whistling, islanders also believed that small actions could have extreme consequences, and that fates could be determined by the smallest details. It was said that if a whelk was put on a fire to roast it would result in seven years of famine, while the direction of the wind on New Year's Day would determine the success or failure of both the year's fishing and crops, for that would be the prevalent direction of the wind for the whole year.[7] Such ideas spoke to the precarious lives and livelihoods of those involved in a coastal economy, one often heavily dependent upon a dominant activity such as fishing.

Indicative of the way that island folklore was also informed by ideas and influences that had existed for longer on the mainland, the will-o'-the-wisp was said to have only reached the Hebridean islands in the early nineteenth century. Will-o'-the-wisps or Jack-o'-Lanterns were often associated with marshy areas and long understood to be dangerous spirits that led people astray with its light, causing them to drown. This mysterious light was first seen in the island of South Uist in 1814. As with most ghost stories, the appearance of this phenomena needed a backstory to explain it. In this case, it was said to be the spirit of a young girl from the island of Benbecula. She had been known for searching the sandy shore for *Galium verum*, a plant used in dyeing local tweed cloth. Her haunting was understood as a punishment for greedily trying to take too much, when limited natural resources should have been shared more equally among the tweed-making communities.

A more fanciful origin story for the appearance of this Jack-o'-Lantern was that it was the spirit of a blacksmith who had been denied admittance to heaven or hell. Begging for a single ember to keep himself warm, he wandered, shivering (explaining the phenomena's fitful or unstable light) as he carried his ember in the dark. In the Hebrides, hell was understood to be a cold place, rather than one of roasting fires. This was informed by the environment in which islanders lived out their lives. In this place of cold mist, rain, drizzle and damp, driving winds and draughts, any suggestion that hell was a place of fire might have been taken as a comfort rather than a punishment.[8]

Brackish Encounters: Selkies, Mermaids, Sea Serpents and Water Sprites

The coast was where a veritable bestiary of marvellous sea creatures could be encountered. One creature not considered when looking at the inhabitants of the open sea in Chapter Three was selkies. These were perhaps the most representative of the coast's distinctive supernatural beings, for while they emerged from the sea, their folkloric accounts revolved around encounters with coastal inhabitants. Projecting human-like qualities onto the appearance and actions of seals laid the foundations for stories of selkies, with tales moving beyond mere affinities to more literal transformations. Selkie stories illustrate how coastal communities, much like mariners at sea, imaginatively anthropomorphized features of the marine environment, seeing something of themselves in the maritime world. To give some credence to these notions, only larger seals were assumed to be selkies, not the smaller, common seals. In the Orkney islands, it was debated whether selkies could only transform on particular days or nights, during certain tides or in certain weather conditions. Unlike the solitary mermaid, female selkies often came ashore in groups to bask on rocks. It was believed that sea birds would warn them of approaching threats, at which point they would all swiftly grab their seal skins and dive back into the sea.

Selkies' removal of their seal skins when ashore, thereby appearing as human, was not just a potential vulnerability but a central plot device in the most common variant of the selkie story. With some expected alterations in detail, that story was as follows. A beautiful selkie or seal woman comes ashore and takes off her seal skin. It is found or taken by a fisherman who hides it. Stranded ashore and unable to return to the sea without her skin, the selkie is coerced into marrying the thief, usually presented as a lonely man whose work or coastal life has prevented him from marrying. Once married, the woman becomes a frugal and thrifty wife, bearing a number of children. As her former amphibious existence is gradually knocked out of her by the drudgery of being a fisherman's wife, she becomes tinged with sadness and regret, looking longingly to the sea from which she has been separated. Sometimes she is seen to conduct conversations with something in the water, although she cannot join it. In other accounts, she never gives up looking for the seal skin, that symbol of her former identity. Some years pass, the children start to grow, and eventually one of them accidentally reveals where her husband had hidden the skin, often in the rafters of the house. Without hesitation, she says a loving goodbye to her children, puts on her seal skin and dives into the surf, finally able to respond to the sea's beckoning call. The husband, realizing what has happened, usually runs down to the shoreline or sees his wife with her male selkie companion, and begs her to return. She refuses, possibly warning that bad luck will come to him if he harms seals (as he may accidentally harm her or her selkie family), and then disappears beneath the waves, never to be seen again.

In the nineteenth century this type of story was told (or at least recorded by predominantly male folklorists) as a tale of 'the one that got away'. Female tellers and listeners may have interpreted it differently, appreciating the fantasized expression of stolen and restored female agency, and in more recent years this story has become popular in feminist (re-)readings of maritime folklore. It offers a relatively rare way in which women could voice their frustrations with domestic drudgery, their callous and controlling husbands, and their loss of identity. In such tales the sea serves as the symbol of freedom and release, a thing yearned for rather than feared. While mariners may have looked longingly to shore as a return to home and safety, the selkie looked upon the sea in the same way. Again, one sees echoes of the gender divide found in mermaid folklore, with male land dwellers and female marine dwellers interacting, but often in uneven and unfulfilling ways.

Male selkies provided another way of exploring domestic and marital problems for those ashore. As handsome as female selkies were beautiful, male selkies were said to be known seducers who came ashore to have sex with young maidens, married women and spinsters. The idea of male selkies conducting illicit affairs with fishermen's wives while their husbands were away at sea might have served as a coded narrative for sexual intrigue within small fishing communities, but equally such tales can be understood as an attempt to promote or shore up sexual mores. In many cases, the male selkie was presented as something of a sexual predator, preying on naive or lonely women and then leaving them, sometimes with inhuman offspring. Yet it was said that a fisherman's wife would take such a lover if her husband had been unfaithful, thereby punishing him for his own unfaithfulness.

In one story from Orkney, it was the wife who initiated the illicit union, with the male selkie appearing as an accommodating lover rather than a seductive rake. A wife, disappointed by her fisherman husband and their life together, took herself to the shoreline and cried seven tears into the sea. A selkie appeared, and the woman told him what she wanted from him. The male selkie returned to her on the spring tide, when he was able to take human form. The wife had to subsequently clip the webbing from the fingers of the children sired by her selkie lover, to disguise their true nature from her husband. The children of such unions were often said to have patches of dry skin, whereas descendants of merfolk had patches of rough skin that resembled scales. In such way skin conditions or blemishes could be given a fantastical explanation.[9] One can only speculate whether the drive behind such stories arose from the paranoia of fishermen who had to repeatedly work away from home or the fantasy of wives who were left behind. Whether featuring male or female selkies, these stories seem to articulate tensions within human relationships ashore, speaking to feelings of entrapment, suspicion, unfaithfulness and infidelity. For female selkies forced into marriage, the relationship was usually presented as a cold one, a mundane and practical convenience lacking the warmth of human love, or the alluring enchantment encountered in stories of coastal mermaids.

These stories of animal–human transformation resonate with the nature of the coast as a liminal space where boundaries met and were crossed. There was also a blurring of boundaries between supernatural entities, especially in the Scottish islands. Selkies shared something of the shapeshifting qualities of the Finn-men, but, like merfolk, they wore special garments that enabled them to travel underwater. That blurring of species continued, for, according to local lore, selkies, merfolk and Finn-men were all known to intermarry with Shetland islanders. Sometimes the idea of mermaids as fallen angels who had been cast into the seas or ocean was also used to explain the existence of selkie folk. Others considered selkies as cursed humans who were forced to assume seal form and live at sea, so that coming ashore and returning to human form was a reprieve. Such tales offered a very different perspective to the selkie-as-enforced-wife story above, reversing the locations that the selkie associated with ordeal and escape.

If the Scottish islands were rich with stories of selkies, nineteenth-century Cornwall abounded with tales of coastal mermaids. Cornish legends suggest that mermaids had been involved in shaping features of the coastal landscape. Seaton had once been a successful fishing town until, according to legend, a local man insulted a mermaid and she placed a curse on it, causing it to be swallowed by sand. At Padstow on Cornwall's northern coast, legend tells of a visiting mariner to the port who shot a mermaid. Details vary as to whether it was to protect himself from being lured beneath the waves or a murderous response to being rejected in love. The mermaid rose up, held out her hand and cursed the port. A storm suddenly blew up as she vowed Padstow would suffer misfortune for the mariner's actions. The storm wrecked many ships and formed the Doom Bar, a sand bank upon which ships have run aground for hundreds of years.[10] While both are clearly retrospective tales to explain topographical features or environmental change, it is interesting that they reach for mermaids as the source of the change. In both cases, the mermaids' powers far exceed anything encountered in the stories explored in Chapter Three, tending to resonate more with stories of the landscape being shaped by the Devil himself.[11]

The ability of mermaids to penetrate inland was seen beyond the British Isles. In his notes on an expedition to the Caribbean in 1806, George Pinckard recorded that the governor of Guyana, 'a sensible and intelligent man', supported the opinion that mermaids existed in the Berbice river. They had been seen by all different races, suggesting they were not simply the product of the cultural beliefs of any one group. However, Pinckard highlighted that the indigenous inhabitants were said to be superstitious about the protection of the mermaids, for if harm came to them people would be plagued 'with every species of ill'. The governor's view was echoed by a planter who declared, 'Nothing . . . is more certain than that mermaids do exist in the rivers of Guiana,' adding that a naval officer had supposedly had one captured, cooked and served up as a meal. Seeking to maintain a sense of old-world distance from these local beliefs, beliefs that nevertheless bore some resemblance to ideas found in the Cornish legends above, Pinckard stated that, without confirmation of their existence, 'we . . . assume the liberty of Englishmen, and still continue . . . to doubt!'[12]

In some tales, those who have adjusted to life underwater return to shore with fatal consequences. In a tale from Sweden, a fisherman was abducted by a mermaid and lived underwater with her. Years later he returned to land to see his former wife remarry. The mermaid permitted this but warned that he must not enter the house where the marriage was being conducted. Whether this was due to the mermaid's prophetic ability or simply not wanting the man to get too close to his former wife, the warning was inevitably ignored. The fisherman entered the building, and a storm tore the roof off. The fisherman was found dead three days later. While presumably the result of injuries sustained in the storm, the story left space for this to be understood as a punishment for defying the mermaid's wishes.[13]

There are echoes here with a tale of a girl who was drowned, but rather than dying lived for many years underwater as a water sprite. One day she swam ashore and was confronted with the beauty of the land, its woods and greenery alive with insects and birds. Longing to go back to her old life ashore, she visited her former village but was unrecognized by family and friends. Saddened, she returned to the water that evening, becoming a water sprite once more. Two days later, the girl's mutilated corpse was found washed up on the sands. Again, it was unclear if this is to be understood as the water sprite being harshly punished for venturing ashore, or if she had somehow killed herself, realizing that she was no longer truly at home either on land or at sea.[14] Both spoke to the tragedy of being caught in a liminal space between land and water, formerly part of human society but now outside it.

The coast could also be where folkloric creatures from further inland could be encountered. In one Cornish legend, one John Taprail encountered a group of piskies (or pixies) sheltering under a boat that had been pulled up onto the beach one night. He observed that one of the group was tossing gold pieces into their hats as if dealing out cards. With greed overcoming the good sense to not provoke or intrude upon piskies, John hid behind the boat and surreptitiously introduced his cap into the circle where the money was being distributed. Sure enough, coins were added to the additional hat. With the piskie coming to the end of his generous sharing of wealth, and with a growing sense of the risk he was taking, John withdrew his hat and made off with his loot. He had made it some way back to his house before the piskies realized they had been duped and gave chase. So close were they to capturing the thief that when he reached home and slammed the door shut behind him, the piskies were left holding the tails of his sea-coat outside. Given their reputation, one might have expected a door to provide flimsy protection from some vengeful piskies, but, for this story at least, the message seemed to be that humans could, just occasionally, get the better of the fairy folk.[15]

While most coastal encounters involved aquatic humanoids, a group of ladies and gentlemen, including a noted clergyman, found themselves up close and personal with a 'sea monster' on 26 September 1871. It occurred at the Diamond Rocks, Kilkee, County Clare, on the Atlantic coast of Ireland. The party had been watching the Atlantic waves crashing against the rocks when a huge monster suddenly appeared about 70 yards out from where they stood. It was later reported as having

> an enormous head, shaped somewhat like a horse, while behind the head and on the neck was a huge mane of

> seaweed-looking hair which rose and fell with the motion of the water; the eyes were large and glaring, and, by the appearance of the water behind, a vast body seemed to be beneath the waves.

All in the party agreed that it was 'the most gigantic creature they had ever seen'. One of the ladies in the party nearly fainted, while all were left shaken by the creature's 'dreadful appearance'. Despite this, the witnesses suggested that the monster looked exhausted, rising and falling with the waves, until it finally vanished after some minutes. Rather than being something dredged up by sailors in response to mysterious sightings in the mid-Atlantic, this creature had, in broad daylight, intruded upon a pleasant coastal stroll. British newspapers reprinted the report from the *Limerick Chronicle*, including the speculations of Philip Henry Gosse, a renowned naturalist. Rejecting the idea

Unknown artist, 'Startling appearance of a monster sea-serpent off Kilkee on the Irish coast', from the *Days' Doings*, VII/177 (21 October 1871).

that it was an actual sea serpent, he suggested it was more likely some species of nearly extinct prehistoric sea creature, with a long neck like that of a Plesiosaurus.[16] Nothing, it seems, was beyond the realm of possibility in that strange and ever-shifting space between land and sea, past and present.

The Return of the Dead

While mermaids were content to perch on the shoreline, ghosts were inclined to drag themselves up to the front door and let themselves in. As indicated in Chapter Four, ghosts expressed a connection between land dwellers and seafarers, and the coast was where the spirits of drowned sailors returned home, back to a place that their lost corpses could never reach. Such stories demonstrate the complex relationship coastal communities, especially fishing communities, had with the sea. On the one hand, it offered an abundance of resources and a fair living. On the other, that temperamental and dangerous environment extracted a dreadful tax on the lives of loved ones. Coastal ghost stories were a way for communities to talk about the brutal fact that misfortune and loss were part of the maritime way of life. While such tales may have been told to frighten and warn, they also spoke to sadness, to what grief can inspire us to wish for, even if a spectral return could never provide the comfort the grieving desired. While the coast was a place of return, those who returned transformed, supernaturally sea changed into ghosts, were usually denied any final rest ashore.

This is seen in a tale of nineteenth-century Normandy fishermen. The local community was expected to pray for those drowned at sea. If the prayers were insufficient, it was said that a storm would gather and a previously lost ship would appear at sea and swiftly race into the harbour. When it pulled up alongside the quayside, ropes would be thrown and caught by the crew who secured the vessel. Widowed wives and their children would congregate, recognizing their dead loved ones on board. They would cry out, seeking communication, but the crew would remain oblivious. When a bell sounded at midnight, a sea fog would swiftly roll in and when it passed a few minutes later the ship had vanished.[17]

Along with suggesting that the failings of landlubbers might be responsible for a ghost ship's return to shore, this story clearly demonstrates a yearning for the dead to be reclaimed from the sea and to return home. To the living, the lost mariners existed in limbo. Unfound and unreturned, neither definitely dead nor alive, theirs was a perpetual state of undead uncertainty. The story also suggests the deceased's yearning to return to the fixity of the shore, for their journey's end. Yet the phantom crew's lack of awareness or communication with their loved ones and the ease with which the fog erased them, returning the vessel to sea, ultimately showed that such longing was in vain. The lost fishermen would forever belong to the ocean. Such accounts read like the pained wish-fulfilment of grieving families confronted with absence, coming to terms with the way the ocean callously took living, vibrant family members and simply swallowed them forever. Here the ocean's illusion of erasing history, leaving no sign of mariners' passing, took on wounding, haunting qualities. The monuments to the lost were erected in broken hearts back home.

There were tales that spoke to such a longing for a reunion by lovers that death would not divide them. Such a tale was told of St Levan, a fishing village in Cornwall. Whatever realities it may or may not have originally been based on, as told it had clearly been coated in legend. A handsome sailor was going to marry the most beautiful girl in those parts when he returned from sea. After many months, news finally returned that the young man's ship had been lost with all on board. In her grief, the young woman spent many a day wandering the cliffs and looking out to sea, hoping against hope that the sailor would return. Then, one night, a violent storm hit the coast, and the young woman awoke to somebody calling her name over the raging wind and the roaring waves crashing ashore. Looking out of the window of her cottage, she saw her former lover, soaked, seaweed in his hair, his eyes shining in his pale face. The woman knew he was a ghost, and although the storm was fierce she did not hesitate to join him outside. He led her down to a cove and invited her to get into a rowing boat that he pushed into the churning surf. Again, she did not hesitate, and the ghost rowed them out into the water, past the dangerous rocks. They were never seen again. It was said that the ghostly sailor had taken his would-be wife to live with him in a cave beneath the sea.[18]

Most encounters with the dead were not so romantic, and many tales spoke to a dread of being confronted with the horrors of maritime revenants. The undead that emerged from the sea were given various names. In Iceland drowned seafarers were a particular variant of the restless, reanimated corpses known as Draugr. In Norway they were known as Draug or 'Gongers'. Appearing in the wet clothes in which they had drowned, their stories reinforced the belief that bodies washed up ashore needed to be buried in a churchyard; if not, they would remain as restless as the waves. In Denmark they were known as Strand Varsler and were said to watch over the corpses of the drowned who had been washed ashore. A woman who took a ring from a dead body on a beach was chased by a Strand Varsler. Described as gaunt, with a green face ruined by decay, its hair and clothes soaked with water, it chased the screaming woman off the beach. Similarly, English sailors supposedly feared picking up any object on the shore that had washed up from a wreck at sea, believing that the drowned owner would come to claim it and them too.[19] Such beliefs spoke to a sense of repressed guilt or remorse among the living ashore: survivors' guilt for fellow seafarers, and the emotional pain of parents and spouses who had to live with the knowledge that they had likely played a part in sending their loved ones out to sea.[20]

Maritime ghosts also tried to communicate with the living. Given the spirit world's knowledge of the future, their calls or cries were often taken as warning of doom or imminent death. In his *Description of Greenland*, Hans Egede included descriptions of several eighteenth-century maritime phantoms, among them a 'sea spectre' known as the Draw. This shapeshifting entity was said to herald maritime disasters such as shipwrecks with its 'frightful and ghastly howling', serving as a marine equivalent of the Banshee, although it was also known to speak too. The Draw was something of a trickster, being said to move equipment around once the fishermen had gone to sleep, but leaving nothing behind but a foul smell. Egede noted that 'fishermen will not suffer the truth of this tale to be questioned'.[21] According to Robert Hunt's *Romances of the West of England*, at night Cornish fishermen avoided walking near places on the shore where wrecks had occurred. It was believed that the spirits of those who had drowned still haunted the shoreline and fishermen declared they had heard the voices of the dead calling their names. This was known as the 'hailing of the dead', with the idea that the dead were summoning those seafarers who were soon to join them.[22]

Indicative of coastal communities' collective memory of lost seafarers and the sheer numbers that died at sea over the years, some folkloric accounts suggested that the dead massed on beaches. The spirits of drowned sailors supposedly haunted Corryvreckan in the Hebrides. They were heard to wail before the arrival of a storm, lamenting the losses it would bring. At the 'Bay of the Departed' off the coast of Brittany, ferrymen would be summoned by supernatural forces in the middle of the night to take the souls of those who had drowned to Sein, a nearby island. Fishermen claimed the ferryboats were so loaded with the wailing and weeping souls of the dead that the vessels sat low in the water as they made their way over to the island. Once there, the souls were organized and sorted by invisible beings. Their task finished, the ferrymen were released from their service and rowed home to await the next summons. Similarly, further down the coast at Guildo, phantom ferrymen were said to take the souls of the drowned in their spectral skiffs over the 'treacherous sands'. Locals were so frightened of witnessing this that none would venture near the place at night.[23] At Sent, also on the Brittany coast, it was believed that skeletons of the drowned paraded along those parts of the coast where shipwrecks had resulted in deaths. Such a macabre parade served as a powerful visual or, if based on hearsay, at least imagined representation of the many lives taken by the Atlantic, especially when many of those bodies remained forever lost to the ocean.

Other coastal ghost stories confronted local communities with a legacy of guilt or complicity in past crimes. There is a particularly ghoulish, physical quality to some of the maritime ghosts on the eastern seaboard of the United States. Skeletons were said to crew a phantom barque in the sea off Dead Man's Island in the Gulf of St Lawrence, and a similarly skeletal band were said to be seen around Orr's Island, Maine. These legends are thought to have developed in the era when coastal wreckers sought to plunder the cargo of ships that had run upon rocks. The stories' emphasis on skeletons, on decayed physical remains rather than ethereal phantoms, demonstrated an element of not just fear but revulsion. They drew attention to the corporeality of the dead, to the grotesque influence the sea has on bodies submerged underwater. Beyond the Gothic theatrics of a skeletal crew was an awareness that local wreckers – possibly the ancestors of these shoreline communities – may have had a hand in causing or at least profiting from those death.

Stories could also offer some vicarious pleasure in thinking that past villainy could be punished. St Just in Cornwall was home of a former wrecker and suspected pirate who had enticed ships onto the rocks by tying a lantern to a horse and walking it along the cliffs, giving the impression that it was a boat light ahead, indicating a safe passage to shore. Ships lured by the false beacon smashed themselves to pieces on the rocks before the cliffs. Further establishing the man's cruelty, it was said that he would take rings from the fingers of survivors who had struggled ashore and then hit them on the head and throw them back into the water to drown.

When the wrecker finally lay dying at the end of his life, he was beset with fear that those he had killed might be waiting for him. The man's house was located by the coast but visiting clergymen claimed they could hear the booming sound of the waves inside the man's room. Sensing the Devil was near, they tried to repel him with prayers, but finally abandoned their efforts as futile when he returned as a fly and buzzed about the wrecker's face. As the hour of the wrecker's death approached, a fierce storm brewed out at sea. At its heart was a square-rigged black ship with black sails. In some accounts, it waited just off the cliffs where the wrecker had committed his crimes. The black clouds rolled towards the dying man's house and, at the moment of the wrecker's death, the wind roared through his house and took his soul. Then the storm retreated, and the vessel turned and headed back out to sea. In another version, the ship itself comes ashore, passes over the wrecker's house and snatches up the evil man's soul as it glides by.

Unfortunately for the dead wrecker, his story did not end there. When his coffin was being taken to the churchyard for burial, it was followed by a large black pig. Those bearing the coffin said it felt too light to contain a body. At the churchyard another fierce storm raged, forcing the bearers to abandon their burden and take shelter in the church. When they finally ventured outside again, the only thing left of the coffin was the handles and a few nails, the rest having been destroyed by lightning. Given the variations in telling, it is unclear whether the ship took the wrecker's soul and the lightning his body, or whether the ship had merely been a symbol of death, and his soul was later taken by the mysterious black pig. What is clear is that, given the presence of the Devil, a demonic pig and a death ship, supernatural forces were evidently keen to have both the wrecker's body and soul by way of punishment for his deeds. Horace Beck indicated that an almost identical story was told in Labrador, even including a voice heard to say, 'The hour is come but not the man,' when the ship appears. However, this second account from the other side of the Atlantic omits the dramatic follow-up in the churchyard.[24]

The idea of coastal spirits was updated and adapted in the early twentieth century. In nineteenth-century Cornwall phantom lights observed before stormy weather were known as 'Jack Harry's lights'. They were understood as dangerous, for they deceived mariners into thinking a vessel was in distress. The vessel would supposedly resemble one that was doomed to suffer disaster in the coming storm. As with similar atmospheric phenomena such as St Elmo's fire, these lights were sometimes understood to be the souls of dead mariners. Towards the end of the First World War, mysterious lights were seen flashing on the Cornish coast. These were said to be the spirits of British mariners drowned by the German navy. Like the wreckers of old, they sought to lure enemy vessels onto the rocks to cause their destruction. As Christina Hole observed, 'This tale is probably a local embroidery added to the far older legend of Jack Harry's Lights.'[25]

The returned undead and the spectres that wandered the coastlines of western Europe spoke to a deep unease among coastal dwellers about the sea as a resting place. Such tales suggested that those lost at sea could not rest: their spirits were doomed to wander, denied a proper burial. Therefore coastal dwellers were denied the comforting sense of the dead being fixed in place. Even when the dead came back to their coastal homes, they rarely stayed for more than a brief visit before the sea reclaimed them or they had to leave upon the coming of the dawn. These brief forays ashore also meant that ghosts of the drowned did not travel far inland but remained confined to the coast as the closest point of contact with the sea or ocean.

Such tales afford us glimpses into the mindset of seafarers, fishermen and their families ashore, frequently revealing dark and painful places full of mental anguish and grief. Such was the strength of the emotional connection between coastal landlubbers and their seafaring loved ones that they could draw the spirits of the dead across distances, both from land to sea (as seen in Chapter Four) and, as here, back to shore. While seafarers often spoke of landlubbers with disdain, ghost stories serve to remind us that coastal communities were inexorably linked to the precarious maritime environment and the livelihoods that were eked out of it. Fishermen and other mariners risked their lives, but it was those anxiously waiting back home that had to bear the emotional wounds, lingering grief and longing inflicted by the ocean.

Coastal communities could also be haunted in a different way, not by individual spectres but by legends of lost villages or drowned settlements that had been claimed by ever-encroaching sea waters. Local stories commonly suggest that church bells could still be heard when people passed over a submerged village. Perhaps the most famous in England is the lost Suffolk town of Dunwich. Once an important part of medieval trade networks in the North Sea, this sizable port had more than four hundred houses, eight churches and an estimated population of around 4,000 people. From the fourteenth century, storms, erosion and the encroaching sea caused it to gradually become submerged, so that by the early nineteenth century its population was under 250 residents, most of their town being underwater.

More fanciful stories, echoing those of Atlantis, linked drowned cities and towns to a disastrous flood. Bretons told of the lost city of Is (or Ker Ys or Ker-Is), located in the Bay of Douarnenez on the Brittany coast. Built on a low plain, it was protected from the Atlantic by a wall with sluice gates, and was ruled by King Grallon. His daughter, Princess Dahut, was the villain of the piece. Said to be lustful and wicked, she stole the key to the gates from around her father's neck, possibly at the behest of the Devil, who had disguised himself as one of her lovers. Dahut opened the gates and the seawaters surged in. The king managed to escape on a horse but his daughter, whom he attempted to save, fell into the waters and was drowned. The story was clearly a product of its age, intended to convey a moral message about the dangers of lustful women, with Princess Dahut being punished by the very forces her evil had unleashed.

In the nineteenth century Bretons claimed to have heard Is's bells underwater and seen the remains of its buildings beneath their boats. Steeples had even been said to appear at low tide. The drowned settlement became linked to a prophecy that if Is should ever rise again, Paris would sink.[26] The feudal, fairy-tale nature of this story clearly located it in a distant past. While we may not know how it was told, received or interpreted by Bretons, in the context of the revolutionary movements that were developing in later eighteenth-century North America and Europe, one cannot help thinking this may have contained a concealed political allegory, especially with Is being directly associated with the fate of Paris. More immediately, tales of submerged settlements served as a melancholic reminder that communities once thought prosperous and enduring had been lost to the sea, that the permanence of human settlements and cultures was a self-aggrandizing illusion. Such stories spoke to the constant struggle in which the insistent might of the ocean would ultimately prove more powerful than the apparent indomitability of the land. The sea's triumph was simply a matter of time: a haunting by the future, rather than the past.

Fakelore and the Telling of Tales

As the location where foreign contraband was smuggled ashore, coastal areas were sites of illegal activities. Coastal landscapes were full of caves, bays, coves and cliffs that could facilitate this illegal economy, and tight-knit communities could be complicit in activities such as smuggling or wrecking. To cloak their work, fakelore, knowingly false folkloric-type tales, could be disseminated to ward people away from specific areas. Along the north Norfolk coast in the nineteenth century, tales used to circulate of a huge demon dog called Black Shuck. Sometimes described as headless, yet somehow possessing fiery eyes or sometimes a single eye and a mouth that breathed fire, it was said to pursue pedestrians at night. A sighting of Black Shuck was taken as a sign of death, usually for the unfortunate individual who encountered it. Yet it was suggested that this terrifying hellhound may have originated as 'a trick of the old smuggling days', when 'a pony made hideous with black cloth and . . . a dark lanthorn tied to his head' was sent along the lanes where the smugglers transported their kegs.[27] Such tales fitted with inland rather than maritime accounts of similar giant hellhounds such as the Skriker and the Barghest.

Similarly, the 'Lady of the Lantern' was a ghost said to haunt a spot of coast near St Ives in Cornwall. The story went that the woman had survived a shipwreck, but her baby had drowned and was lost at sea. Even after her death, the diligent mother's pale ghost continued to haunt the shoreline, endlessly searching among the rocks with a lantern for her dead child. Her appearance was taken as a sign of some forthcoming disaster. In other cases, lights flittering over the rocks at night were said to be the spirits of the drowned looking for their corpses, which the tide may have washed ashore.[28] Such tales seemed designed to explain mysterious lights on the beach at night and to keep people away from whatever illicit activity was being conducted there. The likelihood of this tactic being successful is questionable. Evidence from nineteenth-century British towns and cities would suggest that rumours of ghosts tended to attract rather than repel local attention. Into the mid-nineteenth century newspapers still occasionally reported on local communities spilling out into the streets at night in their hundreds or even thousands to catch sight of a rumoured ghost.[29]

This creation of a supernatural deterrent was also seen in Dieppe, France. In the nineteenth century local fishermen told of fairies holding a fair or bazaar at a certain time of year on a cliff that overlooked the sea. The fairies were understood as dangerous entities who lured humans with their music and their enticing goods of rare beauty. Only those fishermen who averted their gaze and did not look at the fairies' enchanting wares would escape. If they did look, or let themselves be swayed by the fairy music, they would pursue their gleaming prize, though with each attempt to touch it the object would move away from them. The pursuit would draw them to the cliffs, where they would blindly stumble over the edge, falling to their deaths in the churning waters below.[30] Such a tale might have served as a warning against practical dangers near cliffs, but it could have also served to usefully keep people away for other reasons. Indeed, the story's message was plainly spelled out: don't look.

On the eastern seaboard of the United States, coastal or island ghost stories often told of malevolent spirits guarding buried treasure. Again, such tales may have been intended to keep people away from certain locations.[31] Grisly tales could serve to intimidate in other ways. Horace Beck told of an early twentieth-century urban legend as to why there were no 'guinea boats' (fishing vessels crewed by Italians from Boston) in the harbour at Portsmouth, New Hampshire. An Italian mariner had supposedly killed the wife of a local fisherman who was then wrongly accused of her death. A storm prevented the fisherman from being taken to Portsmouth jail and he took his opportunity to escape the policemen who had seized him. He got to the shore, launched a dory and rowed out into the stormy waters. The wronged husband was never seen again, but shortly afterwards, his wife's killer was found dead aboard his vessel, his hand cut off at the wrist. A fellow crew member claimed to have seen a man in oilskins rowing away in a dory. For eighteen years afterwards, whenever Italian crews came into Portsmouth harbour, one of their number was supposedly mutilated on their boats at night, with their eyes being stabbed or their ears, noses or feet being severed. Eventually, they stopped coming. As with most ghost stories created in retrospect, the tale explained the absence of the Italian boats, but it may have also served as a means of intimidation, to keep fishing rivals away.[32]

Certain figures of rural and coastal life could be romanticized as anti-authority folk heroes, including poachers and coastal smugglers. Smugglers' daring and ingenuity could be understood as the common man getting one over on revenue officials and the restrictive forces of law and order. Wreckers were harder to frame in this way, for they profited from maritime disasters that were likely to have resulted in a considerable loss of life. Given that drowning weighed so heavily on the minds of coastal and seafaring communities, this callous, vampiric profiting from misfortune tended to inform wreckers' portrayal as villains. As the Cornish wrecker story above illustrated, there was a cathartic satisfaction to such figures receiving a supernatural comeuppance.

Cathryn Pearce has examined the way in which aspects of eighteenth- and nineteenth-century Cornish wrecking, especially the folkloric elements involving fake lights guiding ships onto coastal rocks or people extinguishing lighthouse beacons, were themselves something of a popular myth.[33] The perpetuation of such ideas tended to play into a view of coastal communities as insular, deceptive and harbouring dark secrets. It is interesting to note that folkloric tales tended to individualize the wrecker as a deliberate agent of destruction, conveniently distracting from the wider communal culpability that came with their opportunistic pilfering of cargo washed ashore as a result of a ship's misfortune at sea. Much as coastal ghosts provided a way of expressing unspoken remorse and regret, so the evil wrecker could become an imaginary scapegoat for those confronted with the guilt of plundering ill-gotten gains from the shoreline. The morality of such activities was muddied, for scavenging 'gifts from the sea' might form an important supplement to coastal communities' legitimate fishing, farming or mining work, communities over whom the prospect of poverty frequently hung like heavy black sea clouds.

Fakelore raises interesting complications for our understanding of coastal folklore. Largely dependent upon scraps of tales gathered by nineteenth-century collectors who may not have distinguished between what was understood as genuinely supernatural and what was understood as a concocted hoax, the coastal tales we have inherited may contain a fair share of fakelore. At the very least, we have to accept that some of the specific local purposes and meanings of these tales are now lost to us. Of course, local people may not have had a clear sense of distinction either, for belief or scepticism about any account was dependent on the individual. Even stories understood as 'genuine' may have had earlier origins in deliberate fabrication.

Added to this was the hesitancy that locals had in sharing their tales and beliefs with an outsider, often for reasons relating to both their social class and geographical origin outside the community. As was noted of the late nineteenth-century Orkney Islander, it was believed, 'often correctly, that educated people held his lore in contempt. When they asked questions on old subjects, he suspected their only object was to make him and his stories objects for amusement.'[34] It was for this reason that informants and go-betweens such as resident clergymen were so important in the gathering of local tales.

This returns us to where we initially launched in Chapter One, back to the ports and coastal communities that served as important sites for the fostering and exchange of maritime supernatural tales and beliefs that seafarers both took to sea and brought back home. Folklorists have long recognized the presence and importance of migratory legends, similar stories that have travelled from one country to another, adapting features of their shared narrative elements to local cultures. Despite their categorization from the mid-twentieth century, the emphasis has been on the geographical reach and proliferation of repeated story tropes, on the distance travelled rather than the actual means by which they were acquired and transmitted overseas.[35] While literary fairy tales developed in their own idiosyncratic ways, oral tales were often part of a freer flowing storytelling trade and culture within the expanding commercial ports and naval towns of the nineteenth-century Atlantic world.[36]

Existing at the meeting point between urban and maritime cultures, eighteenth- and nineteenth-century port communities seemed to have an openness to supernatural tales. A case of poltergeist activity in a mansion in Plymouth, Massachusetts, in 1733 provides a case in point. Josiah Cotton had rented the Phillips mansion to a number of tenants, but they left, refusing to pay the remainder of the lease. They claimed the building was plagued by the ghost of Thompson Phillips, a former merchant sea captain and Cotton's deceased son-in-law, and other evil spirits. A strange pale blue light was said to have been seen in the house, and the building was full of strange sounds. Cotton, seeing a threat to his finances if the mansion gained a reputation for being haunted, took his former tenants to court for slander in 1734. Deploring the ignorance and credulity of the common folk of Plymouth, Cotton found himself up against the strength of local belief in devils, spirits and supernatural forces.

Digging into the cultural soil of eighteenth-century Plymouth, this is not that surprising. The town was infused with both radical New England religion and popular magical thinking, said to be 'as rife here about as they were . . . before the Salem [witchcraft] tragedy' nearby. It was also a seaport, where the gossip in the taverns and homes of merchant sailors returned from sea included 'remarkable accounts of sea monsters, St Elmo's Fire, and shipboard apparitions'. Both maritime and terrestrial notions of supernatural wonder informed the mindset articulated by Cotton's previous tenants. Whether or not it was a scam to break a lease, a shore-based equivalent of sailors inventing ghost stories to justify deserting a ship, Cotton lost the two legal actions he brought against his former tenants. This suggests that when it came to accounts of ghosts in eighteenth-century Plymouth, the tide of opinion was against an individual who looked down upon the supernatural beliefs of his fellow townsfolk.[37]

Within ports, inns and taverns served as important points of contact, interaction and exchange of supernatural stories. Once alcohol had loosened tongues in the taverns of nineteenth-century Portsmouth, England, conversation was known to turn to an exchange of tales about ill-fated vessels, ghost ships and sea monsters.[38] Such stories impressed a sense of the strangeness of seafaring upon landlubbers. In turn, they might reciprocate with their own local ghost stories, possibly regurgitating narratives informed by street ballads, newspaper accounts or regional folklore. Portsmouth was home to the Royal Navy, and many Portmuthians who were not in the service itself worked in the town's dockyard to maintain the fleet. People tend to see ghosts that fit with their surroundings, so it is little surprise that nineteenth-century Portsmouth, a town full of sailors and soldiers, had more than its fair share of ghostly seamen. Accounts suggest that the thing that usually identified them as ghosts was their 'antique clothing'.

Victorian Portsmouth's accounts of local supernatural occurrences were put to different uses to those of Cotton's eighteenth-century tenants. Here ghost stories informed a sense of a rumbustious local identity in a town that was attempting to improve its image and acquire some civic respectability. Local stories about the ghost of a sailor who emerged out of a closet in the room in which he had previously killed a young woman, or the discovery by an overnight guest at the Blue Post Inn that his unexpected room companion was the ghost of a sailor killed in a brawl, informed a popular memory of a wilder, more debauched period in the town's history. At the same time, it subtly questioned attempts to recreate the naval seaman as a heroic figure of nation and empire in the second half of the nineteenth century. Living with and alongside such men, many of Portsmouth's inhabitants knew them to have feet of clay. The increasing stories of civilian ghosts in the late nineteenth and early twentieth centuries also served to bolster a sense of the town as its own place, not merely as a servant to the Navy.[39]

Away from pubs and inns, supernatural storytelling was conducted at home too. It was noted that in the Orkney Islands people spent the long winter nights gathered around the cottage fireplace

> listening to the often tedious and long-winded, but spontaneous flow of old tales, from the lips of men and women who believed in the truth of what they told; and, more essential still, those narrators had not a doubt but that their fireside hearers believed in what they heard.[40]

In other places taletelling did not simply fall to a gathering of family, friends and neighbours, but to itinerant storytellers. Cornwall had its wandering droll tellers who told their stories in local farmhouses. It was said of one 'Uncle' Anthony James, a nineteenth-century droll teller who seasonally employed his talents on the Lizard, a peninsula in southern Cornwall, that everyone knew his stories but wanted to hear how he told them. He had 'much to tell about ghosts, witchcraft, and conjuration . . . and of many other things which were equally wonderful and fraught with interest to us simple folk at the Land's End'.[41]

As befits littoral spaces, sites of meeting and of tidal comings and goings, the maritime supernatural was a product of interaction between land and sea-based cultures, not purely the creation of an isolated and enclosed tribe of seafarers. Ports and coastal settlements were places where both the import and export of supernatural beliefs and narratives were conducted. They were places where future seafarers might first become aware of such a worldview through accounts of supernatural experiences brought ashore with mariners, crews who, in turn, picked up comparable land-based narratives and beliefs that existed on the coast or trickled down to it from the hinterland and were then carried back out across the seas. The supernatural seafaring mentalities explored in this book often began at home, ashore, and the experience of returning there or journeying to other coasts served as an opportunity to continually reinforce and reinvigorate such ideas. A place of safety that was repeatedly forsaken for the potential dangers of the seas, the shoreline marked the site of welcome return for mariners, the point at which their navigation of the hazardous ocean and its maritime world of omens, magic, deadly phantom ships, aquatic marvels and monsters had proven successful once again.

8
Remaking Our Nautical Fears

Some of the monsters, ghosts and superstitions explored in this book may seem oddly familiar, despite very few of us having taken to the seas for any length of time. This is because many of these features of the maritime imaginary have been taken, repeated and adapted as elements of our ever-evolving popular culture. As seen with mermaids and sea serpents, this preceded the eighteenth and nineteenth centuries. This final chapter explores how various aspects of the preceding chapters have been repackaged, updated and disseminated through literary and cinematic fictions from the nineteenth to the twenty-first century. In exploring illustrative examples that mark the development of this cultural amplification and extension of the oceanic fantastical, it will examine why certain maritime tropes have proved more adaptive than others.

As we have seen, folklore was often a complex fusion of oral and literary influences, with these dual expressions of the maritime fantastical long co-existing and co-mingling in ways that are often not easily separated into neat chains of cause and effect. While nautical folklore and literary fantasy both contained strong elements of entertainment, the shift in the dominant modes and forms of maritime storytelling wrought significant changes in its intended audience and the use of its supernatural and fantastical tropes. Most obviously, the shift from oral to literary to cinematic form, coupled with a nineteenth-century denigration of mariners' 'superstition' and 'ignorance', disconnected those tropes from their former pragmatic functions within seafaring communities, both on board ship and in port. Instead, landlubbers' literary and later cinematic stories appropriated elements of the maritime fantastical to become ways of imagining the ocean and expressing their own cultural concerns. These ranged from an articulation of the Gothic otherness and non-human weirdness of oceanic spaces to unease about the environmental consequences of nuclear weapons. More recently, it has furnished us with metaphors of ecohorror, expressing our ecological concerns and culpability in what has become unofficially termed the Anthropocene.

A fantasized play space for the imagination, the vast, unknown depths of the ocean provided endless possibilities from which the haunting wrongs of the past, newly awoken monsters or alien presences might emerge. While such depictions mean the ocean has remained a point of origin for imagined threats and hidden secrets, it is typically only when the monster lumbers ashore and threatens coastal cities that landlubbers are forced to truly confront its horrors. In turn, our cultural consumption of such entertainment further distances us from the ocean, rendering it an essentially imaginary space beyond our known, terrestrial world. Rather than being perceived as just a natural ecological system, the Atlantic of the imagination has continued to carry the reek of vengeful spirits, titanic monstrosities, old gods and malevolent forces upon its briny breeze.

The Nautical Gothic

The modern maritime fantastical has followed the shifting aesthetic concerns of the various literary genres through which it has floated since the eighteenth century, from the dark lens of the Gothic supernatural, through the unsettling strangeness of weird fiction, to the wonder and menace of science fiction. In doing so it has voyaged from nautical horrors akin to and likely informed by supernatural folklore to a science-fictional reframing of the thrills and threats of the unknown in more secular terms, as alien biologies and technologies, or as cryptozoological monstrosities.

Strongly echoing the supernatural elements of previous chapters, Samuel Coleridge Taylor's evocative poem *The Rime of the Ancient Mariner* provides a nightmarish imagining of the sea's terrors. Published in 1798, it borrowed heavily from extant folkloric beliefs and knitted together elements explored in a number of previous chapters. An aged mariner tells his tale to a wedding party who are drawn into his story by its extreme and fantastical events. Driven south to the Antarctic, his ship had been guided out of the ice by an albatross that the mariner then shot. Evoking folkloric notions about sea birds bearing the soul of dead sailors, this rash action brings misfortune to the ship and crew. The mariner's angry shipmates make him wear the dead bird around his neck, a symbol of his guilt. Becalmed near the equator and dying of thirst beneath 'a hot and copper sky' and a 'bloody Sun', the mariner observes the slow approach of a ship. When it arrives it is a true nautical horror, a ship's rotting corpse rather than a spectre, a revenant with its ribs showing and sails as thin as gossamer. It bears Death and a pale woman, 'Nightmare Life-in-Death'. They play dice for the souls of the crew, the woman winning the mariner, Death the other two hundred men. All die, except for the mariner, who is punished by continuing to live. As he comes to appreciate the creatures of the ocean, the albatross falls from him. His dead comrades are reanimated by spirits and this 'ghastly crew' steer the ship, which is driven forwards by supernatural forces rather than the wind. He heads home but his rotted vessel sinks as it nears land. Only the mariner survives, pulled from the water by a man and a boy in a boat. Once ashore, the mariner is compelled to tell his story, passing it on as part of his curse. Both haunted and contaminated by his strange

Gustave Doré, 'Beyond the shadow of the ship, I watched the water-snakes', engraving from Samuel Taylor Coleridge, *The Rime of the Ancient Mariner* (1876).

experiences, the mariner's fate echoes the purgatorial existence of those who sail the *Flying Dutchman*.[1]

A powerful example of nautical Gothic literature, Coleridge's hallucinogenic nightmare of a poem articulated a range of ideas explored in this book: the sea and the elements as both a site and a means of divine punishment and purgatorial endurance; oceans as strange locations of extremes, of ice and heat, of deadly becalmed stillness and destructive whirling movement that pulls the vessel down; a place of death, rotted ghost ships, the possessed corpses of dead mariners, and 'a thousand thousand slimy things'. Perhaps most of all, it expresses the infectious power of supernatural storytelling, of how fantastical ideas are conveyed from mind to mind, living parasitically, serving as a metaphorical means of talking about psychological and spiritual journeys as much as human confrontation with the ocean.

Written during the first wave of Gothic literature in the late eighteenth century, Coleridge's poem was a harbinger of the rise of the nautical Gothic novel in the 1830s. The 1820s to 1850s saw the growing popularity of seafaring stories on both sides of the Atlantic, both in terms of maritime fiction and sailors' biographies.[2] At the same time, Gothic literature was moving on from its eighteenth-century origins of tales frequently based in medieval and early modern Europe, adapting to the cultural developments of the nineteenth century and expressing anxieties about modern urban and nautical environments too. As Emily Alder has noted, the sea is ripe for Gothic interpretation. As in land-based tales set in castles, monasteries and dungeons, mariners were incarcerated aboard claustrophobic ships, subject to the potential tyranny of officers and the abuse of crew members. The ocean was 'boundless yet oppressive', a wild, sublime environment full of dangers on the surface, with hidden monsters and secrets lurking in its dark depths. This took on a strong psychological dimension, with the ocean's surface and depth serving as 'interfaces between life and death, chaos and order, self and other'.[3]

Although it may have faded as a credible entity by the nineteenth century, eclipsed by interest in the possibility of the sea serpent, the Kraken still captured the minds of writers and artists ashore. In 1830 a young Alfred Tennyson penned *The Kraken*, a poem that presented the mythical beast as the embodiment of the might and mystery of the unfathomable depths. Asleep deep within the 'abysmal sea', the ancient beast has dwelled for many an age, attended by 'enormous polypi' and feeding upon 'huge sea-worms'. All life in the deep seems frighteningly large, and yet none compares with the monstrous scale of the Kraken, a creature so vast that it denies the poet's ability to describe it as anything other than 'the slumbering green', an allusion that effectively blurs its boundaries and form with the ocean around it. In effect, it returns the Kraken to its former status as an embodiment of human fears of the unknown and unknowable ocean. Given mariners' concern for omens and misfortune, the poem fittingly ends with the suggestion that the Kraken will slumber in the deep until stirred by some apocalyptic event: 'Then once by man and angels to be seen, in roaring he shall rise and on the surface die.'[4]

Some of the most significant Gothic-inflected nautical literary tales of the nineteenth century were written by authors with experience of seafaring, including Frederick Marryat, Herman Melville and Joseph Conrad. Melville served on several whaling ships between 1841 and 1843, and enlisted in the U.S. Navy from 1843 to 1844 before returning home to write *Moby-Dick*. A novel drenched in nautical superstitions and metaphorical allegory, it has more than its share of haunting scenes. Captain Ahab's vessel, the *Pequod*, is a Gothic horror in itself. Possessing an old-fashioned and weather-stained 'original grotesqueness', with aged and wrinkled decks, it is 'a cannibal of a craft, tricking herself forth in the chased bones of her enemies', with her bulwarks 'garnished like one continuous jaw, with the long sharp teeth of the sperm whale'. Rather than a turnstile wheel, it is steered by a tiller 'carved from the long narrow lower jaw of her hereditary foe'.[5] A hybrid of old ship and whalebone, it is a vessel of singular purpose and death. Reminiscent of the description of sea-ravaged derelicts and Coleridge's death ship, it is but one foreshadowing of the fate of the crew in a story full of superstitious omens and foreboding. The abnormally white Moby-Dick is not a typical sperm whale, although it remains more an exaggerated reality of a cetacean than an unnatural monster. Embodying the callously implacable power of the sea, its eventual confrontation with Ahab's crew highlights the frailty of humans and the misplaced significance of their ambitions when set against maritime nature.[6]

By contrast with Melville, Edgar Allan Poe was no mariner, though he had crossed the Atlantic as a boy in 1815 to be schooled in England for a few years. Some of his stories touched upon coastal and maritime Gothic horrors. His short story 'King Pest' (1835) is set in a plague-infested London docks, a dark, Gothic waterfront space. Two sailors on shore leave escape from a pub without paying for their drinks and hide in a quarantined part of the waterfront, a place of decay and noxious fumes. The story illustrates how among the many imports and exports that passed through ports, those important points of contact between civilization and the maritime frontier, one must include diseases from overseas. In an undertaker's shop that closely resembles the cramped space of the forecastle where common sailors lived, the two sailors encounter the embodiment of disease, King Pest, and his court of diseased grotesques, seated on piled coffins and drinking from a skull. Poe's description reads as if he were describing a satirical scene sketched by the Georgian caricaturist James Gillray. One of the sailors relates Death directly to the figure of Davy Jones. There is an overt theatricality to this strange encounter, and King Pest is revealed to be a stage actor. Underpinning the story are the contradictory views of ports. For sailors they offered temporary escape from the discipline and confinement aboard ships, and freedom to indulge in deprived pleasures. From the view of urban authorities, 'sailor town' districts, areas of ports given to the boisterous needs and entertainment of seafarers, were marked by drunken, raucous and unruly behaviour that needed to be curbed and contained.[7]

This contradiction extended to perceptions of ships and the ocean itself. Popular culture encouraged landlubbers to romanticize ships and seafaring as representative of escape, freedom and adventure. For sailors, seafaring involved navigating the endless potential of danger and misfortune, while the coast represented a return to safety, the solidity of land and an escape from harsh, authoritarian conditions. Alder's notion of the ship as a place of Gothic incarceration was demonstrated in Poe's 'The Premature Burial', in which the cramped sleeping bunks aboard ship encourage a man to dream that he has been buried alive. The association between ships and coffins is repeated in 'The Oblong Box' (1844), Poe's short story about a shipwreck near Cape Hatteras, North Carolina, another part of the ocean known as the graveyard of the Atlantic on account of the many wrecks there. This story tells of a passenger who conducts a ruse, with his dead wife stored in a coffin-like box in his staterooms while her maid pretends to be his wife in her place. When the ship is damaged in a hurricane, the man drowns, pulled beneath the waves by his having attached himself to the box containing his wife's body. The fate of the ruined vessel and the deaths incurred played to mariners' superstitions that transporting dead bodies on board ships would bring misfortune.

As a wilderness beyond civilization, the oceanic voyage represented the classic Gothic journey from the known into the unknown. In the story 'MS Found in a Bottle' (1833) the unnamed narrator's ship is driven towards the South Pole by a simoom (a hurricane combined with a sandstorm). He encounters a huge black galleon, a ship that has seemingly grown over time. With echoes of folkloric death ships, the *Flying Dutchman* and Coleridge's Ancient Mariner, it is crewed by elderly sailors who cannot see the narrator but who seem to welcome a cessation to their voyage as the ship reaches Antarctica. At the story's climax the vessel is drawn down into a whirlpool, the narrator casting his bottled manuscript into the sea at the very final moment. Poe's *The Narrative of Arthur Gordon Pym* (1838) presents a broadly similar if more developed story. A blend of travelogue and spiritual allegory, Pym's journey towards the Antarctic in the later part of the novel becomes reminiscent of the strange otherworldliness of Coleridge's poem, with a rain of ash and the appearance of a shrouded white apparition. Poe's poem 'City under the Sea' (1845, published in an earlier 1831 version as 'The Doomed City') provides a literary take on those strange, oddly illuminated underwater worlds that formed part of mariners' folkloric tales. Representative of Poe's haunting visual aesthetic, his gloomy, phantasmagorical city of the dead eventually sinks as hell rises beneath it in a red glow.[8]

Sounding the Death Knell of Maritime Folklore

The scope for literature to expand the realm of the maritime fantastic was aided by the later nineteenth-century push by educated commentators to claim that genuine belief in maritime folklore was dying out. Such 'superstitions' were, it was said, the cultural remnant of an age of sail that was fading away. This formed part of a broader denigration of folkloric beliefs in this period, a movement that took contradictory forms. On the one hand it rejected the lingering presence of such 'ignorance' and 'superstition' in a self-consciously 'modern' age. Indeed, even the idea of folklore's *lingering* traces informed the framing of the attack, used to minimize its existence and to present it as the remains of worn-out ideas that lacked contemporary relevance or vitality. Newspapers frequently referred to credulous and superstitious sailors, with articles that gently belittled mariners' (former) supernatural thinking as if they had been naive and ignorant children. On the other hand, there was a scramble to capture scraps of these supposedly archaic maritime cultural beliefs before they vanished. As W. Clarke Russell observed in the *Newcastle Weekly Courant* in 1888, the old romanticism of seafaring had been eradicated by 'steam . . . education, the march of science, and above all, Time'. For his part, he was pleased to see accompanying beliefs in mermaids, the witchcraft of Finns and supernatural omens scattered beneath the keel of his modern ship.[9]

This reference to ship design was pertinent to the argument about modern change. Steam-powered, ironclad ships were no longer beholden to the wind or the tides, nor the anxieties they had previously created. As the nature of seafaring changed, so the maritime workforce was presented as more rational and less boisterous: technologically minded mechanics whose steam engines had disconnected them from the vagaries of the sea and the elements. Stokers were the embodiment of a new maritime proletarian worker, mere appendages to an engine that had to be kept fuelled and fed. Reduced to the practical concerns of shovelling sufficient coal to keep the ship driving forward, there was less need for the old-fashioned clutter of gods, magic or omens. In 1885 the *Ladies' Treasury* claimed that modern ships had become 'almost unsinkable' and, with the removal of danger, sailors no longer continued their tradition of passing on lore that presaged good or bad fortune.[10] In the same year, Fletcher S. Bassett's *Legends and Superstitions of the Sea and Sailors* declared that mention of sea monsters or other strange maritime phenomena was now likely to provoke laughter rather than wonder, modern science having supposedly disproved such things.[11]

This narrative of the disenchanting effect of modernization has been increasingly challenged by historians.[12] As indicated time and again through the various chapters of this book, maritime supernatural beliefs did not simply disappear with the advent of steamships but persisted well into the twentieth century. The statements of nineteenth-century commentators should not be taken at face value, for they often expressed what critics wanted to happen, rather than what was happening. Proof of this is seen in the fact that one finds those critics having to repeatedly make the same claims about a decline of supernatural beliefs over several decades, such ideas proving far more tenacious and adaptable than expected in the face of 'modern' attitudes. That said, despite these historical realities, the claim that supernatural beliefs were fading was oft repeated and the perception proved persuasive, at least to those educated landlubbers who were already inclined (at least publicly) towards such a view.

Updating and Re-Imagining: Early Science Fiction and Weird Maritime Literature

The distancing of supernatural beliefs into a romanticized but disappearing age of sail seems to have encouraged writers to find new ways of re-enchanting oceanic spaces, making them fictive playgrounds for strange and fantastical encounters. This further removed the ocean as a reality, turning it into a colourful stage where its dangers and wonders could be safely consumed by armchair readers. Nineteenth-century literary speculation about strange undersea worlds that could not, at the time, be reached formed a precursor to the 'scientific romance' or science fiction that the likes of H. G. Wells would move into space at the turn of the twentieth century. Captain Nemo's submarine, *The Nautilus*, in Jules Verne's *Twenty Thousand Leagues under the Sea* (first serialized between 1869 and 1870) served as a proto-spaceship, its underwater travels a precursor to space adventures in which humans exist in hostile environments and explore strange and wondrous non-terrestrial landscapes. Yet when Nemo undertakes a nocturnal visit to the submerged temples of Atlantis, the description takes on a Gothic tone. Traversing a petrified, underwater forest with fish swimming in the branches, and surrounded by deep abysses and dark crevices containing menacing giant crustaceans and dangerous octopuses, the explorers come upon the ruined temples, arches, aqueducts and streets of Atlantis.[13] The scene is full of Gothic intensity, with eerie, melancholic ruins backlit by the plutonic, elemental force of lava burning from an underwater volcano. Nemo is held 'petrified in mute ecstasy' as he contemplates Atlantis's lost and fallen civilization. With literary theatricality, Verne even has the moonlight dimly pierce the darkness a thousand feet below the Atlantic's surface, rendering the ruins beautiful and haunting.

The late nineteenth and early twentieth century saw the flourishing of what was termed 'weird fiction'. Short stories such as Algernon Blackwood's 'The Willows' (1907) and Arthur Machen's 'The Terror' (1917) evoked environmental horrors, speaking to an unease about our relationship with nature even as marvels of modern engineering such as RMS *Titanic* were being touted as symbolic of our mastery over it. Those stories suggested that nature might possess sentience and possibly malevolence towards humans, an idea that, as we have seen, chimed with mariners' apprehensive view of the ocean. Like the Gothic before it, the weird destabilized and undermined a sense of accepted order and reality, exposing previously unrecognized but innate forces and entities that intend us harm.

A key author of the maritime weird was the Edwardian English writer William Hope Hodgson. While some of his work drew upon older tropes, such as the phantom ship that attacks a transatlantic vessel in *The Ghost Pirates* (1909), its vertical

Alphonse de Neuville, 'A walk under the waters', illustration from Jules Verne, *Twenty Thousand Leagues under the Seas* (1871).

emergence from beneath the waves, masts first, directly borrowed from the *Flying Dutchman* legends, his nautical fictions often updated the supernatural paraphernalia of maritime lore. As a literary trope, the ghost ship had become overfamiliar and rather tired. In its place, Hodgson created weird new nautical menaces, things that often took the form of voracious fungal entities and sentient moulds that transformed ships and sought to consume any seafarers who were unfortunate enough to stumble upon them. In this, they served to update the Ancient Mariner's talk of looking upon 'the rotting sea' and 'the rotting deck . . . where dead men lay'. Hodgson's nautical horror stories frequently drew readers in with the familiarity of older, maritime Gothic tales, the discovery of an old derelict in the fog or dark marking the haunting return of the past to the present. Yet having played to readers' expectations, Hodgson would then reveal his story's weird element. This usually introduce a pseudoscientific rationale, one that emphasized biological rather than supernatural monstrosities: natural lifeforms that were strangely unnatural in their actions or animation.[14]

Hodgson's 'The Stone Ship' (1914) is a haunted house story at sea. A thousand miles west of Africa, a ship encounters a strange, calcified vessel. The stone ship's unusual appearance possesses 'a certain horribleness', with one mariner commenting, 'She's a proper Davy Jones ship . . . she stinks like a corpse.' A group of mariners investigates, and the tension builds as they explore below deck and eventually discover a stone man within the transformed ship. Unease finally gets the better of them and they hurriedly leave. The story serves as a literary exercise in creating tension in which the mariners' supernatural fears initially seem justified, and then, in Scooby-Doo fashion, are torn down through a rational explanation of all we have read. The ship's calcification is explained as a result of its many years underwater, the vessel having been briefly pushed to the surface by underwater seismic activity. The strange sounds heard earlier by the mariners were sea creatures brought to the surface in the same manner, while an accompanying foul stench was that of deep-sea slime similarly cast up to the surface. Stripped of its supernatural trappings, the story leaves the reader with disturbing impressions, of the strangeness of life in the deep seas, and of the stone ship making the mariners' familiar place of work and 'home' both uncanny and otherworldly. Grotesquely transformed through the ocean's ecological powers of metamorphosis, the ship from the past returns as a stone tomb, a rare solid ruin in a watery environment that does not leave visible markers of the vessels it swallows.

The ocean's innate challenge to our 'natural' sense of space, contrasting fixed, horizontal terrestrial space dominated by human habitation with the shifting verticality of the non-human deep, may help explain why tales of the Sargasso Sea seemed to prove so enduring at this time. The legends suggested it possessed its own weird qualities, being neither quite land nor sea, but existing in a strange state beyond the ways we usually delineate, understand and therefore exert a sense of control over space. Other writers had earlier promoted the idea of the Sargasso Sea as the Atlantic's ruined graveyard of ships, but it provided a popular location for Hodgson's Atlantic weirdness.[15] Often this involves natural threats, kept hidden for most of the story so that readers are left suspended, uncertain about the weird or natural status of such dangers until near the end. Killer octopuses lurk in the Sargasso weeds in 'From the Tideless Sea' (1906) but the 'thing' in 'The Thing beneath the Weeds' (1913) is made deliberately ambiguous, its presence suggested mainly by sounds and smell as it remains concealed by both sea mist and the blanket of weeds. Only near the end is it revealed as a giant squid. 'The Boats of the "Glen Carrig"' (1907) is also set in the Sargasso Sea but is presented as a historical account written in 1757. Encountering lost wrecks caught in the weeds, huge crabs and an attack by a giant 'devil fish' (octopus), the story takes a weirder turn when the survivors of a shipwreck have to repel assaults by tentacled 'weed men'.

Mariners' lore tended to focus on surface phenomena such as weather or the sighting of natural and possibly unnatural creatures. By contrast, Hodgson's horror fiction explored a fascination with the process of bodies or ships undergoing grotesque transformations, his stories expressing a revulsion at boundaries and distinctions being dissolved, individuality lost, as our surface forms are conquered and consumed by virulent lifeforms. In doing so it spoke to the essentially alien nature of the marine environment and its transformative effects upon shipwrecks (and bodies) that had become part of underwater ecologies. Rather than terrestrial supernatural tropes adapted to maritime life, these expressions of biological weirdness formed a new way to articulate the strange, dynamic and fluid nature of the nautical world to land dwellers. Hodgson's early twentieth-century weird fictional encounters involved confrontation with the otherness of slime, mould and tentacles, things natural but radically different in their non-human qualities. In doing so, they reiterated that while the ocean served as an endless repository of wrecks, corpses, cargo and of all the human misfortune, violence and tragedy that brought them to the depths, it was its immense non-human scale and nature that imposed itself on the mind.

Hodgson had been a merchant mariner in his youth, and his nautical horror stories suggest that the experience, including possible bullying by crew members, left him with an uneasy relationship to the sea and seafaring. Nowhere is this better expressed than in his unsettling little tale 'Out of the Storm' (1909), in which the ocean itself is the malignant entity, showing its 'death-side' by sinking a ship and drowning all on board.[16] As an experienced sailor he would probably have had little trouble signing up for service in the Royal Navy during the First World War, but he clearly avoided a return to sea. Opting instead to serve as an artilleryman in the British Army, Hodgson was killed in a bombardment at Ypres, Belgium, in April 1918.

In the postwar period, other writers continued to adapt maritime folklore and express the horrors of the seas in Hodgson's fleshier, less supernatural terms. This was seen in Robert W. Sneddon's 'On the Isle of Blue Men' (1927), a tale about an attack on the inhabitants of a lighthouse in the Outer Hebrides by a horde of tentacled, froglike, blue-skinned creatures. Sneddon seems to have borrowed his slick and slimy monsters from Hebridean folklore, with the blue men of the Minch being malevolent human-sized creatures said to dwell in the strait between Scotland's Inner and Outer Hebrides, creating storms, capsizing vessels in jeopardy and drowning seafarers. The story makes much of the lighthouse as a nautical Gothic site, a beacon of light and protection yet also a point of eerie isolation at the very extremities of human civilization. Like ships, lighthouses were predominantly male working environments and it is noted that no woman had ever set foot on the island. Echoing the misogyny sometimes expressed in fishermen's lore, the lighthouse keepers disagree over a prophecy that the arrival of a red-haired woman, part of a couple seeking shelter from a storm at sea, heralds the attack of the mysterious 'blue men'.[17] Lighthouses were places of extreme solitude and isolation, with the elements likely to play tricks on the mind, fostering misperceptions and even the risk of mental instability. This may help explain their tendency to attract accounts of haunting. However, in Sneddon's story one sees the supernatural spectrality of the nineteenth-century tales continuing to give way to the more corporeal horrors of nautical weird fiction.

These earlier science fiction and weird tale influences converged in the writing of H. P. Lovecraft. Despite living in Providence, Rhode Island, for most of his life, Lovecraft's maritime stories suggest he was no great lover of the ocean. In his 1927 essay 'Supernatural Horror in Literature', Lovecraft claimed that humans have a deep, instinctual fear of the unknown, and that the success of a weird fiction tale resided in how well it fostered a sense of dread in the reader as a result of describing contact with unknown entities or powers. The thrills and chills of his cosmic horrors were built on the self-realization of humans existing on a tiny island of ignorance and frailty, surrounded by a vast, strange and potentially hostile universe. Channelling Jules Verne's emphasis on scientific plausibility mixed with Hodgson's jarring confrontation with the strange, stories such as 'Dagon', 'The Call of Cthulhu' and 'The Shadow over Innsmouth' saw Lovecraft explore the horrors of submarine extra-terrestrial or extra-dimensional monsters and amphibious entities. In these stories the oceanic depths served as a spatial substitute for the cosmic unknown, with the added jolt that the hidden horrors had been present and closer than expected for centuries.

Lovecraft's short story 'The Temple' (1925), tells of the discovery of Atlantis by a lone survivor on a crippled German U-boat in the Atlantic during the First World War. With no hope of rescue, the narrator is eventually drawn to the mysterious light and possibly imagined chanting from a huge underwater temple in the drowned city. The temple's titanic dimensions resonate with Lovecraft's later description of R'lyeh, the sunken 'corpse-city' where Cthulhu, one of the 'Great Old Ones', powerful and malevolent cosmic beings that have the status of deities, is imprisoned. Although located in the southern Pacific Ocean, R'lyeh clearly owes a debt to legendary stories of Atlantis and Lemuria. In the third part of 'The Call of Cthulhu' (1928) a series of misadventures leads a Norwegian sailor, Gustaf Johansen, and fellow crew members to discover R'lyeh, an uncharted island citadel of mud, ooze and 'Cyclopean masonry'. From within one of its 'slimy vaults' they accidentally free Cthulhu from his slumber.

Echoing Tennyson's description of the Kraken, this 'gelatinous green immensity' instantly dispatches three unfortunate mariners, and another goes mad at the sight of the gigantic creature. Johansen uses the vessel on which they arrived to ram Cthulhu, then escapes in a delirium. Eventually rescued, he is left scarred by memories of the encounter. R'lyeh sinks back beneath the waves, supposedly trapping Cthulhu once again, for if it had freed itself, Lovecraft tells us, 'the world would by now be screaming with fright and frenzy.'[18] A key story in Lovecraft's Cthulhu mythos, its sense of dread arises from our understanding of the world being violently ruptured by this brief marine revelation. Humanity is confronted not just with the existence of a frighteningly powerful entity but also the larger ramifications of what its presence on Earth means, in terms of both a radically altered understanding of the past and an ominous future. Like Tennyson's Kraken, Lovecraft's Cthulhu embodies not just our fear of the unknown but the unknowable, each possessing an inscrutable, inhuman patience as they wait for the apocalypse.

Lovecraft's maritime tales could also offer more insidious horrors too. In 'The Shadow over Innsmouth' (1936) the town's humanity has been corrupted by interbreeding with amphibious sea creatures. Like Hodgson's fungal horrors, the story indulges in the revulsion of slow bodily transformation, with humans succumbing to the influence of more virile lifeforms that turn them away from the land and towards the seas. The inhabitants of Innsmouth serve as an unsettling reminder of our amphibious ancestry, of that now alien form that once enabled land-based life to move from its origins in the sea.[19] These maritime stories marked a significant break from the nautical Gothic of the nineteenth century, dispensing with the supernatural in favour of purely evolutionary and secular threats. Cthulhu is a twentieth-century Leviathan in a world in which there is no benevolent God to vanquish it. Just as Jules Verne's story of the ocean provided a precursor for space stories, so in turn the horror of Lovecraft's cosmic powerlessness and inferiority in the face of ancient beings echoes the age-old awareness of human insignificance when confronted by the ocean.

From a point of relative obscurity at the time of his death in 1937, Lovecraft's dark star has continued to rise over twentieth and especially twenty-first century horror and science fiction. Cthulhu has become a touchstone word and symbol for an intelligent, alien monstrosity that compels us to come to terms with a radically de-centred view of our place in the world. Confronted with the power of such non-human entities, we are dethroned from our own self-importance, realizing that neither the world nor our place in it is as we have long assumed it to be. Clearly inspired by Lovecraft's work, more recent authors have created better written, character-driven stories. Good on monstrous threats and big ideas, Lovecraft never really seemed to care much for the anaemically sketched human characters who encountered them. By contrast, Caitlin R. Kiernan's *Andromeda Among the Stones* (2003) and *Houses Under the Sea* (2006) and John Langan's *The Fisherman* (2016) draw upon similar ideas of sea gods, amphibious transformation or huge sea monsters to tell disturbing, fantastical, but also poignantly human tales.

The shift of the maritime fantastical from the supernatural to science fiction continued into the second half of the twentieth century. Prior to twenty-first-century popular culture's burgeoning appetite for stories of magic and folklore, this was the predominant way in which sea monsters and other encounters with the maritime unknown were reframed and rationalized. John Wyndham's *The Kraken Wakes* (1953) took its title from Tennyson's poem but was inspired more by its apocalyptic theme than the monster itself, for there is no Kraken in this science-fiction novel. The story opens with strange fireballs streaking into our atmosphere and disappearing into the deepest parts of the earth's oceans. From there the novel evolves into an maritime version of H. G. Wells's *War of the Worlds.* First, the aliens attack ships and drive humans off the seas. Then they begin to make incursions on coastal communities in strange biological rather than mechanical 'sea tanks', dragging their unfortunate captives beneath the waves. Humanity's collective resistance is weakened by Cold War suspicions. When they eventually start to have success in repelling the invaders, the aliens melt the polar ice caps, causing sea levels to rise. Cities and countries are flooded, and human society breaks down as those who have lost their homes scramble to take and defend higher ground. With our increasing concern about global warming and rising sea levels, the book's final depictions of humanity's struggles in the face of submerged landmasses have acquired a disturbingly prophetic note, a grim vision of the future in which we may not require alien invaders to bring about similar catastrophe.[20]

Cinema, Sea Monsters and the Return of the Supernatural

Literature's power to perpetuate and reinvent the fantastical elements of maritime lore and oral legend was eclipsed by the development of film as the twentieth century's most pervasive form of mass culture. This was evident early on in cinematic history. Georges Méliès, a French pioneer of early twentieth-century cinema, produced an underwater fantasy extravaganza in his 1907 *Under the Seas* (*Deux Cents Milles sous les mers ou le Cauchemar du pêcheur*). Méliès' cinematic work had a strong inclination towards fantasy, fairy tales and science fiction, and this fourteen-minute silent film depicts the undersea dreams of a fisherman, squeezing in encounters with mermaids, sea monsters, naiads and nymphs.

While cinema has drawn upon all aspects of the maritime supernatural imaginary explored in previous chapters, some have proved to have a more enduring appeal than others, and none more so than sea monsters. This comes as little surprise. As seen with the later nineteenth-century publication of sea serpent images, giant monsters possessed the greatest visual spectacle. As they usually remain unseen at first, audiences' imaginations are typically teased by witnessing the creature's destructive power in the form of wrecked ships, or its aftermath in the huge footprints left amid tornado-like destruction. Having been allowed to build in the mind, the cinematic payoff arrives when the monster finally comes ashore, and audiences are treated to the spectacular reveal.

As part of the 1950s fad for 'creature features', sea monsters often spoke to new anxieties about radiation and its environmental impact in the atomic age. *The Beast from 20,000 Fathoms* (1953) fused the science fiction, horror and action genres in a way that would often be replicated when it came to cinematic monsters from the deep. Based on Ray Bradbury's short story 'The Fog Horn', the film tells of a dinosaur released from its frozen state by the testing of an atom bomb in the Arctic Circle. The creature travels back to its old spawning ground in what has become

Production still from *Under the Seas* (1907, dir. Georges Méliès).

mid-twentieth-century New York. It gave rise to innumerable films in which ancient creatures are freed or natural creatures are mutated into gigantic monsters by human recklessness, after humans test atom bombs with little thought for the fauna in the region. Underlying this was often a concern about the dangers of scientific and military technology, although individual scientists or servicemen were typically the heroes who ultimately save the day.

Timothy Beale notes how, once a movie monster is understood by science, its days are numbered. Often initially presented through legends or its worship as a sea god by geographically remote or non-Western communities, once the monster is fitted into a rational, naturalized framework, scientific ingenuity can be brought to bear on stopping it. As Arnold Schwarzenegger's character in *Predator* declares, 'If it bleeds, we can kill it.' As with the fate of the Kraken in the nineteenth century, once the monster is turned from mythic beast to natural lifeform, both its status and the fear it evokes is diminished. The unfortunate message that frequently derives from such a narrative is a celebration of human science and knowledge, an attitude that risks reinforcing the hubris that led to the monster being disturbed or released in the first place.[21]

The idea of monsters freed or created by atomic testing was made popular by *Godzilla*. Originally a Japanese film (*Gojira*, 1954), an Americanized version followed in 1956. At least initially, Godzilla, an irradiated reptilian monster with radioactive breath, embodied the destructive force of the atomic bomb. Given the horrors of Hiroshima and Nagasaki, it spoke to a deep unease about that destructive power now held in the hands of mere mortals. An Atomic Age offspring of the mighty Kraken, Godzilla came to illustrate the positive and negative potential of nuclear power, variously adopting the role of titanic threat or heroic defender of humanity, battling other gigantic foes on our behalf.

The 1961 British film *Gorgo* (1961), featuring a sea monster captured off the west coast of Ireland, was clearly influenced by the success of Godzilla. Rather than the freakish byproduct of nuclear fallout, this is a cryptozoological beast that harks back to ancient legend. It is taken to London, where it is put on display for commercial gain. The story twist comes when its even larger mother arrives to free it from captivity. The film encourages a degree of sympathy for the monsters. The mother tears up London to find its child but, once reunited, they leave, impervious to the pathetic weapons of the military. Once again, the hubris of humans who thoughtlessly chain monsters with the goal of turning them into profitable spectacles raises questions about our own callousness. We, these films suggest, mistakenly see the world and its creatures as ours to use as we wish. Monster movies serve as pushback, a violent reminder that they are not, and that our intrusion, ambition, assumptions and shortsightedness will have consequences. Like Lovecraft's earlier science-fiction horrors, cinematic sea monsters work to unsettle our assumptions about a human-dominated status quo.

Godzilla's repeated returns may have been motivated by a desire to grind more money out of a popular cultural icon, but the films unintentionally illustrate how underlying anxieties, whether about nuclear power or ecological concerns, can never be neatly or decisively resolved. If sea monster films were intended as ways of vicariously exorcising our fears about such horrors, they often seem to encourage the wrong message. The onus is nearly always on resisting the intrusion of the monstrous, revelling in its destruction and having the threatened status quo restored before the end credits, a status quo that resembles that which exists outside the cinema. In winning, we blunder on as before, blinded by victory and basking in our own ingenuity. When we fail to attend to the larger underlying eco-message that the film may have slipped in, the regained sense of security encourages us to ignore the anxieties or guilt that the monster expressed, thereby denying that such things are baked into that status quo. The symbol may be temporarily destroyed, but the issues that it symbolizes, be it technological or ecological concerns, have not gone away. If monster movies play out our attempt to measure our power against the non-human world, then, by default, we view that relationship in terms of confrontation, us or it, rather than recognizing our part in its release or creation.

This is seen in Roland Emmerich and Dean Devlin's blockbuster *Godzilla* (1998). New York frequently serves as a symbolic shorthand for Western capitalism, culture and complacency in American science-fiction films, and Emerich repeatedly destroyed it in a series of apocalyptic movies in the late 1990s and early 2000s.[22] After Manhattan is trashed, the film ends with the reassuring defeat of the giant reptile, albeit with its subterranean hidden eggs holding out the possibility of a sequel if it had been more successful. Although an almost direct repeat of *Godzilla*'s basic premise, *Cloverfield* (2008) was far edgier in its willingness to entertain less certain outcomes. The colossal, misshapen monster that emerges from the ocean is still cutting a path of destruction through New York when the 'found film' movie ends.

Other marine monster films have tended to stick with presenting them as scientific mutations or extra-terrestrial life forms, a more acceptable way of framing them for later twentieth-century audiences who had come to understand the supernatural as something largely confined to the cultural margins. There was a notable flurry of underwater science-fiction horror films set in the Atlantic at the end of the 1980s, with *Leviathan* (1989), *DeepStar Six* (1989) and *The Rift* (1990) all arriving in cinemas or on video in short succession. The most high-profile submarine film of that year, *The Abyss* (1989), avoided schlocky horror for an underwater take on *Close Encounters of the Third Kind* (1977). Such Atlantic-based horrors have continued into the present with *Sea*

Fever (2019), its story of sea monster larvae and bodily infection obtaining an additional and unintended resonance as the world was beset by COVID-19. While sea monster movies have proven adept at reflecting our evolving cultural and environmental concerns, they continually articulate a sense of the primeval force of marine nature and our sense of vulnerability before it.

More overtly supernatural tales such as ghost ship films have proven less adaptable, essentially serving as floating haunted house stories. In this they speak to eighteenth- and nineteenth-century mariners' sense of ships not as a means of freedom but as a place of prolonged incarceration from which there is no easy escape. Despite the obvious title, *Ghost Ship* (1952), a British film directed by Vernon Sewell and set in the English Channel, was more a thriller than ghost story, although it contains some supernatural elements, including an onboard séance. More of a direct update was *Death Ship* (1980). Set in the Caribbean, it involved a cruise ship's collision with a mysterious freighter, a derelict vessel that is revealed to be a haunted Nazi torture ship. Perhaps most notable in recent years is Netflix's *1899* (2022). Set aboard a ship taking immigrants across the Atlantic to New York, the series plays to traditions of maritime haunting and weirdness before gradually morphing, once again, into science fiction.

Given how we had become conditioned to thinking of seafaring horrors and the maritime fantastical through a science-fictional framing, the return of old-fashioned maritime folklore in the historical fantasy franchise *Pirates of the Caribbean* came, at least initially, as something of a pleasant surprise. The distance of its vaguely eighteenth-century setting allowed audiences to re-engage with nautical supernatural lore, safe in the knowledge that such beliefs have long since passed. The franchise indulges in an array of supernatural lore and legend purloined from maritime folklore and pirate literature. The five films (to date) feature cursed treasure, magical objects, undead pirates, the Kraken, Davy Jones (and a visit to his locker), a sorceress-turned-sea-goddess, mermaids, vengeful ghosts and two separate love stories woven around the *Flying Dutchman* legend. If Davy Jones's tentacled face owes something to Lovecraft's Cthulhu, his undead crew's physical transformation as a result of service aboard the *Flying Dutchman* – their bodies becoming increasingly adorned with starfish, barnacles, shells, gills or shark fins – offers a nod to Hodgson's weird fungal horrors. Hybrids of land and sea, man and fish, they are also a mélange of maritime folklore and weird literature. This rich banquet of maritime supernatural fantasy is made digestible by the comic tone set by Johnny Depp's Captain Jack Sparrow, variously a daring swashbuckler and a cowardly rogue who sashays around like a drunken catwalk model. Mockingly aware of earlier swashbuckling films, *Pirates*' embracing of supernatural motifs and maritime folklore seemed to be a key ingredient in enabling its box office success when more conventional predecessors such as *Cutthroat Island* (1995) had flopped.

Beneath the fun, there is a problematic exoticizing of the Caribbean in the franchise. Despite a European colonial presence, the world of the *Pirates* films is clearly positioned on the margins of civilization, far removed from the influence of the Enlightenment. It is home to a lively outlaw culture of hedonistic excess, a place where roguish individuals value the old oral knowledge of legends and the power of creolized magical beliefs. The message, it seems, is that only on the far side of the Atlantic, far from the heartland of modernizing Europe, in a place that mixes Black and white cultures, can the maritime supernatural flourish and be indulged.[23]

This depiction forms part of an older Hollywood tradition of 'othering' Caribbean cultures and spaces, best seen in earlier zombie films set in Haiti. Unlike the roaming hordes of zombies that have been let loose on cinema and television since George

Romero's seminal *Night of the Living Dead* (1968), these earlier films focused on the issue of masters, control and loss of agency. In the context of the Caribbean, this made the zombie a powerful metaphor for slavery and colonialism, while the use of voodoo to turn people into zombies reinforced associations between Black and creole cultures and derogatory ideas about 'backward' supernatural beliefs. Interestingly, two such films, *White Zombie* (1932) and *I Walked with a Zombie* (1943), both tell of white women being controlled through voodoo and zombification by white men. While *White Zombie* features both Black and white zombified labourers as minor, passing screen presences, its story suggests that it was deemed less problematic to present the control of white women than Black men in the 1930s. The film's melodramatic storyline certainly fits with a longer, nineteenth-century literary tradition of villainous men using supernatural powers to control women. Still, one is struck by the lack of Black characters in *White Zombie*. Racial difference is almost erased in its white depiction of Haitian society. It may not have been that race was avoided so much as rendered invisible.[24]

If *Pirates of the Caribbean* reconnected modern cinema audiences with nautical supernatural ideas, *The Lighthouse* (2019) provided one of the most visually powerful representations of the maritime weird in recent cinema. Set on a New England island in the 1890s, it captures the strange, imprisoned experience of nineteenth-century lighthouse keepers. The audience is beset with bleak, disturbing and surreal black-and-white images, of forlorn landscapes, mermaids and tentacular horrors (again), of old superstitions surrounding the ill fortune that comes from killing seabirds, and of the claustrophobic descent into insanity. It is, the film suggests, at the very geographical fringes of civilization, at the psychological limits of isolation, where maritime horrors come lapping ashore.

Playing with Monsters: The Atlantic as a Fictional Space

In ending, we return to giant monsters, for the cinema screen seems to delight in their outlandish size and scale. The Kraken has returned to its classical origins and the Mediterranean in *Clash of the Titans*, appearing in both the 1981 original and, considerably enlarged, in the 2010 remake. It also had a key role as a gigantic, tentacular menace in *Pirates of the Caribbean: Dead Man's Chest* (2006). The enormous size that had once ruled it out as a zoological reality has, in time, become the very thing that appeals when it is employed as spectacular cinematic effect towards a film's climax. Via the nineteenth-century's solidifying of its association with giant cephalopods, and, perhaps more significantly, the gradual saturation of Lovecraftian horror within modern mass culture, the Kraken has come to haunt the screen more than any other sea monster. While the Kraken was not traditionally understood as tentacular, being more associated with disappearing islands or else deemed indescribable due to its incredible size, it has become so now. The Kraken's tentacles have become the symbol of marine alterity and monstrosity, different not just to human limbs but to all other animal appendages such as wings or fins. Throughout its long transition from myth and legend to poetry, weird fiction and film, the Kraken has always spilled beyond our ability to conceptualize it in its entirety, its form never fully revealed, its nature and purpose always remaining unknown. In this, it continues to serve as a monstrous metaphor for the fearsome ocean itself.

This shift towards using older supernatural and monstrous tropes purely as entertainment is illustrative of land dwellers' increasing detachment from the reality of the ocean. Nineteenth-century industrialized nations such as France and Britain may have seen the rise of the seaside resort as a healthy holiday break from crowded, polluted towns and cities, but even these made the ocean remote. Seaside towns were about pleasant beaches and coastal vistas, the immediate shoreline, not the raw and turbulent vastness of open waters. The nineteenth century saw successive waves of transatlantic migration from Europe to the United States, with numbers reaching a peak in 1907. However, one imagines that, for most, attention was more on the destination than the ocean between, a monotonous steam-powered trudge to fresh starts and imagined opportunities ashore. Later, once the ocean became subject to industrialized processes of food harvesting, consumers were required to give little thought to where such food came from. It was the very remoteness of the ocean from our daily lives and concerns that has enabled it to be imagined as a fantastical space, a process that furthered that sense of detachment. The draw of the vast ocean and the unknown deep remains, but its otherness and unknowability has been repeatedly reframed over time, turning from the supernatural and the Gothic to the weird and the science fictional. Rather than one form of presentation wholly superseding the former, it has led to an expansion of the way we imagine oceanic spaces and their inhabitants. As a result, the Atlantic is once again full of monsters, as full as when Olaus Magnus first created his Carta Marina map, but now it is pixelated, distributed and widely consumed as part of a popular culture that is enduringly fascinated by the fantastical.

This marks a shift from previous chapters, where the possibility of supernatural occurrences, magical powers and monstrous creatures was entertained as real, for practical purposes, at least by some. Of course, there was always a knowingness to maritime folklore too, with personal investment in its content and ideas existing on an ever-shifting spectrum from belief, through amusing entertainment, to its dismissal as ignorant nonsense. Over time, the tantalizing possibility of its reality has eroded as its practical functions have faded. Now, film audiences suspend disbelief, indulging the Kraken or Godzilla onscreen because we know they do not exist, or exist only as part of an imaginative projection onto the Atlantic. They have changed from folklore to what Michael Dylan Foster has termed the 'folkloresque', a popular cultural perception, presentation or performance of folklore, rather than folklore itself.[25]

Where mythology once made the seas and oceans supernatural through personifying them as gods and goddesses, framing them so as to reflect human nature, the literary and cinematic trends of the past two centuries have posited a popular reframing of the oceans as non-human and alien. Storytelling, once mariners' way of connecting to and explaining the oceanic environment, has in recent centuries encouraged our distancing from it, turning it into a fictive space where we never need to get our feet wet. At the same time, as blue and green environmental issues become ever more pressing, our previous relationship to the maritime world has also shifted. Where once sailors constructed an elaborate web of nautical folklore, legend, practices and beliefs to offset the sense of vulnerability caused by a lack of control over the ocean, now we are confronted with the unease of our excessive and uncontrolled effects upon it. Such circumstances call for new types of stories to reconnect us to the oceans, or for us to recognize new insights long buried in the depths of older maritime tales.

Epilogue: Past Tides and Future Shores

We have long understood the oceanic world through storytelling, and as a place saturated with stories. It was in such ways that our ancestors granted it sentience or created humanlike deities that explained its turbulent nature. They told of ghosts upon its surface and huge monsters, strange aquatic beings and lost realms in its depths. They also told of magical protections, ritual observances and how to recognize omens in the marine environment, signs that granted insight into seafarers' fortunes and fate. Such stories encouraged a fragile sense of human influence on but never over the ocean. In doing so, those narratives shifted the ocean from something wholly natural and oblivious to humankind, to something that appeared responsive to our actions and understandable from our human perspective. Viewed through the lens of our own image, human qualities were imprinted on sea goddesses and seals, winds and waves. Even its surface and depth were readily appropriated as metaphors for our conscious and subconscious mind. To borrow an analogy from the French anthropologist Claude Lévi-Strauss, we took the raw natural existence of the ocean and culturally cooked it into something we could digest.[1]

Although always intrigued by seafarers' richly imaginative engagement with the ocean, landlubbers have long had the luxury of feeling remote from such concerns, and that sense of detachment has only increased over time. Secure in our sense of modern technological progress, there is a tendency to view the maritime supernatural worldview explored here as a quaint imaginative relic of a former age. Our detachment from the ocean has made us complacent, neglectful and blind, largely oblivious to the fact that over 90 per cent of our global trade is still conducted by maritime shipping.[2] Whereas the implacably callous ocean once prompted fear, for most people today it is a distant and largely imagined spectacle, a site of monster-movie fictions, a place to play on a beach holiday, an environmental news story or a beautiful television documentary at best. Yet now we face new maritime anxieties, born of changes in which we are implicated, fears that force us to realize that we are not as detached from the ocean as we thought.

Our previous search for magical influence over the capricious forces of nature has been far surpassed by our more prosaic impact upon the ocean. Once its seemingly vast and limitless power engendered notions of our trespass upon realms of sea gods and goddesses. Since the late twentieth century, and with increasing volume, we have begun to tell a very different narrative, of how our assumed mastery of nature has led to us having a detrimental effect on the planet. The past two hundred years of industrialization has forced the oceans to absorb 525 billion tons of carbon dioxide emissions resulting from the increased burning of fossil fuels, a figure that amounts to almost half of all such emissions in that period. If that were not bad enough, the chemical reaction of such vast amounts of carbon dioxide with sea water has gradually altered the oceans' pH levels, resulting in them becoming more acidic in that same two hundred years. In addition, the oceans have had to absorb much of the heat produced by greenhouse gases, with warming water being pushed to ever-greater depths. The Atlantic, like the other major oceans of the world, is subject to melting polar ice and the threat of rising sea levels, overfishing, plastic and chemical pollution, and the disruption or destruction of underwater ecosystems.[3] Accompanying an awareness of our impact on the oceans is the concern that such transformations may now be beyond our control. Unlike the struggle faced by seafarers for centuries, our fight is no longer simply against the ocean but increasingly for it.

These are some of the marine features of what has been termed the Anthropocene, an unofficial term coined in the 1980s but popularized since the 2000s, in which the modern era is defined by the impact that human activity has had on the planet's complex ecosystems. Yet even this term presents an odd amalgam of human hubris, responsibility and guilt, one in which we both stand apart from and understand ourselves as having a deleterious effect upon nature. In considering that relationship, we can take our pick of analogies from that rich body of maritime lore and legend that accompanied the advent of the modern age. We have become the monsters. Our industrialized exploitation of the seas is the modern Kraken guzzling up resources. We are the arrogant Vanderdecken of the *Flying Dutchman*, ignoring warnings, unable to escape the haunting legacy of our previous actions but forced to look to a future made from their consequences. We may want to point fingers at various Jonahs, but we know this is the result of more than just one convenient scapegoat. We are all complicit, aspiring to or unwilling to give up lifestyles that come with environmental costs we bill to the future. As with the drowned revenants who haunted the shoreline, it will be our coastal communities who first bear witness to the tragedies and threats returned by the sea. The Anthropocene even evokes the classic Gothic trope of suppressed guilt or horrors creeping back or resurfacing, the past's curse falling upon the present, the present's inaction casting a long shadow over the future.

Such grim ideas may invite us to sink into a fatalistic abyss, a Charybdis of existential angst. However, the stories and beliefs explored in this book provide us with a different message, urge a different response. The ocean prompted fear of both natural and supernatural dangers, but it was how mariners responded that was important. Magic, omens and observances engendered a feeling of protection, influence and foresight. Nautical tales imparted a sense of knowledge, insight and understanding of the ocean's secret nature. Regardless of the efficacy of magical charms and practices, or whether supernatural tales were more fiction than fact, magic and storytelling enabled mariners to operate and endure at sea, to have at least some sense of agency in conditions that made them all too aware of their vulnerability and insignificance. The marine environment unquestionably stirred apprehension in seafarers and anxiety in their loved ones back home, but, ultimately, this book can be understood as a history of hope as much as fear.

This previous seafaring mentality can usefully be taken as a means of approaching the future too. Magic and storytelling alone will not save us from the environmental changes that we are helping to bring about, but the underlying qualities and attitudes to which they spoke might. Hope, will, adaptability and endurance, the bones beneath the skin of magical beliefs and supernatural observances, are powerful psychological resources. For mariners, this was alloyed to a need to work collectively and, especially in the age of sail, to be responsive to the caprices of nature. This is not to suggest that mariners were proto-environmentalists, although they were certainly attuned to and highly observant of all manner of meteorological changes in the marine environment. For the most part, they were labourers toiling with and against the ocean to complete their work and return home safely. In the face of dangers and the ocean's long history of shipwreck and loss, it was about mentally armouring themselves, their actions and supernatural knowledge affording faith in a better outcome and a safer passage than the unfortunates who went before. Such attitudes did not allow the weight of the past to submerge the prospects of a better future. Of course, such hopes were not always fulfilled, and the ocean continued to take its share of lives and ships. But mariners' hope was not a vague or wishy-washy brand of optimism, for it was tempered by action: a hope not simply derived from wishing but from doing. We too need to do, rather than continually deferring action and change to an imagined future.

With a mariner's pragmatism, we must also accept that trying to hold on to a presumed environmental status quo is an illusion, for like the tides all is in flux. We can try to navigate the flow or fight against it. In the Anthropocene era, the world has become a ship, one that requires us to work collectively, as crews did, if we are to advance beyond our current and seemingly unending stupor of environmental anxiety. Rather than simply viewing the ocean as a monstrous threat, perhaps we would be better served by recognizing its potential as what Robin Kundis Craig and Jeffrey Mathes McCarthy term 'a medium of connectedness . . . an agent of mutual transformation', one that can promote alliances, collaboration and resilience.[4]

This book has shown how generations of mariners pitted themselves against the fear and challenges of the ocean with courage and a sensitivity to the marine environment around them. Maritime storytelling and an accompanying net of magical and supernatural beliefs provided a way of expressing, sharing and communicating both concerns and curiosity. Talk of gods, ghosts, mermaids and monsters served to articulate thoughts and feelings stirred by an oceanic wilderness that exerted a powerful psychological impact upon those who moved through it. Much maritime magic and folklore was about negotiation, adaptation and vigilance, looking to signs in nature and adjusting behaviours accordingly to avoid misfortune and enhance the chances of survival. While stories of the Kraken suggested it was too large or incomprehensible ever to be overcome by human efforts, those same tales also offered instruction as to how seafarers might survive and even co-exist with such a frightening beast. Such ideas may seem fanciful now, colourful if somewhat salty fragments of a fantastical imagination from a previous age. Yet we should not be so quick to dismiss them or the value they may still possess. Beneath all the barnaclelike accrual of magic, marvels and monsters, those seafaring attitudes can still teach us how to confront our own environmental fears as we attempt to navigate the turbulent currents of an uncertain future, seeking its unknown shores.

REFERENCES

Introduction: Casting Off

1 Jerry Foster, 'Varieties of Sea Lore', *Western Folklore*, XXVIII/4 (1969), pp. 260–66.
2 See Gillian Bennett, 'Geologists and Folklorists: Cultural Evolution and "The Science of Folklore"', *Folklore*, CV (1994), pp. 25–37.
3 William Jones, *Credulities Past and Present, Including the Sea and Seamen, Miners, Amulets and Talismans, Rings, Word and Letter Divination, Numbers, Trials, Exorcising and Blessing of Animals, Birds, Eggs, and Luck* (London, 1880), pp. 6–7.
4 For an example, see 'Sailors' Superstitions Defy the Age of Reason', *New York Times*, 5 August 1923.
5 See, for example, Marcus Rediker, *Between the Devil and the Deep Blue Sea: Merchant Seamen, Pirates and the Anglo-American Maritime World, 1700–1750* (Cambridge, 1987); Brian J. Rouleau, 'Dead Men Do Tell Tales: Folklore, Fraternity and the Forecastle', *Early American Studies*, V/1 (2007), pp. 30–62; and David M. Hopkin, 'Storytelling and Networking in a Breton Fishing Village, 1879–1882', *International Journal of Maritime History*, XVII/2 (2005), pp. 113–39.

1: Seafaring and Sea Fearing

1 'Storm Tossed Sons of the Ocean', *Huddersfield Chronicle*, 10 December 1873, p. 3.
2 David M. Hopkin, 'Storytelling and Networking in a Breton Fishing Village, 1879–1882', *International Journal of Maritime History*, XVII/2 (2005), p. 121, and Daniel Vickers with Vince Walsh, *Young Men and the Sea: Yankee Seafarers in the Age of Sail* (New Haven, CT, 2005), p. 108.
3 Edmund Burke, 'A Philosophical Enquiry into the Origins of Our Ideas of the Sublime and Beautiful', in *The Works of the Right Honourable Edmund Burke*, vol. I (London, 1887), pp. 111 and 132.
4 Frederick E. Bolton, 'Hydro-Psychosis', *American Journal of Psychology*, X/2 (1899), pp. 216–19.

5 Alan J. Jamieson, Glenn Singleman, Thomas D. Linley and Susan Casey, 'Why Don't People Care about the Deep Sea: Fear and Loathing', *ICES Journal of Marine Science*, LXXVIII/3 (2020), p. 799.
6 William Chase Greene, 'The Sea in the Greek Poets', *North American Review*, CXCIX/700 (1914), pp. 429 and 430.
7 Ibid., pp. 432 and 443.
8 William Jones, *Credulities Past and Present, Including the Sea and Seamen, Miners, Amulets and Talismans, Rings, Word and Letter Divination, Numbers, Trials, Exorcising and Blessing of Animals, Birds, Eggs, and Luck* (London, 1880), p. 1.
9 Christopher P. Magra, 'Faith at Sea: Exploring Maritime Religiosity in the Eighteenth Century', *International Journal of Maritime History*, XIX/1 (2007), p. 97.
10 David Vincent, *Literacy and Popular Culture: England, 1750–1914* (Cambridge, 1989), pp. 64–5.
11 Psalm 107, verses 23–30, King James Bible.
12 Thomas Smith, *A Practical Discourse to Sea-Faring Men: Preached in Falmouth, First Parish, Lord's-Day, April 28th 1771* (Boston, MA, 1771).
13 Magra, 'Faith at Sea', pp. 97–100, and Jones, *Credulities Past and Present*, p. 39.
14 Amy Mitchell-Cook, *A Sea of Misadventures: Shipwreck and Survival in Early America* (Columbia, SC, 2014), pp. 4–5.
15 Magra, 'Faith at Sea', pp. 88–9.
16 Tim Flannery, ed., *The Life and Adventures of John Nicol, Mariner* (New York, 1997), pp. 147–50, and Magra, 'Faith at Sea', pp. 104–5.
17 R. L. Hadfield, *The Phantom Ship and Other Ghost Stories of the Sea* (London, 1937), pp. 172–3 and 179.
18 Ibid., p. 67, and Horace Beck, *Folklore and the Sea* (Mystic, CT, 2005), pp. 474–5.
19 'Davy Jones's Locker', *All the Year Round*, 23 November 1889, pp. 498–500.
20 Tobias Smollett, 'The Adventures of Peregrine Pickle', in *The Novels of Tobias Smollett* (London, 1821), p. 227.
21 Hadfield, *The Phantom Ship*, p. 173.
22 James Montgomery, ed., *Journal of Voyages and Travels by the Rev. Daniel Tyerman and George Bennet, Esq: Deputed from the London Missionary Society, to Visit Their Various Stations in the South Sea Islands, China, India, &c. between the Years 1821 and 1829*, vol. I (Boston, MA, 1832), pp. 23–4.
23 David Cashman, 'King Neptune, the Mermaids, and the Cruise Tourists: The Line-Crossing Ceremony in Modern Passenger Shipping', *Coolabah*, 27 (2019), pp. 90–105.
24 J. A. Teit, 'Water-Beings in Shetlandic Folk-Lore, as Remembered by Shetlanders in British Columbia', *Journal of American Folk-Lore*, XXXI/120 (1918), pp. 196 and 200.

25 Christina Hole, 'Superstitions and Beliefs of the Sea', *Folklore*, LXXVIII/3 (1967), p. 184.
26 Angelo S. Rappoport, *Superstitions of Sailors* (London, 1928), p. 134.
27 Jones, *Credulities Past and Present*, p. 7.
28 Hole, 'Superstitions and Beliefs', p. 187.
29 'Storm Tossed Sons of the Ocean', *Huddersfield Chronicle*, 10 December 1873, p. 3.
30 'The Superstitions of Sailors', *Bristol Mercury*, 2 June 1855, p. 6.
31 See Isaac Land, *War, Nationalism, and the British Sailor, 1750–1850* (Basingstoke, 2009); Mary Conley, *From Jack Tar to Union Jack: Representing Naval Manhood in the British Empire, 1870–1918* (Manchester, 2017); and Brad Beaven, '"One of the Toughest Streets in the World": Exploring Male Violence, Class and Ethnicity in London's Sailortown, 1850–1880', *Social History*, XLVI/1 (2021), pp. 1–21.
32 Marcus Rediker, *Between the Devil and the Deep Blue Sea: Merchant Seamen, Pirates and the Anglo-American Maritime World, 1700–1750* (Cambridge, 1987), p. 179.
33 Marion Bowman, 'Vernacular Religion and Nature: The "Bible of the Folk" Tradition in Newfoundland', *Folklore*, CXIV/3 (2003), p. 288.
34 See Brian J. Rouleau, 'Dead Men Do Tell Tales: Folklore, Fraternity and the Forecastle', *Early American Studies*, V/1 (2007), pp. 30–62.
35 Magra, 'Faith at Sea', p. 93.
36 Hopkin, 'Storytelling and Networking', pp. 129–30 and 133.
37 David Hopkin, 'Storytelling, Fairytales and Autobiography: Some Observations on Eighteenth- and Nineteenth-Century French Soldiers' and Sailors' Memoirs', *Social History*, XXIX/2 (2004), p. 187.
38 Críostóir Mac Cárthaigh, 'The Cultural Context of Legend Telling in a West Kerry Fishing Community', *Folk Life*, LV/2 (2017), pp. 151–66.
39 Rouleau, 'Dead Men Do Tell Tales', p. 54.
40 Hopkin, 'Storytelling and Networking', p. 131.
41 W. B. Yeats, *The Celtic Twilight* (London, 2018), p. 135.
42 Hopkin, 'Storytelling and Networking', pp. 129 and 131. For more on the social and political role of telling fairy tales, see Jack Zipes, *Breaking the Magic Spell: Radical Theories of Folk and Fairy Tales* (Lexington, KY, 2002).
43 Hopkin, 'Storytelling, Fairytales and Autobiography', p. 197.
44 Kelby Rose, 'Nostalgia and Imagination in Nineteenth-Century Sea Shanties', *Mariner's Mirror*, XCVIII/2 (2012), pp. 147–60.
45 Charles Tyng, *Before the Wind: The Memoir of an American Sea Captain, 1808–1833* (New York, 2000), pp. 57–9.
46 'A Strange and Deplorable Coincidence', *Western Mail*, 31 October 1870, p. 2.
47 Hadfield, *The Phantom Ship*, p. 23.

2: Maritime Magic and Omens

1 Peter McIntosh, *History of Kintyre*, 3rd edn (Campbeltown, 1870), pp. 21–2. See also Richard M. Dorson, *Buying the Wind: Regional Folklore in the United States* (Chicago, IL, 1964), pp. 32–5.
2 Sir Walter Scott, *Rokeby; A Poem in Six Cantos* (Edinburgh, 1813), p. 70.
3 'Sailors' Superstitions Defy the Age of Reason', *New York Times*, 5 August 1923.
4 Thomas Waters, *Cursed Britain: A History of Witchcraft and Black Magic in Modern Times* (New Haven, CT, 2019), p. 133. See the online catalogue of the Museum of Witchcraft and Magic, Boscastle, for examples of maritime magical charms.
5 William Jones, *Credulities Past and Present, Including the Sea and Seamen, Miners, Amulets and Talismans, Rings, Word and Letter Divination, Numbers, Trials, Exorcising and Blessing of Animals, Birds, Eggs, and Luck* (London, 1880), p. 112.
6 Anon., 'The Belief in Charms', *Folklore*, XXVIII/1 (1917), pp. 98–9, and Owen Davies, *Supernatural War: Magic, Divination, and Faith During the First World War* (Oxford, 2019), pp. 148–9.
7 Christina Hole, 'Superstitions and Beliefs of the Sea', *Folklore*, LXXVIII/3 (1967), p. 186.
8 Richard Esmond, *The Charm of Old Portsmouth* (Portsmouth, 1959), p. 39.
9 Henning Henningsen, 'Coins for Luck under the Mast', *Mariner's Mirror*, LI/3 (1965), pp. 209–10.
10 Jones, *Credulities Past and Present*, p. 65.
11 'Superstitions of the Sea', *Chicago Daily Tribune*, 30 September 1906, p. D14.
12 R. L. Hadfield, *The Phantom Ship and Other Ghost Stories of the Sea* (London, 1937), p. 192.
13 Henningsen, 'Coins for Luck', p. 206, and Leland P. Lovette, *Naval Customs, Traditions and Usage*, 4th edn (Annapolis, MD, 1959), p. 49.
14 Henningsen, 'Coins for Luck', p. 208.
15 'Sailor Superstitions', *Chicago Daily Tribune*, 15 August 1920, p. 2.
16 Rev. Walter Gregor, *Notes on the Folklore of the North-East of Scotland* (London, 1881), p. 198.
17 'Drowning Superstitions', *Science*, XVIII/461 (4 December 1891), p. 309, and Jones, *Credulities Past and Present*, pp. 93–4.
18 'Odd Superstitions: Ill Luck Follows Those Who Rescue the Drowning', *Chicago Daily Tribune*, 14 July 1895, p. 37.
19 Hole, 'Superstitions and Beliefs', p. 188.
20 'Sea-Folks Superstitions', *New York Times*, 8 August 1897, p. 9.
21 'To Quiet Sailors' Superstitions', *Chicago Daily Tribune*, 13 March 1898, p. 46, and Jones, *Credulities Past and Present*, p. 91.
22 Ada Goodrich-Freer, 'The Power of Evil in the Outer Hebrides', *Folklore*, X/3 (1899), p. 272.

23 'Superstitions about Friday', *Chicago Daily Tribune*, 5 December 1892, p. 10.
24 See Ronald Hutton, *The Rise and Fall of Merry England: The Ritual Year, 1400–1700* (Oxford, 1994).
25 'Local News', *Leeds Mercury*, 2 February 1858, p. 2.
26 Hole, 'Superstitions and Beliefs', p. 185.
27 David Cordingly, *Women Sailors and Sailors' Women: An Untold Maritime History* (London, 2001).
28 Hole, 'Superstitions and Beliefs', p. 186.
29 David M. Hopkin, 'Storytelling and Networking in a Breton Fishing Village, 1879–1882', *International Journal of Maritime History*, XVII/2 (2005), p. 133, and Jones, *Credulities Past and Present*, p. 7.
30 Hole, 'Superstitions and Beliefs', p. 185.
31 'Sailors' Superstitions Defy the Age of Reason'.
32 Hadfield, *The Phantom Ship*, p. 182.
33 'The Credulous Mariner', *New York Times*, 30 March 1884, p. 14.
34 'The Sailors and the Hen', *Weekly Irish Times*, 6 March 1886, p. 2.
35 Hadfield, *The Phantom Ship*, p. 194.
36 Fletcher S. Bassett, *Legends and Superstitions of the Sea and of Sailors in All Lands and at All Times* (Chicago, IL, 1885), pp. 144–6, and Angelo R. Rappaport, *Superstitions of Sailors* (London, 1928), pp. 56–8.
37 'Superstition of Sailors', *Weekly Irish Times*, 28 July 1888, p. 2.
38 'Sailors' Superstitions Defy the Age of Reason'.
39 Hadfield, *The Phantom Ship*, p. 182.
40 'The Credulous Mariner'.
41 Jones, *Credulities Past and Present*, p. 79.
42 Gregor, *Folklore of the North-East of Scotland*, pp. 199–200.
43 Jones, *Credulities Past and Present*, p. 116.
44 Ibid., p.118.
45 Gregor, *Folklore of the North-East of Scotland*, p. 200.
46 Lizanne Henderson, 'Witch Belief in Scottish Coastal Communities', in *The New Coastal History: Cultural and Environmental Perspectives from Scotland and Beyond*, ed. David Worthington (Cham, 2017), p. 243.
47 King James, *Daemonologie, In Forme of a Dialogue, Divided into Three Books: By the High and Mighty Prince, James* (1597), Book 2, chapter V, p. 47, and Hadfield, *The Phantom Ship*, p. 181.
48 Henderson, 'Witch Belief', p. 241, and Gregor, *Folklore of North-East Scotland*, pp. 199–200.
49 Goodrich-Freer, 'The Power of Evil', p. 282.
50 Robert Hunt, *Popular Romances of the West of England; or, The Drolls, Traditions, and Superstitions of Old Cornwall*, 2nd series (London, 1865), pp. 108–9.
51 'Scottish Sailors Cling to Superstitions', *New York Times*, 8 July 1928, p. 72.

52 Richard Henry Dana, *Two Years Before the Mast* (Boston, MA, 1911), pp. 47–8.
53 Proceedings of the Old Bailey Online, ref. t18670408–415 (8 April 1867), and 'Law and Police', *Pall Mall Gazette*, 12 April 1867, p. 8.
54 'Sea-Folks Superstitions', p. 9.
55 'Sailors of Superstition: The Old Salt Tells Why It's a Good Thing to Take a Hint', *New York Times*, 9 September 1900, p. 12.
56 Jones, *Credulities Past and Present*, pp. 12–13.
57 'Sailor Superstitions'.
58 Hole, 'Superstitions and Beliefs', p. 189.
59 Wilbur Bassett, *Wanderships: Folk Stories of the Sea with Notes upon Their Origin* (Chicago, IL, 1917), p. 60.
60 'He Killed the Albatross', *Chicago Daily Tribune*, 28 June 1890, p. 2, and 'Due to a Deadly Albatross', *Chicago Daily Tribune*, 13 July 1890, p. 25.
61 'Sailor Superstitions' and Hadfield, *The Phantom Ship*, pp. 198–9.
62 Rappaport, *Superstitions of Sailors*, p. 33, and Jones, *Credulities Past and Present*, p. 76.
63 'Sea Superstitions', *Chicago Daily Tribune*, 15 August 1920, p. 2.

3: Supernatural Beings and Fishy Tales

1 'A Mermaid', *Dumfries and Galloway Standard*, 29 July 1857, p. 3.
2 See Vaughan Scribner, *Merpeople: A Human History* (London, 2020).
3 Erich Pontoppidan, *The Natural History of Norway*, vol. II (London, 1755), pp. 186–95.
4 J. A. Teit, 'Water-Beings in Shetlandic Folk-Lore, as Remembered by Shetlanders in British Columbia', *Journal of American Folk-Lore*, XXXI/120 (1918), p. 189.
5 Ibid., pp. 187–8.
6 Ibid., p. 196.
7 William Jones, *Credulities Past and Present, Including the Sea and Seamen, Miners, Amulets and Talismans, Rings, Word and Letter Divination, Numbers, Trials, Exorcising and Blessing of Animals, Birds, Eggs, and Luck* (London, 1880), p. 27.
8 'Sailor Superstitions', *Chicago Daily Tribune*, 15 August 1920, p. 2.
9 Armand Landrin, *Monsters of the Deep and Curiosities of Ocean Life*, trans. W. Davenport (London, 1875), pp. 271–2.
10 Gerald K. Gresseth, 'The Homeric Sirens', *Transactions and Proceedings of the American Philological Association*, CL (1970), pp. 204, 210–11.
11 Landrin, *Monsters of the Deep*, p. 268.
12 Boria Sax, 'The Mermaid and Her Sisters: From Archaic Goddess to Consumer Society', *Interdisciplinary Studies in Literature and Environment*, VII/2 (2000), p. 44.
13 Pliny the Elder, *The Natural History of Pliny*, trans. John Bostock and H. T. Riley (London, 1855), pp. 362–4.

14 Landrin, *Monsters of the Deep*, p. 262.
15 Hans Egede, *A Description of Greenland*, 2nd edn (London, 1818), p. 80.
16 See Ambroise Paré, *On Monsters and Marvels*, trans. Janis L. Pallister (Chicago, IL, 1984), pp. xxvi and 107–36.
17 See ibid., pp. 109–10.
18 Sax, 'The Mermaid and Her Sisters', pp. 47–8.
19 Landrin, *Monsters of the Deep*, p. 289.
20 William Bottrell, *Traditions and Hearthside Stories of West Cornwall*, vol. I (Penzance, 1870), pp. 65–71.
21 Teit, 'Water Beings in Shetlandic Folk-Lore', pp. 188–9.
22 David MacRitchie, 'The Finn-men of Britain', *Archaeological Review*, IV/1 (1889), pp. 7–8.
23 Teit, 'Water Beings in Shetlandic Folk-Lore', p. 195.
24 Ibid.
25 Paula T. Connolly, 'Breaking the Surface: Mermaids and the Middle Passage', *Marvels and Tales*, XXXV/1 (2021), pp. 79–93, and, Jalondra A. Davis, 'Crossing Merfolk Narratives of the Sacred', *Shima*, XV/2 (2021), pp. 52–5.
26 Ras Michael Brown, '"But the Mermaid Did Not Rise Up": The Death of a Simbi in the Carolina Lowcountry', *Southern Quarterly*, XLVII/4 (2010), pp. 120–50.
27 For more on Mami Wata, see Alex van Stipriaan, 'Watramama/ Mami Wata: Three Centuries of Creolization of a Water Spirit in West Africa, Suriname and Europe', *Matatu, Journal of African Culture and Society*, XXVII/1 (2003), pp. 321–37, and Henry John Drewal, 'Interpretation, Invention, and Re-Presentation in the Worship of Mami Wata', *Journal of Folklore Research*, XXV/1–2 (1988), pp. 101–39.
28 Jones, *Credulities Past and Present*, pp. 24–5.
29 Ibid., p. 21.
30 Karl Banse, 'Mermaids-Their Biology, Culture, and Demise', *Limnology and Oceanography*, XXXV/1 (1990), p. 152.
31 Pontoppidan, *The Natural History of Norway*, pp. 194–5.
32 'London', *Hampshire Chronicle*, 10 December 1810, p. 2.
33 See Robert Hamilton, *The Naturalist's Library: Mammalia*, vol. VIII (Edinburgh, 1839), pp. 286–8.
34 Teit, 'Water Beings in Shetlandic Folk-Lore', pp. 188–90.
35 Margaret Robinson, 'Some Fabulous Beasts', *Folklore*, LXXVI/4 (1965), pp. 284–7. For more on early modern ideas on monstrosity, see Laura Lunger Knoppers and Joan B. Landes, eds, *Monstrous Bodies/Political Monstrosities in Early Modern Europe* (Ithaca, NY, 2004), pp. 1–22.
36 See Vaughan Scribner, '"Such Monsters Do Exist in Nature": Mermaids, Tritons, and the Science of Wonder in Eighteenth-Century Europe', *Itinerario*, XLI/3 (2017), pp. 520–25.

37 See Benoît de Maillet, *Telliamed; or Conversations between an Indian Philosopher and a French Missionary on the Diminution of the Sea*, ed. and trans. Albert V. Carozzi (Urbana, IL, 1968), and H. Brink-Roby, '*Siren canora*: The Mermaid and the Mythical in Late Nineteenth-Century Science', *Archives of Natural History*, XXXV/1 (2008), pp. 1–14.
38 See Beatrice Laurent, 'Monster or Missing Link? The Mermaid and the Victorian Imagination', *Cahiers Victoriens et Edouardiens*, 85 (2017), pp. 1–17.
39 Henry Lee, *Sea Fables Explained* (London, 1883), p. 28.
40 Landrin, *Monsters of the Deep*, p. 297.
41 Laurent, 'Monster or Missing Link?', pp. 6–7.
42 'Nature's Puzzle World No. 17: Sea Creatures That Pass for Mermaids', *Weekly Irish Times*, 30 July 1932, p. 17.
43 Lee, *Sea Fables Explained*, p. 45. See also pp. 36–44.
44 Landrin, *Monsters of the Deep*, p. 262. See 'The Mermaid' and 'The Merman', in Alfred, Lord Tennyson, *The Works of Alfred, Lord Tennyson* (London, 1893), and Matthew Arnold, 'The Forsaken Merman', *Selected Poems of Matthew Arnold* (London, 1886), p. 104.
45 Joseph Kestner, 'Edward Burne-Jones and Nineteenth-Century Fear of Women', *Biography*, VII/2 (1984), pp. 95–122.
46 'The Albert Palace', *The Era*, 24 April 1886, p. 10.
47 'With Neptune's Daughter and Her Mermaids', *New York Times*, 25 November 1906, p. X1.
48 Hans Christian Andersen, 'The Little Mermaid', in *The Penguin Book of Mermaids*, ed. Cristina Bacchilega and Marie Alohalini Brown (New York, 2019), pp. 107–30.
49 'Jack Jones's Adventures among the Mermaids', *Boy's Standard*, 14 March 1891, pp. 276–8.
50 See Carole G. Silver, *Strange and Secret Peoples: Fairies and Victorian Consciousness* (Oxford, 1999).
51 Simon Young, 'Mermaids, Mere-Maids and No Maids: Mermaid Place Names and Folklore in Britain', *Shima*, XV/2 (2021), pp. 183 and 187, and Simon Young, 'Mermaid Toponyms in the West Indies: Traditional and Non-Traditional Names', *Shima*, XV/2 (2021), p. 207.

4: The Haunted High Seas

1 R. L. Hadfield, *The Phantom Ship and Other Ghost Stories of the Sea* (London, 1937), pp. 5–6.
2 Owen Davies, *A Supernatural War: Magic, Divination, and Faith During the First World War* (Oxford, 2019), p. 224. For an example, see Mass Observation Archive, File Report 1315, 'Death and the Supernatural', 18 June 1942.
3 Wilbur Bassett, *Wanderships: Folk Stories of the Sea with Notes upon Their Origin* (Chicago, IL, 1917), pp. 55–6.
4 Ibid., pp. 48–9.

5 See Hadfield, *The Phantom Ship*, p. 15.
6 Julia Mix Barrington, 'Phantom Bark: The Chronotype of the Phantom Ship in the Atlantic World', *Gothic Studies*, XIX/2 (2017), p. 61.
7 Willard Hallam Bonner, 'The Flying Dutchman of the Western World', *Journal of American Folklore*, LIX/233 (1946), pp. 286 and 287, and Horace Beck, *Folklore and the Sea* (Mystic, CT, 2005), pp. 457–60.
8 Bonner, 'Flying Dutchman', p. 287.
9 Bassett, *Wanderships*, p. 51, and Hadfield, *The Phantom Ship*, p. 16.
10 Herman Melville, *Moby Dick* (Ware, 1992), pp. 243–9.
11 Bassett, *Wanderships*, p. 51.
12 Ibid.
13 William M. Hutchison, *The Phantom Ship, A Nautical Ballad, Words and Music Composed by William M. Hutchison* (London, 1896), British Library ref. H2601.a.(11.).
14 Bassett, *Wanderships*, pp. 50 and 61, and Hadfield, *The Phantom Ship*, p. 177.
15 'How Many Shipwrecks Are There?', www.worldatlas.com, accessed 21 October 2024.
16 See *Science*, 4 December 1891, XVIII/461, pp. 309–10.
17 Beck, *Folklore and the Sea*, p. 462.
18 Helen Rozwadowski 'Ocean's Depth', *Environmental History*, V/3 (2010), pp. 521 and 524.
19 See Hadfield, *The Phantom Ship*, pp. 84–5, and Sophia Kingshill and Jennifer Westwood, *The Fabled Coast* (London, 2014), p. 96.
20 Fletcher S. Bassett, *Legends and Superstitions of the Sea and of Sailors in All Lands and at All Times* (Chicago, IL, 1885), pp. 346 and 348.
21 Beck, *Folklore and the Sea*, p. 470.
22 Ibid., pp. 463–4.
23 Ibid., p. 472.
24 Walter Scott, *Letters on Demonology and Witchcraft* (Ware, 2001), pp. 212–14, and Bassett, *Wanderships*, p. 59.
25 Beck, *Folklore and the Sea*, pp. 470–71.
26 Hadfield, *The Phantom Ship*, p. 29.
27 Davies, *A Supernatural War*, p. 87.
28 Helen Creighton, *Maritime Folksongs* (St John's, Newfoundland, 1979), p. 113, and 'Far, Far at Sea', Bodleian ballad Roud No.V387 (Harding B11 (476).
29 'The Yarmouth Tragedy, or The Constant Lovers', Bodleian Library ref. Bod 5718, Roud No. 187.
30 Creighton, *Maritime Folk Songs*, pp. 113 and 116–17.
31 Paul Cowdell, '"I have believed in spirits from that day unto this": "The Ghostly Crew", Ghostlore, and Traditional Song', *Folk Music Journal*, XI/4 (2019), p. 82.
32 Ibid., p. 88.

33 'Literary Extracts' *Evening Telegraph*, 18 April 1910, p. 6.
34 'Ghost Stories', *Boston Investigator*, 6 April 1870, p. 388, and Cowdell, '"The Ghostly Crew"'. 'The Ghostly Crew' was said to be well known on the northeastern seaboard, from Labrador down to Maine.
35 Barrington, 'Phantom Bark', p. 69.
36 Hadfield, *The Phantom Ship*, p. 33.
37 Bassett, *Wanderships*, pp. 41–4.
38 Ibid., pp. 54–5.
39 See 'Phantom Ships' (by Mico Keno)', *The Herald of Revolt*, IV (4 April 1914), p. 41.
40 Charles Dickens, *The Christmas Books* (London, 1994), p. 18.
41 Jones, *Credulities Past and Present*, p. 86.
42 'Meteorological Superstitions', *Cambridge Chronicle and Journal*, 17 October 1823, p. 4.
43 Hadfield, *The Phantom Ship*, p. 19.
44 Beck, *Folklore and the Sea*, pp. 455–6, and Hadfield, *The Phantom Ship*, p. 41.
45 Hadfield, *The Phantom Ship*, pp. 42–3.
46 'Mysterious Occurrence at Sea', *Exeter and Plymouth Gazette*, 14 February 1873, p. 3.
47 Kingshill and Westwood, *The Fabled Coast*, pp. 452–3.
48 Beck, *Folklore and the Sea*, p. 465.
49 'The Ghost Ship of the North Sea', *New York Times*, 11 December 1927, p. SM20.

5: Monsters of the Deep

1 'The Great Sea Serpent', *The Times*, 14 October 1848, p. 3; 'The Great Sea Serpent Again', *The Times*, 23 October 1848, p. 6; 'The Sea Serpent', *The Times*, 2 November 1848, p. 3.
2 Stephen T. Asma, 'Monsters on the Brain', *Social Research*, LXXXI/4 (2014), p. 954.
3 Cornelia Catlin Coulter, 'The "Great Fish" in Ancient and Medieval Story', *Transactions and Proceedings of the American Philological Association*, LVII (1926), p. 41.
4 Thomas Wright, ed., *St Brendan: A Mediaeval Legend of the Sea* (London, 1844), p. 7 and 46–7.
5 Lindsay J. Starkey, 'Why Sea Monsters Surround the Northern Lands: Olaus Magnus's Conception of Water', *Preternature: Critical and Historical Studies on the Preternatural*, VI/1 (2017), pp. 31–62, and Chet Van Duzer, *Sea Monsters on Medieval and Renaissance Maps* (London, 2013).
6 'Man in Whale's Stomach. Rescue of a Modern Jonah', *Aberdeen Journal*, 29 July 1891, p. 6.
7 Armand Landrin, *Monsters of the Deep and Curiosities of Ocean Life*, trans. W. Davenport (London, 1875), p. 41.

8 Henry Lee, *Sea Monsters Unmasked* (London, 1883), p. 2.
9 Stephen Asma, *On Monsters: An Unnatural History of Our Worst Fears* (Oxford, 2009), p. 64.
10 Erich Pontoppidan, *The Natural History of Norway*, vol. II (London, 1755), p. 218.
11 Ibid., p. 212.
12 Hans Egede, *Description of Greenland*, 2nd edn (London, 1818), p. 86, footnote 29.
13 Ibid., pp. 86–9.
14 Lee, *Sea Monsters Unmasked*, p. 3.
15 Thomas Holcroft and William Hazlitt, *Memoirs of the Late Thomas Holcroft: Written by Himself; And Continued to the Time of His Death, from His Diary, Notes, and Other Papers* (London, 1816), vol. III, letter V, pp. 224–6.
16 Landrin, *Monsters of the Deep*, pp. 41, 44 and 62.
17 Henry Lee, *Sea Fables Explained* (London, 1883), p. 48.
18 'Yarns about the Sea Serpent Still Persist', *Sea Breeze*, 30 (1926), pp. 14–15.
19 Landrin, *Monsters of the Deep*, p. 56, and Lee, *Sea Monsters Unmasked*, p. 40.
20 John Gibson, *Monsters of the Sea, Legendary and Authentic* (London, 1887), p. 86.
21 Pontoppidan, *The Natural History of Norway*, p. 213.
22 Landrin, *Monsters of the Deep*, pp. 47–8.
23 See, for example, 'Appearance of the Green-Eyed Monster', *Morning Republican*, 25 November 1873, p. 1.
24 Lee, *Sea Monsters Unmasked*, p. 51.
25 J. A. Teit, 'Water Beings in Shetlandic Folklore', *Journal of American Folklore*, XXXI/120 (1918), pp. 181 and 196–7.
26 'Battles for His Life with Big Sea Monster', *The St John's Daily Star*, 11 September 1920, p. 16, and '"Sea Serpent" Story from Port Saunders', *Western Star*, 15 September 1920, p. 1.
27 'Sea Monsters of Old', *Sea Breeze*, 13 (1909), p. 11.
28 See Isaiah 27:1 and Job 41 for biblical descriptions of Leviathan. For Aristotle's comments on sea serpents, see *Aristotle's History of Animals in Ten Books*, trans. Richard Cresswell (London, 1887), pp. 39 and 255.
29 Lee, *Sea Monsters Unmasked*, p. 56.
30 Pontoppidan, *The Natural History of Norway*, p. 196.
31 See Edward J. Lenik, 'Mythic Creatures: Serpents, Dragons, and Sea Monsters in Northeastern Rock Art', *Archaeology of Eastern North America*, XXXVIII (2010), pp. 17–37.
32 John McAleer, '"As pretty a thing as I have ever seen": Animal Encounters and Atlantic Voyages, 1750–1850', *Journal of Maritime Research*, XXII/1–2 (2020), pp. 5–23.
33 Holcroft and Hazlitt, *Memoirs of the Late Thomas Holcroft*, vol. III, pp. 227–8.

34 'The Sea Serpent's Immortal Coils', *New York Times*, 15 July 1934, p. 8, and Gibson, *Monsters of the Sea*, pp. 35–9. See also W. Soini, *Gloucester's Sea-Serpent* (Charleston, SC, 2010).
35 'The Great Sea-Serpent', *Illustrated London News*, 28 October 1848, p. 264, and Lee, *Sea Monsters Unmasked*, p. 80.
36 See 'The Fossil Sea Serpent', *Illustrated London News*, 4 November 1848, p. 278.
37 For the evolving debate, see *The Times*, 14, 26 and 28 October and 2, 10, 14 and 21 November 1848, and also the *Illustrated London News*, 25 November 1848, p. 331.
38 'The Sea-Serpent Arrived', *The Leader*, 20 April 1850, p. 79.
39 'Wonders', *The Leader*, 7 September 1850, p. 563.
40 'The Sea Serpent Again', *Chicago Tribune*, 4 December 1869, p. 3.
41 C.G.M. Paxton, 'Driven Mad by the Sea Serpent: The Strange Case of Captain George Drevar', *Mariner's Mirror*, CVII/3 (2021), p. 312.
42 Ibid., p. 311.
43 See 'The Sea Serpent', *Irish Times*, 15 January 1877, p. 3.
44 'The Sea Serpent', *Shields Daily Gazette*, 29 November 1875, p. 3.
45 See Paxton, 'Driven Mad by the Sea Serpent', p. 315.
46 George Drevar, *The Great Sea Serpent and Sperm Whale Conflict* (Sydney, 1889).
47 'Another Sea Serpent', *Weekly Irish Times*, 27 September 1879, p. 2.
48 'The Sea Serpent Again', *Irish Times*, 27 May 1899, p. 8.
49 'The Great Sea Serpent', *Douglas Jerrold's Weekly Newspaper*, 28 October 1848.
50 'Wonders', p. 563.
51 *Daily Telegraph*, 6 September 1878, p. 5.
52 See 'The Sea Serpent Caught', *Chicago Daily Tribune*, 29 August 1885, p. 13, and 'Miscellaneous News', *Ipswich Journal*, 13 August 1885, p. 4.
53 'The Sea Serpent at Cuchendall', *Irish Times*, 17 June 1899, p. 7.
54 'Yarns about the Sea Serpent Still Persist', *Sea Breeze*, 30 (1926), pp. 14–15.
55 See *Illustrated London News*, 28 October 1848, XXIII, p. 264 (*Daedalus*); 13 June 1857, XXX, p. 570 (Table Bay); 20 November 1875, LXVII, p. 515 (*Pauline*); 11 February 1905, CXXVI, p. 7; 30 June 1906, CXXVIII, p. 13; 28 July 1906, CXXIX, p. 18.
56 Gibson, *Monsters of the Sea*, pp. 66–7.
57 'Yarns about the Sea Serpent Still Persist', p. 15.
58 See '"Sea Monster" Seen in Loch', *Evening Telegraph*, 23 May 1933, p. 6, and 'Loch Ness "Monster" Again', *Dundee Courier*, 1 June 1933, p. 3.
59 'Sea Monster Finds Another Champion', *New York Times*, 29 December 1933, p. 23.
60 See G. J. Galbreath, 'The 1848 "Enormous Serpent" of the Daedalus Identified', *Skeptical Inquirer*, XXXIX/5 (2015), pp. 42–6, and

R. L. France, 'Imaginary Sea Monsters and Real Environmental Threats: Reconsidering the Famous Osborne, "Moha-Moha", Valhalla, and "Soay Beast" Sightings of Unidentified Marine Objects', *International Review of Environmental History*, III/1 (2017), pp. 63–100. For historical accounts of sea serpents, see A. C. Oudemans, *The Great Sea-Serpent: An Historical and Critical Treatise* (Leiden, 1892); Lt Commander R. T. Gould, *The Case for the Sea Serpent* (New York, 1934), and B. Heuvelmans, *In the Wake of the Sea-Serpents* (London, 1968).

61 Gibson, *Monsters of the Sea*, pp. 77–8.

6: Weird and Enchanted Geographies

1 D. R. McAnally, *Irish Wonders; The Ghosts, Giants, Pookas, Demons, Leprechawns, Banshees, Fairies, Witches, Widows, Old Maids, and Other Marvels of the Emerald Isle; Popular Tales as Told by the People* (Boston, MA, 1888), pp. 67–76. For more on O'Brasil, see Bob Curran, *Lost Lands, Forgotten Realms: Sunken Continents, Vanished Cities, and the Kingdoms that History Misplaced* (Franklin Lakes, NJ, 2007), pp. 61–9.

2 Stith Thompson, *Motif-Index of Folk-Literature: A Classification of Narrative Elements in Folktales, Ballads, Myths, Fables, Mediaeval Romances, Exempla, Fabliaux, Jest-Books, and Local Legends* (Bloomington, IN, 1958), p. 982.

3 For examples, see Thomas Wentworth Higginson, *Tales of the Enchanted Islands of the Atlantic* (New York, 1899).

4 Thomas Johnson Westropp, 'Brasil and the Legendary Islands of the North Atlantic: Their History and Fable. A Contribution to the "Atlantis" Problem', *Proceedings of the Royal Irish Academy: Archaeology, Culture, History, Literature*, XXX (1912–13), p. 246, and Malachy Tallack, *The Un-Discovered Islands: An Archipelago of Myths and Mysteries, Phantoms and Fakes* (Edinburgh, 2016), p. 45.

5 Sophia Kingshill and Jennifer Westwood, *The Fabled Coast* (London, 2014), p. 459.

6 Westropp, 'Brasil and the Legendary Islands', pp. 227–8.

7 See Francis Parkman, *France and England in North America, Part 1: Pioneers of France in the New World* (Boston, MA, 1902), pp. 193–4 and 226–8, and Tallack, *The Un-Discovered Islands*, p. 138.

8 Westropp, 'Brasil and the Legendary Islands', pp. 255–7, and Kingshill and Westwood, *The Fabled Coast*, pp. 413–14.

9 Barbara Freitag, *Hy Brasil: The Metamorphosis of an Island: From Cartographic Error to Celtic Elysium* (Amsterdam, 2013).

10 Westropp, 'Brasil and the Legendary Islands', p. 257.

11 See ibid., p. 240, and Tallack, *The Un-Discovered Islands*, pp. 68–71.

12 Kingshill and Westwood, *The Fabled Coast*, p. 376.

13 See *Egils Saga*, trans. Bernard Scudder (London, 2004), and T. W. Rolleston, ed., *The High Deeds of Finn and other Bardic Romances of Ancient Ireland* (London, 1910), pp. 22–50.
14 Hans Egede, *A Description of Greenland* (London, 1818 edn), pp. 183–5 and 202–5.
15 Angelo S. Rappoport, *Superstitions of Sailors* (London, 1928), p. 28.
16 See William Bottrell, *Traditions and Hearthside Stories of West Cornwall*, vol. I (Penzance, 1870), pp. 66–9.
17 Ignatius Donnelly, *Atlantis in the Antediluvian World* (New York, 1882). See also Frank de Caro, *Folklore Recycled: Old Traditions in New Contexts* (Jackson, MS, 2013), pp. 136–40.
18 Helena Blavatsky, *Isis Unveiled: A Master Key to the Mysteries of Ancient and Modern Science and Theology*, vol. I, 4th edn (London, 1878) pp. 593–4.
19 Sir Wyville Thomson, *The Atlantic: A Preliminary Accounts of the General Results of the Exploring Voyage of HMS Voyager*, vol. II (New York, 1878), pp. 15–17.
20 'The Sargasso Sea', *Chambers Journal of Popular Literature, Science and Art*, 19 May 1897, p. 309 and 311.
21 'The Graveyard of the Atlantic', *London Journal*, 8 April 1905, p. 297, and 'The Sargasso Sea', *Expository Times*, XVII/8 (1906), pp. 44–5.
22 R. L. Hadfield, *The Phantom Ship and Other Ghost Stories of the Sea* (London, 1937), p. 179.
23 'Sargasso Sea is Not as Bad as Painted', *Dundee Courier*, 25 July 1910, p. 7. For scientific interest in the Sargasso Sea, see W. G. Farlow, 'The Vegetation of the Sargasso Sea', *Proceedings of the American Philosophical Society*, LIII (1914), pp. 257–62, and M. Gordon, 'Sargasso Sea Merry-Go-Round', *Scientific Monthly*, LIII/6 (1941), pp. 542–9.
24 'Notes from All Quarters', *Western Gazette*, 6 March 1914, p. 12.
25 'Sargasso Sea Secrets', *Aberdeen Journal*, 5 January 1925, p. 7.
26 'Mysterious Sea of Seaweed', *Dundee Courier*, 2 March 1925, p. 4.
27 'Back from Dread Sargasso Sea', *Dundee Courier*, 31 July 1925, p. 4.
28 'Grim Ocean Graveyard – Mystery of the Sargasso Sea', *Nottingham Evening Post*, 6 February 1930, p. 4.
29 C. E. Ashworth, 'Flying Saucers, Spoon-Bending and Atlantis: A Structural Analysis of New Mythologies', *Sociological Review*, XXVIII/2 (1980), p. 359.

7: Coastal Folklore: Bringing It Back Home

1 'Is It a Ghostly Attack? Mysterious Bombardment of a Lighthouse on the Texas Coast', *Washington Post*, 25 October 1888, p. 3.
2 Jason Marc Harris, 'Perilous Shores: The Unfathomable Supernaturalism of Water in 19th-Century Scottish Folklore', *Mythlore*, XXVIII/1–2 (2009), p. 6.

3 Christina Hole, 'Superstitions and Beliefs of the Sea', *Folklore*, LXXVIII/3 (1967), p. 184, and Rev. Walter Gregor, 'Fishermen's Folklore', *Folklore*, II/1 (1884), p. 355.
4 Ada Goodrich-Freer, 'More Folklore of the Hebrides', *Folklore*, XIII/1 (1902), p. 37, and Fletcher S. Bassett, *Legends and Superstitions of the Sea and of Sailors in All Lands and at All Times* (Chicago, IL, 1885), p. 468.
5 Goodrich-Freer, 'More Folklore', pp. 51–2.
6 Ibid., pp. 32 and 47–9.
7 Ibid., pp. 37–8 and 40.
8 Ibid., pp. 43–4.
9 W. Traill Dennison, 'Orkney Folk Lore', *The Scottish Antiquary, or, Northern Notes and Queries*, VII/28 (1893), pp. 175–6, and J. A. Teit, 'Water-Beings in Shetlandic Folk-Lore, as Remembered by Shetlanders in British Columbia', *Journal of American Folk-Lore*, XXXI/120 (1918), pp. 191–3.
10 Robert Hunt, ed., *Popular Romances of the West of England; or, The Drolls, Traditions, and Superstitions of Old Cornwall* (London, 1908 edn), pp. 151–2, and Enys Tregarthen, *North Cornwall Fairies and Legends* (London, 1906), pp. 51–69.
11 See Jeremy Harte, *Cloven Country: The Devil and the English Landscape* (London, 2022), pp. 44–64.
12 George Pinckard, *Notes on West Indies: Written During the Expedition Under the Command of the Late General Sir Ralph Abercromby* (London, 1806), vol. III, Letter 1, pp. 7–8.
13 William Jones, *Credulities Past and Present, Including the Sea and Seamen, Miners, Amulets and Talismans, Rings, Word and Letter Divination, Numbers, Trials, Exorcising and Blessing of Animals, Birds, Eggs, and Luck* (London, 1880), p. 24.
14 Ibid., p. 27.
15 Ibid., pp. 32–3.
16 'A Strange Sea Monster', *Western Daily Press*, 5 October 1871, p. 3.
17 R. L. Hadfield, *The Phantom Ship and Other Ghost Stories of the Sea* (London, 1937), p. 83.
18 Ibid., pp. 48–9.
19 Ibid., p. 63, and Bassett, *Legends and Superstitions*, pp. 468 and 471.
20 Alexander Hay, '"From Beneath the Waves": Sea-Draugr and the Popular Conscience', in *Beasts of the Deep: Sea Creatures and Popular Culture*, ed. Jon Hackett and Sean Harrington (East Barnet, 2018), pp. 11–25.
21 Hans Egede, *A Description of Greenland* (London, 1818 edn), pp. 86–9, footnote 29.
22 'Drowning Superstitions', *Science*, 4 December 1891, pp. 309–10; Bassett, *Legends and Superstitions*, p. 471; Hadfield, *The Phantom Ship*, p. 121.
23 Hadfield, *The Phantom Ship*, p. 121; Jones, *Credulities Past and Present*, p. 92; Bassett, *Legends and Superstitions*, p. 471.

24 For variants, see William Bottrell, *Traditions and Hearthside Stories of West Cornwall* (Penzance, 1870), pp. 247–9; Horace Beck, *Folklore and the Sea* (Mystic, CT, 2005), p. 466; Hadfield, *The Phantom Ship*, pp. 49–51; and Sophia Kingshill and Jennifer Westwood, *The Fabled Coast* (London, 2014), pp. 45–6.

25 Hunt, *Popular Romances of the West of England*, p. 136, and Hole, 'Superstitions and Beliefs', p. 189.

26 Bassett, *Legends and Superstitions*, p. 479.

27 John T. Varden, 'Traditions, Superstitions, and Folklore, Chiefly Relating to the Counties of Norfolk and Suffolk', in *The East Anglian Handbook and Agricultural Annual for 1885*, ed. P. Soman (Norwich, 1885), pp. 74–5.

28 Hunt, *Popular Romances of the West of England*, pp. 143–6, and Hadfield, *The Phantom Ship*, pp. 104–5.

29 Owen Davies, *The Haunted: A Social History of Ghosts* (Basingstoke, 2007), pp. 90–94.

30 Jones, *Credulities Past and Present*, p. 31.

31 Paul Cowdell, '"I have believed in spirits from that day unto this": "The Ghostly Crew", Ghostlore, and Traditional Song', *Folk Music Journal*, XI/4 (2019), pp. 80–81, and Hadfield, *The Phantom Ship*, p. 35.

32 Beck, *Folklore and the Sea*, pp. 468–9.

33 See Cathryn Pearce, *Cornish Wrecking, 1700–1860: Reality and Popular Myth* (Woodbridge, 2010).

34 Traill Dennison, 'Orkney Folk Lore', p. 173.

35 See Reidar Thoralf Christiansen, *The Migratory Legends: A Proposed List of Types with a Systematic Catalogue of the Norwegian Variants* (Helsinki, 1958).

36 Nicholas Jubber, *The Fairy Tellers: A Journey into the Secret History of Fairy Tales* (London, 2022).

37 Douglas L. Winiarski, '"Pale Blewish Lights" and a Dead Man's Groan: Tales of the Supernatural from Eighteenth-Century Plymouth, Massachusetts', *William and Mary Quarterly*, LV/4 (1998), pp. 515–16.

38 W. H. Saunders, *Tales of Old Portsmouth,* Portsmouth Central Library ref. 942.2792, p. 43.

39 Karl Bell, 'Civic Spirits: Ghost Lore and Civic Narratives in Nineteenth-Century Portsmouth', *Cultural and Social History*, XI/1 (2014), pp. 51–68.

40 Traill Dennison, 'Orkney Folk Lore', p. 173.

41 Bottrell, *Traditions and Hearthside Stories*, p. 63.

8: Remaking Our Nautical Fears

1 Samuel Taylor Coleridge, 'The Rime of the Ancient Mariner', in *Samuel Taylor Coleridge: Selected Poems* (London, 1996), pp. 81–100.

2 See Hester Blum, *The View from the Masthead: Maritime Imagination and Antebellum American Sea Narratives* (Chapel Hill, NC, 2008).

3 Emily Alder, 'Through Oceans Darkly: Sea Literature and the Nautical Gothic', *Gothic Studies*, XIX/2 (2017), pp. 1–2.
4 Alfred Lord Tennyson, 'The Kraken', in *Penguin Classics Selected Poems: Tennyson* (London, 2007), p. 7.
5 Herman Melville, *Moby Dick* (Ware, 1992), p.71.
6 For more on the Gothic elements of *Moby-Dick*, see Fadi Ali Abdelsalam and Baker Bani-Khair, 'A Psychological Study of the Gothic Marine Locales in Herman Melville's *Moby Dick*', *Theory and Practice in Language Studies*, XIV/5 (2024), pp. 1510–16.
7 See Brad Beaven, 'The Resilience of Sailortown Culture in English Naval Ports, c. 1820–1900', *Urban History*, XLIII/1 (2016), pp. 72–95.
8 All the stories mentioned here can be found in Edgar Allan Poe, *The Complete Tales and Poems of Edgar Allan Poe* (London, 1987). See also Dan Walden, 'Ships and Crypts: The Coastal World of Poe's "King Pest," "The Premature Burial," and "The Oblong Box"', *Edgar Allan Poe Review*, X/2 (2009), pp. 104–21.
9 'Sketches of Maritime Life' *Newcastle Weekly Courant*, 31 August 1888, p. 5.
10 'Fishermen's Superstitions', *Ladies' Treasury: A Household Magazine*, 1 December 1885, p. 684.
11 Fletcher S. Bassett, *Legends and Superstitions of the Sea and Sailors in All Lands and at All Times* (Chicago, IL, 1885), p. 11.
12 See Karl Bell, *Magical Imagination: Magic and Modernity in Urban England, 1780–1914* (Cambridge, 2012), and Jason A. Josephson-Storm, *The Myth of Disenchantment: Magic, Modernity, and the Birth of the Human Sciences* (Chicago, IL, 2017).
13 Jules Verne, *Twenty Thousand Leagues Under the Sea* (London, 1994), pp. 261–7.
14 Although not set in the Atlantic, see Hodgson's short stories 'The Voice in the Night' (1907) and 'The Derelict' (1912) as good examples.
15 See Julius Chambers, *Missing: A Romance. A Tale of the Sargasso Sea* (New York, 1896), and Thomas A. Janvier, *In the Sargasso Sea* (New York, 1898).
16 For the various stories indicated here, see Jeremy Lassen, ed., *The Ghost Pirates and Other Revenants of the Sea: The Collected Fiction of William Hope Hodgson*, vol. III (New York, 2018).
17 See Robert W. Sneddon, 'On the Isle of Blue Men', in *Our Haunted Shores: Tales from the Coasts of the British Isles*, ed. Emily Alder, Jimmy Packham and Joan Passey (London, 2022), pp. 275–305.
18 See 'The Call of Cthuhlu', in H. P. Lovecraft, *H. P. Lovecraft Omnibus 3: The Haunter in the Dark* (London, 2000), pp. 61–98.
19 For more on Lovecraft's maritime stories, see Antonio Alcala Gonzalez, 'From the Sea and Beyond: Lovecraft's Sea Monsters', *Gothic Studies*, XIX/2 (2017), pp. 85–97.
20 John Wyndham, *The Kraken Wakes* (London, 1953).

21 See Timothy Beales, *Religion and Its Monsters*, 2nd edn (London, 2022), pp. 155–65.
22 In addition to *Godzilla*, see *Independence Day* (1996) and *The Day after Tomorrow* (2004).
23 For more on this, see Andrea Shaw Nevins, *Working Juju: Representations of the Caribbean Fantastic* (Athens, GA, 2019), pp. 49–58.
24 Ibid., pp. 59–66.
25 Michael Dylan Foster and Jeffrey A. Tolbert, eds, *The Folkloresque: Reframing Folklore in a Popular Culture World* (Boulder, CO, 2016), p. 5.

Epilogue: Past Tides and Future Shores

1 Claude Lévi-Strauss, *The Raw and the Cooked*, trans. John and Doreen Weightman (New York, 1969).
2 OECD, 'Ocean Shipping', www.oecd.org, accessed 25 October 2024.
3 Robin Kundis Craig and Jeffrey Mathes McCarthy, ed., *Re-Envisioning the Anthropocene Ocean* (Salt Lake City, UT, 2023), pp. 8–9.
4 Ibid., p. 30.

BIBLIOGRAPHY

Abdelsalam, Fadi Ali, and Baker Bani-Khair, 'A Psychological Study of the Gothic Marine Locales in Herman Melville's *Moby Dick*', *Theory and Practice in Language Studies*, XIV/5 (2024), pp. 1510–16

Alder, Emily, 'Through Oceans Darkly: Sea Literature and the Nautical Gothic', *Gothic Studies*, XIX/2 (2017), pp. 1–15

Andersen, Hans Christian, 'The Little Mermaid', in *The Penguin Book of Mermaids*, ed. Cristina Bacchilega and Marie Alohalini Brown (New York, 2019), pp. 107–30

Anon., 'The Belief in Charms', *Folklore*, XXVIII/1 (1917), pp. 98–9

Aristotle, *Aristotle's History of Animals in Ten Books*, trans. Richard Cresswell (London, 1887)

Arnold, Matthew, *Selected Poems of Matthew Arnold* (London, 1886)

Ashworth, C. E., 'Flying Saucers, Spoon-Bending and Atlantis: A Structural Analysis of New Mythologies', *Sociological Review*, XXVIII/2 (1980), pp. 353–76

Asma, Stephen T., 'Monsters on the Brain', *Social Research*, LXXXI/4 (2014), pp. 941–68

—, *On Monsters: An Unnatural History of Our Worst Fears* (Oxford, 2009)

Baker, Margaret, *Folklore of the Sea* (Newton Abbot, 1979)

Banse, Karl, 'Mermaids: Their Biology, Culture, and Demise', *Limnology and Oceanography*, XXXV/1 (1990), pp. 148–53

Barrington, Julia Mix, 'Phantom Bark: The Chronotype of the Phantom Ship in the Atlantic World', *Gothic Studies*, XIX/2 (2017), pp. 58–70

Bassett, Fletcher S., *Legends and Superstitions of the Sea and Sailors in All Lands and at All Times* (Chicago, IL, 1885)

Bassett, Wilbur, *Wanderships: Folk Stories of the Sea with Notes upon Their Origin* (Chicago, IL, 1917)

Beales, Timothy, *Religion and Its Monsters*, 2nd edn (London, 2022)

Beaven, Brad, '"One of the Toughest Streets in the World": Exploring Male Violence, Class and Ethnicity in London's Sailortown, 1850–1880', *Social History*, XLVI/1 (2021), pp. 1–21

——, 'The Resilience of Sailortown Culture in English Naval Ports, *c.* 1820–1900', *Urban History*, XLIII/1 (2016), pp. 72–95

Beck, Horace, *Folklore and the Sea*, 2nd edn (Mystic, CT, 1996)

Bell, Karl, 'Civic Spirits: Ghost Lore and Civic Narratives in Nineteenth-Century Portsmouth', *Cultural and Social History*, XI/1 (2014), pp. 51–68

——, *Magical Imagination: Magic and Modernity in Urban England, 1780–1914* (Cambridge, 2012)

Bennett, Gillian, 'Geologists and Folklorists: Cultural Evolution and "The Science of Folklore"' *Folklore*, CV (1994), pp. 25–37

Blavatsky, Helena, *Isis Unveiled: A Master Key to the Mysteries of Ancient and Modern Science and Theology*, vol. I, 4th edn (London, 1878)

Blum, Hester, *The View from the Masthead: Maritime Imagination and Antebellum American Sea Narratives* (Chapel Hill, NC, 2008)

Bohn, Henry G., ed., *Fosteriana,* Con*sisting of Thoughts, Reflections, and Criticisms of John Foster* (London, 1858)

Bolton, Frederick E., 'Hydro-Psychosis', *American Journal of Psychology*, X/2 (1899), pp. 169–227

Bonner, Willard Hallam, 'The Flying Dutchman of the Western World', *Journal of American Folklore*, LIX/233 (1946), pp. 282–8

Bottrell, William, *Traditions and Hearthside Stories of West Cornwall*, vol. I (Penzance, 1870)

Bowman, Marion, 'Vernacular Religion and Nature: The "Bible of the Folk" Tradition in Newfoundland', *Folklore*, CXIV/3 (2003), pp. 285–95

Brink-Roby, H., 'Siren Canora: The Mermaid and the Mythical in Late Nineteenth-Century Science' *Archives of Natural History*, XXXV/1 (2008), pp. 1–14

Brown, Ras Michael, '"But the Mermaid Did Not Rise Up": The Death of a Simbi in the Carolina Lowcountry', *Southern Quarterly*, XLVII/4 (2010), pp. 120–50

Burke, Edmund, 'A Philosophical Enquiry into the Origins of Our Ideas of the Sublime and Beautiful', in *The Works of the Right Honourable Edmund Burke*, vol. I (London, 1887)

de Caro, Frank, *Folklore Recycled: Old Traditions in New Contexts* (Jackson, MS, 2013)

Cárthaigh, Críostóir Mac, 'The Cultural Context of Legend Telling in a West Kerry Fishing Community', *Folk Life*, LV/2 (2017), pp. 151–66

Cashman, David, 'King Neptune, the Mermaids, and the Cruise Tourists: The Line-Crossing Ceremony in Modern Passenger Shipping', *Coolabah*, 27 (2019), pp. 90–105

Chambers, Julius, *Missing: A Romance. A Tale of the Sargasso Sea* (New York, 1896)

Christiansen, Reidar Thoralf, *The Migratory Legends: A Proposed List of Types with a Systematic Catalogue of the Norwegian Variants* (Helsinki, 1958)

Coleridge, Samuel Taylor, *Penguin Selected Poems* (London, 1996)

Conley, Mary A., *From Jack Tar to Union Jack: Representing Naval Manhood in the British Empire, 1870–1918* (Manchester, 2017)
Connolly, Paula T., 'Breaking the Surface: Mermaids and the Middle Passage', *Marvels and Tales*, XXXV/1 (2021), pp. 79–93
Cordingly, David, *Women Sailors and Sailors' Women: An Untold Maritime History* (London, 2001)
Coulter, Cornelia Catlin, 'The "Great Fish" in Ancient and Medieval Story', *Transactions and Proceedings of the American Philological Association*, LVII (1926), pp. 32–50
Cowdell, Paul, '"I have believed in spirits from that day unto this": "The Ghostly Crew", Ghostlore, and Traditional Song', *Folk Music Journal*, XI/4 (2018), pp. 76–98
Craig, Robin Kundis, and Jeffrey Mathes McCarthy, eds, *Re-Envisioning the Anthropocene Ocean* (Salt Lake City, UT, 2023)
Creighton, Helen, *Maritime Folk Songs* (St John's, Newfoundland, 1979)
Curran, Bob, *Lost Lands, Forgotten Realms: Sunken Continents, Vanished Cities, and the Kingdoms that History Misplaced* (Franklin Lakes, NJ, 2007)
Dana, Richard Henry, *Two Years before the Mast* (Boston, MA, 1911)
Davies, Owen, *A Supernatural War: Magic, Divination, and Faith during the First World War* (Oxford, 2019)
—, *The Haunted: A Social History of Ghosts* (Basingstoke, 2007)
Davis, Jalondra A., 'Crossing Merfolk Narratives of the Sacred', *Shima*, XV/2 (2021), pp. 52–71
Dickens, Charles, *The Christmas Books* (London, 1994)
Donnelly, Ignatius, *Atlantis in the Antediluvian World* (New York, 1882)
Dorson, Richard M., *Buying the Wind: Regional Folklore in the United States* (Chicago, IL, 1964)
Drevar, George, *The Great Sea Serpent and Sperm Whale Conflict* (Sydney, 1889)
Drewal, Henry John, 'Interpretation, Invention, and Re-Presentation in the Worship of Mami Wata', *Journal of Folklore Research*, XXV/1–2 (1988), pp. 101–39
Egede, Hans, *A Description of Greenland*, 2nd edn (London, 1818)
Esmond, Richard, *The Charm of Old Portsmouth* (Portsmouth, 1959)
'Far, Far at Sea', Bodleian Library ballad ref. Harding B11 (476), Roud No. V387
Farlow, W. G., 'The Vegetation of the Sargasso Sea', *Proceedings of the American Philosophical Society*, LIII (1914), pp. 257–62
Flannery, Tim, ed., *The Life and Adventures of John Nicol, Mariner* (New York, 1997)
Foster, Jerry, 'Varieties of Sea Lore', *Western Folklore*, XXVIII/4 (1969), pp. 260–66
Foster, Michael Dylan, and Jeffrey A. Tolbert, eds, *The Folkloresque: Reframing Folklore in a Popular Culture World* (Boulder, CO, 2016)
France, R. L., 'Imaginary Sea Monsters and Real Environmental Threats: Reconsidering the Famous Osborne, "Moha-Moha", Valhalla,

and "Soay Beast" Sightings of Unidentified Marine Objects', *International Review of Environmental History*, III (2017), pp. 63–100

Freitag, Barbara, *Hy Brasil: the Metamorphosis of an Island: From Cartographic Error to Celtic Elysium* (Amsterdam, 2013)

Galbreath, G. J., 'The 1848 "Enormous Serpent" of the Daedalus Identified', *Skeptical Inquirer*, XXXIX/5 (2015), pp. 42–6

Gibson, John, *Monsters of the Sea, Legendary and Authentic* (London, 1887)

Gonzalez, Antonio Alcala, 'From the Sea and Beyond: Lovecraft's Sea Monsters', *Gothic Studies*, XIX/2 (2017), pp. 85–97

Goodrich-Freer, Ada, 'More Folklore of the Hebrides', *Folklore*, XIII/1 (1902), pp. 29–62

—, 'The Power of Evil in the Outer Hebrides', *Folklore*, X/3 (1899), pp. 259–82

Gordon, M., 'Sargasso Sea Merry-Go-Round', *Scientific Monthly*, LIII/6 (1941), pp. 542–9

Gould, R. T., *The Case for the Sea Serpent* (New York, 1934)

Greene, William Chase, 'The Sea in the Greek Poets', *North American Review*, CXCIX/700 (1914), pp. 427–43

Gregor, Rev. Walter, 'Fishermen's Folklore', *Folklore*, II (1884), pp. 353–7

—, *Notes on the Folklore of the North-East of Scotland* (London, 1881)

Gresseth, Gerald K, 'The Homeric Sirens', *Transactions and Proceedings of the American Philological Association*, CL (1970), pp. 203–18

Hadfield, Robert, *The Phantom Ship and Other Ghost Stories of the Sea* (London, 1937)

Hamilton, Robert, *The Naturalist's Library: Mammalia*, vol. VIII (Edinburgh, 1839)

Harris, Jason Marc, 'Perilous Shores: The Unfathomable Supernaturalism of Water in 19th-Century Scottish Folklore', *Mythlore*, XXVIII/1–2 (2009), pp. 5–25

Harte, Jeremy, *Cloven Country: The Devil and the English Landscape* (London, 2022)

Hathaway, Donna, *Staying with the Trouble: Making Kin in the Chthulucene* (Durham, NC, 2016)

Hay, Alexander, '"From Beneath the Waves": Sea-Draugr and the Popular Conscience', in *Beasts of the Deep: Sea Creatures and Popular Culture*, ed. Jon Hackett and Sean Harrington (East Barnet, 2018), pp. 11–25

Henderson, Lizanne, 'Witch Belief in Scottish Coastal Communities', in *The New Coastal History: Cultural and Environmental Perspectives from Scotland and Beyond*, ed. David Worthington (Cham, 2017), pp. 233–49

Henningsen, Henning, 'Coins for Luck under the Mast', *Mariner's Mirror*, LI/3 (1965), pp. 205–10

Heuvelmans, Bernard, *In the Wake of the Sea-Serpents* (London, 1968)

Higginson, Thomas Wentworth, *Tales of the Enchanted Islands of the Atlantic* (London, 1899)

Holcroft, Thomas, and William Hazlitt, *Memoirs of the Late Thomas Holcroft: Written by Himself; And Continued to the Time of His Death, from His Diary, Notes, and Other Papers*, vol. III (London, 1816)

Hole, Christina, 'Superstitions and Beliefs of the Sea', *Folklore*, LXXVIII/3 (1967), pp. 184–9

Hopkin, David M., 'Storytelling and Networking in a Breton Fishing Village, 1879–1882', *International Journal of Maritime History*, XVII/2 (2005), pp. 113–39

—, 'Storytelling, Fairytales and Autobiography: Some Observations on Eighteenth- and Nineteenth-Century French Soldiers' and Sailors' Memoirs', *Social History*, XXIX/2 (2004), pp. 186–98

Hunt, Robert, *Popular Romances of the West of England; or, The Drolls, Traditions, and Superstitions of Old Cornwall* (London, 1908 edn)

—, *Popular Romances of the West of England; or The Drolls, Traditions, and Superstitions of Old Cornwall*, 2nd Series (London, 1865)

Hutchison, William M., *The Phantom Ship, A Nautical Ballad, Words and Music Composed by William M. Hutchison* (London, 1896), British Library ref. H2601.a.(11)

Hutton, Ronald, *The Rise and Fall of Merry England: The Ritual Year, 1400–1700* (Oxford, 1994)

Jamieson, Alan J., Glenn Singleman, Thomas D. Linley and Susan Casey, 'Why Don't People Care About the Deep Sea: Fear and Loathing', *ICES Journal of Marine Science*, LXXVIII/3 (2020), pp. 797–809

Janvier, Thomas A., *In the Sargasso Sea* (New York, 1898)

Jones, William, *Credulities Past and Present, Including the Sea and Seamen, Miners, Amulets and Talismans, Rings, Word and Letter Divination, Numbers, Trials, Exorcising and Blessing of Animals, Birds, Eggs, and Luck* (London, 1880)

Josephson-Storm, Jason A., *The Myth of Disenchantment: Magic, Modernity, and the Birth of the Human Sciences* (Chicago, IL, 2017)

Jubber, Nicholas, *The Fairy Tellers: A Journey into the Secret History of Fairy Tales* (London, 2022)

Kestner, Joseph, 'Edward Burne-Jones and Nineteenth-Century Fear of Women', *Biography*, VII/2 (1984), pp. 95–122

Kingshill, Sophia, and Jennifer Westwood, *The Fabled Coast: Legends and Traditions from around the Shores of Britain and Ireland* (London, 2012)

Knoppers, Laura Lunger, and Joan B. Landes, eds, *Monstrous Bodies/ Political Monstrosities in Early Modern Europe* (Ithaca, NY, 2004)

Land, Isaac, *War, Nationalism and the British Sailor, 1750–1850* (Basingstoke, 2009)

Landrin, Armand, *Monsters of the Deep and Curiosities of Ocean Life*, trans. W. Davenport (London, 1875)

Lassen, Jeremy, ed., *The Ghost Pirates and Other Revenants of the Sea: The Collected Fiction of William Hope Hodgson*, vol. III (New York, 2018)

Laurent, Beatrice, 'Monster or Missing Link? The Mermaid and the Victorian Imagination', *Cahiers Victoriens et Edouardiens*, 85 (2017), pp. 1–17

Lee, Henry, *Sea Fables Explained* (London, 1883)

—, *Sea Monsters Unmasked* (London, 1883)

Lenik, Edward J., 'Mythic Creatures: Serpents, Dragons, and Sea Monsters in Northeastern Rock Art', *Archaeology of Eastern North America*, XXXVIII (2010), pp. 17–37

Lévi-Strauss, Claude, *The Raw and the Cooked*, trans. John and Doreen Weightman (New York, 1969)

Lovecraft, H. P., 'Supernatural Horror in Literature', in *The H. P. Lovecraft Omnibus 2: Dagon and Other Macabre Tales* (London, 1994), pp. 421–512

—, *The H. P. Lovecraft Omnibus 3: The Haunter in the Dark* (London, 2000)

Lovette, Leland P., *Naval Customs, Traditions and Usage*, 4th edn (Annapolis, MD, 1959)

McAleer, John, '"As pretty a thing as I have ever seen": Animal Encounters and Atlantic Voyages, 1750–1850', *Journal of Maritime Research*, XXII/1–2 (2020), pp. 5–23

McAnally, D. R., *Irish Wonders; The Ghosts, Giants, Pookas, Demons, Leprechawns, Banshees, Fairies, Witches, Widows, Old Maids, and Other Marvels of the Emerald Isle; Popular Tales as Told by the People* (Boston, MA, 1888)

McIntosh, Peter, *History of Kintyre*, 3rd edn (Campbeltown, 1870)

MacRitchie, David, 'The Finn-Men of Britain', *Archaeological Review*, IV/1 (1889), pp. 1–26

Magra, Christopher P., 'Faith at Sea: Exploring Maritime Religiosity in the Eighteenth Century', *International Journal of Maritime History*, XIX/1 (2007), pp. 87–106

de Maillet, Benoît, *Telliamed; or Conversations between an Indian Philosopher and a French Missionary on the Diminution of the Sea*, ed. and trans. Albert V. Carozzi (Urbana, IL, 1968)

Marryat, Frederick, *The Phantom Ship* (Stroud, 2006)

Melville, Herman, *Moby Dick* (Ware, 1992)

Mitchell-Cook, Amy, *A Sea of Misadventures: Shipwreck and Survival in Early America* (Columbia, SC, 2014)

Montgomery, James, ed., *Journal of Voyages and Travels by the Rev. Daniel Tyerman and George Bennet, Esq: Deputed from the London Missionary Society, to Visit Their Various Stations in the South Sea Islands, China, India, &c. between the Yearss 1821 and 1829*, vol. I (Boston, MA, 1832)

Mortensen, Peter, '"Half Fish, Half Woman": Annette Kellerman, Mermaids, and Eco-Aquatic Revisioning', *Journal of the Fantastic in the Arts*, XXIX/2 (2018), pp. 201–22

Nevins, Andrea Shaw, *Working Juju: Representations of the Caribbean Fantastic* (Athens, GA, 2019)

Oudemans, A. C., *The Great Sea-Serpent: An Historical and Critical Treatise* (Leiden, 1892)

Pare, Ambroise, *On Monsters and Marvels*, trans. Janis L. Pallister (Chicago, IL, 1983)

Parkman, Francis, *France and England in North America, Part 1: Pioneers of France in the New World* (Boston, MA, 1902)

Paxton, C.G.M., 'Driven Mad by the Sea Serpent: The Strange Case of Captain George Drevar', *Mariner's Mirror*, CVII/3 (2021), pp. 308–23

Pearce, Cathryn, *Cornish Wrecking, 1700–1860: Reality and Popular Myth* (Woodbridge, 2010)

Pinckard, George, *Notes on West Indies: Written During the Expedition Under the Command of the Late General Sir Ralph Abercromby*, vol. III (London, 1806)

Pliny the Elder, *The Natural History of Pliny*, trans. John Bostock and H. T. Riley (London, 1855)

Poe, Edgar Allan, *The Complete Tales and Poems of Edgar Allan Poe* (London, 1987)

Pontoppidan, Erich, *The Natural History of Norway*, vol. II (London, 1755)

Rappaport, Angelo, *Superstitions of Sailors* (London, 1928)

Rediker, Marcus, *Between the Devil and the Deep Blue Sea: Merchant Seamen, Pirates and the Anglo-American Maritime World, 1700–1750* (Cambridge, 1987)

Robinson, Margaret, 'Fabulous Beasts', *Folklore*, LXXVI/4 (1965), pp. 273–87

Rolleston, T. W., ed., *The High Deeds of Finn and other Bardic Romances of Ancient Ireland* (London, 1910)

Rose, Kelby, 'Nostalgia and Imagination in Nineteenth-Century Sea Shanties', *Mariner's Mirror*, XCVIII/2 (2012), pp. 147–60

Rouleau, Brian J., 'Dead Men Do Tell Tales: Folklore, Fraternity and the Forecastle', *Early American Studies*, V/1 (2007), pp. 30–62

Rozwadowski, Helen, 'Ocean's Depth', *Environmental History*, XV/3 (2010), pp. 520–25

Saunders, W. H., *Tales of Old Portsmouth*, Portsmouth Central Library ref. 942.2792

Sax, Boria, 'The Mermaid and Her Sisters: From Archaic Goddess to Consumer Society', *Interdisciplinary Studies in Literature and Environment*, VII/2 (2000), pp. 43–54

Scott, Sir Walter, *Letters on Demonology and Witchcraft* (Ware, 2001)

—, *Rokeby; A Poem in Six Cantos* (Edinburgh, 1813)

Scribner, Vaughan, *Merpeople: A Human History* (London, 2020)

—,'"Such Monsters Do Exist in Nature": Mermaids, Tritons, and the Science of Wonder in Eighteenth-Century Europe', *Itinerario*, XLI/3 (2017), pp. 507–38

Scudder, Bernard, trans., *Egil's Saga* (London, 2004)

Shaw, Philip, *The Sublime* (Abingdon, 2006)

Silver, Carole G., *Strange and Secret Peoples: Fairies and Victorian Consciousness* (Oxford, 1999)

Smith, Thomas, *A Practical Discourse to Sea-Faring Men: Preached in Falmouth, First Parish, Lord's-Day, April 28th 1771* (Boston, MA, 1771)
Smollett, Tobias, 'The Adventures of Peregrine Pickle', in *The Novels of Tobias Smollett* (London, 1821), pp. 197–528
Sneddon, Robert W., 'On the Isle of Blue Men', in *Our Haunted Shores: Tales from the Coasts of the British Isles*, ed. Emily Alder, Jimmy Packham and Joan Passey (London, 2022), pp. 275–305
Soini, Wayne, *Gloucester's Sea Serpent* (Charleston, SC, 2010)
Starkey, Lindsay J., 'Why Sea Monsters Surround the Northern Lands: Olaus Magnus's Conception of Water', *Preternature: Critical and Historical Studies on the Preternatural*, VI/1 (2017), pp. 31–62
Stipriaan, Alex van, 'Watramama/Mami Wata: Three Centuries of Creolization of a Water Spirit in West Africa, Suriname and Europe', *Matatu, Journal of African Culture and Society*, XXVII/1 (2003), pp. 321–37
Tallack, Malachy, *The Un-Discovered Islands: An Archipelago of Myths and Mysteries, Phantoms and Fakes* (Edinburgh, 2016)
Teit, J. A., 'Water-Beings in Shetlandic Folk-Lore, as Remembered by Shetlanders in British Columbia', *Journal of American Folk-Lore*, XXXI/120 (1918), pp. 180–201
Tennyson, Alfred Lord, *Selected Poems: Tennyson* (London, 2007)
—, *The Works of Alfred Lord Tennyson* (London, 1893)
Thompson, Stith, *Motif-Index of Folk-Literature: A Classification of Narrative Elements in Folktales, Ballads, Myths, Fables, Mediaeval Romances, Exempla, Fabliaux, Jest-Books, and Local Legends* (Bloomington, IN, 1958)
Thomson, Sir Wyville, *The Atlantic: A Preliminary Accounts of the General Results of the Exploring Voyage of HMS Voyager*, vol. II (New York, 1878)
Traill Dennison, W., 'Orkney Folk Lore', *The Scottish Antiquary; or, Northern Notes and Queries*, VII/28 (1893), pp. 171–7
Tregarthen, Enys, *North Cornwall Fairies and Legends* (London, 1906)
Tylor, Edward Burnett, *Primitive Culture*, vol. II: *Religion in Primitive Cultures* (London, 1871)
Tyng, Charles, *Before the Wind: The Memoir of an American Sea Captain, 1808–1833* (New York, 2000)
Van Duzer, Chet, *Sea Monsters on Medieval and Renaissance Maps* (London, 2013)
Varden, John T., 'Traditions, Superstitions, and Folklore, Chiefly Relating to the Counties of Norfolk and Suffolk', in *The East Anglian Handbook and Agricultural Annual for 1885*, ed. P. Soman (Norwich, 1885), pp. 70–124
Verne, Jules, *Twenty Thousand Leagues Under the Sea* (London, 1994)
Vickers, Daniel, with Vince Walsh, *Young Men and the Sea: Yankee Seafarers in the Age of Sail* (New Haven, CT, 2005)
Vincent, David, *Popular Literacy and Culture: England, 1750–1914* (Cambridge, 1989)

Walden, Dan, 'Ships and Crypts: The Costal World of Poe's "King Pest," "The Premature Burial," and "The Oblong Box"', *Edgar Allan Poe Review*, x/2 (2009), pp. 104–21

Walsham, Alexandra, *The Reformation of the Landscape: Religion, Identity, and Memory in Early Modern Britain and Ireland* (Oxford, 2011)

Waters, Thomas, *Cursed Britain: A History of Witchcraft and Black Magic in Modern Times* (New Haven, CT, 2019)

Westropp, Thomas Johnson, 'Brasil and the Legendary Islands of the North Atlantic: Their History and Fable. A Contribution to the "Atlantis" Problem', *Proceedings of the Royal Irish Academy: Archaeology, Culture, History, Literature*, xxx (1912–13), pp. 223–60

Winiarski, Douglas L., '"Pale Blewish Lights" and a Dead Man's Groan: Tales of the Supernatural from Eighteenth-Century Plymouth, Massachusetts', *William and Mary Quarterly*, LV/4 (1998), pp. 497–530

Wright, Thomas, ed., *St Brendan: A Mediaeval Legend of the Sea* (London, 1844)

'The Yarmouth Tragedy, or The Constant Lovers', Bodleian Library ballad ref. Bod 5718, Roud No. 187

Yeats, W. B., *The Celtic Twilight* (London, 2018)

Young, Simon, 'Mermaids, Mere-Maids and No Maids: Mermaid Place Names and Folklore in Britain', *Shima*, xv/2 (2021), pp. 176–200

—, 'Mermaid Toponyms in the West Indies: Traditional and Non-Traditional Names', *Shima*, xv/2 (2021), pp. 202–20

Zipes, Jack, *Breaking the Magic Spell: Radical Theories of Folk and Fairy Tales* (Lexington, KY, 2002)

ACKNOWLEDGEMENTS

In undertaking this voyage through the supernatural history of the Atlantic, I have been blessed with the support of crew mates and fellow travellers who have each played their part. As ever, I must first thank Jo for giving me the time and space to work on yet another weird and wonderful project about monsters, magic and stuff that might have caused other wives to abandon ship years ago. My love and gratitude are fathomless.

In terms of providing ongoing encouragement, I would like to thank my gang of fellow rogues and writers who meet in Portsmouth's taverns and share fragments of books and stories in progress – William Sutton, Alison Habens, Matt Parsons, Tom Sykes, Victoria Leslie, Sue Harper and Paul Valentine. My colleagues in the University of Portsmouth's Centre for Port Cities and Maritime Cultures have been equally supportive, and I would especially like to thank Professor Brad Beaven. His leading research on the social history of port cities informed various points in this book.

I would like to thank Dave Watkins for commissioning this book. The timetable for completing it was knocked way off course by the COVID-19 pandemic. I am extremely thankful to the staff at Reaktion Books for their understanding in this matter. In particular, I would like to thank David Hayden for his patience and guidance. I have been struck by the enthusiasm and professionalism of the Reaktion team throughout the publication process, and would like to thank Alex Ciobanu, Helen McCusker, Martha Jay and Fran Roberts for their help in getting this book launched into the world.

While venturing into the past, the book's final consideration of ecological anxieties and the power of storytelling naturally turns my thoughts to the future and therefore my sons. It has been a pride and privilege to watch you grow into the young men you have become. I wish you bold adventures and the courage to face the future, be it fair weather or foul.

This book is dedicated to Luca and Evan.

PHOTO ACKNOWLEDGEMENTS

The author and publishers wish to express their thanks to the sources listed below for illustrative material and/or permission to reproduce it. Some locations of works are also given below, in the interest of brevity:

Alamy Stock Photo: pp. 130 (Chronicle), 195 (Robert Estall Photo Agency), 200 (*bottom*; Ian Fleming), 202 (Chronicle), 203 (*bottom*; Chronicle); Archivist/AdobeStock: p. 242; Bridgeman Images: pp. 196 (Christie's Images), 206 (photo © Léonard de Selva); The British Museum, London: p. 197; from J. W. Buel, *Heroes of Unknown Seas and Savage Lands* (Philadelphia, PA, 1891), photo Library of Congress, Washington, DC: p. 28; from Samuel Taylor Coleridge, *The Rime of the Ancient Mariner* (London, 1876), photos Bibliothèque nationale de France, Paris: pp. 74, 264; from T. Dibdin, *Songs, Naval and National, of the Late Charles Dibdin* (London, 1841), photo University of California Libraries: p. 39; Disney/Kobal/Shutterstock: p. 207 (*bottom*); from John Gibson, *Monsters of the Sea: Legendary and Authentic* (London, 1887): p. 201 (*bottom*); Harvard Art Museums/Fogg Museum, Cambridge, MA (bequest of Grenville L. Winthrop, 1943.462), photo © President and Fellows of Harvard College: p. 198; Heritage Auctions, HA.com: 203 (*top*), 204, 208; Lewis Walpole Library, Yale University, Farmington, CT: p. 137; Library of Congress, Prints and Photographs Division, Washington, DC: p. 175; Museu Calouste Gulbenkian, Lisbon: p. 194 (*top*); Museum Kunstpalast, Düsseldorf: p. 201 (*top*); National Archives at College Park, MD: p. 148; The National Gallery, London: p. 194 (*bottom*); Nowaczyk/Shutterstock.com: p. 205; from A. C. Oudemans, *The Great Sea-Serpent: An Historical and Critical Treatise* (Leiden and London, 1892), photo Smithsonian Libraries, Washington, DC: p. 179; from Caspar Plautius, *Nova typis transacta navigatio*... ([Linz], 1621), photo Wellcome Collection, London: p. 156; powerofforever/iStock.com: p. 67; private collection: pp. 110, 193, 200 (*top*); Robarts Library, University of Toronto: p. 31; from *La Sainte Bible selon la vulgate* (Tours, 1866), vol. II, photo Bibliothèque nationale de France, Paris: p. 171; from Gaspar Schott, *Physica curiosa, sive mirabilia naturae*... (Würzburg, 1667), vol. I, photo ETH-Bibliothek Zurich: p. 86; Skagens Museum: p. 207 (*top*); from *Stories from Hans Christian Andersen* (Boston, 1890): p. 199; from Jules Verne, *Vingt mille lieues sous les mers* (Paris, 1871), photo Bibliothèque nationale de France, Paris: p. 273; Wikimedia Commons (public domain): p. 282.

INDEX

Page numbers in *italics* indicate illustrations